FOREVER UNDONE

J. SAMAN

Boston World Family Tree

This family tree is simply a reference if needed. Each book is a complete standalone.

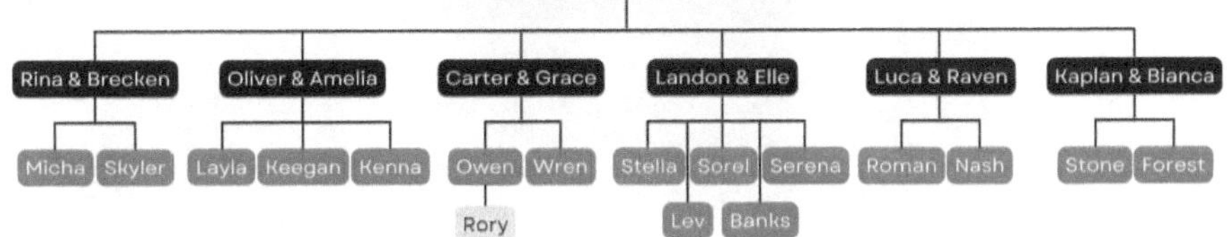

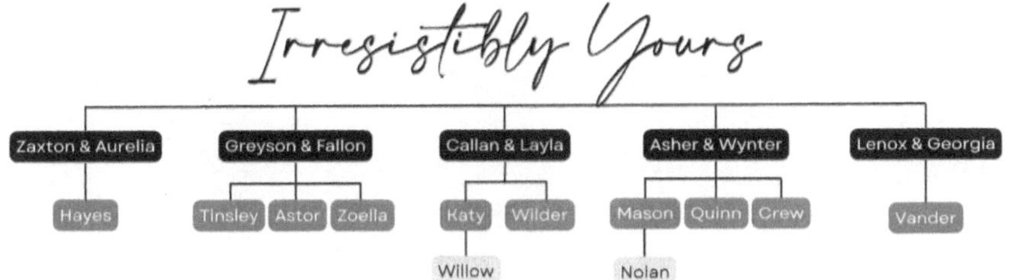

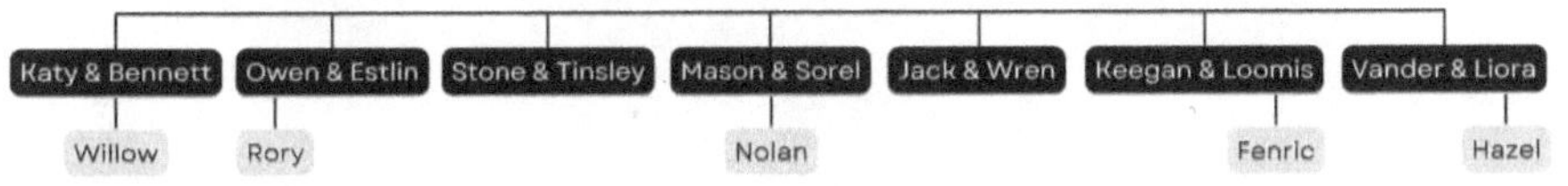

1

ASTON

The heat surrounding me is pleasantly suffocating, even as it draws a layer of sweat on my forehead. That could also be the small buzz I'm rocking after three beers and three shots of tequila. I can't remember the last time I did this, and I hadn't realized how much I needed a night out until now.

A Boston penthouse party wasn't exactly on my bingo card when I came home to visit from LA but given everything that's happened in the last six months, there was no way I was going to say no. Especially when my parents told me they'd happily hold onto Zoey for the night.

Heavy-based music pumps through the room, and all around me is a conglomerate of Boston elite. Billionaire doctors, movie stars, pop stars, and professional athletes are everywhere you look. Myself included in the first category, but as I've been living and working as a doctor in LA for the last seven years, I hardly fit in here.

"Hey," Micha yells in my ear. "Want another drink?"

I've known Micha my entire life. Not only are our parents best friends, but so are we, to the point where we even went to college and medical school together, and he's my daughter's godfather. He's like a brother to me and has been by my side through everything.

"The answer to that is yes," Bennett states for me, eyeing the end of my beer. He was my resident during my intern year in LA, and we've low-key kept in touch over the years. Now he lives here in Boston and is friends with my friends and married to Micha's cousin. Small world with how that works.

I think about this as I scan the dimly lit room. "Sure. What the hell."

Micha nods, and the three of us make our way through the crowd over to the large bar lining the wall. There are pink and red decorations everywhere, and every woman, and even some of the men, is dressed in variations of either color. I'd never heard of people having Valentine's Day parties before, but here we are.

"You made it!" Stone, whose penthouse this is, yells so he can be heard over the noise of the party. "How's your little princess?"

"She's good. Hanging in there. She's with my parents tonight." I finish off the beer in my hand and set my empty down. "She made me promise to make her heart-shaped pancakes in the morning since that's a Valentine's tradition Astrid started last year."

Stone nods, that familiar look of pity creeping into his eyes. I hate that look. I don't know why I said all of that. I'm so out of sorts I don't even recognize myself anymore. Finding out my wife was sleeping with someone else was a blow, but discovering she was not only in love with him but also going to marry him hit even harder. Our divorce was finalized last week, and I brought Zoey to Boston so we could both get away.

A hand slaps my back, and I turn to see my older brother, Alden, with a lazy smile lighting up his hazy eyes. "Good. You're drinking."

I laugh. "I've been drinking."

"Even better. Now we just have to get you laid. Listen, there's someone here I want you to meet," he begins, but I'm already shaking my head. "Just one drink with her," he persists. "She's smart, funny, and sexy as hell."

A glass is placed in my hand, and reflexively, I stare down at the clear liquid, wondering if another shot is a wise decision but not caring all that much either.

"Don't push that if he's not ready, man," Micha defends.

A frown hits my lips before I can stop it. I don't remember the last time I had sex. I was working bastardly long hours, and having a kid sort of changes your life, realigns your priorities, and removes options. Also, you know, my wife was fucking someone else.

I had a one-night stand with Astrid. I met her at a club and screwed her in a back room. Three months later, she tracked me down at the hospital and told me she was pregnant.

We started dating, and things were good. Great even. I fell fast and hard for her. We got married and had Zoey, and it was as it should be, even with the end of my residency and the start of my fellowship. Or so I thought. Clearly, I was wrong, and Astrid wasn't happy even if I was. Or she simply fell out of love with me and in love with someone else.

"I live in LA and am certainly not dating anyone," I explain.

"Who said anything about dating?" Alden quips, and Bennett rolls his eyes at him. "You know the saying *get under someone new to get over someone old*? Well, that's what you need."

The thought of meaningless sex is as appealing as it's unappealing, but I simply give him a noncommittal nod instead of replying.

"Well, it's still good to see you, and I'm glad I was able to drag you out." Micha holds up his glass.

"Yes!" Bennett declares. "To saving lives instead of taking

them. To the right woman instead of the wrong one. And to our beautiful daughters."

"I'll drink to that." I clink my glass with theirs and down the tequila in one smooth go. A shudder runs through me, and I set my empty glass on the counter. "I'm going to find the bathroom."

Stone points in the direction of a long corridor. "Any of the bathrooms in one of the bedrooms will be your best bet."

"Got it." I slap his shoulder and give my brother, Micha, and Bennett a fist bump. "I'll find you guys."

With that, I head toward the hall Stone mentioned. The alcohol warms my belly and lightens my steps. I nod hellos and smile at random people I pass, including a few women who give me *come fuck me* eyes that don't hold a lot of interest for me.

I reach the first bedroom on my right and open the door to find it quiet and dark. It smells faintly of perfume, something easy and light and equally appealing. I find myself taking a deeper inhale and then laughing to myself. Shit. I'm definitely drunk.

It takes me a moment to adjust to the darkness of the room, and on my right are two closed doors. The first one turns out to be a closet. I move toward the other door and open it to find a fogged mirror and a woman standing before it with wavy, damp blonde hair hanging around her bare shoulders. Before I can take in more of her, a loud pop sounds from somewhere in the distance, and the lights go out.

Complete darkness falls, so absolute it feels like I've been struck blind. The party noise beyond the bathroom and bedroom sparks with surprised yelps, nervous laughter, and a few theatrical screams.

"Shit!" someone who I think is Stone yells from somewhere in the penthouse. "No one move. The power went out. Let me see what's going on."

"Oh my god!" the woman in the bathroom exclaims. "This is

dramatic. Good thing I finished getting cleaned up before this. You didn't see anything, did you?"

"Huh? Is that meant to be ironic?"

"No. I wasn't dressed."

"Oh," I reply automatically, heat curling up the back of my neck at the thought. I rub it away with my hand. "No. The lights went out just as I opened the door. I didn't see anything. I was looking for the bathroom."

"You found it. I thought I locked the door. A friend accidentally spilled pink punch in my hair and down the top of my dress. I was in here washing it out of both. Crap, I seriously can't see anything."

"Me neither. Are you okay?"

She gives a nervous laugh. "I mean, I'm not great considering the situation, but I think it's better in here than out there."

Given the loud murmurs and panicked hush outside the bedroom door, I'm inclined to agree with her. It's complete sensory deprivation in here, and a little eerie if I'm being honest. I hear her move and note the soft rustle of fabric against skin. Is she getting dressed? The thought sends a rush of unexpected lust through my body.

"I think we're stuck in here until the lights come back on."

"Probably," she agrees, and I hear her shift again, closer to me now, and with it I catch the light, sweet scent I admired when I came into the bedroom.

It's her perfume. A smile curls up my lips.

"Though being trapped in a dark bedroom with a stranger isn't the worst Valentine's scenario I can imagine."

Suddenly I'm aware of how close we are, how intimate darkness can be. The alcohol in my blood makes me brave, or perhaps just reckless, as I inch toward her, my pulse thrumming with excitement at the darkness and the woman.

"What would be the worst scenario?" I ask, my voice lower.

"Being *alone* in the dark," she answers simply. "Or, you

know, there being a psycho killer in the apartment going from room to room to slash up unsuspecting women."

I chuckle. "Watch a lot of horror movies, do you?"

"Enough to know the half-naked, unsuspecting blonde always gets it first." She cracks up. "Wow, that sounded insanely dirty. More like a porn than a horror film."

My smile grows. "It did, but I'm not complaining. Are you still half-naked?" I don't know why I ask. Or why my voice drops to a seductive timbre.

"Not anymore. Not that you'd be able to see either way."

Her voice is light. Soft. Almost sugar-coated. Combined with the way she smells, she practically has me under some kind of hypnotic spell. I want to touch her. I want to smell her skin. Taste it. Taste *her*.

"True," I agree and change course. "Your date must be missing you?"

She laughs, the sound full and uninhibited, making me chuckle in return. "That was the worst way to ask if I'm here with someone."

"Probably. I'm a bit out of practice." I blink, willing my eyes to see through the darkness, to find her, even if it's just an outline, a flash of her eyes, something to go by.

"At what? Flirting with women in the dark?"

"Yes," I admit.

"Well, this is the most practice I've ever had."

"Huh?"

"I've never flirted with anyone in the dark before."

"I find that hard to believe."

"You shouldn't. It's the truth. I'll have to scratch this off my bucket list."

My hand fumbles forward until I find silky fabric covering her hip. "Not a very exciting bucket list," I tell her. "What else is on it?"

She releases a breathy laugh, probably from my hand on her body, but she's not pushing me away. "Skydiving."

I slide up to the curve of her waist and hold her. She's short. A lot shorter than I am. I can tell that by where my hand is and the feel of her breath as it meets my neck.

"I've done that," I tell her. "It's exhilarating and definitely something to try at least once in your life. What else do you have? Spice it up for me."

"Are we getting dirty now? I don't typically tell my spicy fantasies to strangers in dark rooms."

I shift in front of her and drag my thumb back and forth on her hip. "That's because you haven't tried it before. Another thing we can scratch off your bucket list. Who better to bare your dirty secrets to?"

"Now we're onto secrets?"

"The dirty kind," I remind her, bringing my other hand to her other hip and testing boundaries.

"Because I can't see you and you can't see me?"

I find myself smiling again, her lightness somehow making the weight I haven't been able to shake more bearable. "Exactly."

"Hmm. Okay. You tell me one of yours, and I'll tell you one of mine." Her body brushes mine as she moves, the feel of her soft tits against my shirt makes my cock pulse as it shoots a fresh jolt of desire straight through me. She's getting me hard, and if she keeps moving, she's going to feel it.

"I like your voice. And I like the way you smell. A lot. I like how you feel too. You're soft and sweet and sexy."

"See, you're better at this than you were giving yourself credit for."

"Yeah?" I tease. "Are my moves working?"

"Absolutely. I like that you think I'm all those things. Even if you haven't seen me." She touches the junction of my neck and shoulder just beneath the collar of my shirt, and the feel of her small, warm hand on my skin sends a shiver down my spine.

Then my hand is on her cheek, and I'm kissing her. Hard. No soft introduction or light, testing peck. I kiss her because I'm a little drunk and a lot excited, and it's been so fucking long, and I've been so goddamn miserable for what feels like an eternity that I don't know how to hold back. Her lips are full and delicious, tasting faintly of cranberry and champagne, likely from the punch she mentioned.

But the best part? She makes this tiny, surprised noise that instantly becomes a moan before her mouth opens beneath mine. And there's nothing tentative about her either. She's kissing me back with equal fervor, her body sliding up mine as she climbs to her tiptoes in her shoes. Our tongues meet and our heads tilt, and I pull her closer, one hand tangled in her hair, the other at the small of her back.

Her body is warm and yielding against mine, curves fitting perfectly along the planes of my chest. Something between a sigh and a whimper emanates from the back of her throat, and it resonates through my entire body.

The kiss deepens, turning hungry. My hand slides lower, following the curve of her spine to her ass, where I squeeze and pull her against me so she can feel how fucking hard she's made me. She gasps and arches into me, and I'm dying to rip the top of her dress back down so I can take her tits in my hands.

Her palms slide under my jacket, pushing it off my shoulders, and I let it fall to the floor, lost in the sensation of her touch, the heat of her mouth, and the way her body responds to mine. I've never had a kiss like this. One that I feel in every nerve of my body, every pound of my heart. It's not even the alcohol because I've been plenty more drunk and kissed plenty more women.

It's her. This woman. This kiss.

Time loses meaning in the darkness. I don't know how long we stand here kissing like teenagers, our hands exploring with increasing boldness. I just know I never want to stop.

My fingers find the zipper at the back of her dress, and just as I begin to lower it, there's a flicker, a hum, and suddenly the lights are back on, harsh and unforgiving after the ceaseless darkness.

We both startle back, and I blink, momentarily blinded, only to find myself staring into a pair of wide green eyes that I know all too well. Eyes I've seen a hundred times across dinner tables and at family gatherings, but never this close, never darkened with desire.

Oh my god. Holy shit.

"Aston?!" she exclaims, taking another step back and covering her mouth with one hand as she adjusts her tits in her dress with the other. I dive down to grab my jacket, and hastily shove my hands back into it, angry, frustrated, or just simply fucked.

Why did it have to be her? That kiss... the way she felt...

"Skylar." It ends there. Because I just made out with my best friend's little sister. A best friend who is in the other room. Fuck! I haven't seen her in forever. Not since she was a college kid, eighteen or nineteen, at a party that Micha dragged me to so we could keep an eye on her, and she threw up on me. That was... five years ago?

Jesus. What have I done? She wasn't someone I could kiss. Or want to do more with. Shit.

"We shouldn't have done that," I mumble, scrubbing my hands up and down my face, feeling like a world-class asshole. "I didn't know it was you. Your brother is right out there." The things I said to her... the things I would have done...

Guilt swarms me like a pack of rabid bees.

"Relax. It's not like I tell Micha who I kiss."

I laugh caustically into my hands. "That's not exactly the

point, and you know it. This was a giant mistake. On both our parts."

She opens her mouth, but before she can say anything, the door bursts open, and someone walks in. Thankfully it's not her brother. The tequila in my stomach roils, threatening to rebel. I have to go back out there and talk to Micha and pretend like I didn't just kiss the hell out of his baby sister. Pretend like she didn't make me hard and hungry and excited. Like she didn't make me feel alive for the first time in so long.

"Hey," the woman says, and I realize I know her, too. Awesome. Braelyn blinks her large brown eyes at us, shifting back and forth between both of us. "I've been looking for you," she says to Skylar. "We should get going."

Skylar nods. "Yeah."

That's all she says, but now she's not meeting my eyes. And without a word to me, she walks off to join her friend, leaving me standing here in shock and torment.

I just fucked up. Big time. But even worse, I have a gnawing urge to run after her and do it all over again. And that's something that can never happen.

2

———

SKYLAR

Two years later

"What the hell?" I cry at the ominous crunch from beneath my platformed heel and feel the buckle of cardboard beneath my weight. I step back, nearly dropping my cute clutch purse when I see what it is. A warm and anxious flutter rolls through me because there's a giant red heart-shaped box—now partially crushed on one end—and a huge ultra-soft-looking teddy bear with a card perched in its arms right in front of my door. "Oh my god."

Crouching down, I set my purse on the top step and snatch the card. Nerves shake me. Both the good and the bad kind. The good, because hello, chocolate, and a teddy bear. The bad because I have no idea who sent me these, but I worry it's the last person I ever want sending me anything.

I glance up and down the sidewalk but don't see anyone I know. Not that I expected to see Josh lurking. He's more subtle than that. Still, a girl can never be too careful. I open the envelope with a shaky hand and pull out the pink heart-shaped card.

Hope you enjoy these. We're so proud of you and love you so much. Happy Valentine's Day. Love, Mom and Dad.

A warm, gooey sensation fills my insides. I'm proud of myself, too. And I'm relieved. Not that I expected Josh to send me anything, but I'm grateful he didn't. I'd hate to throw out all this chocolate and cut up the bear. What a waste that would have been.

With a sigh, I push the bear and card back inside, lock up, awkwardly pick up the large box of chocolates and my purse, and get my ass going, already late to meet my friends. I had a six-year-old with pneumonia who took a turn for the worse, and I wouldn't leave until she was stable. Then I had to run home, shower, and change my clothes.

A few blocks up, I turn the corner and spot my friend Roman's restaurant, Roundhouse, overflowing with people waiting in the cold February night for a table. I quicken my pace just as the phone buzzes in my purse. I pull it out and am not shocked to see it's Braelyn.

Braelyn: Where are you?

Me: About to walk in.

I tuck my phone back in my purse, zip it up, and swing it behind me so I can slip it back onto my shoulder when the heavy leather connects with something—*someone*—and a sharp intake of breath is followed by a string of profanities.

"Oh my god, I'm so sorry!" I spin around to find a tall man doubled over, one hand on his knee, the other on his lower abdomen. "I didn't see you. Where are you—oh." A small laugh escapes my lips. His hand is actually covering his groin. "Wow. I'm really sorry."

"Yeah," he manages, his voice tight. "You sound like it."

"No, really. I am. I didn't mean to hit you. Especially not... there. I sometimes have strange reactions to things at inappropriate times. That had to hurt. My purse is heavy." Another laugh that I poorly attempt to disguise as a cough, and he looks up at me through watering, pain-etched eyes, sending a jolt of recognition through me. His blond hair is longer now, styled differently, but his sharp-as-cut-glass blue eyes are unmistakable. "Aston?" His name escapes my lips before I can think better of it.

Aston Hughes, my brother's best friend, squints through his pain. "Skylar?" His voice holds the same low timbre I remember from two years ago on this exact night, though currently strained an octave higher. "Did you assault me on purpose, or is this how you greet all your brother's friends?"

"Just the ones I don't like," I quip, only to slap a hand over my mouth. I really need to grow a filter. At least he didn't say *all men you make out with in the dark*. Heat climbs up my neck. "It was an accident." Though part of me isn't entirely sorry, and I can't even explain why that is. I never really liked Aston. He was always a little too arrogant and asshole-ish for me. His appalled look when he realized he had been kissing me didn't help that. Nor the fact that immediately after, he called me a mistake and said it never should have happened.

"Some accident," he mutters, finally straightening to his full height. Damn. I forgot how tall and broad he is. "You always did have impeccable aim."

I threw up on him at one of my college parties that Micha dragged him to. Yep. Lovely reminder.

I roll my eyes at him. "And you always did have a flair for dramatic reactions." I adjust my purse strap, distancing the weapon from potential repeat offenses. "What are you doing back in town? Are you visiting your parents or simply stalking me down for another kiss?"

My eyes close, and I blow out a slow breath. I didn't want to mention that night to him but seeing him has me frazzled for some reason. He chuckles lightly, and my eyes slowly peel open, mortification crawling up my face, making my skin itchy and hot.

"No. Sorry to disappoint you on that. I just moved back."

"Oh." I do some sort of owl blink. "I hadn't heard."

The streetlight catches in his hair, turning it the color of wheat fields in late summer, and his square jawline has the type of stubble I imagine would tickle my hand and feel deliciously scandalous against my inner thighs. Not that I'd ever know, and I certainly won't be finding out. Unfortunately, he's ridiculously gorgeous and wears it with the confidence and arrogance of a man who knows it.

"It was a quick decision. You look..." He trails off, his gaze taking me in fully for the first time.

"Amazing," I finish for him.

"Different is what I was going to say."

I frown before I can stop it, and I hate that's my first reaction. This is why I left Josh. This is why I'm working on myself and rewiring my brain.

"Different is not a compliment, and you're staring," I point out, one eyebrow arched.

His hand rubs the back of his head, and a slow smirk curls up his lips. "I'm shocked to see you, I guess. And I'm not going to compliment you."

I bristle. "What's that supposed to mean?"

"You're Micha's sister. Whatever I want to say, I shouldn't. I'm trying to reconcile the girl who kissed the hell out of me with the woman standing before me, and I'm struggling a bit with that." He gestures vaguely at me.

"Hey! You kissed me first, and I didn't kiss the hell out of you."

His smirk grows into a devilishly seductive smile, and he

runs his thumb along his bottom lip in a bastardly distracting way. "I beg to differ."

My jaw drops. "Are you intentionally trying to be a jerk and embarrass me?"

"Are you actually this immature and easy to rile? It was a simple, drunk kiss. A mistake. Nothing to be embarrassed about."

I hate all of that for far too many reasons, and it naturally raises my hackles. "Just a mental note for your future. Women don't generally love it when you call us immature and a mistake. It makes you sound not only like a condescending dick but also a total asshole. Besides, you just said I kissed the hell out of you. Which is it?"

"Both. You kissed the hell out of me, and it was a mistake."

I cross my arms, holding the box of chocolates closer. "Now that we've cleared that up, I'm going to go. I'm twenty-five minutes late." Except I don't move, and I don't know why. I kind of want to kick him in the shins for what he said to me, yet there's a part of me that wants to see what he'll say next.

"Yes. I should, too. I'm meeting some people in there as well." He doesn't move to leave either.

"Small circles in our world. Anyone I know?" Micha is in Sudan, so I know it's not him.

His lips twitch. "My brother and a few other guys. Yeah, you know them. A couple are your cousins."

"That's who I'm meeting up with too. Though likely different people from you because I'm not meeting up with Alden."

"He's too old for you anyway."

I laugh lightly. "So are you."

His eyes round as if he's now realizing our age difference. "Very true. But you're not so young anymore, despite how Micha still speaks about you." He clears his throat and notes the candy in my arms. "That's a lot of chocolate. From your boyfriend?"

For some reason, I don't want to answer him. Micha knows I broke up with Josh recently, as I moved into his house after I moved out of Josh's apartment. But the last thing I want to talk about with Aston Hughes is my ex-boyfriend or the fact that my parents sent me a Valentine's Day present because of him.

"Can I have one? I think you owe me for the nut shot."

With a sigh, I shift the box, and he opens the lid. "All dark chocolate."

"My favorite."

"These look expensive. This guy must like you."

I try not to frown. I really, seriously do. He picks up one that I'm positive is chocolate-covered caramel—my freaking favorite —and pops it in his mouth, and for a moment, I watch him chew before I force myself away.

I cover the box and bring it back into my chest. "I'm gonna head in. It was good to see you, Aston."

"You don't mean that."

"It's what people say, though you didn't say it."

He holds up a hand as he licks a bit of chocolate and caramel from his lips. "But I was thinking it. I promise."

I roll my eyes at his charming smile just as I feel another buzz in my purse. "My friends are wondering where I am."

"Mine too, likely."

"I'll see you around."

"As long as you don't run into me."

I wince. "Sorry again about that."

"No, you're not."

A slow smile spreads across my face, and I wink at him. "Not entirely. Welcome back to Boston. Try not to kiss any random women in the middle of a blackout tonight. You never know who they might turn out to be."

Now it's his turn to frown. "My kissing random women days are behind me."

"Somehow I doubt it." His phone rings in his pocket. "I'll let you get that."

"Yeah. You should go, and so should I."

There's something in the way he says that. Something that catches and sticks. Something that makes me think he almost doesn't want me to go. Except I know that can't be the case. Not with Aston Hughes.

3

SKYLAR

I race inside, glancing around as I bypass the hostess and head for the back. Braelyn throws her hand up in the air when she spots me, waving me down manically and making me laugh. I'm the last to arrive as Hayes, Roman, Quinn, Crew, and Forest are already here with her. These people are not only my lifelong best friends, my ride or die, but are more or less my family. Especially Roman and Forest, who are actually my cousins.

"Hey!" I exclaim. "Sorry I'm late." I pull down on the brim of Crew's Rebels hat as I give him a hug. "Look at you. Already falling into team mode. Or is that so you can keep a low profile while out in public?" Crew is a tight end in the NFL and had been living in LA along with Forest, but both moved back last month for different reasons. Crew came after a trade deal with the Boston Rebels was made. A team where Quinn and Crew's dad is the coach, and their brother, Mason, is the quarterback. Since both Forest and Crew moved back, it feels complete for all of us.

"Both," he tells me. "Though in here, Roman is the celebrity, not me."

Roman flips him off, but it's true, so he can't deny it.

"How cute. You brought us chocolates..." Quinn trails off with a small laugh when I set them down on the large table. "That look like they've been run over," she finishes.

"That's because I stepped on the box when I found them outside my door tonight."

Everyone falls silent as they stare at me.

"Don't get your panties in a twist. They're from my parents, not Darth Sidious." I smart.

"Is that what we're calling the dickhead now?" Forest questions.

"Works for me." I take a sip of the dirty martini they ordered for me as I look around the restaurant, people-watching while noting the couples and non-couples. Valentine's Day is such a strange holiday.

Quinn whistles through her teeth and tugs the box in her direction to slip the lid off. "All dark chocolate. Of course. Couldn't you like milk chocolate? You know, for the rest of us?"

"Sorry. My parents only get me the good stuff."

"Pass them here," Crew demands of his twin. Without waiting for her to comply, he slides the box over, picks one up, and takes a bite. His face pinches up in disgust when he realizes it's orange cream and spits it out into a napkin before he goes for another. "Fudge. Better. They're good. It was nice of your parents to get you these."

A round of appetizers is placed in front of us, and I close the box of chocolates in favor of a tuna and avocado wonton.

"Hell, I have a fiancé, and all I got from him was an orgasm this morning before he left for work," Braelyn jokes.

Hayes laughs and tosses his arm over the back of the booth behind my shoulder. "You're telling me your billionaire fiancé didn't get you a present?"

"Don't start with that again."

"You brought it up."

She sticks her tongue out at him. "Considering we're getting married in a couple of months and will have more gifts than we know what to do with, I don't need much else right now other than the orgasms."

Roman, usually the quiet one of us, makes a disapproving noise in the back of his throat. "Please don't make me hear more about sex with Adam. My ears are still bleeding from the last time."

"Or maybe that's from your last opponent," Forest teases. Roman is not only a famous Michelin-starred chef and owner of several restaurants here in Boston and around the world, but he's also part of an underground boxing ring. Except the joke is, he rarely, if ever, gets hit. "Still, he's right. No talking about sex," Forest laments, sipping his soda. "It's been way too long for me."

I snort. "Try never having an orgasm from your partner."

Everyone grimaces, and for good reason. My vagina is broken. Or at least men don't speak its language because I can make myself come, but thus far, I haven't met a man who can meet that challenge.

It frustrated the hell out of Josh. It didn't take long before he started criticizing and blaming me for it. The man was nothing if not mean and belittling while packaging it as love. The best thing I ever did was leave him, and my main regret is that I didn't do it sooner.

"Probably better off with toys than boyfriends," Quinn states. "Trust me when I say, even the non-asshole ones tend to be disappointing in the flesh. Think about my ex."

I point at her. "Exactly."

"How about we not talk about this anymore? Particularly about you using toys," Crew groans, and Quinn tosses a piece of ice from her drink at him.

"Forget that bullshit," Braelyn exclaims, turning back to me.

"We need to work on finding you a real man. A man who loves and appreciates you for who you are."

I sigh.

When you grew up as the awkward, nerdy girl who didn't come into her own until very late in the game and was subsequently teased and criticized relentlessly, or used for your family name and connections, sometimes trusting a person in bed takes a bit of time. When I first started having sex in college, I didn't have a lot of self-esteem to pull me through in a healthy or positive way, and I mostly did whatever my partners wanted. They were drunk guys at parties. Not boyfriends, and I wanted them to like me.

So, I faked it.

Then it became a thing. I couldn't come with a partner. Josh was my first boyfriend. He showered me with love and adoration until he didn't. Until he became cruel and I was weak, and when he still couldn't make me come, I faked it with him too because it was easier and safer than facing his reaction. The eggshells that man always had me walking on could make feet bleed.

Whatever. I don't want to talk about Josh or any other guy.

"Or we could just not tonight," I grumble.

"To being single and anti-Valentine's Day," Quinn jumps in, saving me as she holds up her Manhattan, and we all toast to that.

"All I know is, the next guy you end up with shouldn't be some random dick," Hayes states. "The guy who takes your orgasm card will be a lucky bastard and better know it, or he'll have to face us."

Crew gives him a fist bump. "Damn straight."

I blow them each a kiss and change the subject. "Speaking of random dicks, I bumped into Aston Hughes outside. Actually, I nailed him in the nuts with my purse."

Hayes chokes on his beer. "You what?"

"It was an accident!" I protest. "Mostly."

"That's so classically you," Forest says.

"Right? I swear. But it was still random running into him."

Braelyn is the only person who knows about the kiss. I didn't tell anyone else. Our circle is too small, and I didn't want it somehow getting back to my brother by accident.

Quinn grins, her eyebrows bouncing. "What are the odds? How did he look?"

"Annoyingly good," I admit. "And apparently, he's moved back to town."

"He moved back with his daughter," Forest explains. "His ex-wife died about six months ago, and he felt it was time for a change for them."

"Oh." I forgot that happened. Micha flew home from somewhere in Asia for the funeral and stayed in California with them for a week after. I don't remember the details around their relationship or her death, but I know they had a daughter, Zoey, because Micha is her godfather.

"He's here with my brother and a few of the other guys," he continues. "I spoke to Aston briefly last week before he moved back. We used to hang out sometimes and go hiking when we both lived in LA. He's living with his parents until he finds something better." His dark eyes rattle with realization. "I should have thought about it sooner, but he's going to be working at the hospital with you." He points at me.

That pulls me up short. "What?"

"He's a pediatric trauma surgeon."

"Oh yeah. I forgot." Because for two years, I've tried not to think about Aston Hughes or the powerhouse kiss he nailed me with and then regretted. The thought of him working at my hospital with me makes my stomach churn and my chest flutter. I work in the MSICU, or medical-surgical intensive care unit, at Boston Children's Hospital. I'll see him. I'll see him a lot.

Crew leans forward, his elbows on the table. "You don't look so happy about this."

"It's fine," I lie and drain my martini.

"This is better than a rom-com," Braelyn declares, signaling the waiter for another round. "The nurse and the doctor with a complicated past, forced to work together saving children's lives..." She fans her face. "Maybe he'll make you come for the first time. I bet he's damn good at it." She launches into a rendition of *Frozen*'s "For the First Time in Forever."

I glare at her to watch the complicated past stuff. "It's not a rom-com," I protest ardently. "It's an interesting professional situation at best, and he's not going to be the guy to make me come for the first time. More than likely, we'll ignore each other and be nothing but professional."

"Ah, I see you heard the good news, same as I just did."

I freeze, my insides icing over as my eyes turn into saucers bigger than the moon. I stare at Roman. *Please tell me Aston didn't hear me talk about him making me come for the first time. Which isn't entirely accurate.* Judging by Roman's grimace, he did. Awesome.

"Hey, everyone." Aston shakes hands with Hayes, Forest, Roman, and Crew and gives the women hugs before returning to my side and nudging me with his elbow.

"Is this all true?" I ask. "Are you really working at my hospital?"

"It's not your hospital, Swan. It's our hospital now."

Swan? Before I can even comprehend that nickname, he continues.

"And yes. We'll be working together. I signed the paperwork this morning. Home sweet home."

Just great.

4

SKYLAR

I wake up with a headache that I'm not so affectionately naming Aston. I guess that's what happens when you go to sleep annoyed.

After climbing out of bed, I use the bathroom and brush my teeth, all the while mentally ranting to myself. But really, what does it matter if he's going to be working with me? He doesn't seem to care about the kiss. He even called me immature for still lingering on it. Maybe he's right. I was a bit drunk that night. I kissed a man whom I thought was a stranger in the dark. It turned out it wasn't. Case closed.

I'm not going to let it have power over me. That's become my mantra where men are concerned, and it's now extending to Aston. You can't have a new reality with an old mentality, so here I am. I'll see him at work, and we'll be indifferent, just as I told Braelyn we'd be, and that's that.

With that mental declaration, I head downstairs. The best part of no longer living with Josh is my freedom. And the lack of constant fear. I was having eczema under my eyes, GI symptoms, back and neck pain, and occasionally palpitations. I wasn't sleeping and was jittery and nervous all the time. Afraid to eat something I wanted or listen to music I liked or dress how I wanted or not wear makeup.

I was afraid of my boyfriend, and to have that behind me is the best feeling in the world.

Life of a Showgirl streams through the speakers because it's that kind of morning. I make myself scrambled eggs with turkey sausage and eat them while sipping on my second cup of coffee. The moment I'm done with all of that and have cleaned up the kitchen, I plop my ass down on the sofa to eat my chocolates with a fire blazing in the fireplace and put on *Kill Bill: Volume 1* with the intention of watching Volume 2 before this day is over.

"Just the three of us," I sing to my candy and coffee, but then I hear an odd sound at the front door before the lock disengages. I jump up and freeze with my arms and legs spread wide like that cat getting electrocuted in *Christmas Vacation*. I search around for a weapon, wishing I had one of Uma Thurman's swords, when the door opens.

My heart thunders. Who the hell is here?

People are talking. I grip my mug tighter, ready to chuck it at someone's head if I must. The chocolates are useless. But then two suitcases are shoved through the open door, rolling until they bump into the foyer's wall, but I don't notice them so much because now I'm staring at Aston and the small person who I suspect is his daughter.

"Hi," I shriek, feeling like I got caught being somewhere I shouldn't be, only to remember that I live here. "What are you doing here? How'd you get in?"

Aston looks like he's been struck, blinking about five times. He adjusts his backward navy baseball cap until it's facing forward, with a 617 in a shamrock on the front. So Boston, and it would turn me on if I hadn't decided I hate him. His gaze snags on my bare legs and oversized college shirt as he gives me a once-over similar to the way he did last night.

Only instead of a cute dress and hot-as-fuck platform heels that give my five-foot-two frame six or so extra inches, he's getting me braless, wearing cream shearling Birkenstock slippers, no makeup, and a high, messy bun.

"Um." He glances down at the little version of himself, who's wearing a Disney's Rapunzel dress, then back up at me. "What are you doing here?"

"I asked you first."

He grunts, less than amused. "Micha offered for us to move in here since he's likely not coming back anytime soon. And I've had a spare key to his place for years."

Brothers. I fucking swear. "That's hilarious since he told me I could move in here six weeks ago when I broke up with my boyfriend." Then I remember a vague detail from last night before the martinis started pouring down my throat. "Forest said you were staying with your parents."

"I was. I mean, we were. Then I spoke to Micha on Thursday, and he offered us his place."

"But I live here," I protest, sounding like I'm six and not caring in the slightest. The little girl is eyeing me like I'm a villain in her not-so-happily-ever-after, and I remember that her mom died. "Hi," I say, coming over to her and ignoring her father. And the way I look because fuck him. No more fear. "I'm Skylar. You can call me Sky."

She glances up at the ceiling before returning to me. "Sky? I've never heard that name before. Do you have rainbows? I like rainbows."

I think I might love her. "All women have rainbows. We just have to find the sun through the rain in order to see them."

"Are you a philosopher now?"

I covertly flip off her father without removing my eyes from her.

She studies me and sticks out her hand to me. "I'm Zoey."

I shake her surprisingly firm grip. "Hi, Zoey. I'm Micha's sister and hopefully the bane of your father's existence."

He grunts, but I continue to ignore him.

"Why are you in our new house?"

"That's my question." I glare at her father. "My question for you. Do you have a middle name?"

"Huh?" he blusters at the random question.

"A middle name," I repeat.

"Oliver."

I snort a laugh. "You're kidding me? Your middle name is after my uncle Oliver?"

He shrugs.

"I can't name my headache Aston Oliver Hughes."

"What?"

He's looking at me like I'm crazy. Right now, I might be.

He sighs and shifts his weight, releasing his daughter's hand to pull out his phone. He puts it on speakerphone as he dials up my brother's number, and it does that wacky international ring with an elongated beep and a click about five times before Micha picks up.

"Hey!" he greets Aston. "Any trouble getting in?"

"You mean other than the fact that your sister is squatting here?"

"I am not squatting!" I snap indignantly.

"Oh, shit."

"Uncle Micha!" Zoey scolds.

"Sorry! Crap. Take me off speaker and hand me to my sister."

Aston does exactly that, and I snatch the phone and turn my back to them as I head into the kitchen so they can't hear me eviscerate my brother. "What in the absolute fuck did you do?"

"I messed up. I told Aston that he and Zoey could live in my house because it's unoccupied."

"It's not unoccupied!"

"Yes. That's where I messed up. I completely and totally forgot you moved in after you broke up with Dickface."

"So, what am I supposed to do? Move out? I have to move out?"

"Nooooo. Don't move out. You can't. You have to stay."

My hand flails about. "How?"

"I don't know, but I can't kick out my sister, who just broke up with an abusive man, or my best friend and godchild, who just lost her mother."

"This doesn't work. Not even a little." And he doesn't even know the half of it. I lean my hip against the counter and change the phone to my other ear. "It's weird, Micha. I can't live here with Aston and his daughter."

"Why not?"

"Because I don't even like him!"

"I heard that," Aston yells.

"You're not supposed to be listening," I fire back. "See what I mean," I say, returning to Micha as I walk in a circle between the stove and the island. "I can't live with him!"

Except Micha's laughing. "Why don't you like him?"

Um, how about because he called me immature and a mistake? I go with the second half of my truth. "Because he's an insufferable, arrogant dick and always has been."

He sighs. "Sky, Zoey already has a bedroom at my house, and it's near her preschool."

Hmm. I was wondering why one of the bedrooms had a pink princess theme, but then again, this is Micha we're talking about, and I assumed it had been there when he bought the place and was too lazy to redo it.

"There are three bedrooms, so it's not like you'll have to share. You can still do whatever it is you do, as long as it's not an asshole or a rando in my house."

"Tell me you're kidding."

"On that, no."

I stop my circling. "I'm twenty-five. Like you weren't screwing random women at my age."

"That's not up for discussion."

"Micha!"

"Fine. You're twenty-five. I respect that. Kind of. Not really. You're still my baby sister and should be a virgin until marriage or death. But I won't have to worry about that because Aston will be there, and he'll be my chastity policeman for you on my behalf."

"Micha!"

"Stop saying my name like that. Come on, Sky. Aston will be doing his single-dad doctor thing, and you'll be doing your single-girl nursing thing. You'll hardly overlap. It's not good to live in such a big place by yourself. It'll make me feel better to know you're not living there alone."

"You didn't even remember I was living here."

"That's because I work sixteen-hour shifts in ridiculous conditions, and some days I barely remember my name, let alone what a hot shower feels like. I messed up. But this could be beneficial for everyone. What do you care if Aston and his daughter live there with you?"

Um, how about a lot? I care a lot. But hell, I can't say that now, can I? He thinks Aston and I are indifferent or simply prickly toward each other because that's exactly what we're supposed to be and always have been since I accidentally threw up on him and he treated me like a brat.

"I'm sure he won't be an asshole. In fact, I'll tell him not to be. It'll be good for Zoey to have another female around. She just lost her mother."

I can't live with Aston, but what freaking choice do I have short of moving out today, which isn't exactly possible? And what would be my excuse for running out so fast, especially when he's asking me to be there for a little girl who just lost her mother? Maybe I'm the one making too big a deal out of the kiss. It was two years ago, and he didn't seem flustered by it. Not the least bit rattled. To him, it was a mistake and nothing more.

And last night when he came over to the table, he teased me for a few minutes, chatted with the guys, then excused himself and left. That was that. It wasn't a thing. I'm the one making it so.

"Micha..."

"Please. For me," he begs. "Aston is a single dad. It's a lot. Zoey is five and living in a new city where she has no friends. They need you. You're a pediatric nurse. This is what you do. You help kids in need."

"You're hitting below the belt."

"Actually, I'm hitting your ooey, gooey, soft, sweet-as-spun-sugar heart. Do this for me. Do this for Zoey."

I clench my jaw and close my eyes. "I hate you."

"You're the best. I love you. Put Aston back on the phone."

With a blustery sigh, I head back over to him. Zoey is doing small twirls, so the bottom of her dress flares out, using Aston's hand above her head to guide her along. I used to do those with Micha when I was little. Micha—and Aston—are ten years older than me. I liked having an older brother. I still do. Even when he's acting a bit too overprotective.

"Micha wants to talk to you. Zoey and I can hang out if you want privacy." I hand him back his phone, and without a response, he storms into the kitchen.

"I don't think Daddy is happy you live here," Zoey tells me in that blunt way kids are.

"Tough noogies on him."

She scrunches her nose, not fully understanding.

"Would it be weird for you if I lived here too? At least for a little while."

She shrugs. "Will you sleep in my room or play with my toys?"

I try to hold in my smile. "Nope. Not unless you have really awesome toys and tell me I can play with them first."

She juts her hip out. "Then I'm cool with it."

"You're kind of a sassy pants, aren't you?"

"Daddy says I have the mouth of a troublemaker."

Now there's no holding back my smile. "I do too. I think we'll be fast friends."

"How come you don't like Daddy?"

"Grown-up reasons." And because I need to change the subject from that. "You've stayed here before, huh?"

She nods vigorously. "Uncle Micha has a princess room for me. It's my favorite." Then she frowns, her body sinking in on itself. "Other than my old room at my mom's and stepdad's."

I didn't know she had a stepdad. I wonder if he's still in the picture.

"I get that. Moving is hard. I moved recently too. It's not fun."

She shakes her blonde head, her curls bouncing. Other than the dark eyes, she looks so much like Aston. I never met his ex-wife, so I have no clue what she looked like.

"What was your favorite thing about your old room?"

"My rainbow fairy lights and my pictures."

"We can make some new pictures if you want. I love to draw, and I'm pretty good at it."

A smile lights up her face, but before she can say anything, her father comes back over and interrupts us. "Can I talk to you?" Aston asks, a hard edge to his voice.

"Sure." I smile sweetly at him, which makes his jaw twitch a little. Fun.

"Zo-Zo, you can go up to your room. I'll come get you in a few minutes."

"Okay. Bye, Sky." She jumps up to give me a high five.

"Bye, Zoey. It was fun meeting you."

She scampers up the stairs, and I turn to Aston, only to have him grab me by my arm and drag me back into the kitchen. "You're not wearing pants."

"Your powers of observation are masterful."

He gives me an unimpressed look.

I throw my hands up in the air. "Get over it. You weren't supposed to be here. I was alone. It's not like my ass is showing. Either look or don't."

He grunts. "Micha said he can't kick you out." He paces in front of me. "But we can't live here together. You know that, right?"

I huff a breath. "I already live here, Aston. I have been for six weeks." And this house has become my sanctuary. My happy place. It's a home I feel good and safe being in.

He stops and stands over me, staring down at me as an aggravated growl hits his lips. Before I can comprehend what he's doing, he grasps my hips and lifts me until I'm seated on the counter.

"What the hell?" I swat his hands away.

"You're too damn short to have this conversation with. This is better."

I roll my eyes, fold my arms, and cross my knees, which covers my underwear but manages to hike up my shirt even more. Something I'm positive he notices. "I don't like being manhandled without my permission."

That pulls him up short, and he tilts his head. "What does that mean? You like being manhandled when you do give permission?"

I honestly said it as a joke, but it sounds kind of hot in the right situation with the right guy. "None of your business."

He sighs. "Skylar, these past six months have been hell. Zoey's mother died, and her stepfather decided he didn't want any parenting responsibility for Zoey and essentially booted her out of their house the week Astrid died. I punched him out at the funeral because he had it coming, and I wasn't in the best mental state, and my kid was heartbroken on top of being heartbroken. I broke his jaw, and because he's a lawyer and a dick, he had me arrested for assault and then dragged me through court over it. I had to deal with that and with Child and Family Services coming into my home to make sure Zoey was safe. Can you imagine that? All of that turmoil and upheaval for a five-year-old? Everything is finally settled, and now we're here, trying to restart our lives, but so are you, and now my best friend is telling me you have to stay."

I get it. He's hurting, and they've been through unspeakable pain over the last six months. I'm not insensitive to that, especially for Zoey. But that doesn't stop me from feeling rubbed raw and left outside naked. I don't even know if that makes sense, but that's how it's been for me with nearly every guy in my life. Not my friends and not my father or even Micha. They're men.

I'm talking about guys. Teased and belittled and made to feel small and insignificant. My entire life, that's how it's been for me. I was in a bad relationship for longer than I should have been with a guy who wasn't good to me. With a guy who repeated the same bad behavior others did throughout my life, only worse, while gaslighting me and telling me he loved me. Then he started getting aggressive. It took a while, but I left him. I'm here, and for the first time in my life, I feel strong, capable, and in control.

Now the guy who gave me the best kiss of my life at a party two years ago, the same guy who called me a drunken mistake, is trying to kick me out onto the street.

"Where do you propose I go?" I ask in a small but unmistakably bitter voice. I don't want to cry, but this morning took a miserable turn for me.

"Your parents?"

I laugh. "Why don't you go back to your parents?"

"I can't live with my parents, Skylar. I'm a thirty-five-year-old dad. Zoey needs consistency and familiarity right now, and this house is it. Her bedroom upstairs is it. Micha was going to sell me the house because he doesn't need it or want something so big when he's here a couple of months out of the year."

I frown. Micha never offered to sell me the house. I would have bought it from him.

"I can't live with my parents either," I tell him flatly.

But I also don't want to live with him. Zoey is cool, and I like her, but her father is a dick. A gorgeous dick but still a dick nonetheless. Maybe it's better this way. Maybe it's time I go out and find my own place and make it all mine and start living my best girl life.

"I need two months to find something else. It's not up for negotiation. If you don't like it, feel free to leave."

I hop off the counter and head toward the family room to get my candy and shut off my movie. I'm going to shower and get the hell out of here for a while. Go clear my head and do some deep thinking.

I spin back around. "And Aston? Your daughter, I like. But not you. Stay the hell away from me. I only make mistakes once. Never twice."

5

ASTON

The predawn air is heavy and frozen, my breath pluming out in thick white clouds of vapor. It has me shoving my hands deeper into my pockets and missing the warmth of LA. Nine years there have thinned my blood. But as I navigate the quiet streets, I can't stop wondering if uprooting our lives was the right call after all.

> Mom: Zoey wants to say good morning. Do you have a minute?

I smile, typing back quickly.

> Me: Absolutely.

I check the time and see that I've got thirty minutes before I need to meet with my new boss. The thought of Zoey in her new bedroom, surrounded by half-unpacked boxes, makes my chest tighten. She'd been brave about the move. Braver than I was, but I caught her yesterday staring at a picture of her old preschool class with a trembling lower lip.

"It's just us, Zo-Zo," I told her, smoothing her blonde curls away from her forehead. "Team Hughes against the world, remember? Boston will be fun. An adventure. And we have Grandma and Grandpa and Uncle Alden here."

She'd nodded solemnly, her eyes looking far too wise for a five-year-old. I suppose that happens when you lose one parent at the age of four and a half years old. I tried to keep us in California, but it got to be too hard to do by myself, and Zoey deserves better than that. Better than all the bad memories that plagued us both.

I want her to have a family. I want her to have light. Not simply a dad who works too many hours and most days still feels like he's learning how to be a dad.

My phone rings in my hand. "Morning, Zo."

"Morning." She yawns loudly.

"What are you doing up so early?"

"I wanted to see you before you left."

Guilt slams me in the chest like a two-by-four. "I'm sorry, sweetie. I didn't want to wake you that early. I'll be home in time to take you to the preschool meet and greet later."

"Okay." A pause. "Do you think the other kids are nice?"

"I'm sure they are. You'll make tons of friends." I hope. I seriously fucking hope. "You'll love it as much as you did your last one. Even more so when you start kindergarten this fall. It'll be so much fun."

"I guess. Is Skylar here?"

"I don't know, sweetie. She could be working today too."

"At your new hospital?"

"Yes."

"Will she have dinner with us?" There's no mistaking the hope in her voice.

Great. One five-minute meeting and she's already getting attached. "I don't know. I doubt it. I'm not sure how long Skylar is going to be living with us."

"Oh. Is it because you were mean to her? Because maybe you should say sorry, and then she'll stay."

Seriously? What on earth do I do with this? "Skylar has her own adult life going on. It might just be you and me, and that's okay."

She's silent for a beat. "I guess. I'm gonna go have breakfast."

"Sounds good, sweetie. Have a good day. I love you."

"Love you. Bye."

"All done?" my mother says in the background just as Zoey hangs up, and for a moment, it's so hard to breathe, I feel like I could die. She misses her mother. I know that. It's a hole for her that will never close, and a large part of me worries that with time, she'll forget her, and the hurt will be worse. She's simply forming attachments to any female she encounters. That's probably normal, but we'll see what her new therapist thinks.

Forcing one foot in front of the other, I walk myself into the hospital. I'm only working a half day today, and once she's back in preschool and all settled in, everything will be easier for both of us.

I feel like crap about Skylar.

I haven't seen her since our blowout in the kitchen yesterday. I moved Zoey's and my things in, and I didn't hear when Skylar left. I just know she did and that she didn't come home last night, which shouldn't bother me, but it does. Micha told me to keep an eye on her.

He thinks it's great for all of us if we live together.

And if I weren't attracted to his sister, maybe it would be.

But that kiss... that stupid surprise kiss. It left an imprint on my brain in indelible ink. Every fine detail is glued to my memory. For reasons I can't comprehend, it knocked me sideways and scrambled my brain, and I haven't been right since. The way her hands felt on my skin and the little sounds she made, and the way she tasted and pressed against me, so small and cute as she stood on her tiptoes and moved her mouth and tongue with mine like kissing me was all she'd ever wanted.

But it was Skylar. Not some random, sexy-as-all-sin woman. Skylar!

I told myself it was just a byproduct of everything. That I was drunk and sad and lonely that night, and that the latter two haven't changed so much for me. That Skylar was the first person I'd kissed or flirted with since my divorce. But I know better.

My memory of her was tiny, awkward, shy, too young, and too innocent. The girl had three beers at a college party and threw up. But that's not who she is anymore. She's curves and confidence, with shoulder-length messy blonde hair and green eyes that miss nothing. And the way she talks to me? I wish I didn't like her sassy fucking mouth as much as I do.

Would I even have noticed her if it weren't for the kiss? Would I have thought twice about her? I don't know. But now I don't know how to stop.

My first thought when I realized it was her Saturday night was how pretty she was. I couldn't look away, and she even called me out on my staring, but who could blame me? Then to overhear how she's never had an orgasm?

What's the story with that anyway, because there has to be one? I can't imagine a world where men aren't lined up to make her come. I can't exactly ask Micha either. It shouldn't have piqued my curiosity, and she definitely shouldn't have tickled my interest again. I'm not dating women right now. I have too much on my plate as it is, and I have to focus on my daughter and my new job in that order.

Plus, she works with me, is ten years younger than I am, and is my best friend's little sister. She's in her mid-fucking-twenties, which practically makes me an old man compared to her.

Oh, and she hates my guts because I was a moron and

called her a drunken mistake and said she was immature. She can never know the truth. Skylar Davenport is completely off-limits to me. Which is why she has to move out.

The sooner the better.

The hospital looms ahead, and I plow through, ready for the fresh start being handed to me. After meeting with my boss and talking with the OR and PACU staff, I make my way to the MSICU. The place I've been most anxious to get to today and a place I'll likely spend just as much time as I will in the OR. Skylar was not excited to have me work here. Truth be told, I don't love the idea of working with her either.

"Dr. Hughes." A no-bullshit-looking woman greets me as I step onto the floor. "I'm Suzanne, the nurse manager for the MSICU. Welcome."

"Thanks. I'm happy to be here."

"Let me know if there's anything I can do or if you have any questions."

I glance to my right and find the hallway lined with nurses, all watching me and whispering, some blushing and giggling. I smile at them while I search. It doesn't take me long. Four nurses in, I find a short blonde cocking a hip and folding her arms with a pissed-off scowl on her face as she talks to the redhead next to her.

Now my smile grows, and I wink at her, causing a tittering among the other nurses.

I turn back to the nurse manager. "I was hoping Skylar Davenport could give me a tour of the floor so I have a good lay of the land. I always like to know where things are so I can be prepared should I require an instrument or piece of equipment emergently."

If she's surprised I'm asking for Skylar specifically, she isn't letting on. Then again, I'm positive everyone in this hospital knows that Skylar is part of the Fritz family the way they know I'm a Hughes, which means they likely know how our families are aligned. We both come from famous billionaire families, though the Fritzes are a far larger family than ours and thankfully a hell of a lot more famous.

"Absolutely. It's perfect timing. Her patient was just moved to a floor bed, so she's awaiting her next, which is currently in the OR for at least another hour."

"Great."

I look back at the nurses and don't see Skylar still among them. She walked off, and I can't help my private smile. She hates that I'm here. I shouldn't be playing with this fire. I need to be polite and professional and indifferent. And I will be. I don't want to start off on the wrong foot with any of the nurses, her included. I simply want to clear the air between us and apologize. At least that's what I'm telling myself I'm doing.

Even if getting under her skin so she'll mouth off to me seems to be my new favorite hobby. Clearly, I'm just missing excitement in my life.

"I'll go find her."

Without waiting for Suzanne to direct me, I head down the hall only to hit the wall of nurses.

"Hi, I'm Lacy," one introduces herself.

"I'm Aspira," another comes.

They go on from there until I reach the last one. The redhead Skylar was talking to. Her name is Michaela, and she's smiling at me the way the rest of them are.

"Can you help me?" I ask her. "I'm looking for Skylar. She's supposed to show me around the floor."

"I can do that," one of them offers. "My patient has a procedure in fifteen minutes, so he'll be off the floor."

"Thanks. I appreciate that, but Suzanne told me to find Skylar for this."

The redhead is looking at me with new eyes, sizing me up the way good friends do when they're unsure about a man's intentions.

"Follow me, Doctor."

I do, much to the disappointment of the other nurses. It's been a while since I've had this level of attention. At my old hospital, the nurses and female doctors and staff stopped noticing me that way after my second year of residency and then completely after I got married. After Astrid left me, I was the sad sack of shit and dove into all things work, and no one felt right about flirting with me. They also didn't know I was part of Hughes Healthcare, a chain of community health centers in the Boston area, the way everyone here does.

Alden runs it now since he's the family provider and I'm the surgeon, but I'm still on the board and part of the charity it helps to run.

"She doesn't like you, though all she said was that she knows you," Michaela tells me bluntly.

"Her older brother is my best friend." I tuck in my grin. I don't elaborate. I have no idea how close she is with this woman, and I don't want word getting out that Skylar and I technically live in the same house, even if it's temporary.

"Did you earn her dislike?"

"Yes," I admit. "But in fairness, she was never roses and sunshine to me either."

She always thought I was an arrogant jerk—because I was—and I always thought she was a brat—because she was. But that's not what this is. I've been around her plenty of times in the past, and we've never been more than indifferent.

This is her reacting because we kissed and it was hot, and it would have led to more if the situation and circumstances were different, and she doesn't know how to manage that other than to be antagonistic and think of me as an asshole.

At least that's my psych 101 analysis.

"She's around the corner. Don't make me have to suffer ice cream because of you. I'm lactose intolerant."

I smile down at her. "No unnecessary emotional ice cream eating. I get it."

"Good. Be nice to her."

"That I can't promise." I grin at Michaela and find my cute little swan setting up an empty patient room. I enter and cross the room as she goes through the supply cart.

"I believe I told you to stay away from me. That wasn't me being dramatic."

I approach so I'm standing beside her but not close enough that I can smell her sweet fragrance. "I know. But I don't think that's going to work well with us. We live in the same house and work together."

"How come Micha didn't tell me you were going to be working here?" she asks as she closes one red drawer and opens another, sifting through packs of equipment.

I shrug. "Honestly, I don't even remember if I told him. Our conversations are usually over text because of the time change. I told him I was moving to Boston, and he called and offered me his place, and that was kind of that."

She closes the last bin, staring down at the red cart. "This is my job. I don't want it to be weird."

"Same," I agree. "Nurses are too important, and I rely too heavily on them to have a problem with one."

She nods slowly and turns to look up at me just as I look down at her.

"I don't know what to say about Micha's house other than I'm sorry," I tell her.

She makes a dismissive noise.

"No, really," I protest. "I am."

"But you have no intention of moving out." It's a statement, not a question.

"If it were just me, I would. But Zoey loves that house, and she needs something that makes her smile right now." Which reminds me. "Where did you stay last night?"

A smile curls up her lips. "Elsewhere."

"Did he make you come?"

Fuck. The words slipped out. Angry and jealous sounding too. Awesome. This is why we can't live together.

Her green eyes narrow. "That's an unprofessional question, Doctor."

"Did he?" I press, inching into her a little.

She laughs as if that's the most ridiculous question in the world. "Why do you care?"

Because the thought of her never orgasming before has been silently killing me, and I don't know what's worse—the thought that no one has ever gotten her off before or that someone will, and it won't be me.

Before I can come up with some sort of a response, there's a knock on the edge of the doorway that has us both turning around to find a young surgeon. "Hey, Skylar?" His eyes are all over her with blatant interest. "I was looking for you. Got a second?"

She stiffens beside me. Is this the guy she was with last night?

Oh, hell no.

"Actually, Sky was going to show me around the floor," I state, moving closer to her side and giving him a look a man shouldn't miss. One that says *fuck off*. "I'm the new trauma surgery attending."

He blinks as if he just realized I'm here and straightens his spine. And now his entire disposition changes, reforming into the arrogance of a surgeon and the contempt of a man who doesn't like another man touching what he wants.

"You must be Dr. Hughes. I heard you were joining the team. Welcome. I'm Josh Wesley, an R-3 with trauma."

Which means he works for me. "Excellent. I'm looking forward to working with you. If it's nothing emergent, I'll have

Sky show me around the floor before she finds you for whatever you wanted to talk to her about."

His gaze shifts back and forth between the two of us, narrowing ever so slightly as his jaw clenches. "No. It can wait."

"Perfect." I glance down at Skylar, who does not look happy with me. "Ready?" I place my hand on the small of her back, not even sure what I'm doing or why, but not stopping myself either.

"Of course, Doctor," she all but snarls, and yeah, so much for calling a truce with her.

6

SKYLAR

Would it be wrong to hit the cocky, new, hotshot trauma surgeon in the nuts again? As we walk down the hall, I take a quick glance down at his family jewels and wonder how I could make it look like an accident. Happened once, right? I've also been known to be clumsy on occasion.

"I see you plotting over there. Leave my boys out of this."

"I don't know what you're talking about," I say sweetly.

"Staring at my dick is sexual harassment. What would Josh say about where your curious little eyes are venturing?"

Josh. That's another thing. What the fuck does he want? What is this? Ghosts of bad exes and mistaken kisses day?

"You're an ass."

"Not a dick?"

"Are you always like this?"

"No," he answers with a note of honesty. "It's something about you that drives it out of me."

"Yeah. Like I said. You're an ass."

His head snaps down toward me. "How am I an ass? I simply wanted my tour before lover boy asked you some basic, inane question he already knew the answer to just so he could talk to you." A large hand on my arm that happens to graze my boob pulls me to a screeching halt. "Wait. Is he the guy who bought you the chocolates? Is he who you were with last night? You mentioned an ex, not a new boyfriend."

A bitter laugh catapults from me. "You know I'm twenty-five, right? I graduated from nursing school at the top of my class. I even earned an award for it. I'm a damn good nurse, and I save lives on a daily basis. That means no one gets to play games with me. Not anymore and not ever again."

He frowns. "I'm not playing games."

My hands fly frantically about. "Bullshit, you're not. *Sky was going to show me around,*" I mock his voice. "Never in my life have you ever called me Sky."

"I would have called you Swan, but I felt that was revealing my hand a bit too much, and I didn't want him to think we're together. Just wonder enough to fuck off since I'm his new boss."

"Argh. Stop." I shove at his chest, more than a little frustrated by all things men. "I don't need another big brother playing the role of protector. One is enough. I know Micha asked you to babysit and cockblock me."

He laughs. Kind of loud. "Sure. Yeah. You got it, Swan. No more acting like a big brother. Since that's obviously what I was doing."

I squint at the sarcasm in his voice but move on to the next hot button. "Why do you call me Swan? Is it meant to be ironic?"

His eyebrows take a nosedive. "Ironic?"

I fold my arms over my fleece and adjust the stethoscope around my neck. "Do you think I don't know that people used to call me an ugly duckling? Do you think I didn't hear them when they talked about me behind my back? *'Poor Skylar, so short and awkward, she'll never be tall and graceful. Poor Skylar with those vomit green eyes that are a little too big and lips that are a little too thick and wide and a nose that's a little too small for her face. She'll never be beautiful. Such an ugly duckling'."*

He shifts into me, his hand on my upper arm, and his expression fierce. "Who the fuck said that about you? Not Micha."

His extreme reaction throws me back a step. "No. Not Micha, but everyone else. The kids at school, my dance instructors, and even some parents and teachers." And it didn't stop there. High school kids can be brutal. Especially rich, elitist kids. In college, guys weren't much better and only pretended to be interested in me because of my family.

Then I met Josh after I started here and was so broken and affection-hungry that I fell for his love bombing. All the gifts and gestures and affection. It was incredible. Like waking up to a bright sunny day after a never-ending nightmare. Unfortunately, it wasn't long before he started treating me like shit and making me feel like the old, chewed-up gum you step on in the street and then curse at for being there. They all made me feel so small, so ugly, so insignificant, and useless, but he was the worst of them. And my wake-up call.

"That's pretty fucked up."

I remove his hand from my arm. "No less true, though."

"That's not why I call you Swan." The strong, sober note in his eyes and the hard set of his jaw demand I take him seriously. "I think it suits you. *Beautiful*," he emphasizes, "smart, protective, untouchable, and a little mean. Plus, your skin is so fair, and your hair is so blonde it's almost white." He takes a strand between his fingers, and my belly jumps.

I huff a breath and swat his hand, along with that feeling, away. "I'm not mean."

"You are to me. All of those things, actually."

I close my eyes. "Ugh. Stop. Why are you here?"

"I work here."

I cock an eyebrow, unimpressed with his deadpan response. "I meant, why did you ask for me to show you around?"

He sighs and runs his hands up his face and through his hair before he nods as if coming to some sort of conclusion. "We've somehow gotten on the wrong foot since Saturday night. Perhaps since the kiss. I'm known for being cocky, and I guess I am in a lot of ways, but mostly around my job. I used to be cocky and confident with women, but I haven't been in a very long time, and something about you brings it back out of me. It's kind of addictive."

He holds up his hand to stop me, as he can see I'm about to argue.

"Since my divorce, I'm an idiot a lot. I say stupid things. I'm also really bad at saying the right thing at the right time with women, and a lot of my confidence has vanished. You say you're awkward. Well, I am too now. Then you didn't come home last night, and I feel like shit about it. I don't want to kick you out of the home you've been living in, but I also don't want to live with you. I was hoping to clear the air between us. You're Micha's little sister, and I've known you your whole life. Yet despite my best intentions, I keep setting off stink bomb after stink bomb with you."

My nose scrunches. "That's kind of gross."

He tosses his hands up. "See what I mean? Regardless, it's no less accurate. It's been a rough couple of years for me, and there's something about you that gets me going and makes it so I don't know how to stop. But you're not someone I want to be enemies with, and you're definitely not someone I can flirt with. I'll behave. No more teasing or stepping in with your new boyfriend."

I don't correct him about Josh. Just as I didn't tell him who the chocolates were from. I don't even know why. Maybe old protective instincts die hard. Or maybe it's because I stupidly and immaturely like that he called me beautiful and acted, well, jealous. Even if he was just trying to be brotherly or noble on Micha's behalf or whatever that was. It has been a rough couple of years for him. He got divorced and then lost his ex-wife and had to deal with whatever Zoey's stepdad put him through and is now a single dad.

We all deserve a pass and a second chance.

"Fine. Let me finish showing you around."

He smiles, and I wish he wouldn't. It's a damn good look on him.

"Thank you."

I nod and take him on a tour of the floor, showing him where the storage and supply rooms, the crash carts, and the Pyxis MedStations are. I don't bother with the break room or locker room because he's a surgeon, and they have their own on a different floor. As we walk, I explain that the floor is mostly divided between surgical and medical patients and how we keep them separate to prevent unnecessary exposure and infections.

"Big floor," he notes, looking around now that we're back where we started. "My last hospital had a separate SICU."

"We have forty beds and are one of the highest-volume pediatric ICUs in the country."

He grins. "Now you know why it wasn't such a hard sell for me to move back here."

"Should we come up with rules?"

He peers down at me, stepping in a bit closer than he should. Closer than I'd like. Especially when he smells like expensive manly bodywash and not the hospital. "Rules?"

"Rules for living together. I haven't had a roommate since college, and the only man I've ever lived with was my boyfriend. I don't know how this works, and you're a grown man with a child."

He chuckles lightly. "I think the rules are still the same as they were in college. Stay out of my shit, and I'll stay out of yours. As for cleaning up after myself, as you said, I'm a grown man and a father, and I do that already. I won't eat your food, but since I have a tendency to overbuy groceries for Zoey, you can help yourself to whatever I get. I'm good at making breakfast, but I'm not the best at dinner, so if you want takeout, just let me know and I can order you stuff. No men. No parties."

I smile up at him. "No men?"

He smiles back. "Those were Micha's orders, but I'm not sour on them."

I roll my eyes. "I'm not bringing men home, but that has nothing to do with you or Micha. And the only people I ever have over are my people, who you already know."

"Then we're good. Other than no more hitting me in the nuts or kissing me in dark rooms, I'm not sure what other rules we need. Since you're moving out soon anyway."

I flip him off, and he chuckles.

"Thanks for showing me around. I have to get going. Will I see you tonight?"

I peek up at him. It's annoying how good he looks in blue scrubs. They match his eyes almost perfectly, and his blond hair is a little too long on top, like he's gone a while between haircuts, but it totally works on him. Sucks he's so pretty. And he knows it.

"You're done for the day?"

"Half day. Zoey has a preschool meet and greet."

I smile thinking about that for her. "That's exciting."

"She's nervous. She loved her last preschool. This one feeds right into the kindergarten, so I'm hoping she makes friends."

"She will. She's a great kid."

A soft, prideful smile lights up his face, and it makes something in my chest—and let's face it, my ovaries—go oomph.

"I almost forgot. She asked that I show you. She's your biggest fan now, by the way, in case that wasn't clear." He pulls out his phone and starts scrolling through until he finds a picture and flips his phone around for me to see. She's all blonde hair and dark eyes and big smiles, showing off a missing tooth on the bottom. "Her first lost tooth. It happened right after dinner before her bath. Thankfully, she didn't swallow it. I barely had anything set up for us, and I had to make the tooth fairy come."

"With you as the tooth fairy."

His smile twists. "I'm everything right now. Mom and Dad. Tooth fairy and Santa Claus. She asked if the tooth fairy could fly to heaven to show her mother the tooth. I told her yes and then had a moment of panic when I realized that one day she'll learn there is no tooth fairy and that her mother didn't get to see her first lost tooth, and then she'll hate me for lying. I think I need to read more parenting after loss books."

That last part is said as a joke, as a way to lighten the heavy topic. But it falls flat. My chest pinches, and I soften faster than ice cream in the desert. "I'll be home tonight," I tell him. "I want to hear all about how Zoey liked her new preschool and the tooth fairy."

His eyes hold mine for a long moment before they dip to my lips and then flicker back up. "Thank you," he says in a low tone that instantly makes goose bumps rise on my arms and the back of my neck. "She'll love that."

"Of course." I don't move, and neither does he, and I don't understand any of this. Why I react to him so strongly. I don't like it. "See you later, Doctor." I walk away, but he stops me.

"Hey, Little Swan?" I stop but don't turn back to him. That stupid nickname is growing on me, and that's not a good thing.

"Yeah?"

He doesn't say anything, and curiosity gets the better of me. I turn and look at him, but all the softness he had a moment ago when talking about his daughter is gone. I tilt my head when Josh steps in front of me, blocking my view of Aston.

"Hey. Do you have that second now?"

Aston storms off, and for the second time this morning, I'm tempted to take a shot at a man's nuts.

"No," I answer evenly.

"Sure, you do. Your next patient just got to the PACU, and you're done puppy walking your brother's bestie around."

"How did you know he's my brother's friend?"

He makes a dismissive noise. "Everyone in Boston knows who the Hugheses are, the same as they know who the Fritzes are. Word has already spread around about who he is."

Yes, everyone knows who we are, but there are plenty of moments I'm glad my last name is Davenport and not Fritz. My mom, Rina, is the baby of the Fritz siblings and works part-time as an ICU nurse across town. She and my uncle Landon have probably kept the lowest profile out of all the primary Fritz children, but the rest of my uncles and even plenty of my cousins are as famous as it gets.

"Whatever. Go away."

"Come on. Don't be like that." He shifts his weight, looking sad and broken. "Have you been getting my notes? You haven't mentioned them."

"You mean the ones you shove into my locker? Yes. I've gotten them. And then fed them to the biowaste bin."

He grunts, annoyed by that. "I wouldn't have to leave you notes if you'd just talk to me like an adult instead of acting like a child about this. I still don't understand why you left me."

He just called me a child and doesn't understand why I left him? Ha. That's a good one. "Yes, you do. I told you why."

He shakes his head as if my reasons don't make sense and never did to him, which is probably accurate. He never saw a problem with how he treated me, and on the occasions that I pointed out how it hurt me or even how he was scaring me, he'd be dismissive and call me oversensitive or hormonal or say I was overreacting or making things up or some other variant of that. Still, I'm all set with the gaslighting.

"Can we just... I don't know, get a coffee maybe? Sit and talk since you blocked my number and won't let me call you?"

"There's nothing to say. It's been six weeks, and we're as much over now as we were when I left."

He grasps my shoulders and pulls me closer. His hand goes for my neck, and my pulse speeds up as adrenaline spikes in my veins the way it would whenever he did that. I swat his hand away and suppress my shiver. That won't happen again.

He sighs and holds his hands up in surrender. "I miss you. I was angry when you left, and I know I said some things I shouldn't have that day. You think I did a million things wrong, but you didn't fight for us, and it hurt. But Skylar, I haven't stopped loving you, and I haven't stopped missing you. Come on. It wasn't all bad with us. Most of it was pretty great."

I clench my fists until my nails dig into my palm. It's easy when he looks at me like this and says these things to forget how it was with him. How being with him made me feel. The fear that used to consume me. I think back to that saying that if it costs you your peace, it's too expensive.

"Do you really not understand that you treated me like shit? That you ridiculed me like I was nothing. That you would yell and berate me and talk down to me and insult me. You'd terrorize and intimidate and shame me. You'd squeeze my neck and use your grip on me like a threat."

He looks down at the floor. "I don't recall it being that way. You came down on me a lot too. Nothing I ever did or said to you was good enough. If I didn't like something, it was like I couldn't be honest about it. And let's face it, you're a bit of a drama queen and tend to overreact and make up things that aren't actually happening. But regardless, I never meant to make you feel bad if I ever did. Never. Please give me a second chance."

The fact that he doesn't know and still doesn't see it is scary.

"I need to finish getting my room ready for my patient. My orders are a mess, and I have to sort them out."

"Okay. I'll let you do that. But you know how I feel and what I want. I'll let you think about it, and then we'll talk again later this week."

He leaves me here, and I dutifully go and get ready for my patient and do my job. For eight hours, that's exactly what I do. And I don't think about either of the sharks swimming in my ocean. Even if I know they're still there lurking.

7

***

ASTON

There's no reason I should be edgy right now. Zoey loved the preschool and her new teacher. She starts tomorrow and is excited about it. I spent two hours unpacking and doing laundry and getting us organized and even boxing up some of Micha's things he said I could, so we'd have more room. Tomorrow is my first full and real day at the hospital.

It's all good things. I'm insanely happy about it.

But that hasn't stopped me from stupidly and annoyingly watching the door or wondering what that douche Josh wanted with Skylar. I heard the buzz about him as I walked past the nurse's station. He's her ex. They were whispering about secret notes he leaves in her locker and how they can't understand how someone like her could dump someone like him.

Someone like her.

I didn't comprehend their meaning at first. Skylar is a billionaire. A Fritz. Despite being a total ballbuster, she's a sweet and kind human. She's also seriously fucking beautiful. Her hair and eyes are the stuff of fantasies, and don't even get me started on her curves. So, I didn't get it. I was almost tempted to ask. Until I thought back to what she said about what others have called her in the past.

My swan was called an ugly duckling.

I wanted to tell each of those nurses that a guy like Josh was lucky he ever had a shot with a girl like her, but I kept walking. Kept fuming. Hating myself for all of it. Because if I hadn't already been feeling protective over her after what she told me, I sure as fuck was after that. Even if her battles aren't mine to fight.

Zoey is drawing at the kitchen table while I finish cooking for us. Pasta with zucchini and meat sauce because she'll eat it, and I know how to make it.

"Zo-Zo, finish up. Dinner's almost ready."

She doesn't spare me a glance, just moves faster with her tongue tucked off to the side between her teeth. The pasta is done, and after I drain it, I add it to the meat sauce and toss it all together. Zoey is the worst with veggies, but this sauce has tiny pieces of zucchini hidden and spinach masked as torn-up basil. Thus far, she hasn't noticed and always eats it.

"Drawing away," I tell her as I put the pasta into a bowl.

"Ugh."

I cock an eyebrow. "Really?"

She gives me a glare she's about ten years too young for. "I'm in my art era. I need to decorate my walls with my feels."

I try to contain my smirk. "You can reenter your art era and feels after dinner. And since when are you so into art?"

She shrugs. "You're bossing my space."

"Where are you learning these things? You're five."

"YouTube."

I make a mental note to increase the parental controls on her iPad.

"I used to do art with Mommy," she continues.

Oh. Shit. And I suck because I didn't know that.

She falls quiet, and I place her food in front of her along

with a glass of milk and one of water. I sit beside her, twirling my noodles without bringing the fork to my mouth as I watch her.

"I was never very good at art," I start. "I have a science brain. But your mom used to paint a lot, and it seems you got your art talent from her and thankfully not from me. Would you like that? If I bought you some paints and gave you a space to do that or got you into an art class?"

I get another shrug with a downward glum face as she starts to twirl her pasta, same as I am.

"Will you make me a picture? It can be anything you want."

She opens her mouth to answer when we hear the front door opens and then immediately close. And much to my chagrin, my daughter's face lights up like a Christmas tree.

"Hello," Skylar sings out, only to find us a moment later as she enters the kitchen. "Guess what I found?!" She is practically vibrating with excitement as she pulls two boxes of multicolored fairy lights out of her bag. "I thought maybe after dinner we could set them up in your room. What do you think?"

Zoey flies off her chair and races straight over to Skylar. She throws her arms around her like they're ancient besties, and I'm hit with a pang unlike any I've ever felt. For a moment, all I can do is blink. I'm hot and have chills. Skylar bought Zoey fairy lights for her room. It's beautiful and terrifying. It makes me want to cross the room, thread my hands through Skylar's hair, and kiss her crazy. But worse than that? My kid is already falling in love with her.

Fuck.

"Is that a yes?" Skylar laughs, hugging her back.

"Yes! Yes!" Zoey jumps up and down before she glances back over at me. "Do you think Uncle Micha will mind? Stephen didn't like it when I taped lights to the ceiling."

That's because your former stepfather was a dick.

"I think Uncle Micha will love it. We'll set them up tonight, so you have them as a nightlight. You need to thank Skylar for that very thoughtful gift."

"Thank you! Thank you!" Zoey is jumping like she has springs for feet.

"It was nothing. I was passing a shop and saw them." She looks past me into the kitchen, eyeing the dishes and pots. "Smells delicious. Is there enough for three?"

"Help yourself," I offer, because yes, there's more than enough for three. I might have made the entire box of pasta and doubled the sauce recipe, even if I wasn't sure she'd be home to eat it.

"Awesome. I'm starving. Thank you." She makes herself a bowl, and I try not to notice how she's showered and changed her clothes and how her hair is now down and wavy and she has something light and shimmery on her cheeks and eyelids and how the purple sweater she's wearing hugs her tits just a little too tightly. "Zoey-Zo. Tell me all about preschool, girl. I want every detail."

Zoey is wiggling in her seat, but I point to her pasta, and she scoops up a bite and dutifully shovels it into her mouth.

"They have a really big slide," Zoey tells her.

"Oh. Sounds like fun." Skylar takes the seat on the other side of her, not even sparing me a glance. "What else? Is it a big playground? Those are my favorites."

Zoey nods vigorously. "So big. It also has a bouncy bridge."

"Cool. That sounds amazing. I'm super jealous I can't join you."

Zoey laughs. "Silly, you're too old."

"Don't I know it. Your daddy is even older than I am. But I don't think we're too old to play with each other, are we, Daddy?"

I choke on my pasta, and there's a legit moment when I think I'm going to die or that my life will be in Skylar's hands when I require her to do the Heimlich maneuver. Luckily for all of us, it clears with a few strong coughs.

"Daddy, you okay?" Zoey asks, worry stretched across her face.

I wipe my mouth and take a sip of my water. "Yes. I'm fine. Just went down the wrong pipe."

"That's what she said," Skylar chirps, and I glare at her.

"Is there a reason you're being... impudent?"

Her eyebrows bounce. "Big word, Daddy. And I'm guessing it's because you couldn't say something else. I think it's a little deserved, no? Comes with overstepping boundaries. But since we're both thrust into a hard situation, if I can't beat him, I might as well join him."

None of this should make me hard, but of course it does. My palm tingles with the mental image of putting her on my knees so I can spank her round ass red. Then we'll see who she's calling Daddy.

"Behave," I warn her.

"Or what?" She bats her eyelashes at me, and I clench my fork so tightly I'm shocked I'm not bending it. "Will you punish me for being naughty, Daddy?"

Yes. Yes, I fucking will, and you'll both love it and hate it.

"What are you doing?"

"I don't appreciate you going around telling everyone at work that I'm off-limits."

"What?" comes out a pitch higher. "I didn't do that."

She tilts her head, studying me intently, only for her eyebrows to take a nosedive. "You didn't?"

I shake my head. "No. I left the hospital right after you gave me the tour."

Her lashes flutter. "Oh. But that's what was going around the floor and that's what..." She trails off. "You really didn't?"

"I really didn't. I wouldn't do that." Even if I didn't like the way Josh was looking at her.

"Um. That's curious."

"Well, I didn't. You clearly misheard, or they did. Are you going to apologize?"

She smirks at me. "Nope. You're still kicking me out. Tit for tat." Mercifully, she returns to Zoey. "Promise you'll tell me all about your first day tomorrow?"

"Okay."

"Great. I also heard you lost your first tooth. That's pretty major. Did the tooth fairy come?"

The two of them go back and forth the entire meal as the three of us eat. I'm superfluous. Just the dad, but not the daddy, thankfully. Still, it's difficult to stay mad at Skylar. Zoey hasn't been this animated in months. She's smiling and laughing and even teasing me and Skylar.

She reacts to Skylar in a way she doesn't with me, and I'm more than grateful for it. I don't know why Skylar is being this way with my daughter, or even me, but I don't care. It's everything Zoey needs right now, and I hate the way it turns my cold, dead heart into something that's reluctantly beating harder than it wants to.

I really need to get laid. Or at the very least find a life. One that doesn't include inappropriate thoughts about my best friend's little sister.

8

———

ASTON

The rest of the night is uneventful. I clean up the kitchen, give Zoey a bath, and do our standard nightly routine. Skylar is around, doing her own thing, but other than popping in to say good night to Zoey and checking on how the lights turned out, she doesn't bother me again. And when I close the door to my bedroom, get undressed, and take a shower, it's not Skylar on my brain when I jerk off.

It's some random, faceless, nonexistent blonde.

At least that's what I tell myself as I take my cock in my hand and squeeze the base. My eyes close as a heavy breath exhales from my lungs. I stifle my moan as the hot water hits my muscles, trailing down my body and over my aching cock.

I can't decide how I want her. Standing naked in the warm, steamy water with me or somewhere else. Like a bed or a kitchen counter, where I surprise her, coming in behind her. I'm hard, and she feels it and moans for me.

At first, that's how I imagine her. I rub against her perky ass and reach around to squeeze her tits, but it's not doing it. I want her naked. I want to see her tits and her pussy, and I want her eyes. Pretty green eyes that are filled with desire as they beg me. My fantasy changes and now we're showering together.

She runs her hands through her hair, getting it wet before she locks eyes with me and sinks to her knees. I get a coy smile while she licks her lips and takes my throbbing cock in her hand.

A growl rips from my lungs as I start to pump myself, greedy for her mouth that's now licking the underside of my cock. My forearm hits the marble wall. Shit, that feels good. Her tongue flickers along my shaft, up along a vein before she dives down on me, taking me as deep as she can go. So deep she gags on me and has to swallow.

My fingers thread through her hair, holding the strands back from her face so I can see her.

"That's it," I tell her. "Suck me down."

She moans, and fuck, how I love that. Her hand slides over her tits, where she pulls on her nipples before continuing south to her cunt that's spread open, anxious for her fingers. For my mouth. For my cock. For my cum.

"Are you wet for me, my little swan?"

She nods eagerly. "Yes, but I'm empty. I need you to fill me up. Please, Aston, I need you in my pussy."

I groan because shit. I want that. I want that so fucking badly. I want her tits and her cunt and her ass. I want all of her. I'm dying with the need to taste her. To lick her. To feel her.

"Take my cock down your throat one more time and then stand up for me," I command, picking up the pace of my hand and running my thumb over my head.

She does. My good girl sucks me hard until I see stars, and then stands, her fingers playing with her clit because she's too turned on to stop.

"Does that feel good?"

She lifts her leg to my hip and leans back against the wall to show me as she touches herself. Her pussy is so pretty. So pink and wet and warm. I lick my lips, line my cock up with her opening, and thrust in her as hard as I can. Because that's what she wants. My cock. Me to fuck her. No one else.

"Oh god!" she cries out, and I pump faster into her as I fuck my hand harder.

"Don't stop rubbing your clit. I want you to come on my cock. I'm so close. I can't stop. I can't hold back."

And I can't. I'm right at the edge, and I fuck her and fuck her and fuck her. Feeling how tight she is. Listening to how she moans and begs for me to take her harder, deeper, anyway I want. Her body arches, and her eyes stay on mine, and then she's coming. So. Fucking. Hard.

And so am I. I explode, spurts of cum shooting all over my hand and the wall while I shove my face into my arm to muffle my curses and yells, and God help me, even her name. When I'm done, I collapse against the wall, breathing hard with my heart pounding in my chest.

Dammit!

I push away from the wall, angry and frustrated. I get myself cleaned up, rationalizing that it was just a release. Just a way to blow off steam. That she's the only woman in my life at present so it's natural that I thought of her. I convince myself of it. And when I get in bed to go to sleep, I don't allow her to cross my mind.

That is, until morning comes.

The digital clock on the nightstand reads 4:59. My alarm will go off in exactly one minute, and no matter how much or how little sleep I get, I always wake before it. Another night of fractured sleep behind me, and I groan, reaching for my phone to shut off my alarm so I don't have to deal with that. I'm cloudy, my thoughts feeling like they're wrapped in cotton, fuzzy and indistinct. I'm still not used to the time change.

Today is going to feel like running a gauntlet. Zoey's first day at preschool, starting at the hospital this morning, the smattering of unpacked boxes lining the hallway, and the woman in the bedroom next to mine, whom I can't quite figure out.

I swing my legs over the side of the bed and sit here for a moment, letting the fogginess pass. I scrub my hands up and down my face, use the bathroom, get myself dressed and ready to run into work, and then go to wake up Zoey, but as I step into the hall, I hear noise in the bathroom. I strain my ears, trying to determine why Zoey is already up. She's been waking earlier since the move, wanting to be with me in the morning.

Micha's house is too big for just him, which is why he offered it to us while he's overseas with Doctors Without Borders. "Two years minimum in Sudan," he'd said. "The place will just sit empty otherwise. You'd be doing me a favor, keeping it lived in." As if he weren't the one doing me the favor.

What he failed to mention was that his sister had already moved in six weeks prior.

A thump from the bathroom breaks my reverie, followed by what sounds like a child's voice singing and the faucet turning on. Zoey must be up. I guess that's good. I don't have to drag her out of bed.

"Zoey? You getting ready?" I call softly, twisting the knob on the door to open it without waiting for a response. "Let me help you with—"

The words die in my throat.

It's not Zoey.

Skylar stands there, one hand clutching a white towel around her body, the other frozen in the act of wiping steam from the mirror. Her hair is slick and gold against her neck as water droplets trail down her shoulders, collarbones, and ample cleavage before disappearing beneath the edge of the towel. She looks like she did in my fantasy last night.

But it gets worse. The towel is small. Even for Skylar, who is short. The thing cuts off at her upper thighs, which are curvy and wet like the rest of her—fuck, did I actually just think that? —and smooth, and Jesus, I'm already sweating, and my heart is pounding, and I haven't even started my run yet.

For one excruciating moment, we stare at each other, my hand still on the doorknob, her eyes wide with shock. My dick is growing hard in my track pants, and these bastards are thin and won't hide much. Thankfully, her hateful eyes are glued to my face.

"What the hell?" she finally sputters, clutching the towel tighter. "Get out!"

I backpedal so fast I nearly trip over my own feet. "Sorry! I thought you were—I swear I heard—Zoey sometimes—" My brain short-circuits, unable to form a coherent sentence while the image of her wet skin burns itself into my retinas and, unfortunately, my memory.

"Ever heard of knocking?" Skylar's voice rises, her free hand groping for something on the counter before she comes up with a hairbrush, which she brandishes at me like a weapon.

"The door was unlocked!" I protest, finding my voice again. "Who doesn't lock the bathroom door?"

"Someone who was used to living alone. If this weren't Micha's house, I would have taken the master from the start. You're lucky I closed the door in the first place. I didn't think about it. It was a habit."

"You seriously have a problem with locking bathroom doors. This is the second time I've walked in on you like..." I trail off.

"Like what?" she challenges.

My eyes narrow. "You know."

"No. I don't. Tell me."

Fucking tease. "Almost naked!" I wave my hand up and down her body.

"Normal people knock before barging into a bathroom." She shifts her weight, and the towel slips a dangerous half inch before she catches it. My eyes betray me, following the movement before I can force them back to her face.

"I thought Zoey was in here," I explain through gritted teeth. "I didn't exactly expect to find you half-naked."

"You're very interested in my current state of dress. Or undress. I'm not half-naked," she corrects, a dangerous glint in her eye. "I'm fully naked under this towel. There's a difference."

Heat crawls up my neck, and my stupid, pussy-deprived cock nods toward her in agreement. *Traitor.* "That's—that's not the point."

"What's the point, Dr. Hughes? That you can't handle seeing a woman in a towel? Are you twelve?" She arches an eyebrow, and I hate how composed she is now despite standing here dripping wet with only a thin piece of fabric between her and my hands. Shit, no, I mean total exposure. Not my hands. I won't be touching her. Not ever.

"The point is you should lock the door," I insist, refusing to be baited. "And while we're at it, if we're going to attempt coexisting in this house, maybe work on wearing more clothes. When we got here you were in nothing but a shirt."

"A long, oversized shirt. Don't exaggerate."

"A very short shirt," I correct.

"Fine. How about you work on knocking before entering and looking a little less?"

"Maybe. Or you could lock the door and wear clothes. If I didn't know better, I'd think you wanted me to look."

She belts out a caustic laugh. "Don't flatter yourself. I'd rather bathe in acid than have you look at me."

I smirk at the exaggerated denial. "Somehow I doubt that, Little Swan."

She squints at me. "You're the one who walked in uninvited. Twice now."

"Except I was invited. I live here now. And hopefully you won't for much longer."

"You're being such an asshole!" She flips me off, and I probably deserve that.

With a gruff breath, I calm myself down because she's right. I am being an asshole. "Sorry. That just came out. I don't want to fight. It's too early for that."

I realize I'm still standing in the doorway while water drips steadily from her hair down her arms and onto the tile floor. I should leave. I should turn around and walk away and pretend this never happened. Instead, I find myself noticing the faint scent of her shampoo or bodywash. It's that scent. The one I liked so much from two years ago that I thought was perfume.

Shit. That smell.

"I agree." She puffs out a breath and sets the hairbrush down. "You're a real charmer in the morning."

No. Now I'm a horny, grumpy son of a bitch. "I haven't had coffee yet. I'm much more charming post-caffeine."

"I already know that's not true." She makes a shooing motion with her free hand. "Go. Make coffee. I'm starting to get cold."

I close the door behind me and blow out a breath. Coffee. I need coffee, and then I need to get Zoey up and both of us out the door. And I need to bleach the image of water droplets on smooth skin from my mind.

This is exactly why living with Skylar Davenport is a bad idea. She takes up too much space in a room, in a conversation, in my head. I have enough complications already. She's not another I can afford.

9

SKYLAR

"Vitals have been up and down all night, but his sats are stable enough with the nasal cannula. His hemoglobin and hematocrit have been holding, but output from his chest tube picked up a little in the last hour, so you might want to mention it to the trauma team this morning during rounds," Alison tells me as I take report from her. "He's been in a decent amount of pain with the rib, clavicle, and arm fractures."

"Poor kiddo."

"For real. This is why whenever I have children, I'll never let them climb trees."

"They're holding off on surgery?" I ask.

"For now. His CT didn't show any bleeding."

"Works for me." I put my pen in my pocket, fold up my piece of paper, and slip it in beside it.

"Hey, I heard you know the new hot attending."

Here we go. It's as if a celebrity walked into the hospital, and now I'm part of it. I was shocked when Aston said he never told anyone that I'm off-limits. Michaela told me she had heard a few of the male residents and a couple of nurses from the

PACU team talking about how Aston told them that I'm his best friend's little sister and no one is to touch me. I was furious. Rightfully so.

But maybe Michaela simply misheard, or that off-limits crap came from Josh. Who knows. Regardless, I heard two techs gossiping about Aston in the café off the lobby this morning as I was getting coffee. I'm seriously starting to wish he worked in a different hospital.

I didn't stay long this morning after the bathroom incident. I said good morning to Zoey and wished her a good first day, but then I got my cute ass out the door.

Aston wasn't dressed for work. He was wearing running clothes, including a shirt that clung to his chest, arms, and abs, showing off every detail of the muscle the man is made of. For a moment, I was tempted to drop the towel until I remembered who he is and that I can't stand him. Oh, and I'm focusing on me and not men.

"Uh-huh," I say noncommittally.

"He's gorgeous. Seriously freaking gorgeous. I helped bring over a patient from the PACU earlier, and he had just gotten there after *running* into work. What is it about a hot, sweaty guy?" She fans her face. "So, tell me, what's he like? Is he as dreamy—"

I stand abruptly, cutting her off. "You probably want to get home. I'm sure it was a long shift."

She giggles. "Or I'll just wait until the new doctor comes in for rounds."

"Unless Sky's already claimed him," Michaela unhelpfully provides, joining us and playing with a pen in her hands. "He's a Hughes. Besides, didn't you hear the gossip going around? He asked for her personally yesterday for a tour."

I glare at her. "It wasn't like that."

"No?" Michaela questions, smirking mischievously at me.

"No," I reply adamantly, a little miffed that she's teasing me like this, especially in front of other people. "He's my brother's best friend. That's all."

Alison tilts her head at me until recognition dawns on her face. "Oh. Right. Wow. For some reason I always forget you're a Fritz. Maybe it's because your last name is different." Her eyes go wide with interest. "So, if you're not dating him, is he single? Give me all the details."

I sigh. "I'm not involved in his personal life enough to know anything."

"You won't mind if I make a pass at him?"

"Or any of us single women." Michaela laughs, shoving the pen in her chest pocket and adjusting her stethoscope. "Because damn, he's hot. Skylar shouldn't get all the hot men around here."

Something sticky and weird churns in my stomach. The milk in my coffee from the café must have gone bad. "Go for it," I tell them, scratching at a sudden itchy spot on the back of my neck. "He's all yours. Josh too, for that matter. I want nothing to do with trauma surgeons."

"Talking about me already?" comes a voice from behind me, and I close my eyes. There really is no escaping this man. As much as I like Zoey, I need to find my own place stat.

I turn and find Aston in full surgeon mode with a cup of coffee in his hand, blue scrubs on with his long-sleeved shirt pushed up to the elbows, revealing strong, tan forearms. His blond hair is a little damp from a shower, and his jawline, which really should be illegal for how chiseled it is, is smooth. Then there's the smug look in his blue eyes.

"Hi," Alison says with a breathy rasp. "We didn't get a chance to meet this morning. I'm Alison."

"Hi Alison. I'm Aston." He shakes her hand, and I think Alison is going to pass out. "Nice to meet you." He nods at Michaela. "Good morning, Michaela."

"Good morning, Doctor." Her face is as red as her hair, and I don't think I've ever seen Michaela blush for anyone.

"Are you ready for rounds?" He asks me like I'm a child and don't know how to do my job.

"Yes." That's all I say.

"Excellent. Because, as luck would have it, I believe my first patient here is yours." He doesn't seem happy about that, and neither am I.

"He was my patient overnight. I'm happy to stay and talk you through him," Alison offers, inching closer only to have Michaela do the same on the other side of him, and seriously, ladies? Way to play it cool.

"That's kind of you, but I'm sure Skylar can likely manage it."

Ass.

"Come with me, Doctor." I turn on my heels and head toward my patient's room. In a half-beat, he's beside me, one of his strides equaling two of mine. "You know this is a professional environment, and being a condescending dick doesn't go over well with the nurses."

"I don't know what you're talking about. Those nurses seemed to like me a lot. You're the only one who can't stand me."

"That's because your pretty face doesn't earn you bonus points with me. I know who you are underneath."

He chuckles. "So, I shouldn't comment on the fact that you think I'm good-looking."

"No. You shouldn't. And I won't comment on how you stared at my boobs this morning in only my towel. Regardless, maybe you should stop being a dick and telling me how to do things."

"I didn't tell you how to do things," he defends as we reach the outside of the patient's room. "I gave you a helpful suggestion. Like locking a bathroom door."

"That's not a suggestion. That's being bossy."

He makes a tsking noise and shakes his head. "Oh no, Little Swan. That's survival."

I peek into the patient's room and find him awake despite the early hour. His parents are in there with him, postures tense with worry.

I turn back to Aston and peer up at him. "No more *Little Swan* or any swan for that matter. We're at work."

He nods solemnly. "You're right. Professional only."

"You're early," I tell him. "I haven't even seen my patient yet or done my evaluation."

"Yes, but the overnight trauma team said he's a close watch, and I wasn't thrilled with what I saw on his CT. I'm sure we can evaluate him together."

"Fine. Alison mentioned how she didn't like his chest tube output over the last hour or so and that he's in a lot of pain."

"Let's go take a look." He pans his hand for me to enter first. "Lead the way, Nurse Davenport."

I resist the urge to flip him off again. Instead, we walk into the room together. "Good morning. I'm Skylar. I'll be your nurse today. This is Dr. Aston Hughes. He's the trauma surgeon in charge of your case."

The parents greet us and give us both a rundown of what happened. Parker is a tough kid but is clearly hurting and scared. Both Aston and I go through our exams and questions.

"I'm thinking I'm going to take you into the OR this morning, Parker," Aston announces as he places his stethoscope back around his neck.

"Is that really necessary?" his mother asks. "The doctor who admitted us said they'd just observe him."

"Yes, but his chest tube is putting out more blood and fluid than I'm comfortable with, and his oxygen saturation level is a bit lower than I'd like. I want to take a look and make sure we're not missing anything. We need to keep his lungs clear to prevent infection and help with healing."

Her husband puts his arm around her and pulls her into his side, but he gives Aston a firm nod.

"Hey, Parker," Aston says, walking over to him and taking a seat on the side of the ICU bed. "Have you ever been inside an OR before?"

Parker shakes his head.

"They're pretty cool, but if you don't know what to expect, they're a little scary. I'll have the nurse show you everything before they put you to sleep. You won't feel a thing. I promise. When you wake up, you'll be pretty tired, and we can give you medicine to help with your pain. But I'm hoping I can also do something about that when I'm operating. Sound good?"

"Yes," he says softly.

"Good stuff. You're a brave guy. I can see that already." He turns back to the parents.

"I'll have anesthesia come in and speak with you, and we'll get consents, but I'd like to get him in the OR sooner rather than later." He stands and nods to me for us to step out.

"I'll be back in a bit," I tell them.

We step out into the hall, and Aston logs into my computer to start inputting orders and get the OR going.

"Are you going to freeze his nerves to help with his pain?" I ask as I stare over his shoulder and take note of what he's doing.

"If I can, that's my plan. I have a feeling one of those broken ribs is poking something it shouldn't be. He's bleeding from somewhere."

"I agree. He doesn't look right to me. How did Zoey do getting off this morning?"

"Good," he replies, typing away. "She was excited, which helps. We'll see if she liked it tonight."

"People are gossiping about us," I whisper, keeping my voice low so it doesn't carry.

He throws me a side-eye. "I know. I heard a bit of it this morning, and someone already asked me how I know you. It seems like the gossip is mixed and a bit jumbled. It wasn't from me. I swear."

"I believe you. I just don't like it." It was probably Josh talking shit. Had to be. "But with that, we really need to keep our professional distance."

He nods as he logs out and faces me. "I agree. The last thing I want is someone thinking we're together and having you ruin my chances with all the nurses."

I roll my eyes at him, and his lips bounce up into a teasing smile.

"Anything specific you want from me?" I ask, getting back to work. "He already has a large bore IV and has been typed and crossed."

"Keep the parents from freaking him out too much." He cants his head. "You could come watch me in action."

My eyebrows bounce. "I beg your pardon?"

"In the OR."

"Why would I want to do that?"

"You might like me more if you saw what I can do with my hands. I'm very talented, and I know you've been missing that action in your life."

My jaw drops. "I can't believe you said that. Didn't we just say we were going to be professional?"

He smirks. "No one's around. That was for your bullshit at dinner last night. Now we're even and can both stop getting off on riling the other up."

"But you already know I have trouble getting off."

He grunts, and I laugh.

"Did I really rile you up?" I don't know why I ask. It's a dumb question. There is no good answer either way. That's the old Skylar, who cared too much about the opinions of others, and because of that, I don't allow him to answer. "Forget that." The last thing I want is more gossip about me. I already had plenty after I broke up with Josh. I give him a shove so he'll back up. He's too close and smells incredible. "Take good care of my patient in surgery, Dr. Hughes."

"I plan to, Nurse Davenport." He takes another step back. "Incidentally, I'm taking your Josh into the OR with me. Anything I should know about him?"

Only that he's not my Josh anymore, and you make me feel a million times more sexy and desirable than he did the entire time I was dating him, which is freaking sad and pathetic.

"Nope. But he's a surgeon's surgeon."

"What does that mean?"

I snort a sardonic laugh. "He's cocky and arrogant and thinks he's God. Same as you do. I'm sure you'll get along just fine."

He stares into my eyes for a long, silent moment as if he's attempting to read something within me. Finally, he blinks and, without another word, walks off.

"I doubt that," he calls back to me, still facing ahead. "See you later, Skylar."

Then he's gone, and I wish he hadn't answered. I wish he had left it where it was. I really need to cut out all toxic and unavailable men from my life. I'm not doing myself any favors by continuing whatever this is with Aston.

I head into the break room and slip my phone from my pocket to pull up my group chat with my friends.

Me: I can't live with him. It's official. You have no idea the morning I've had with him.

Forest: Aren't you at work?

> Me: Yes. That's why I'm bitching about him. I work with him too, remember?

> Braelyn: Did you murder him yet or just fantasize about it?

> Roman: Murder is messy. Psychological warfare is cleaner.

> Me: You'd know. Maybe I need you to teach me your ways, Obi-Wan.

> Hayes: Or you could just TALK to the man. Revolutionary concept, I know.

> Quinn: Riiiight. Spoken like a true man to blame the woman.

> Hayes: Fine. Fair. But that's not how I meant it. Explain what's going on, and we'll advise.

I hesitate, trying to summarize the complicated reality of living with Aston and Zoey without revealing too much of my conflicted feelings. Or my history with Aston and the kiss.

> Me: He opened the door on me this morning after my shower, thinking I was Zoey. Then we fought, sorta, and now we're still at each other at work. It's not good, and it's certainly not healthy.

> Braelyn: At each other sounds promising...

> Me: Not like that. Professionally at each other.

Sorta. Not really.

> Me: He's trauma surgery and I'm ICU. There is no avoiding him. He's a good father and, I'm sure, an excellent surgeon, but he's stubborn, opinionated, and often infuriating.

Roman: So, he's the male version of you. No wonder you clash.

Quinn: Or maybe that's why there's tension. *Looking emoji*

Me: NOT HELPING.

Crew: Have you called that realtor I recommended? He's great and found me my place in two weeks.

Me: Not yet. I haven't had time.

Quinn: Call him. For your sanity. Living with a single dad who is your brother's BFF whom you have tension with is a recipe for bad decisions.

Hayes: Like that time Braelyn hooked up with her professor.

Braelyn: WE AGREED NEVER TO SPEAK OF THAT.

I laugh out loud, grateful for friends who know exactly how to lighten my mood.

Me: Fine. I'll call the realtor after my shift. Happy?

Forest: It's not for us, babe, it's for you.

He's right, of course. It's for me that I need to do this. The sooner I get away from Aston, the better.

10

———

ASTON

Did I request Josh Wesley to assist in my surgery? Yes, I did. Why? Well, that's a bit more complicated. I told myself it's what a new attending should do. That I need to evaluate the surgical expertise of my residents. I tacked on that I was playing the role of big brother interrogator in honor of Micha since Josh is Skylar's ex, who doesn't seem to be entirely out of the picture.

But here I am, barely an incision deep, and I want to strangle the guy across my table holding the retractor. It's not even necessarily because of Skylar. The guy is a douche.

"Wow. Those are a lot of broken ribs," Josh notes like the rocket scientist he is. "What kind of parents allow their child to climb a tree in winter? They should be brought up on charges."

"The kid was having a sleepover, and they snuck out of their house, and one friend dared the other to climb to the highest branch," I tell him. "Kids do stupid shit, especially when they're with friends and especially when they're dared."

"It's still criminal."

"Clearly you're not a parent or were ever a child who did

stupid shit," I deadpan. "And maybe a little less judgment and a little more retraction."

"I never did stupid shit like this kid did. Why are we even in here? The overnight trauma team didn't feel the kid was surgical."

Yeah. I want to strangle him.

"I disagree with their assessment."

Thankfully, he does as I ask, even as he calls my judgment into question.

"Ah. There it is. See that?" I use my probe to point to the cracked rib stabbing straight into his diaphragm, causing it to bleed into the pleural space. "That's why we're doing surgery. Because a first-run CT doesn't always show small leaks, and sometimes you have to follow your instincts. That's what trauma is. Instinct and guts. If we had done nothing, it would have only been a matter of time before the loss of blood caught up to him and he went into shock. Or developed a wicked pneumonia because his lungs were filled with blood and fluid."

Dr. Wesley isn't amused that I just proved him wrong when he was blatantly trying to be a disrespectful prick to me. It's not something I'll forget. I get to work on the diaphragm and cracked ribs surrounding it while not allowing him to assist. Fucker can watch and mope about it.

"So, you're Micha's best friend, huh?" he muses as if he's simply making polite conversation to fill the silence. The fact that he's using Micha's name and not saying Skylar's brother's best friend tells me he wants me to know he's familiar with Skylar. He knows her, and he knows her family situation.

"Since birth," I reply evenly without removing my eyes from the field.

"Then you must know Skylar pretty well."

There has already been gossip going around about me and Skylar. It's amazing what you can hear in a hospital when you simply stand still and listen. Skylar was right that someone did deem her off-limits, but it wasn't me. I'm guessing, since he's bringing her up now, it was the asshole on the other side of the table from me, and that message was for me and no one else.

There's also some buzz that she and I are a thing after I requested her to show me around the floor yesterday. I'm not one for gossip, and I typically don't give a shit what people say about me. But I'm guessing Skylar cares.

Actually, I know she does.

Still, that doesn't stop the part of me that wants to drive the proverbial scalpel into him just a bit.

"Yes." That's all I say because I know it'll rile him up like nothing else, and it's vague enough that there's not much others can read into it.

"How well can that be, though? You've been living in LA, and she's a lot younger than you."

I peer up at him and cock an eyebrow. "Something you're intimating at, Dr. Wesley? Cauterize that bleeder, please?" I ask the scrub nurse on my left.

"You seemed a bit territorial over her yesterday morning when you had her show you around the floor."

I've never been in an OR and had another surgeon directly ask me about a coworker. Especially not in this way. I feel like I'm in one of the medical soap operas or something.

"I don't know about that," I reply, keeping my tone even. "I was on a time crunch, and as you said, Skylar is my best friend's little sister."

"I just didn't know if she had told you or if you were already aware that Skylar and I were together for over a year and a half."

There are a few things that I picked up on in that.

One, a year and a fucking half? No. I didn't know *that*. Because I kissed Skylar two years ago, and maybe it was my single dad status or the fact that I was recently divorced at the time or that I was finishing up my fellowship, but I haven't dated anyone.

Two, he used the past tense when speaking about their relationship, which means the chocolates likely weren't from him, and she wasn't out with him last night before she came home looking too pretty for words. So that's something right there. They're not reconciling. Or at least she's not actively getting back together with him. Something I shouldn't care about or feel relief from, but I'm not going to analyze that right now when I'm busy analyzing him.

Three, and this is likely the most important, he's still very interested in Skylar and wants me to know it. Wants me to know she's his and therefore can't be mine.

"She didn't mention you to me, but we don't exactly spend a lot of time talking about our exes."

That was stupid. I know that was stupid. But fuck him. And it was still vague enough that no one could say much.

He makes a tantrum-style noise I'm positive he's regretting now. It shows his hand way too much.

"Lived together for a year and everything."

So, he's the dick she broke up with before she moved into Micha's. It makes sense. It also makes me want to interrogate him and break his bones for hurting her, however he did. Because if he weren't a dick, I wouldn't be forced to live with her, and she wouldn't enter into my thoughts because that wouldn't be an option. Not that it is now.

But I can't help but wonder what broke them up. Or if she loved him. If he broke her heart or if she felt relief when it ended. And how, legit how, after a year and a half together, was he unable to make her come? What's up with Skylar's lack of orgasms? Is it physical, mental, or shitty partners?

Whatever the reason, whatever all of this is or even isn't, I want to watch him squirm. Just enough so he feels it. So he knows she's no longer his. Even if she'll never be mine.

"That must be difficult for you, considering she's moved on."

"What?" flees his lips, and I realize I'm completely talking out of my ass now. I have no clue who sent her the chocolates or where she was after work yesterday, when I know she got off at three and didn't come home until after six. I've simply assumed she was with this guy, but now that I know she wasn't, I don't mind torturing him a bit.

He couldn't even get her off. Which for some inexplicable reason makes me smile behind my mask.

"Someone sent her a massive box of dark chocolates—her favorite—for Valentine's Day." I tilt my head, the light coming from beneath my surgical glasses illuminating just how much blood has pooled in this kid's lungs and how badly these ribs are fractured. "Let's drain all this blood and get his lungs cleaned up. Then I want to place a patch here and redirect the ribs so they'll heal faster and better. And I want to freeze the nerves. Poor kid's been in a lot of pain."

"I'll ready the cryo," the circulating nurse tells me.

"Let's hang a unit of type specific," the anesthesiologist says. "That's a lot of blood you're suctioning out of his lungs."

"That'd be great. How are his vitals?" I ask.

"Holding steady, but his BP is dipping a little. The blood will bring it back up."

"Perfect."

"She's not with anyone," Josh picks up without caring about what we're doing in the surgery. "I'd know."

I peek up at him before I glance around the room, noting all the eyes on us, all the curious, gossip-loving eyes. It's insanely unprofessional.

I shrug indifferently. "If you say so." Now that the blood is drained from the lungs, I get to work on repairing the diaphragm before we can place the patch and freeze the nerves surrounding his broken ribs. "Perhaps you should focus more on the patient and less on nurses you're no longer dating. Especially while in my OR, Dr. Wesley."

He doesn't seem to care about the gossip-loving nurses and techs in the room. He's steaming, visibly fuming, which is no easy feat considering we're masked and goggled up. Whether it's because I told him Skylar is dating someone else or because I called him out on it, it doesn't matter. I don't like him. I don't want him seeking Skylar out or talking to her, or even so much as looking at her. Maybe it's better if she continues to live with me.

Then again, I haven't told anyone she is. And as far as I know, she hasn't either.

It's a secret, and I'm not sure why, when it's innocent. A simple misunderstanding.

Smartly, Dr. Wesley keeps his mouth shut for the rest of the surgery while I save this little boy's life.

"I'll scrub out and speak to the parents," he announces and goes to leave the OR without waiting for my response.

"You can do that," I call out to him before he reaches the OR doors. "Because we all know you've been completely useless in this surgery. How you got into this program is a mystery to me. But if you ever behave this way in my OR again, caring more about a previous relationship instead of your patient, I will write you up. As it is, this was not the best first impression to make with me, Doctor. I expect better next time. Is that understood?"

He turns back to me, his eyes narrowed slightly, but otherwise he's cool and composed. "Understood."

The door opens and swings shut behind him, and I step back to allow the tech and nurses to finish up and get the patient ready to move to the PACU.

"Is it always like this here in the OR?" I ask. "What's with all the drama?"

"He started chasing Skylar the moment he set foot in this

hospital as an intern and saw her," Marion, one of the nurses, informs me.

"Skylar thought it was a Fritz thing at first," Erica, the circulating nurse, states. "Owen, Stone, Luca, and Kaplan Fritz all checked in on her when she started here three years ago, and word spread fast about her family. Plus, everyone knows her mother is Rina Fritz Davenport. There's no hiding it if you're a Fritz in this city, as I'm sure you know as a Hughes."

"So, he was money- and fame-seeking?"

They all share bewildered looks. "That's what Skylar thought," Erica continues. "She didn't believe his intentions were honorable, and she pushed him off for more than half a year, but he wore her down. They started dating and got serious quickly. They were adorable as a couple. Always together and smiling. Then six weeks ago, out of nowhere, Skylar reportedly broke up with him and moved out."

I blink, a little taken aback by that.

"No one knows why or what happened, and neither of them talked about it," Marion explains. "This was the first time he's mentioned it, though we all know he puts notes in her locker and makes it so his patients are her patients."

Interesting. And he brought her up to me, so either he's threatened by me or thinks I have insider information that I was willing to share.

"Clearly he's not over her," Marion says with a light giggle in her voice.

"Or he's still after the money and fame," Erica states. "I mean, no offense to Skylar. I think she's amazing, but they don't quite... match up, if you know what I mean."

My jaw clenches. "No. I don't know what you mean."

She instantly backtracks at my harsh tone. "Nothing. Just that, I don't know. Never mind. That came out wrong."

Yeah. I bet it fucking did. How does anyone look at Skylar and not see what I see? I don't get it. But women are different, I guess. Josh clearly sees more. Or he saw a broken-down woman who would build up his ego and worship him.

"All I'm saying is that it doesn't seem like he's ready to give up," she finishes.

No. It doesn't seem like he is, and they're feeding on it. Drama makes the hospital go round.

But if I didn't like him before, I like him even less now. And I sure as hell don't want him anywhere near Skylar.

I leave the OR to speak to the parents despite Josh doing it and observe from slightly across the MSICU as Skylar tends to him and his parents. Pediatrics isn't just about the child you're treating. It's about the parents, too, and Skylar seems to get that. She's in the room as much as she's out of it, laughing and chatting and answering questions.

So, here's my dilemma. My moral quandary, I guess you could say.

I'm severely attracted to my best friend's little sister.

She's everything I was never interested in until I kissed her, and now she's everything I don't know how to escape.

I want to see her in a towel. In an oversized T-shirt. In only my hands. In nothing at all. I want to hear her chatting with my daughter like they're besties, and I want to open bathroom doors that should be locked and find her soaking wet and biting my head off. I want her fiery and angry and tender and sweet. I want her as the nurse for all of my patients, and I want her nowhere near any of Josh's or even him.

But I can't have her like that. Not like any of that.

So, what do I do? I'm honestly not sure. I've known loneliness for so long it's become the only color I wear. I'm tired of it. This is my fresh start, and the woman who I can't evict from my thoughts is the one I need to evict from my life.

11

ASTON

"How are things at the hospital with your new position there?" Dr. Tudor, Zoey's new therapist, asks in the serious yet soft way she has when she asks questions. She wanted a one-on-one with me after her second meeting with Zoey yesterday, though we've talked on the phone several times already. I lean forward, my elbows dig into my thighs, and my hands rub together. I hate answering personal questions.

"It's good. Challenging. The cases are tough, and I like the overall flow and system they have going." My hands rub a little harder. "I work with Skylar Davenport, who is Micha's younger sister."

"The woman temporarily living in your new home?"

I nod, my gaze on the foot of her chair. "Yes."

"Is she part of what's making your new role challenging?"

I nearly laugh at that, but as it is, I don't even allow a smile to escape. Still, I answer honestly. "Partially, yes. We... clash. I don't know. Maybe hot and cold is a better description."

"In what way?"

I glance up, hating how she's scribbling down notes on me.

A cold sweat breaks out across the back of my neck as I think back to when social services came and interviewed me about what kind of parent I was with Zoey. What kind of person I was. And if I were fit to care for my child.

"We just butt heads and don't get along well."

"How is she with Zoey?"

"Great, actually. Zoey seems to like her, and the feeling is mutual with Skylar. Skylar is young and full of energy, which Zoey responds to."

"But you're still determined to have her move out? Even if she's already bonding with Zoey?"

I inwardly sigh. "I think that's best. Like I said, Skylar is young, and other than being Micha's sister, she's not a permanent fixture in Zoey's life. Living with her is a complication."

She uncrosses and recrosses her legs as she straightens her spine, and here it comes. "I'm going to level with you, Aston. The next few months to the next couple of years are crucial in Zoey's life. She's been through enormous trauma and has a severe fear of abandonment along with an anxious-preoccupied attachment disorder, meaning she craves intimacy and latches on fast, afraid to let go and lose someone."

"You picked all of this up from two forty-five-minute sessions with her?"

"Yes," she says simply, almost pityingly.

I wince and cover my face with my hands. "I know," is all I can manage because I do. I've seen it. She's had a horrible year, and it's shaped her in ways that keep me up at night as I try to think about how I can fix this for her.

"She needs stability in her life," she continues. "That includes the people in it. People she can rely on. More than just you."

"I'm trying to give her that. It's why we moved back here. She has my parents and even my brother." Alden picked her up from school yesterday and spent all afternoon with her. He took her to the aquarium and bought her ice cream and a new stuffed penguin she's been sleeping with. Hearing her squeal about it all last night reminded me why moving back to Boston was the right choice for her.

"And that's fantastic. But right now, she needs consistency. Not the uncertainty of fluctuation." She lets that sit for a moment. "Let's plan to have another talk next month after I've had some more sessions with Zoey, and we can see how things are going."

"Sure."

Numbly, I get to my feet and make my way home, my head spinning. Before long, I'm parking and dragging myself up Micha's front steps, my shoulders hunched and my brain heavy. Today was a particular motherfucker. Seven back-to-back trauma cases, two emergency surgeries, and a mountain of administrative paperwork have left me hollowed out, and then this chat with Dr. Tudor.

It's only been a couple of weeks here, and I already can't help but feel like I'm failing Zoey. That no matter what choice I make or how I do it, I'm doing it wrong. All I want is to collapse on the couch with Zoey tucked against my side, maybe order pizza, and watch one of her cartoon movies until we both drift off to sleep. Simple comfort to counterbalance the chaos. But when I push open the front door, the scene that greets me isn't what I expected at all.

My parents were supposed to pick Zoey up and bring her home while I met with Dr. Tudor. So what in the East Jesus am I looking at now?

The kitchen table is covered in construction paper, markers, glitter—God help us, it's pink and extra sparkly—and what appears to be dozens of cut-out paper dolls. Zoey sits cross-legged on one of the chairs, her tongue poking out between her teeth in concentration as she carefully applies glue to a paper figure. Beside her, propped up on her knees but somehow making the position look graceful, is Skylar. Her hair is pulled back in a messy bun, blonde strands escaping to frame her face. There's a smudge of glitter on her cheek beneath her left eye that makes her look like a bedazzled football player.

"And this one can be Mommy," Zoey explains, holding up a paper doll with wild curls drawn in black marker. "She's watching from heaven, so she needs extra sparkles."

"That makes perfect sense," Skylar replies, her voice gentle in a way I've never heard directed at me while she cuts her paper people. "People who love us are like stars. We can't always see them, sometimes they're even hidden from us, but they're always there watching over us."

"Do you think that's what Mommy is doing?"

Skylar glances up, and the smile she gives my daughter makes my chest clench. "Absolutely. You make your mommy smile every day."

"Do you think she hears me when I talk to her?"

"Without a doubt, she does. Your mom is always with you. That's what makes mommies so special."

"Daddy!" Zoey spots me and scrambles off her chair before launching herself at my legs. I drop my bag and scoop her up, breathing in the scent of strawberry shampoo and glue.

"Hey, Zo-Zo. What's all this? Where's Grandma and Grandpa?"

"I told them I had her," Skylar supplies. "I was already home, and there was no sense in them staying while I was here."

"Me and Skylar are making paper people! Look!" She wiggles to be put down and drags me by the hand to their art project. "This is you, and this is me, and this is Mr. Penguin, and this is Mommy in heaven, and this is Uncle Micha in Africa, and this is Uncle Alden, and this one is Skylar!"

I study the paper figures. Mine is tall with a stethoscope made from a silver pipe cleaner. Zoey's has wild curls like her mother's, only hers are in yellow marker, and what appears to be a cape is on her back. Skylar looks like a blonde princess covered in pink glitter, and Micha and Alden look indiscriminate. "Wow. Look at all of us."

Skylar rises from the chair, brushing glitter from her jeans. "Isn't it amazing? She did such a great job."

"Yeah," I agree. "I love it."

"I want to put them on the wall in my room."

"Sure," I tell her. "We can tape them up after dinner."

"Let's clean this up so we can get ready to eat then," Skylar suggests.

"Okay," Zoey singsongs.

Skylar bobs her head to the side, and I follow. "She told me she wanted to draw a picture of her mom. That she used to draw a lot with her and had pictures all over her walls. I remember one of the art therapy workers making paper people with the kids on the floor a few months back, and I thought this might be a fun way to do that. She showed me which box had all of her art stuff in it. I hope that's okay. She seemed excited to do this."

Something warm and unexpected blooms in my chest. For seven months, it's been me trying to navigate Zoey's grief alongside my own. Much the way it did with the fairy lights last week. Having someone else in this space, someone who seems to instinctively understand what my daughter needs, is both a relief and a complication.

"Thank you," I say, the words inadequate but sincere. "It was really kind of you to take the time to do that with her."

She waves me off as if it was nothing when it's actually everything, then gestures toward the kitchen. "There's lasagna in the oven. It's my aunt Elle's recipe, which means it's amazing. Zoey told me she likes lasagna."

I squint at her accusingly so I don't kiss her. "Are you trying to be nice to me?"

She laughs and tosses her hands up. "Not really, no. But I like your kid."

"Not me," I state, not as a question.

"Definitely not you. I'm a nurse for a reason. We think doctors are shmucks."

I choke. "Shmucks?"

"It's Yiddish. Dr. Schwartz taught me it. He's my favorite intensivist."

"Are you sleeping with him too?"

I get a glare mixed with an eyebrow raise. "Too?"

"Josh."

She visibly stiffens as if she doesn't want to talk about him. "No. Dr. Schwartz is older than my father, so ew. And Josh... no."

There's a lot there I want to question but don't feel deserving of the answers to. Especially after all she's done for Zoey tonight, who's making an obscene mess of trying to clean up but is trying all the same simply because Skylar asked her to. We've been living together for over a week, but I haven't seen her much. We dodged each other effectively, and either she or Zoey and I were out much of the weekend, and this week was busy for all of us.

"You're very interested in my sex life, Doctor. Is that to report back to Micha or for your own personal knowledge?"

"I just want to know who you're going to be dragging in and out of the house while we live here together."

"Dragging?" She laughs. "They come crawling." She gives me a wink.

"Ah, but they don't make you come when they do."

She huffs. "What is it with you and my friends being so obsessed with a man getting me off? They're orgasms. I can't imagine they're all that different from the ones I give myself."

Heat sears through me at the thought of her getting herself

off, but before I can explore that, the timer on her phone goes off. Thank god, right?

"Oh. The lasagna." She flies over to her phone to shut off the alarm and then heads into the kitchen.

I follow her, watching as she slides on oven mitts and retrieves a bubbling dish that fills the air with the scent of tomato and herbs.

"You didn't have to do this," I say.

"I like cooking. Stella and Aunt Elle used to teach Roman and me when we were kids. You'd never believe the concoctions he and I created over the years."

I can't help my grin. "Your family is..."

"The best?" she finishes for me. "For sure."

"Is massive, is actually what I was going to say. And special."

She beams, and what is it about her? Why am I drawn to her wide smile and mossy green eyes and adorable, short, curvy body? She's everything I should never notice but seem to more and more.

I nod and move on, watching as she moves efficiently around the kitchen while I start setting the table, pouring milk for Zoey and hitting up Micha's extensive wine fridge for myself and Skylar because I could use a glass—or six—of wine tonight, and I bet Skylar could too.

It's easier when I dislike her. So much easier. So, for now, I pour us some red wine and start sipping on it and try not to think beyond that. But she brushes past me. It's innocent. A nothing of a move. Except with it comes her hair beneath my face, the soft texture tickling my chin, and her scent hits me like a bullet.

Before I know what the fuck I'm actually doing, I grab her arm, spin her around, set my glass of wine down so I can cup her face, and then I kiss her. Thankfully, some fucking intelligence and rational thought hit me at the last second, and instead of her mouth, I move to her cheek right at the corner of her lips.

She startles against me, but I hold her steady, not increasing the kiss or even moving, but breathing and fucking smelling and just feeling her. It's been two years since I've felt this, and it's as perfect as it was that night. Only tonight I'm not drunk, and I have no excuse for what I'm doing, so I pull back and pick up my wine and create some distance.

She stares up at me, a million questions in her eyes. "For Zoey," I manage even though my tongue feels impossibly thick in my mouth. "For the fairy lights and the drawing and making dinner and just giving her some peace and normality." I swallow. "I just... thank you."

She gives me a small, uncertain nod, but thankfully, my impulsivity dies there. "It's hot. We're ready." Her voice is low. Quiet. She throws me an eye. "The salad is in the fridge. Can you grab it?"

"Sure. Absolutely." Fuck! Why the fuck did I fucking kiss her?

We settle at the table, Zoey chattering about preschool and her new friend Maci, who has two moms and a turtle named Bob. Skylar asks about pets and favorite weekend activities and if she likes museums, because there's a museum of ice cream in Boston and she's anxious to go.

I listen. I nod and smile and eat.

But there's no escaping it. Skylar is spending time with my child. I'm spending time with Skylar. We're spending time together, the three of us. This is exactly what I need to avoid. Complication. Attachment. Vulnerability when I need to be strong for Zoey.

Skylar isn't going to be permanent. Which means she needs to go. And not just from this house. But from all the other places she's starting to creep into.

12

SKYLAR

I really need a haircut, but honestly, who has time for that? I shift my part around, only to settle on putting it up into a high ponytail. I'm nervous, which is ridiculous. I'm only looking at apartments, not being auctioned off to the highest bidder and forced into an arranged marriage. Though that's pretty hot and sexy in my books, so maybe... argh! I'm a mess. Looking doesn't have to equal buying, and I might find something that I love.

I don't know why I'm freaking out. Something just feels off today.

My mom was supposed to join me this morning, but she ended up driving out to my grandparents' compound along with all of my uncles to talk Fritz family business. She asked that I postpone this for another day or do it tomorrow on Sunday, but I just want to get the ball rolling and don't want to put it off.

Aston has been cold and keeping his distance from me since I made lasagna and hung out with Zoey a couple of nights ago. Well, since the almost kiss. And right on cue, my stomach flutters. It happens every damn time I think about it or replay it in my head.

I appreciate him being distant after that, and it's been fine. What I want actually, and what I tried to do for the full week we were living together before that, but instead of making things easier, it's felt more strained. Maybe that's just me since I seem to be the only one feeling the tension, but it's another reason to go sooner rather than later.

I smear on a coat of pink lipstick and ignore the churning of my stomach as the smell of coffee, bacon, and French toast wafts its way up to my room. My stomach is off this morning, like the rest of me, and I know it's just those nerves, but even the idea of coffee is off-putting.

The doorbell rings and I jump. Shit. How did it get this late? I run and open my door to ask Aston to get the door, but I hear the heavy stomps of his feet, so I take the extra second and shove a few last-minute items into my large, gray leather purse, slip into my Monroe leather boots, and fly out the door to the stairs when I hear Aston talking with my realtor.

"I'm here for Skylar Davenport," he says. "I'm Elliot Abernathy."

"Good for you. Is she expecting you?"

"Yes. Of course she is."

"I doubt that. She hasn't come down for coffee yet, and she never misses coffee."

"Um. Well. I don't know what to say to that other than she's expecting me."

"I'm coming," I call out as I hit the bottom step and walk over to the door. Aston turns, and his eyes widen when he sees me before they drag up and down my body. By the time they reach my face, they've narrowed, and his features have hardened and turned almost accusatory. I blow past him and greet Elliot. "Hi. Thanks for coming to pick me up. It's lovely to see you."

"You too." He glances over at Aston on my right, who's only wearing a white T-shirt and flannel pants with an old-school Rebels hat on his head, his hair annoyingly sexy as it tickles out from the bottom of it. Though I think that last observation is only mine. His gaze snaps back to mine. "Are you ready to go?"

"Yes. Let me grab my coat."

"She'll be right with you." Aston slams the door in Elliot's face, and I turn on him.

"What the hell are you doing?"

"Who is that guy?" he hisses, aware that Zoey is in the next room.

I cross my arms, not liking his tone. "That's none of your business." I mean, I could tell him it's my realtor, but I shouldn't have to explain myself to him, and I'm not about to start now.

"It is when you bring strange men to the house where my daughter lives. That was one of our rules, remember?"

My eyes flash, but I settle for a small, dismissive laugh instead. "First of all, he's not a *strange man*. Second, I didn't *bring him to the house*. He's picking me up. And third, I don't owe you explanations about my personal life."

Without waiting for him to reply, I push past him toward the closet, set my purse on the floor, and pull out a camel-colored cashmere coat and slip my hands through the sleeves.

"So, you're dating again?" he asks, almost incredulous but with a very distinct edge I don't like the sound of.

I pause, my back to him as I button my coat. "Would it matter if I were?"

"Yes. No. It's just... it's been, what, only seven weeks since Josh? That's a bit fast, don't you think?"

I whirl around, my eyes blazing. "Don't you dare bring Josh or my past relationship into this. You don't know anything about that, and you certainly have no right."

"I'm just concerned—"

"Oh?" I snort a laugh. "Is that what you are?"

"Yes," he barks defiantly. "What else would I be? I don't like you bringing strange men to our house, and I don't want to see you make yet another mistake. Or is this simply some fun you're trying to have? You know, see how many guys it takes to get you to the finish line for once."

I gasp, my jaw dropping. "You son of a—" I cut myself off and settle for a glare. "You have no right to judge me or the things I do. You're not my brother or my boyfriend."

"Thank god for that."

I point at him. "I seriously don't like you."

He chuckles. "The feeling's mutual, Little Swan."

"Don't call me that."

"Why not? We both know you like it." He smirks. Bastard.

"You're an ass, and I'm late for Elliot. Move!" I practically shove him out of the way of the door.

He grabs my arm. "Don't go out with him."

I jerk away from him. "Give me one reason why I shouldn't?"

He stares down at me, his jaw locked tight. That's what I thought. No, thanks.

"Bye, Zoey," I call out to her so my voice will carry across the first floor and into the kitchen. "See you later, babe."

"Bye, Sky!" she chirps, oblivious to the standoff between me and her father since she's focused on something on her iPad.

I pick up my purse and nudge past him, heading out the door to a waiting Elliot, who looks nothing short of perplexed and uneasy. Who can blame him?

"Everything okay?"

I plaster on my Fritz-Davenport smile. The one I've been trained to deliver since birth. Even if I'm silently fuming. "Perfect. Let's go. I'm anxious to see the places you have lined up for me."

"Great. Okay." He pans his hand down the steps toward a waiting Mercedes SUV, but as he helps me up, I glance back up at the house and catch sight of the shutters snapping shut. Was Aston watching us? I don't know what that was all about. All I know is I can't make heads or tails of Aston Hughes, and I don't want to. Men are officially bad for my health.

"This one is a bit closer to the hospital, which I know was on your list of desirables," Elliot tells me as we head up the elevator in one of the larger buildings in this complex. "The apartment has two bedrooms, two full bathrooms, a large state-of-the-art kitchen, a dining area, and a family room with an unobstructed view of the Back Bay Fens."

"Sounds nice," I tell him, but the truth is, not much today has been. I don't know if it's me or the encounter I had with Aston, or perhaps maybe I'm coming down with something, but I haven't felt well all morning.

He unlocks the apartment, and we step inside to bright lights and dull gray skies outside the window. Snow is starting to fall, and it would be cozy, but nothing right now is. Elliot continues to tell me more about the building amenities and things like that, but a wave of nausea comes over me so fierce that it has me running straight for what I seriously hope is a bathroom. Mercifully, it is, and I slam the door shut behind me, lift the lid for the toilet, and vomit nothing but bile into it.

"Skylar, are you all right?" Elliot questions behind the door, concern in his voice.

"Yes," I manage as I wipe my mouth with the back of my hand. Ugh. "I just need a moment."

"Of course. Take your time."

A few dry heaves rattle through me, but my stomach seems to have settled, and the vomiting stops. I flush the toilet and wash my hands and mouth. I'm a disaster with mascara running down my cheeks. I do my best to clean myself up, and when I step out of the bathroom, Elliot is across the apartment, standing against the island in the kitchen.

"I'm so sorry," I apologize.

He waves me away. "No worries. These things happen. Do you want to see the rest of the apartment or just go?"

"I'm here," I tell him as I glance around and start back for the kitchen so I can get a better look at it.

"I suppose that's why you're looking for two bedrooms," he muses, and I stop short and pivot to look at him.

"Pardon?"

A knowing glint hits his eyes, but he holds his hands up in surrender. "I get it, and I won't say anything more. But when my fiancée started skipping coffee and throwing up out of nowhere, we figured out pretty quickly she was pregnant. It also makes sense why your brother was so protective of you when I arrived."

I'm impersonating a goldfish. Or perhaps an owl. Or more like I'm a motherfucking deer in headlights because what the actual fuck? My first reaction is no. And that *no* carries a lot of meaning behind it. No, I can't be pregnant. No, it can't be Josh's because that would mean a lot of bullshit, and I cannot have that bullshit, any of it, in my new life.

He must catch on that I'm panicking because he pauses and tilts his head before a blush like a wildfire takes over his face. "Oh. Crap." His hands stretch out toward me. "I'm sorry. Listen, I didn't mean to—"

"No. Um. Yeah." I laugh. There's absolutely no humor to it. "I think maybe I should go."

He nods. "I'm so sorry. Can I drive you anywhere?"

I shake my head. "I think I just need to walk."

"Of course." I've never seen another human look more awkward or uncomfortable before, and I'm a nurse. "Can I call you next week? See if you want to reschedule?"

"Yes. I'd appreciate that."

Before he can say anything else, I fly out of the apartment and back into the elevator. The flight down takes forever, but I can't catch my breath, so it might as well take days. I'm not even making sense. Because holy shit. Holy freaking shit! I might be pregnant.

I make it outside into the freezing February afternoon. Snow is coming down a bit heavier, and I know we're supposed to get a few inches or so. I don't know what to do. I just know I can't do it alone.

With a tremulous hand, I slip my phone from my purse and call Braelyn.

"Hey," she answers on the third ring. "How'd it go? Did you find a place?"

"Are you working?" I ask instead of answering her.

She's silent for a beat. "Yes. Why? Are you okay? You sound…"

"Can I come see you?"

"Always."

"Is anyone else there right now?"

By anyone else, I mean anyone else in my family or our extended network of people who are more or less like family. A lot of them work at MGH, which is her hospital, and a lot of them also work in the ER, where she's a nurse.

"Jack and Wren are here." Wren is my cousin on my mother's side, and Jack is her husband and also my cousin, but on my father's side. It's confusing as hell. Welcome to my life.

"Is there a way I can get in without them knowing?"

"Come to the ambulance bay and text me when you get here. I'll have a room waiting. Is there anything I need waiting in it?"

I gulp. "I threw up just now. After not having anything to eat or drink. Not even coffee."

Another long silence. "I got you. Just text when you get here."

She disconnects the call, and since I'm nowhere near her hospital, I Uber over there and text as I walk along the hospital toward the back entrance of the ER. Braelyn is here waiting for me, a nervous look on her face.

"I have a room, but things are starting to pick up in there, so we have to move fast. I'm technically on my lunch break, so I shouldn't be bothered."

I pull my dark-haired friend in for a hug. "Thank you."

"Don't thank me yet. You have to pee in a cup."

"Right." I hiccup a half-sob and swallow it down.

She takes my arm and pulls me inside straight into the bathroom. "Pee and bring it back with you. You know the drill."

She shuts the door behind me, and I lock myself in, staring down at the small, clear plastic cup in my hand. I might not be pregnant, but in my gut, I know I am. My breasts are a little tender, and I threw up. Then in the Uber over, I realized I was due for my period two weeks after I moved into Micha's, and I never had it. I remember writing it off as stress at the time.

Now here I am.

I pee into the cup, wash my hands, and open the door to find Braelyn waiting for me.

"When was your last period?" she whispers as we walk down the hall, my head cast down and my body angled toward the wall. I don't come here often. Hardly ever, actually. But that doesn't mean someone couldn't recognize me.

"About two months ago, I think. I'm due this week for it."

"So, you missed your last?"

I nod as we enter a room, and she closes the glass door and the curtain for privacy. "I thought it was the stress of leaving Josh and trying to crawl out from all of the emotional damage he did. Honestly, I didn't really track it. I was on the pill forever, but then shortly before I left him, I stopped the pill for that cycle because I kept missing days. I think it was stress. I think I knew I was going to leave him, and my head was too full. But we used condoms. Every fucking time."

"Shit, Sky. Okay. Do you want to do the dip, or do you want me to?"

"You."

"I have three sticks."

I swallow and sit on one of the chairs in the room instead of the gurney. I don't want her to have to change the sheets for me, and I can't handle the notion of being the patient and not the provider.

Braelyn gloves up, and the sticks go in, and then we wait. But it doesn't take long. The moment the control shows, a second pink line forms immediately below it. On all three sticks.

"Well then." She disposes of the sticks and her gloves and comes to sit beside me. She takes my hand, and my head falls to her shoulder, and the first of my tears comes.

"I'm pregnant."

"Do you want to discuss options?"

"I know my options."

"We can still talk about them if you want. There's no shame or judgment."

"Thank you for that. That's why you're an incredible nurse. I can't yet, though."

"We're here for you. All of us. No matter what you decide."

I can't speak, so instead I squeeze her hand. Because I know and I love her, and I love my friends, and I love my family. I'm so blessed with them.

"Are you going to tell him?"

"I..." A sob escapes. "I left him for a reason."

"I know."

"I don't want him to be the father of my child." That's when I lose it. Because Josh was a monster. He was verbally and emotionally abusive with the threat of physical abuse. For over a year, practically from the moment I moved in with him, he was like that. And I lived with it for far longer than I should have.

I was the girl no guy had ever wanted to date. Who had been teased and ridiculed because I wasn't pretty. I had big, thick glasses and bad teeth that needed two rounds of braces, and I was short and chubby and awkward with hair so blonde it's practically white that never sat right on me and a face with features that never quite fit together.

I was the ugly duckling. A very late bloomer.

By the end of college, I felt better about myself, and then when I started as a nurse at Children's and caught the eye of Dr. Josh Wesley, I was over the moon. Incredulous, too. I thought he was after my money or family, but he assured me it was me he wanted. And for six months, it was incredible.

He was everything. And the things he wasn't, I overlooked or ignored or explained away. He tried to make me have an orgasm. I couldn't. I was still that duckling with a lot of self-esteem issues that I was working on, but they weren't all gone either. Anytime we'd have sex and I wouldn't finish, he became angry and resentful and mean. I started faking orgasms so he'd feel better about himself. I started wearing more makeup, even to bed, so I'd wake up with some on because he told me I wasn't pretty without it.

He'd be stressed from work and come home and take it out on me, complaining and belittling everything I was doing. Everything I was. My music was awful. My cooking sucked. My clothes were hideous and made me look fat. He'd rage if another guy talked to me. He'd call me any bad name he could think of whenever he drank a little too much or even when he didn't. Stupid. Ugly. Fat. Frigid. Useless. Embarrassing. And any synonym for those he could conjure up.

Then it progressed. He'd take my neck in his hand, sometimes he'd squeeze, sometimes he'd just threaten to. But the threat was real, and it was there. He had all the power over my life, and I had none. I couldn't sleep. I hardly ate. I was scared all the fucking time. Terrified one wrong move or word would throw him over the edge. I distanced myself from the people in my life because I was afraid they'd see what I'd become.

When I'd build up enough courage to call him out on his behavior, he'd tell me I was being crazy or overly emotional or find another way to brush it off and gaslight me.

Naturally all of this was interspersed with loving moments. With tender moments. With good days. Enough so that I'd rationalize his behaviors. I'd tell myself it's just a bad day at work or he's just a little stressed, and if I loved him, I'd take the good with the bad. That's what people in relationships do. He loved me, right?

And I wasn't perfect. Maybe he was right about some of those things. A lot of those things. After all, I'd heard them most of my life from other people who didn't claim to love me. So maybe he was right. Maybe I was lucky he loved me, and I should accept the bad for the good.

Those were the horrible, toxic, destructive thoughts I'd have.

I never told anyone. Not until after I left him. I felt so much shame and humiliation, I couldn't bear for anyone to know. He was the first guy to ever want me, and maybe this was just how it went for girls like me. I didn't really get what was happening or what he was doing. Not fully. Not to the extent I should have.

Not till we had an in-service on spotting signs of abuse in our patients, and then I saw it all, clear as day.

I called Micha in Africa and sobbed to him for an hour. I don't know why I called him. Maybe because he was so far away and couldn't do much other than listen. He told me if I didn't leave him immediately and start demanding better for myself, he was going to fly home and make me. I packed my things and moved them into his place before I went home and told Josh that I was leaving him. I was afraid that if my things were still there, he would be able to convince me to stay.

I left him, and for the last seven weeks, I've made myself believe that I am beautiful. That I am special. That I am deserving of every incredible thing this world has to offer me. I've become more of the woman I want to be. The one with confidence. The one living her life for herself and no one else, while not taking the shit men like to hand out. It's a work in progress, but I've been working it, and fighting for it, and really starting to own it.

Now I'm pregnant with his baby. And I have no idea what I'm going to do about it.

13

"Ah! It's snowing!" Zoey shrieks, jumping up and down like a wild child in front of the window. "Daddy, look. It's snowing!"

"I see, sweetie." I laugh despite my foul mood. I don't know why it's eating at me as much as it is. It's exactly as Skylar asked. What do I care if she dates? It's good if she does. Preferable even. All I know is I'm stupidly fixated on it. Wondering where she is with him. What they're doing. If he's making her smile and laugh. If she's letting him touch her, kiss her, do more...

I blow out a frustrated breath.

I'm just lonely, and it's been way, way too long since I've been with a woman.

"Do you want to go out—" My words get cut off as my phone rings. I pull it from my pocket and see it's my mother. "Hi Mom," I answer.

"Hi! How would you feel about Zoey having a sleepover here tonight? I have a new princess baking kit that Rina bought me for her, and I thought it would be fun to have a princess tea party with it. It'd also give you a chance to go out and have some adult time for yourself."

I snicker. "Adult time?"

"I'm not going to ask how you spend it. I just know you need it."

Was she reading my mind?

"Hold on. Let me ask her."

"Zo-Zo, do you want to sleep at Grandma and Grandpa's tonight and do a princess baking thing and a princess tea party?"

"Yes!" she screams at the top of her lungs and starts running in circles around me.

I laugh. "I take it you heard that?"

"I did." My mom laughs, too. "Great. We'll be by to pick her up in a bit before the snow gets bad."

"Thank you. She's excited, and I appreciate it."

"I'm glad. See you soon."

She disconnects the call, and Zoey and I go upstairs to pack her overnight bag, including the perfect princess dress to go with whatever they're baking and for the tea party. In the meantime, I text my brother and a few friends to see what—if any—their plans are for tonight. We all agree to meet up at The Hill, and the first real smile I've had all day cracks across my lips.

Maybe this is what I needed. Just a night out with the guys without all the stress.

My parents arrive a few minutes later, and I kiss Zoey goodbye as I remind her to behave for Grandma and Grandpa, though it's an unnecessary caution. She's always an angel for them, saving her rare meltdowns exclusively for me.

"Have fun with Uncle Alden and Uncle Bennett, Daddy," she says, giving me an extra squeeze. "Be good with them."

I bite back a smile at her parroting of my own instructions. "Yes, little sassy pants."

My parents give me a wink, then twenty minutes later, I push through the door of The Hill, a bar not too far from the hospital but far enough that I'm not thinking of work. I spot my brother and friends at a corner table, already deep into what appears to be a hell of a lot of food and a round of drinks.

"There he is!" Alden calls, rising to pull me into a back-thumping embrace. "The prodigal surgeon returns to the land of the living."

"Barely," I admit, settling into the empty chair they've saved for me. "It's been a rough first couple of weeks home, but I'm glad we were able to make this work."

"Here. Take this. You look like you need it," Stone says, handing me a double shot of something clear.

I take a whiff. Tequila. Without thinking, I swallow it down in one large gulp.

"How's Micha's place?" Jack asks. He's still in scrubs, which tells me he just got off work. He works in the ER across town at MGH.

"Good," I answer as I blow out a harsh, tequila-tinted breath. "It's great, and Zoey loves it."

"And living with Skylar?" Mason questions. I don't ask how he knows that. His younger siblings are Quinn and Crew, and I know they're close with Skylar. As Skylar once said to me, there are small circles in our worlds.

I shrug indifferently, hoping I'm fooling them. "She's great with Zoey." Not a lie either.

No one knows about the kiss. To them, Skylar is simply Micha's baby sister. They don't know how we fight or how I look at her or even the thoughts that enter my mind. Life was somehow easier and harder back in LA. But it was predictable. Now, nothing is.

I throw my hand up in the air and catch the waitress's attention so I can order myself a beer.

Bennett studies me from across the table. "That bad, huh?"

I deflect. "Meh. It's fine. Tell me what's up with you guys."

For the next hour, conversation flows easily as we discuss

what Mason is doing during the off-season—he's an NFL quarterback for the Boston Rebels—and then inevitably Jack, Bennett, Stone, Owen, Alden, and I morph into talk of hospitals and patients since we're all doctors, despite our different specialties, though Stone does tell us how he's buying a new sailing boat.

The Celtics play on the TVs over the bar, and I settle in, laughing and drinking and relaxing for the first time all week. Perhaps longer.

Bennett waits until the others are engrossed in a heated debate about the Rebels and their coaching situation since Mason's father, Asher, is thinking of retiring, before sliding into the empty chair beside me.

"So," he says without preamble, "I thought you should know, the women are anxious to set you up with someone and have already been conspiring on it."

I nearly choke on my beer. "Please tell me you're kidding."

"The Fritz women have a complex intelligence network that the CIA would envy." His smile is kind but knowing.

I can't argue that. It's true. "Please let your wife know I'm all set. I have enough on my plate right now and frankly, no time for dating. The thought of being set up sounds awful."

"Because you're living with Skylar?"

"No. Not because of Skylar." Only as I say that I'm not entirely sure I mean it.

Bennett nods, tracing a pattern in the condensation on his glass. "Must be good for Zoey to have her around, though. Skylar is amazing with kids. She's babysat Willow a few times. I'm sure it's helping Zoey adjust to the move and to the new school."

I exhale slowly, measuring my response. "Yes. She has been very helpful with Zoey, and they get along great. Unexpectedly so."

That catches his attention. "Why unexpected?"

"Because Skylar and I, we seem to..." I struggle for the right word. "Clash."

Bennett laughs. "I'm glad to hear that."

That stops me, and I turn my focus away from the TV and over to him. "Not like that. It's not like that."

He gives me an *if you say so* shrug.

"Look," Bennett continues, his voice dropping so the others can't hear. "I get it. The balancing act is brutal. When Willow was born, I nearly tanked my chief role trying to be Superdad and Supersurgeon simultaneously. Katy too, and now she's pregnant again, which makes me even more worried with her type I diabetes."

"How do you manage?" I ask, genuinely curious. Bennett and Katy seem to have the perfect setup. Both successful surgeons, their daughter is thriving, and their marriage is solid. Clearly, I failed somewhere along the way with my marriage, and now it's just me and Zoey.

"I stopped trying to do it all myself." He meets my eyes directly. "Pride is the enemy of parenting, man. I had to learn to accept help from Katy's parents, from my mom, and from friends. Even from the daycare and a nanny Willow adores, whom I initially resented for having time with my kid that I didn't."

"It's not just pride," I admit, the shots and Bennett's steady presence loosening my tongue. "It's fear. Zoey's already lost her mother, and her fucker of a husband tried to get her taken from me too. Her therapist mentioned some emotional trauma from that and even attachment disorders. My parents are amazing, but she needs stability I'm not sure I know how to give her. That's why I can't date right now. I can't have women in and out of her life. She'll have that when Skylar moves out, and she's already attached to her."

"That's a valid concern," Bennett agrees quietly.

"And there's the small matter of us working at the same

hospital, living in the same house, and having a history of... complications."

Bennett's eyebrows rise, and am I really this cheap of a drunk? Shit. I hadn't meant to say anything. "Complications? That's a new euphemism."

Heat crawls up my neck. "It was one kiss. Two years ago. At a party."

"Must have been some kiss if you're still thinking about it."

Before I can formulate a suitably dismissive response, Alden swoops in, handing us a fresh round of shots. "What are you two whispering about? Patient gossip? Women? Both?"

"Aston's love life," Bennett quips with perfect casualness. "Or lack thereof."

"Ouch," I mutter, taking the offered shot, but thankfully, the conversation has been steered into safer waters.

Three hours later, I climb out of my Uber alone. Alden tried, as he does, to get me to meet someone, and as much as I miss the hell out of sex, my head is too much of a mess. I don't want to bring someone home, and the thought of fucking some random woman and then trying to escape the moment the condom comes off feels... I don't know. Juvenile, maybe. Prickish for sure.

I'd like to meet someone. That's the problem. I was married, and I didn't hate it. I loved it actually. She just didn't love it with me. But it's as I told Bennett, I don't have that luxury right now.

Unlocking the door, I open it, lock it back up, then stop in my tracks when I head for the kitchen to get a glass of water. Skylar is sitting on the sofa staring into the fire, so lost in thought I'm not sure she heard me come in.

There's no TV on, and she's so still it instantly has me unsettled.

"Skylar?" I question softly, not wanting to startle her. For some reason, I didn't think she'd be home. I figured her morning date would have turned into all night or that she'd be out with her friends.

Her head swivels in my direction, her shock at seeing me evident in her features, but it's her face that has my brows drawing in and me crossing the room toward her with deliberate steps. She's a mess and has visibly been crying for hours.

"Hey. Oh. Um." Hastily, she wipes her cheeks, but the attempt is futile. "I didn't hear you come in."

"Are you okay? What's wrong?"

She laughs and shifts on the sofa to hide from me. "I just finished a really sad movie."

"With the TV off?"

She glances up at the black screen and emits another humorless, shaky laugh. "I turned it off after."

I take the chair kitty-corner to where she is on the sofa and lean forward so I'm almost in her space, unable to stop myself as fury pulses through my veins. "Was it your date? Did he hurt you?"

She keeps her head tucked down, but she shakes it. "No. It wasn't that, and it wasn't a date. He was my realtor."

Oh. Relief I have no right to hits me straight in the gut. Then I think about how I behaved, how jealous I acted. I clear my throat. "Then what is this?"

She goes to stand. "It's nothing. Just a bad night. I'm going to bed."

I stand too, intercepting her and taking her by the wrist so I can gently sit her back down. I take the seat directly beside her and box her in a little, even though she won't meet my eyes. "Bullshit. Tell me."

"What do you care?" she snaps, but that won't work with me.

"I care. Now tell me who hurt you."

"No one hurt me. Like I said, it's just a bad night."

"I don't believe you."

"Nothing happened," she grits out, growing aggravated.

"Again, bullshit. Talk to me," I demand, my voice climbing in frustration.

Fresh tears well in her eyes. Instinct and worry take over, and I cup her face with one hand while putting the other around her and drawing her head to my shoulder.

"Shh. It's okay. I've got you. You're safe. I promise." I kiss the top of her head, and she hiccups out a whimper that breaks my fucking heart. "Please tell me what happened. You're scaring the shit out of me, and my mind is going wild. Do I need to kill someone?"

I get a watery laugh, but I'm actually not kidding. I will murder the motherfucker.

"Was it Josh?"

She sobs, and her face digs into my shirt while her hands grip it. For a moment, all she does is cry, and I don't know what to do other than hold her and console her and promise her that whatever it is, I'll fix it. Fuck, I have to fix this. I can't handle her tears. They're ripping me apart.

Skylar is a ballbuster and tough as nails and sweet as pie. She should never know this kind of sadness or pain or whatever this is.

"Little Swan, tell me. Whatever it is, I'll make it better for you."

"You can't," she whispers, her voice drenched in agony.

I draw her chin up until her eyes meet mine. "Tell me," I implore.

"You'll tell Micha or someone else, and I can't..." She trails off with a shake of her head.

"You and I already have secrets I haven't told Micha or anyone else." Then I nearly choke since I did tell Bennett about the kiss tonight. But he's not going to say anything. Bennett isn't like that. "I swear. Whatever it is, I won't tell anyone."

Her eyes search mine, and finally she whispers, "I'm pregnant," and my world shuts down completely.

14

SKYLAR

Fear ripples through me. I shouldn't have told Aston of all people, but after I left Braelyn at the hospital, I walked all the way back here in the cold and the snow, doing nothing but thinking. I'm scared. That's the not-so-simple truth. I'm freaking terrified of not only being pregnant but also of what being pregnant with Josh's baby will mean for my life.

I'm not ready for anyone to know yet. I'm not ready for this to be my story. Not until I have it figured out a bit more. Until I have a strategy and feel strong and capable instead of weak and powerless. But then Aston came home and demanded answers while holding me and promising to help me and take care of me and make all of this better.

Aston.

My brother's best friend. The man who fights with me one minute, then is colder than ice the next. Now he's staring at me like he's never seen me before, an opera of emotions flashing across his face one by one.

"Pregnant?" he finally utters.

I don't bother answering. It's not really a question anyway.

"How?" His eyes snap shut, and he shakes his head at his stupid question. "Josh's?"

"Yes."

His eyes open, and he's calmer now, more clinical. Doctor mode. "Does he know?"

"No."

"How far along are you?"

I shrug. "No clue. My guess is somewhere around eight weeks."

"Okay." His head bobs up and down as he absorbs this, but then his eyes flicker with something before they turn clinical again just as fast. "Are you keeping it?"

"I think so. I'm not... well, I'm not a hundred percent sure, but I think so. I have money and family and a good, stable job with great insurance. It's much sooner than I wanted, but I have it a lot easier than many other women in my position."

"Then the tears are because of Josh?" he questions, and I swallow and stare down at my hands knotted in my lap. Shockingly, my tears have stopped. Something about telling him brought me an odd calm.

"I don't want him to be the father of my child."

"He wants you back. I've only had a couple of interactions with him, but it's clear as day. It wasn't me who claimed you as off-limits. It had to be him."

"I worry that once he finds out I'm pregnant, it'll make him more determined. He'll make this even harder. I know he will. He'll be everywhere. And he wasn't... good to me. I can't go down that road with him again. I can't, but more importantly, I won't. So, yeah, that's going to be tough. And I don't particularly want him in my child's life, but I'm not sure how to work that."

"Was he physically abusive with you?"

"No. Well, not really. He never hit me or anything. But he was emotionally and verbally abusive. And the threat of physical stuff was very much there."

"Motherfucker," he hisses, releasing me to scrub his hands up and down his face. "That son of a bitch motherfucker." His posture is rigid, and he looks as though he's trying to calm himself down with deep breaths and bouncing knees. His reaction is stronger than I was expecting. "I'm shocked your friends haven't killed him," he grits out. "Especially Roman. That guy is scary."

I snicker thinking about my big, burly, wolf-eyed, tattooed, bad boy friend who actually has the heart of a puppy. "They wanted to. Especially Roman because yeah, he can be scary. I wouldn't mess with Forest either, and he was ready to lead the charge. None of them ever liked him. I wouldn't let them do anything. He wasn't worth it, and I was so relieved to be free of him I just wanted distance and never to look back. I didn't want to engage with him or start something. It wasn't for them to fight my battle. It was my job, and leaving him is how I did that. I hadn't realized what it felt like to take a breath because I had been held underwater for so long and forced to drown."

"You know I can ruin his life," he notes, not exactly kidding. He twists to look at me. "He technically works for me. I'm his attending, and he's a third-year. I can make his life hell."

I pan a hand toward him. "Knock yourself out, but you don't need to get involved or fight my battle either. It's my mess."

"We're both a mess," he says with a weird sort of chuckle. I can smell the beer on his breath, but I can't tell if he's drunk or not. He doesn't seem like it, but Aston is reserved and doesn't show his hand easily.

"Yes." I fall back against the cushion, staring at the dancing flames in the hearth. "We most definitely are."

"How do you work with him?"

I toss my hands up. "Most of the time, it's work. Other than him dropping notes in my locker and making sure I see him a couple of times a day. He was mad at me for breaking up with him and sulked about it, so he didn't outright confront me until the other day. The doctors round and input orders electronically, or we do it for you, and I don't have to bother you unless I need something, and even then, I can text it."

"You're brave. Braver than I am."

"I'm not. I'm a coward who doesn't want anyone at work to know what he did to me because I'm ashamed I stayed for as long as I did, and I don't want the gossip. I'm a Fritz. We avoid gossip like the plague."

"I hated seeing my ex-wife. I hated seeing her husband even more."

"The guy who tried to get you in trouble with family services?"

He brushes the hair flopping onto his forehead back. "Yep. I'm not sad he's out of Zoey's life, but I hurt for her that she lost so much all at once. She's struggling with it. Big time. And I'm failing her no matter how hard I try."

"You're not failing her. She's a great kid, but I get it. I'm pregnant with the baby of a guy I'm not sure how I'll get rid of, and you have a new job and a little girl who just lost her mother and is heartbroken with it. Life can be a bit of a bitch when it wants to be."

"Absolutely."

"If only there were some magic fix that would eliminate Josh from my life and help Zoey through her grief. I'd give anything for that. For all of us."

"Yeah," he whispers, lost in thought, but a moment later, his hands meet the top of his head, and he twists his torso to fully face me. But he's not just looking at me. He's locked on my face, but his mind is moving so fast I can't tell if he actually sees me or not. "Wait. What did you just say?"

My brows scrunch. "Huh? Which part? I said a lot."

"No. Yes, you did say a lot. But you said..." He stops himself. "Holy shit, Skylar."

"What?"

"What if there was a magic fix? Something we could do to get Josh to stay away from you and to help Zoey through her grief."

I shake my head in confusion. "What are you talking about?"

He shoots off the couch and starts to pace, his body half illuminated by the fire, casting him in weird shadows I can't drag myself away from. A half beat later, he drops into the opposite chair he was originally in and covers his mouth with his hand, his gaze once again locked on my face.

"You need help getting Josh off your back."

"Yes," I say slowly, my heart starting to pound at the way he's saying that and his strange behavior.

"I need more stability and consistency for Zoey."

"Okaaay…" I draw out the word.

"Jesus, I'm either drunk or insane, but it makes so much sense. Actually, it's fucking brilliant." His hands cover his face, and he laughs into them.

"Dude, what? I've had enough insanity for one day. How about you skip the drama and suspense? I don't think my heart can take any more."

He falls to his knees and scoots over until he's right in front of me, not touching me but close enough that we can be eye to eye. "Skylar, what if we got married?"

For a moment, all I can do is blink at him. Because there is no way I could have possibly heard him say that. It must have been a different word. Married, harried, larried, which isn't even a word.

I sit up and squint at him. "I'm sorry. I totally hallucinated. Long day and all. Can you repeat that?"

His blue eyes are wild yet focused. I've never seen anything like it. "If you're married, then Josh can't try to win you back. The most he can be is a father to the baby if he chooses, and you can set boundaries because you'll be married, which looks more stable should you ever have to go to court over it. Trust me on that. I lived it with Zoey and my ex. On the flip side, Zoey adores you and talks to you, and you seem to get her."

"Uhhhh..."

His hands shoot out toward me. "I know. I know this sounds nuts, but hear me out. You don't move out. You stay because we're married, and you help me with Zoey. You give her love and friendship and consistency and the home life she so desperately needs. And I play the part of your husband to help you and the baby stay safe."

"I broke up with him seven weeks ago, and you expect him to believe you and I are in love and want to get married?"

He tosses his hands in the air. "It's a stretch, but we've known each other our entire lives, and our families are very close. Plus, we kissed two years ago before you got together with him. Past precedent."

"You're not an attorney."

"But there's a history between us, Skylar. One you and I might not like now, but we can use to our advantage should we need to."

He grows more animated, getting carried away and almost excited by the idea. He's obviously drunk. He has to be. No sober man would suggest getting married like this.

"Maybe you should get some sleep. You know, de-alcoholize or whatever."

"I'm not drunk. I had two beers and two shots with a lot of food, and I'm a tall guy with a lot of muscle."

I roll my eyes at him. Always so cocky, this one. "At least you're not full of yourself."

"Skylar, focus here and listen to what I'm saying. I think we should get married."

"But... we don't... even like each other."

He smiles, and it's scarily beautiful and terrifying. "Which is why this will work so well. It'll be contractual. Business. Not love."

I'm not sure I can even begin to process this. Yet oddly some remote part of my brain is trying, and it's growing in me like a virus. "So, we'll be as we are now, but married to help each other out?"

"Yes. Exactly."

"Um. Wow." I brush my hair away and press my hands into the back of my head. "You're serious?" I pull my knees up to my chest and wrap my arms around them for distance. I feel vulnerable right now. I know I do. With that, I need to force myself to think clearly. Logically. And not strangle him because I think he's actually trying to help with his harebrained scheme.

"One hundred percent."

"What about our families?"

He hitches up a shoulder and climbs back up onto the sofa, keeping plenty of space between us, which I appreciate. "We should probably tell them. Eventually, they'll find out anyway, and we can be honest about it. The only person we don't want to know the truth is Josh. And I'd probably rather Zoey not know we're married, but I don't want to lie to her either, so we'd have to figure that part out. Maybe we'll just tell her you and I are special friends and wear rings to show that. It'd only be for like a year or two. Just long enough that the baby is born and things are settled and in place for you with that, and so that Zoey is in a better, more secure place emotionally."

"What about Micha?"

"It's not real. I'm protecting his baby sister. How can he object?"

Fair. Okay. "What about sex?"

A wry twist of his lips has my fingers and toes tingling, but thankfully, he charts a different course when he says, "No sex. That would be a very bad idea and complicate and confuse things we're not going to let get complicated or confusing. No outside relationships, and if one of us ends up meeting some-one, well, we'll discuss it and figure it out then."

"I think that'll be you over me. I'm the pregnant one. Who wants to fuck a pregnant woman when it's not even their kid?"

God, that's so sad. Then again, it's not as though I've enjoyed sex all that much. But I'd like to. Eventually, I'd like to. That seems like more of an impossibility now, but hey, I'm young. I still have time for hot, steamy, orgasm-inducing sex.

"Honestly, I can't tell you not to have sex for two years. That's crazy. Just don't brag to me about it or anything if you do."

He gives me a look, one I can't decipher, but redirects with, "What do you think?"

I look toward the fire, watching the gas flames dance while my mind runs sprints uphill. Weirdly... my first instinct is to say yes. Because he's right. If I'm married to another man, Josh can't do anything to try to win me back or manipulate me into being with him because of the baby or any of that bullshit. He'll have no argument for it, and he can't hurt me that way. I'll have a ring—literally—of protection around me and the baby. Hanging out with Zoey and being her friend isn't exactly a hardship either. I want to help her through this. She's a good kid who's been dealt a crappy hand.

I'm a pediatric nurse. Helping kids is what I do. So, I'm clearly getting the better end of this deal. I love this house, and I adore Zoey, and it's nothing more than what she and I have already been doing.

But that's just crazy. I can't *marry* him.

Not when there's the flip side. The side that has me living with Aston for two years, all the while not dating or having sex or even being touched or kissed. That feels like a recipe for disaster. For loneliness and heartache. I'll either grow to resent him for this or...

I can't think like that. If I agree to this, I have to think of Aston Hughes from an emotionally detached place. We'll be acquaintances. Roommates. Two people who simply co-exist in the same house. That's it and nothing more.

We only have one life. And it likes to play tricks on us. It likes to give us a run for our money. It likes to challenge us and make us sad and greedy. It enjoys our pain. Our suffering. But beneath all that, if you're able to see past it, there's light. There's love. There's happiness and laughter. I have to believe that. With what I do and all I've seen, I have to believe that.

I do believe that.

So, this pregnancy isn't the thing that will stop me. It's the thing that will teach me how to rise above and be better than I ever imagined. I'm going to be strong for this baby. I'm going to do what's right for it. And I'm going to fucking protect it.

I blow out a breath, my heart as heavy as my limbs that sink me into the sofa.

It's not as though my love life was going to be dancing from the club rafters anyway. I'm pregnant, and then I'll have a newborn.

Wait...

Holy shit.

Am I actually considering this?

I should tell her to forget it. Say that I'm drunk or kidding or whatever will erase my offer. But I don't. I continue to stare at her pretty, tear-stained face and force myself to believe that this isn't the wrong decision. That it's the absolute right one.

That this is exactly what Zoey needs in her life, even if it's with the last person I want in mine. But that doesn't make it any less stupid or precarious. At least I'm self-aware, and with that, I can hopefully navigate my mental and physical ship into safe, non-turbulent waters.

Skylar is pregnant, and her ex is a monster. I knew he was trouble for her within five minutes of being in the OR with him. He was too aggressive. Too territorial for an ex. And he hurt her. To the point where she left him and doesn't want him to be the father of her child. I don't know the details, but that's extremely telling of the type of man he is.

I don't like him for her, and it had nothing to do with my own... whatever I have with her. I don't want her near him. I don't want his talons to curl back around her and not only suck her in but also steal her away.

More importantly, she doesn't want that, and she's afraid of him. Maybe not physically, or maybe she is and isn't fully letting on about that, but psychologically, she's afraid of him. And that can be just as terrorizing. I know. I've seen it in patients. In their families, too. I won't let that happen to her. I won't.

It's like I told her. I care. I do. I'm not sure how or why or in what form, but I care.

If I had a little sister and Micha was the front-line defense against a guy like Josh, I'd want him to do anything he could to keep her safe. She needs my help, and I want to help her, but she'll also save Zoey in the process. I can't ask for more than that. Zoey adores her, and she needs her, and that's where my head will be.

Nowhere else.

If Skylar weren't already off-limits to me before, she'd become a dark, forbidden forest, riddled with creatures that will maim and kill me if I go near them.

And with that, I think I need a moment. A moment to be fully sober and to think about what I've just done. About what this will mean for the next couple of years of my life. I've not only asked Skylar to be part of our lives but to be my wife. *My wife*. A role I never took lightly, even when my ex did.

I'd never sleep with someone else, whether the marriage is fake or not. I'd have a band on my finger and a pregnant wife at home. So no, there'd be no other women. But since I won't have this woman either, I have to seriously consider what I'm potentially giving up.

I blow out a breath and stand, walking over to the fireplace and dropping my forearms on the mantle so I can hang from them and stare into the fire, keeping my back to Skylar. She's been silent since I asked if she was going to do this, and suddenly, I don't have it in me to push her to say yes.

I haven't had motivation with women. Not since my

marriage ended. Not since... fuck. Not since that goddamn kiss. But I was sorta kinda not really okay with that. I swallowed down excuses of too much work and being a single father to Zoey and not being quite ready to meet someone new.

Now that seems even farther away, even more untouchable, but it'll be worse because I'll be living with Skylar.

"Yes," she says softly, so softly it's almost a breath and not even a whisper, but I hear it all the same. My eyes close, and my insides plummet. I've never felt such a strangling mix of grief and gratitude. Of regret and relief.

Slowly, I right myself and turn. Her eyes are especially green and glowing with the reflection of the fire, and her shoulder-length blonde hair is all over the place. Her face is puffy and red, but god, she's so pretty. And fuck! That's not a thought I should be having. Not right now with her saying...

"I'll marry you," she continues, her voice a bit stronger. "It'll be messy, and I don't think Josh will believe any of it, but I suppose it doesn't quite matter whether he does or doesn't. The marriage will be legal and binding, and he can't fight that. My family is going to freak the fuck out. You know this. Yours will too, but thankfully, we can tell them both at the same time, and then they can freak out together."

"Which they will. We'll have to tell them you're pregnant."

She looks down at her hands. "I need to see an OB first." She coughs out a laugh. "Not one of my family members either. I don't really want to tell anyone until I'm further along. A lot can happen in the first trimester, as you know."

"Do you want to wait to get married until that point?"

She glances back up at me. "Do you?"

"No." I fold my arms over my chest and lean back against the stone on the side of the fireplace. "I think the sooner we get married, the less it looks like we did it because you're pregnant. And that could be something he'd fight back on with you. If we get married before people know about the baby, it looks like we're so in love we got swept up in it."

She thinks about this for a minute. "Braelyn is the only one who knows. And considering the date of my last period and how my cycles work, I figure I'm about eight weeks along."

"An OB won't ultrasound you now anyway unless you're having issues. They'll ultrasound at your screening, around twelve weeks-ish."

She wraps her arms tighter around her legs. "We'll get married and I'll see an OB. If there's an issue with the pregnancy, we'll get a divorce the fastest way we can, but I'll still stay in Zoey's life."

"You wouldn't—"

"I want to, Aston. If that means you need me to live here a while longer or have regular hangouts with her, then I'll do it. I want to be a stable entity in Zoey's life. The marriage part of this is more for me, and you know it."

I shift my weight and put my hands on my hips. She's right about the marriage being more for her than for me. But if it doesn't work out with the baby, she's offering to be part of Zoey's life regardless, and I need to honor my part of this too.

"I'm going to tell people that I moved back here for you," I say, thinking this through more. "At work, I mean. That we'd had a thing a couple of years ago that rekindled after you left Josh and we fell in love. That's why I moved into this house with Zoey, and that's why we're married."

"Will this impact your job?"

"No. How can it? It won't impact either of ours. Yes, we work together, but that's hardly a new thing, and I don't supervise or evaluate your work. At the hospital, we'll be professional." My lips bounce. "But you can't be antagonistic toward me anymore. In fact, you can't hate me. At least not in public."

"But in private I still can, right?" She laughs, her head falling to the top of the cushion, and she stares up at the ceiling. "Holy shit. This is so crazy. Remind me why you're doing this again?"

It's a serious question. Yes, I want her in Zoey's life, and yes, that's what I get out of this, but I don't have to be married to Skylar to push that piece of our arrangement.

"Because telling Josh you and I are dating or even engaged wouldn't be enough, and you know it. Not for men like him. As you said, marriage is legal and binding."

Her chin falls, and she meets my steady gaze. "You're willing to do this for me? To *marry* me? To become my lawfully wedded husband, even if it's fake?"

Am I? Fuck. But despite the fierce pounding of my heart and the unease churning in my gut, something else, something stronger than my physical reaction, is having me say a resounding "Yes" like no decision I've ever made before has been more right.

I'm not going to analyze that. I'm helping her and she needs it, and so does Zoey, and I'm positive that's the source of why I'm suddenly trembling, but not from nerves or second thoughts. It's almost as if... I'm excited. But that can't be.

"Thank you. That's... I don't even have words for what that is."

"Mutually beneficial," I offer because that's what this is. A contract. An agreement.

"Yes. You're right. Um." She licks her lips and brushes her hair back from her face. "I'm going to go to bed and think more about everything. I think you should do the same, and in the morning, we'll make the final call and work out more of the logistics if we decide to move forward."

I nod because I don't have words. I already know if she tells me she needs this, I'll do it. I won't hesitate. After all, I offered it, but more than that, we're talking about her safety and the safety of an unborn child, and I won't risk either.

Instead, I leave her here and go upstairs to Micha's bedroom and shut the door behind me. I blow out the breath I was holding and go straight for the bathroom, my hands planting onto the counter and my head slowly rolling up to find my reflection.

I just asked Skylar Davenport to marry me. And she said yes.

I'm going to marry her. So why am I not freaking out the way I should be?

I CAN'T SLEEP. I imagine that's no surprise to anyone. I hardly even spend time in my bed. I pace my room and walk the hall outside her bedroom, debating if I should go in and tell her I was crazy. Because something gruesome dawned on me last night.

Not only will I be married to Skylar, but she'll technically become Zoey's stepmother. When this thing ends, what will happen to that relationship? Am I setting Zoey up for more heartache and pain in order to bring her happiness and stability now? Plus, Skylar will have her own child. Her own family. She'll move on from us and leave Zoey behind. Not because she's cruel or uncaring, but because Zoey won't be her priority. Her new baby will be, which I get. I won't even be able to fault her for that.

That's how it should be for her.

I'd been worried about how I'd react to living with Skylar. How the marriage would impact me and my life. But what about Zoey?

I can't lie to her. She'll see the band on my finger. There will be times when I'll have to call Skylar my wife, not just my special friend. And then there's the baby. How will I explain to Zoey that the baby isn't mine? It isn't ours. What happens when Zoey falls in love with both of them?

There are too many variables with this. Too many uncertainties and things that could not just go wrong but blow up in our faces.

But how do I pull back?

I should, right?

I stare at Skylar's door, closed and quiet, and heave out a breath. I'm so fucked. I asked her to marry me. What have I gotten myself involved in?

With determined strides, I head back into my room, shut my door, and climb into my bed, sitting up against the headboard with my legs under my covers. My phone is resting on my nightstand, fully charged, and I unplug it and set it on my lap, looking at the picture of me and Zoey I have as my wallpaper.

It was supposed to be just us against the world, but the world doesn't care about our best intentions. I need advice. I need to talk to someone.

Normally, I'd call Micha and talk this through. He has an uncanny ability to listen intently and advise brilliantly. Alden, not so much. But Alden is legit the only guy in my world who isn't directly tied to Skylar. Which is why, at some time not even close to dawn, I call him.

"Hey," he grumbles into the phone. "What's wrong?"

"Can I trust you?"

"Huh? What the fuck time is it? Is Zoey okay?"

I smile a bit that he's worried about his niece and press on. "She's fine. She's with Mom and Dad. I need to talk, and I need to be able to trust that your mouth will stay shut."

Random, indistinct noises carry through the phone. "I'm awake. I'm sitting up. Fuck, dude, it's not even five yet. What's going on?"

"Promise me."

"I promise. You don't ever have to question that. You're my brother. My blood."

He means it, and I love him, but I still wish this were Micha. "Skylar is pregnant from a guy who isn't good, and Zoey has PTSD from losing her mother and her stepfucker and has a resulting attachment disorder, so I asked Skylar to marry me."

The phone is silent for so long that I pull it away from my ear to make sure he's still on the line and hasn't fallen back to sleep.

Finally, I get, "Um. Back up. My brain isn't processing correctly yet. Skylar is pregnant with her ex's baby?"

"Yeah. You know him?"

"Of him. I think I might have met him once. I don't remember. But I went to one of Roman's matches, and he and I had drinks afterward, and he not so candidly told me that he was picturing her ex that night when he annihilated his opponent."

I blow out a heavy breath because, fuck. Roman is an emotional guy, and I know he and Sky are insanely close. But that... Shit. Now any thoughts I was having about changing my mind are gone. I have to do this for her. Micha would never forgive me if I didn't take care of Skylar.

Then again, she has a whole network of people, right? I mean, Roman alone is enough to scare anyone. I close my eyes.

"I work with him. He's a third-year."

"Then you can torture him."

"I plan to. But..." I open my eyes and stare sightlessly at the wall.

"She's pregnant with his kid. Okay. Repeat the part about why you're marrying her? Because I'm lost."

I shift and slide down into bed, pulling the blankets higher over me. "Zoey likes her. A lot. Skylar talks to her and does art stuff or whatever with her. I don't even know what it is, but Zoey bonded with her instantly."

"Because she's Micha's sister and is a young woman, which is something Zoey needs in her life after losing Astrid."

"Yes. Because of that, they have a thing I don't have with Zoey."

"You're going to marry Skylar so she stays and helps your kid, and in return you're going to help her fend off her ex?"

"You nailed it."

He whistles through his teeth. "Shit, man. That's a big ask and impacts you way more than her. How long will you stay married?"

"Two years, I think."

"Jesus, Aston. That's not a small amount of time. How are you going to be married to Skylar for two years?"

"I don't know. Maybe it'll be less." My voice climbs because he stated my own panicked thoughts back to me. "We'll be like we are now. Roommates who barely tolerate each other."

He exhales heavily into the phone.

"What would you do?" I throw at him. "Honestly. I need help because I offered her this after a few drinks, but it felt so smart and right at the time. I want Zoey to have security and a normal-feeling home life. Not one where she's getting bounced around between me and her grandparents. I'm trying, but I'm also man enough to admit that I might not be enough. Bennett said tonight that the best thing I can do as a parent is to swallow my pride and admit I need help. That's what I'm doing. Short of quitting my job, which I've honestly considered tonight, I'm not sure what else to do. Zoey needs more than I can give her right now, and Skylar is here, and she also happens to need a lot of help too. Micha is my best friend. Another brother to me. So again, if you were me, what would you do?"

"I..." He trails off. "I guess I'd marry her. I don't know. I'm not sure something like that would have ever occurred to me, but I'm not you. You're always the hero. The good guy. It's who you are, so I get it. But what happens if the marriage falls apart before the two years, or if you meet someone and fall in love, or worse yet, you fall in love with Skylar and she's not there with you or the reverse of that happens?"

"Then…" Now it's my turn to trail off as I rub a hand over my bleary eyes. "Then I don't know. I'm fucked. We're fucked. I worry about all of that."

"But I guess that's anything, right?"

"How do you mean?"

"You had a one-night stand with a woman, and she got pregnant. You did the honorable thing by dating her and marrying her, and you even fell in love with her. It was as it should be until it wasn't. That's kind of life, though. Unpredictable. So you'll marry Skylar for the right reasons and hope it works out despite all the potential complications."

I stare at my closed door. "Skylar is about ten feet down the hall from me. I could go in there now, wake her ass up, and tell her to forget it. I feel like that's what I should do."

"You don't, and you won't. Not if she'll help Zoey and you'll help her with her ex and her baby."

"But what am I risking by helping her?"

"Hopefully nothing, but potentially everything. That's the gamble. But if you don't do this and Skylar moves out and Zoey struggles with that and Skylar has problems with her ex and the baby, will you ever be able to forgive yourself?"

My eyes close as a heaviness sinks in my chest. "No. I won't. So, I guess I'm getting married."

16

———

SKYLAR

"Hey." Michaela nudges me in the back as I get to the Pyxis to pull out some meds. "What are you up to tonight?"

I keep my head down as I punch in my code and the patient's info into the machine. *Oh, you know, just getting married to my brother's best friend. Typical Friday stuff.* "Not much," I reply evenly. "What about you?"

I start to draw up morphine, pushing air into the vial from the syringe and then pulling back on the plunger.

Sunday morning, I came downstairs to find Aston sitting at the counter drinking a lot of coffee and looking resolute. We spent the following two hours talking and working out logistics and even discussing our worries. We only fought, like, three or four times, which I considered a win.

Since then, I haven't seen him much, and he's avoided me. It seems easier that way.

But we did go and fill out and file our marriage license on Monday, and this evening at four thirty, we have an appointment with a judge at city hall to marry us. Alden is coming because Aston told him, and because he did, I have Braelyn coming to be on my side of things and hold me up or help me make a run for it should I come to my fucking senses. Our plan is to tell our families after it's done.

I didn't want a million voices in my head about it, and I think Aston felt the same. The marriage is a decision we made together that benefits both of us, and that's that.

I finish filling up the syringe and go to cap the needle when Michaela hits me with, "I was thinking of asking Aston Hughes out."

The cap goes flying out of my hand and hits the floor before it skitters away, and I nearly drop the uncapped needle of morphine. That bitch would have gone right into my foot. Good thing I have clogs on. But what the absolute fuck?

I glance at her, the needle in my hand like a weapon, before I set it into the plastic bin. We don't use the needle anyway to push the morphine. We only use it to draw it up, and then it gets disposed of since we twist the syringe into a port on the IV.

"Um. Really?" I try to smile. I try for nonchalance. I'm not sure I'm pulling it off.

Michaela laughs at my reaction. "Yes. Bad idea?"

"Oh. No. I was surprised." Yes, it's a bad idea. The man is about to be my husband, and now my friend wants to date him. Just awesome.

"He's hot. And I think he likes me."

It feels like I swallowed a frog. "Why do you think that?" I croak.

She shrugs. "I don't know. It's a feeling I get. I've had a lot of his patients this week, and he spends extra time with them and with me. And yesterday he touched my shoulder."

"Wow. Concrete evidence there."

Shit. I said that out loud.

"I mean, that's great. If you like him."

She tilts her head. "I do. A lot. But do you also like him? You're being weird."

"No," I say quickly. Too quickly. I don't like him, so that part is fine. Really, it is. "I've just known him forever and…" Fuck. I'm messing this up. We had decided not to keep it a secret from people on the floor because we wanted Josh to find out. So, I have to tell her that he and I have secretly been a thing for a bit and that we're in love.

My cousins Stone and Owen work here in the hospital. So do my uncle Luca, who is Roman's father, and my other uncle, Kaplan, who is Stone's father, and you see where I'm going with this. We're going to have to tell our families, and we were going to, but we planned to do it in person with our parents first and then have it trickle down.

Telling Michaela will start the gossip mill before I'm ready for it to be unleashed.

I wasn't sure I was even going to wear a ring, but Aston thought it was essential. He's buying them. I can't handle that. I can barely handle this.

But Michaela and I are friends, and I hadn't really considered how this lie would creep into all the spaces in my life. Or that she'd want to date my soon-to-be husband.

"Well, actually, here's the thing—"

"Hey, got a second?" Josh asks, interrupting me as he comes out of nowhere.

"No," I tell him. "I have to give my patient their morphine."

Michaela beams at him. "Josh, great timing. Can you help me with something for my patient in room eight?"

"No. That's not my patient. Ask Dr. Asshole. It's his."

"I am asking Dr. Asshole."

I snort a laugh and give my friend a high-five because she definitely deserves one for that before I scoot around them. I'm going to have to find time to talk to Michaela, but now isn't it.

"I'll catch up with you," I tell her. "I have more to say on what we were just talking about." She gives me a wave of acknowledgment, and I head straight for my patient without looking back.

But since this is Josh, he's right next to me, walking too damn close. The smell of his cologne makes my already weak and frazzled stomach flip, and not in a good way.

"You've been dodging me all week. How long are we going to do this? Did you get the notes I gave you?"

Yes. I got them. And threw them out as I always do.

It's things like *call me* or *we need to talk* or *I miss you* or *I love you* or *come find me*. It's never *I'm sorry I was a monster* or *I'm going to change* or *you were right and I was wrong*. Not that it would matter. He could tell me he's found Jesus and is volunteering at an animal shelter while getting the therapy he desperately needs and I still wouldn't go back to him.

"I got them." I throw him a sideways glare. "And how long are we going to do what?"

"Stay broken up?"

"Forever?" I quip.

He grabs my arm and pulls me to a stop, then over to an alcove in between two patient rooms. He squeezes my arm tightly, his fingers pressing into my skin as he gets right up in my face. "Don't say that. Don't ever say that to me again."

I try to jerk my arm away. "Let me go."

"Never," he forces between us, his expression serious and absolute. "Never. I will never let you go. I can't. I tried, but it's impossible. Do you not understand that?"

My heart pounds, and protectively, I bring the pink basin holding the syringe lower to cover my stomach. "It's over. You need to learn to accept that."

"Except it's not, and I won't. I'm your boyfriend. Me and no one else." He gives me a meaningful look. "I've been letting you have your spoiled, rich girl temper tantrum because I assumed you needed time and space to fully grasp what this is between us and to get over your emotional bullshit, but the truth is, my patience is wearing thin. Unblock me from your phone."

"No."

He steps into me until our toes are touching, and his face is inches from mine. His voice drops, turning menacing. "Unblock me from your phone, Skylar. Unless you want me to start showing up at your brother's house or following you around from patient to patient."

Jesus. The thought of him showing up at the house with Zoey there terrifies me to no end.

"Do it, Skylar."

"I have to get this to my patient. She's in pain."

"Fine. I'm going with you. Then I'll stand over you while you unblock me. I need a way to be able to talk to you, so the choice is yours on how I do that."

I push against him, but it's useless. He's holding one arm, and the other has a basin with a syringe in it. "No. I said no. We're broken up, and I want you to leave me alone."

His voice turns deathly cold and still, while his grip on my arm is bruising. "And I just told you, that's never going to happen."

"Dr. Wesley," a sharp voice comes from behind him. "Get your hand off Skylar immediately."

Josh's face hardens, his eyes narrowing, but he releases me and turns around to face Aston.

"This doesn't concern you, Dr. Hughes. It's a private conversation between me and Skylar."

"Not in the middle of the hospital, it's not, and not while you're on my service. You've already been paged twice. Now I had to come down here to find you because you ignored them. Wrong thing to do. You're on scut all weekend along with your intern. If I have to have a conversation with you like this again, you won't see the inside of an OR for a month. Am I understood?"

Josh is breathing fire, but he's got nothing on Aston right now. I've never seen more controlled rage in my life. But he's calm whereas Josh is anything but.

Josh turns back to me. "This conversation isn't over."

Without a word to Aston, he storms off, and I release the breath I was holding, working to fight back tears. As it is, I'm trembling.

Aston glances left and right to make sure we're alone and then steps into me without touching me. "Are you okay?"

"Just dandy."

Aston studies me, though his expression doesn't soften. "By five o'clock, you'll be married and safe."

"I don't know if it'll stop him." And what do I do about the baby? I don't want him to know about it. Maybe not ever.

"Hey. It'll be okay. We'll figure it out. We will."

I nod slowly. It's not his problem, married or not. It's mine to figure out, and I will. "Michaela wants to ask you out."

His lips thin at the topic change, and he folds his arms over his chest. "Did you tell her?"

"Do you want to date her and see where it can go?"

"No. I'm not interested in her. Answer my question."

"I didn't have a chance to because Josh showed up. But it's going to complicate things when I do."

He shrugs. "Or maybe she'll be happy for you."

"That I'm pregnant with one guy's baby and marrying another because of it?" I smart.

"Not quite sure that's how you should phrase it. Maybe try telling her you've secretly been obsessed with me for two years but were too afraid to say anything."

"Ha!" bursts out of me as a loud laugh. My nerves are making me a disaster. "Or maybe you're the one who's obsessed."

His lips twitch. "Maybe. Are you sure you're okay?"

"I'll be fine, Dr. Hughes. I'm tougher than I look."

"I believe that." He tucks a piece of hair behind my ear. "Go take care of your patient, and I'll see you later. But if you need me, page me. I'll keep Dr. Wesley off the floor."

With that, he walks off to get back to work, and I do the same. But if I were having doubts about marrying Aston, now those are gone.

BRAELYN'S JEEP PULLS UP RIGHT in front of the hospital, and I climb in. I didn't see Josh or Aston again during my shift, and things got so busy, I didn't have a chance to talk to Michaela. I'll tell her on Monday and explain... I don't know what I'll explain to her. I won't tell her the truth. Michaela is my friend, but she's not my inner people, and as a Fritz, we're taught from a young age to be careful with our trust and secrets.

People target us. They like to exploit us. And they can be wolves in sheep's clothing, though I don't think that's her. Still, it's a secret I don't want getting around or whispered about either.

"Helllooo there, buttercup. How are we feeling on this fine winter's day?"

I give my cheerful friend an impatient look. "You're kidding me with that, right?"

She puts the Jeep into drive and heads out. "Just trying to keep it as light as possible. It's a shame that I can't get you drunk after this."

"You're telling me. If ever there was a time I could use a drink, it's now."

"Instead, we'll have to settle for really amazing Italian food in the North End and pastries after."

I nearly groan as I haven't eaten much today. I had some morning sickness, but it was mostly nerves that wouldn't let me eat. The thought of spicy pasta and cannolis might be enough to get me through.

"Am I crazy for doing this?"

"No. It's not forever. It's to help a child over her hump and to help you while you're growing yours. That's all this is and how you have to think about it."

I nod. She's right.

"I have your stuff at my place all ready for you."

I sigh and turn toward the window and the Boston traffic surrounding us. "It feels weird to get dressed up for this."

"You can't go in scrubs. That's nasty. Besides, it's not like you're wearing white."

"No," I agree. I'm wearing pink, which, in retrospect, I sort of wish I weren't. Pink is my favorite color, and I thought that by wearing it, I'd feel strong and beautiful and confident. But I had always envisioned myself getting married in a pink gown, and now I'm afraid I've ruined that.

Braelyn takes me to her apartment, and I wordlessly shower and change. She does my hair, curling my blonde locks, and helps me with my makeup when my fingers tremble.

"I should be wearing a trash bag."

She gasps, affronted. "Never. You're a Fritz. I don't have your money. I don't have your family's fame. And I don't know all the emotional shit you're battling right now. But you're marrying a Hughes, and when the pictures eventually slip into social media, you need to look like a goddess happily in love on her wedding day."

I watch my reflection as another spiral curl falls behind my head. "Josh threatened me today. He demanded that I unblock him or he'd start showing up at my house or following me around the hospital more. He's held back on the latter. My cousins and uncles work there, and he's a resident. He's not stupid. That's self-preservation. But he was... unhinged. I don't know. It's like from the moment Aston showed up at the hospital, a switch flipped in him. He made me... afraid again."

Braelyn stares at me in the mirror, quietly waiting me out.

"I've been thinking since I found out..." I stare down at my hands. "Am I a horrible person if I don't tell him that it's his?"

Braelyn continues with my hair as if I didn't ask a monumental question. "I don't know. I'm not sure I'd tell him if I were you. Maybe that does sound bad, but to me, it sounds safe. He might question and demand a paternity test. That's something you'd have to be ready for. You have money. A lot of money. And your name goes very far in this town. If you lie or hide it from him, that might not look so great if the truth gets out. But if it were me, I wouldn't want him to know or have any right to my child. He's dangerous. He's destructive. He's selfish and scary and not safe. He's not fucking safe, Skylar. If you tell me he's not the father of your child, I will go to the mattresses over that. Besides, you'll be married, and the baby will look like Aston's whether you confirm that or not. You could also go to your family with this. Your parents."

Tears line my eyes, and I continue to stare at my hands. "I know, and I will. It was hard to tell everyone after I left him, but I did because it was important for them to know. Fritzes are always made out to be perfect. Famous billionaires who run Boston. Our faces and secrets have been splashed across tabloids a million times over, and because of this, my family is very cautious and aware of our appearance to the world. And when you come from a family like that and feel like you're anything but perfect, it's hard to talk about it. I never wanted my secrets out there for others to pick apart and ridicule me the way they have my entire life."

"I know. But this situation is different."

I swallow and nod because I know it is. "Do you know anyone who can fix things like this?"

"Yes," she tells me. "I do."

I do too. Roman and Forest are friends with people in some very dark places. As a result, I know people who could fix this so that Josh, even if he tried to contest paternity, would never know that the baby is his. I just have to figure out how far I'm willing to go with this.

"My mom had an abusive stepfather," she says. "He... well, my mom doesn't talk about it. But I think—in fact, I know, that there are certain reasons why a man should never be a father to a child, especially if he's hurting the mother of that child."

A tear plummets from my eye, but no others follow. "Thank you for being here with me today."

"If not for love and family, then what for?"

"This is the moment for champagne."

She laughs. "But in lieu of that, how about looking like a beauty queen all-star?"

"Not the small duckling?"

Her brows furrow, and she turns serious. "Babe, you've never been that. That was always insecure kids who were threatened by you and felt that bringing you down made them bigger than they actually were. You've always outshone them, and you still do."

That makes another tear fall. "I always do."

"Yes. I'm so glad you finally see it."

I sniffle. "I wish I had seen it sooner. Believed it when you all told me. Then maybe I wouldn't have stayed with Josh as long as I did, and then I wouldn't be here, pregnant and about to marry Aston."

"No going back in time. Only moving forward after we learn from our past."

"I love you."

"Ditto."

I get a wink before Braelyn returns to my hair. Once that's

done, I step into my heels. Killer heels. Five-and-a-half-inch bitches.

I'm ready to marry Aston Hughes. Come what may.

17

ASTON

"Were you able to get in touch with Micha?" Alden asks, handing me my suit jacket.

The rings I bought burn a hole in my pocket, and I think I might have gone too far with the ones I bought for Skylar.

"No. We've been playing phone tag. This isn't exactly something I can text him."

"Why don't you have Skylar talk to him?"

I adjust my tie only to untie it and start again. "Because it has to come from me."

"What are you even going to tell him?"

I catch Alden in the reflection of the mirror, annoyed that he's asking me ten thousand stupid questions right now. At least we're alone here, City Hall all but closed for the day.

"What do you mean? I'm going to tell him I married his sister and hope he doesn't fly home from Sudan to kick my ass."

"Why would he kick your ass? You're helping Skylar, and you're not the one who got her pregnant."

"I know." This fucking tie. I adjust it again, but it still looks like shit.

"Then you have nothing to worry about unless…"

"Unless what?" I bark. "And why can't I get this fucking tie to work?"

"Oh shit, man. You like her," he states, his voice climbing.

"What?" I almost laugh at that. Almost. "You're high."

He straightens, and I can feel him staring at my reflection from behind me. "You do. Why else would you be like this? You're the most in control, always calm under pressure man I know. You're a trauma surgeon for children. You never lose your cool or your shit, but that's what you're doing now."

I work the tie, the silk feeling like it's burning my hands with every flip and knot. "Do you have a point, or are you just being an asshole?"

"You told me yourself that you can fuck women on the side. That the marriage isn't real. I know you're worried about Zoey and how she'll respond to all of this, but it's more than that. You like Skylar. You've got a thing for her."

I bristle. "I don't."

"You *can't.*"

My hands fall to the sides of the sink, and I grip the porcelain as indignation crawls up my skin. "I know."

"But you don't since you're a flustered mess."

I grunt.

"Maybe it's not a bad thing to marry the woman you're falling for. You can convince her to fall in love with you, and you'll both live happily ever after."

I laugh bitterly. "Right. Because that worked out so well for me the first time I tried it. Are we in a romance novel now?"

"No? You also didn't deny that you're falling for her."

I rip the tie from my neck and throw it in the trash with likely more force than necessary and turn on him. I'm getting ready in the bathroom at the courthouse for my wedding. What the fuck am I doing? On top of that, I have to listen to this shit?

I stare my asshole brother down. "I'm not falling for her. It's not like that with us."

"You don't think she's smart then. Or funny. Definitely not pretty. That must be it. I mean, she's curvy in all the right places. Maybe you're not into the curvy ones."

"Shut up. Don't talk about her like that." I give him a meaningful glare and turn back to the sink, regripping it so I don't strangle my brother to death in a federal building.

He's undeterred as he folds his arms and picks at his nails like a douchebag. "So... you *don't* think she's pretty?"

I roll my eyes at him. "You know she's pretty, so cut the shit. Stop baiting me about this."

For a flicker of a moment, he turns serious. "Is it because the baby isn't yours?"

"No. I don't care about that." The words slip past my lips without any conscious thought, and Alden is all over it.

"Holy fuck, dude." He jumps up and down and points at me like a sixth grader. "You do like her."

I spin back around, clenching my fists and growing more agitated by the second. "I don't. We fight constantly. She's a complete pain in my ass. I'm not sure we've ever had a civil or even friendly conversation. She drives me crazy."

His eyebrows bounce. "She does all that with you, huh? Drives you crazy?"

"Yes!" I state emphatically.

"Oh. Well then. I hadn't realized. In that case, marry her. You're certainly in no danger of liking her if that's how she makes you feel."

I hate his sarcasm.

"You're not helping anything. She's Micha's baby sister and pregnant with another man's kid, and I'm a single dad with a little girl who has suffered unspeakable trauma. Not to mention I've been down that ugly road before, and it left me in ruin."

His hands go up in surrender. "Fine. You're right. I'm sorry.

Let's go get you married. I'll give you a minute to yourself and make sure everything is ready with the judge."

Alden leaves, and I wish I hadn't thrown my tie out. My palms are sweating, and my heart is racing. The only thing missing right now is Eminem's mom's spaghetti splattered across my suit. Why am I so nervous? It doesn't make sense. It's like what Alden said, I'm always calm. Always in control. Nothing ruffles me.

This afternoon, I was ready to take Skylar into my arms right there in the middle of the floor when Josh had her cornered. I wanted to tell him that she was marrying me and watch his expression when he realized she was going to be mine and not his before I ripped him limb from fucking limb.

After all, that's why we're doing this. So Josh thinks all of that even if it's not true.

I pull out the box from my pocket and open it. Two rings sparkle up at me. One is a five-carat oval diamond bracketed by two diamonds on either side. It cost me more than medical school did, but this is Skylar Fritz Davenport, and I'm Aston Hughes, and if we want it to look real, it's the ring I would have bought her. The other is the diamond eternity band that will fit perfectly beside her engagement ring.

I snap the lid closed, give myself one last fleeting look, and exit the bathroom, only to stop short when I spot Skylar at the end of the hall talking to Braelyn. Skylar is wearing a pale pink long-sleeved dress that hugs her full tits, narrow waist, and curved hips, stopping just above her knees. But from this angle, I can see there's a slit in the back that goes up pretty high, and there's a triangular cutout in the back that peaks between her shoulder blades. Her shoes are the same pink with a mile-high heel that makes her short legs look like they go on forever.

She's demure yet sexy. A teasing, tempting, delicious little siren.

And then there's her hair. Silky, bouncy waves of pale gold

pinned to one side that stop just below her shoulders, so you can see the detail of the back of her dress. Her makeup is light and shimmery, and fuck. Holy fuck. She is every bit the swan I've been calling her. Beautiful and graceful and taking my goddamn breath away.

Christ. What have I agreed to?

In a minute, I'm going to have to hold her hands and look into her eyes and tell her that I'm going to love and honor her until death do us part. Then I'm going to have to kiss her. But it won't be the sort of kiss I want from her. It'll be perfunctory and polite. Indifferent.

It won't be with my hands in her hair and my mouth devouring hers. I won't be able to pull her body into mine and press against her the way I did the first time I kissed her. There will be no tasting her with a promise of more later.

I'm such a fool.

This is why I was such a mess when she left with that guy last weekend. It's why I hated Josh on sight, before he ever challenged me in my OR. It's why I've hardly looked at or thought about another woman since my lips were melded to hers two years ago.

One kiss two years ago. It was one fucking kiss, and it was two motherfucking years ago. I don't even like Skylar. She's young and bratty, and there isn't anything about her that should hit me this way.

I don't know what it is, and I can't explain it.

I thought it was grief and loss and bitterness about my ex. I thought it was loneliness and possibly some depression and boredom and frustration. I didn't know it was Skylar. Not really. Not in this hitting me over the head and slamming into my chest sort of gruesome detail.

Because when I look at her right now, like this, and then think about marrying her, like the actual logistics of it, my pulse speeds up and my skin tingles, and my stupid dick is getting hard. I'm getting hard from looking at the woman I'm about to marry. From the thought of kissing her and putting my ring on her finger and being able to call her my wife.

I'm getting. Fucking. Hard.

I don't know how to do this because I can't get hard over her. I can't want to call her my wife with something akin to possessive pride. And I can't be hungry for her lips on mine or that sexy body beneath me.

I drag a hand across my smooth, clenched jaw. Two years. It'll be two years of nothing while being surrounded by her. It's not my baby, and she doesn't even like me, and both of those should be enough of a deterrent, but they're not.

I don't care that it's not my baby. I like that she doesn't like me.

I spot Alden coming out of the small ceremony room they have here, and he stops when he sees me, his eyes wide with worry before they slowly slide across the room to Skylar, who still hasn't noticed us. She's busy having her own mental crisis, so unlike the one I'm currently having.

Why did he have to say any of that to me? Would I be feeling like this now if he hadn't? He turns back to me with a sympathetic expression and a flattening of his lips. That's it. It's not gloating or cocky. It's almost commiserative. Like he gets it, and maybe he does. He was in love with Skylar's cousin Keegan, and now Keegan is married to someone else.

But he was right. I have a thing for my best friend's little sister. I'm about to marry her. And she wants nothing to do with me.

That last thought has me straightening my spine and pushing away from the bathroom. My shoes tap on the floor, and she hears it because her head swivels in my direction and her eyes round as they lock with mine.

"Hi," I greet her and Braelyn. "You look beautiful. Are you ready?"

She gives me a slow, rolling blink. Likely because my tone is flat and emotionless.

"Yes. I'm ready."

"Great. I got you this." I pull out the box, open it, and hand her the diamond ring. I don't slip it on her finger, and I sure as hell don't get on one knee to propose. I already did that more or less.

She gulps as she stares down at it. "What's this for?"

"You're a Fritz, and I'm a Hughes. We want this to appear as real as possible."

With a jerky nod, she slides it onto her right hand since her left is where I'll be putting her wedding band.

"It's beautiful."

"It's fucking stunning." Braelyn whistles through her teeth. "You've got great taste and look very dapper. I look beautiful too, thanks for noticing, and Alden looks, well, like Alden, so it could be better."

"Hey!" he snaps, but there's no heat in it. They're trying to defuse the tension, and I appreciate that.

I stick out my elbow to Skylar, and she loops her small hand through and holds onto my forearm, my diamond sparkling up at me.

"This is too much," she whispers. "You're already doing too much."

I don't respond for two reasons. One, there's nothing I can say to that. And two, we're now in the ceremony room, and the judge in his black cloak thing is waiting for us with a warm, friendly smile.

"Good evening. Welcome. You both look happy, if not a little nervous."

I chuckle lightly, and Skylar does the same. I glance down at her and bend to kiss her cheek, but more importantly, to whisper in her ear. "This needs to look real. Pretend you love me and try not to argue with me for the next ten minutes." I take a small inhale, just a tiny torture for myself to hold onto, and pull away, releasing her as we greet the judge.

"Both of you over here." He points to the spot in front of his podium. "Aston, you on this side and Skylar on the other. Are these the only people who will be joining us today?" he asks, motioning toward Braelyn and Alden.

"Yes," I answer.

"Great. Let's get started. As you know, this isn't a religious ceremony, so we'll be skipping over those parts. But if there's anything you'd like to say to each other, feel free to do so. Please take each other's hands."

Alden stands beside me, and Braelyn is moving around, taking pictures or videos or both for all I know. But both of them fade into the background as I take Skylar's trembling hands in mine, and we stare at each other.

The judge begins by saying our names before launching into a speech. "The step that each of you is about to undergo is one of the most important events in life that any two people can undertake. It is entering into a union founded upon mutual respect and love. Because of this unique relationship that you both are voluntarily partaking in, your individual lives will change."

My thumb drags over the ring on her finger, and she squeezes my hand. I squeeze hers back and take a step closer, almost magnetized. Her green eyes are sparkling, and I can't look away. I don't even want to blink.

"If you are sincere with your pledge that you are about to make to one another today, I will now have you exchange vows followed by rings. Do you, Aston Oliver Hughes take Skylar Fritz Davenport to be your legal wedded wife, to love her, comfort her, honor her, and keep her, forsaking all others, for so long as you both shall live?"

I stare into Skylar's green eyes and say, "I do."

Skylar sucks in a breath as the judge turns to her, repeating the same words for her.

"I do," Skylar states.

"Aston, please place the ring on Skylar's finger and say, 'With this ring, I thee wed.'"

I pull the boxes out of my pocket and hand one to Braelyn, then open the other. I pull out the diamond band and slip it onto her left ring finger. "With this ring, I thee wed."

Tears roll down Skylar's cheeks as the judge instructs her to do the same with me. Skylar slides the cold, platinum band onto my finger and whispers, "With this ring, I thee wed."

"Let these rings be given and received as a token of your affection, sincerity, and fidelity to one another. Skylar and Aston have consented together in wedlock and have witnessed the same before this company and pledged their vows to each other. By the authority vested in me by the State of Massachusetts, I now pronounce you husband and wife. You may kiss your bride."

I release her hands and do exactly as I wanted to do when I first saw her. I cup her face, slide my hands up into her hair, and lower my lips to hers. The first touch comes with a spark. A current that has me tilting my head and seeking more of it. Her lips are sticky with gloss and sweetness, and I press in deeper, shifting my body so we're flush, and her heart pounds against mine.

Her hands grip my biceps, but for this moment, she's not pushing me away, simply holding on, and I go with it. Blood thrums through my veins, and much like it was two years ago, her kiss awakens every nerve ending I'm comprised of. It'll only be this once, so I hold her tight as I move her lips with mine.

I kiss her. Deep and steady but not nearly as passionately as I'd like.

The moment I split her lips with my tongue, she pushes me back and stares up at me, her eyes dark and glazed. I want more. I want to do that again, and I start to when Braelyn lets out an excited cheer.

"Ah! That was amazing. Congrats, you two!"

I force myself back and put a smile on my lips. Skylar does the same, only now she won't look at me. We thank the judge, and Skylar gives Braelyn a hug while Alden throws his hand around my shoulder and gives me a poor bastard squeeze.

"Let's get you drunk," he whispers in my ear as he leads me toward the exit. Skylar and Braelyn are already ahead of us. Skylar throws me a backward glance over her shoulder, offers me a tight smile, then continues on without me.

"Yes," I say to him. "Let's."

18

SKYLAR

"How long have you two been married?" the waiter at La Bella Mia asks us.

"It's our wedding night," Braelyn tells him. "That's why we're celebrating."

The waiter gives her a happy, indulgent smile. "That's fabulous. Congrats. This cake is on the house. Thank you for celebrating with us."

"No, thank you. That pasta was delicious."

He leaves us with our cake and the glowing candle in it. I cock an eyebrow at my friend, but she unrepentantly shrugs.

"What? It's free cake."

"Our wedding night?"

She beams a smile at me. "Is it not, sugar plum?"

"If only. Then I wouldn't be pregnant or married to Aston."

"You mean the man who kissed you sideways until all you saw were spinning lights?"

"Ha! So funny."

"Make a wish before this candle drips wax all over my chocolate frosting."

I close my eyes and make a wish because right now I need

all the wishes I can get. With one exaggerated blow, I knock that candle out, and Braelyn cheers for me like she did when I turned six.

"Nice." She goes straight for her fork. "You do know this won't stop me from going down the street for the pastries I was promised, right?"

"Girl, I'm pregnant. We're getting the big box."

She holds her fork up to clink it with mine. "This is why I love you. But you have to try this. It's orgasmically good." She gulps, crumbs of chocolate cake sticking to her lips. "Shit. I'm sorry."

"It's fine. I'll have a real orgasm one day."

"Do you remember when we were little and thought boys had cooties?"

I nod. "Simpler days." I fork a bite of cake into my mouth, and though it's not the wedding cake of my dreams—that's champagne cake with strawberry cream filling and buttercream frosting—this is damn close.

"When are you going to tell everyone else about the pregnancy?"

"If I can avoid it, after I have the ultrasound in three weeks."

"You can tell them before that."

"I know. I might have to if it spreads around the hospital."

"They'll be on your side. Even Aston's."

I don't reply, just continue to shovel more chocolate into my mouth.

"Are we going to talk about the kiss? Or the vows? Or the ring?"

I shake my head. "It's not real."

She hooks her brown curls behind her ears like she's about to get down to business with me, her brown eyes telling me I'm not fooling her for a second. "He kissed you. And bought you an epic ring."

"So it would look real."

"Do you really believe that?" She's genuinely asking. "Because, and I'm not trying to stir drama, I'm really not, but... he looked at you like... and then he kissed you like..." She glances up as if searching for the right words. "Like he meant it."

"He didn't," I say reflexively, though that kiss certainly had my toes curling in my heels and my stupid pussy getting wet. Pregnancy hormones are bitches like that, or so I've been told. They make sluts out of the most pious chicks. Not me, of course.

"Fine. Tell me one dirty thing you want done to you that you'd never admit to."

I belt out a laugh. "What?"

"I mean it. It's our wedding night. This is sacred trust ground. You tell me yours, and I'll tell you mine."

I lean back in my seat, taking my fork loaded with chocolate cake with me. It's milk chocolate and therefore inferior, but I'll manage it. I nibble on it as I think. "I just want to feel beautiful under someone's touch. I want them to be so crazy with desire that they can't hold back. I know that's not dirty or slutty or sexy. I'm not going to ask him to tie me up—though I do think that's hot—and I'm not going to ask him to put me over his knee and spank me—though I wouldn't say no to that either. But for starters, I want a guy I feel comfortable enough with that I have a real orgasm."

Her elbow digs into the table, and she rests the side of her head against her hand. "I love that for you, and I know you'll get it. You will. For me, I want a guy who can handle my spirit without breaking it. But I also want to be pushed to my limits to see how far I can go. You know?"

"Is that not Adam?"

She considers this for a moment. "Sometimes I think it is. Sometimes I can get him past his comfort zone, and he'll dominate me a bit. Sometimes I'm not sure he knows what to do with me and finds me more amusing and cute than anything else. "

"Maybe Adam has a hidden dominant in him?"

She glances down at her ring. "I don't think so. But it's okay. It's a fantasy, right? Not reality. Maybe we don't get all the things. Maybe we get most of them and learn to live without the rest."

"Maybe. No one is perfect. No situation is either. But that doesn't mean I'll settle for less than I deserve again."

"I'll drink to that." We lift our glasses and clink them together. "He kissed you," she says, changing the subject.

I stare down at the plate. "He did."

"Was it good? Like the first time?"

"It was good. Different from the first time."

"Can you not have more of that?"

"Braelyn, I'm pregnant with another man's child and only married to Aston because he wants me to help him with his kid. Yes, he kissed me. But I'm not sure that made me special. He kissed me much harder than that when I was a stranger in a dark room. That kiss was for the cameras. I remember Micha talking about all the women he used to go around kissing. All the women they'd hook up with. I don't have time or space to be another man's doormat, something they can use to wipe their feet on but don't bother to bring inside."

"Then here's to us. Brilliant, bold, guileless, and masters of our own universes. May the men come to us and may fortune follow the routes we pick for ourselves."

"Cheers."

An hour later, I'm walking through the door with a giant box of pastries. I bought extras for Zoey and Aston. My attempt at a peace offering for the latter. He's not a bad man. Actually, I think he's a good man. And now he's my husband, and I don't want to fight with him anymore. I want this to be peaceful and amicable. Not more than that. That's a big fat no for me. But I want this arrangement to work.

Especially if I decide I'm not going to tell Josh the baby is his.

The lights are out downstairs, and the house feels empty. My rings hit a random beam of light coming from somewhere, causing the diamonds to sparkle and dazzle, drawing my focus there.

He bought me so many diamonds. Such beautiful rings.

I moved my engagement ring to my wedding band finger, and the two are just... god, they're stunning. I'm married. It's real and legal. And my family doesn't know. My parents are going to be crushed. My friends too. It's not the first time I've kept secrets from them, but this is different. I'm pregnant with one man's child and married to another, and will I ever get my life on the track I want it to be on?

I thought I was getting there. Until this happened, I really thought I was getting there. My chest feels tight, making it diffi-cult to take in a breath.

"I spoke to Micha," comes from the family room. My head snaps up, and I squint against the dark to find Aston sitting on the sofa alone with not even the fire to keep him company.

My heart picks up an extra few beats. "Did you tell him about the baby?"

"No. That's for you to tell him. I started to tell him we were married, and he cut me off because he had to go."

I laugh. "Sounds like typical Micha."

Aston rises from the sofa and comes into the kitchen. He spots the box and slides it across the stone toward him, untying the red-and-white ribbon wrapped around it so he can open it up.

"I can't decide if he'll be pissed at me or not when I tell him."

"I honestly have no clue," I admit. "He's hard to read like

that. Just when you think you know what he's thinking and how he'll react to something, he surprises you."

Aston picks up a crème puff with a chocolate glaze and takes a bite.

"You shouldn't have done that."

"But these are my favorites." He stares down at the half-eaten crème puff in his hand, and I roll my eyes.

"That's not what I meant. I meant we could have called him together."

"I had to. He's my best friend, and I married his baby sister. A baby sister he's very protective of."

"Right." So his loyalties are forever to him and not me. Which explains everything. The marriage and the extra-level kiss for the cameras. "How will you appease him?"

"I'll tell him I wouldn't have done it unless it was necessary and to help you."

I swallow and nod, pushing myself up onto the counter so I don't have to look at him so directly. I don't know why that bothers me, but it does, and it's stupid. Aston isn't my hero. I'm my hero. He's simply the guy I'm using as my shield while I fight my own battles.

"I need to tell my family. My parents. Micha. Jesus, I need to tell my grandmother."

"Can I not be in the room when you tell Octavia?"

My lips twist into a wry smile. "My grandmother is cooler than you think. Think of all the things my family has put her through over the years. All the scandals."

"Octavia scares me. She's not someone I'd ever want to upset or disappoint."

I snort. "Take a number. She scares and charms everyone. That's her superpower." I pause. Hesitate. "Can I ask you something?"

"Sure," he replies, finishing off the crème puff and closing the lid on the pastries.

"I need you to be very honest."

His eyes meet mine. "Skylar, I feel like that's something we both have to be with each other, so that's how I'll always be with you."

Warmth rolls over me and makes me brave. "I don't think I want to tell Josh the baby is his."

He stands up to his full height and walks around the island until he's pressed against the opposite counter from me. His hands clasp the stone, and he hoists himself up, the same way I did, but now there's no escaping him. His eyes are directly on mine, and we're face-to-face.

"That's not a question."

My head bobs, and I stare down at my hands. "It's different. So different. I don't know everything that happened with you and your ex, and you're nothing like Josh. But, for a minute, can you try to imagine you're him and she's me?" I push out a breath and cover my face with my hands. "No. That isn't right. I don't know." My hands hit my thighs, and I stare over at him. "I just need to know if that's wrong or not. It doesn't feel wrong. It feels safe and right, not just for me, but for the baby. But I also want to think that maybe the knowledge that he's going to be a father will... snap him out of this and make him... I don't know. A better man, maybe."

"I can't imagine my life without Zoey, and while my ex did a lot to hurt me, she gave me her and never made it so that I couldn't see her whenever I wanted to. But I never hurt my ex. Not intentionally or even unintentionally. And I'd never ever hurt Zoey, which she knew. I can't tell you what to do here, Skylar. This has to be your decision and your decision alone. But I will tell you that you have to follow your gut because your instincts are usually right."

I had a feeling he was going to say that, and I obviously still have a lot of thinking to do on this. I don't like the idea of keeping a father from his child. But I don't like the idea of that father being dangerous to my child or using them like a weapon either.

I scrunch my nose at him. "We're married."

A lazy sort of smile curls his lips. "I have the band to prove it." He holds up his left hand.

"Except it's not real. We're not even consummating it."

That smile grows into something dark and sexy. Without a word, he hops off the counter, and suddenly he's in front of me, his hands on either side of my thighs and his face inches away.

"Would it be real if I made my wife come?"

My breath hitches before I can stop it, but I do my best to brush it off. "Ha, ha. You have a real thing about that."

"I do, actually. I have a very big thing about that. It's kept me up at night. It's given me fantasies. It's triggered my voracious competitive side."

I fold my arms, trying to create some distance between us. He doesn't smell like alcohol. In fact, his breath smells like the crème puff, sweet and enticing and forbidden.

"Why?" I tease. "Because your arrogant ass thinks you could go where no man has ever gone before?"

He doesn't even smile. There is no teasing to him when he unequivocally says, "Yes."

I snort, still trying to remain unaffected when, let's face it, I'm not. I'm an emotional baggage mess. I'm the girl who legit could use a screaming orgasm right now the way no other woman could. But let's not confuse things. I mean, the man who is offering said orgasm comes at a price.

"Why?"

"Why what?"

"Why do you want to do that? Just because you're a cocky dick and think you're better at everything than everyone else?"

"Yes," he says again, but he leans in, his nose gliding along my cheek up toward my ear, where he speaks against it. "My sweet little swan, I'd be more than happy to show you just what kind of cocky dick I can be. But I think for this, for tonight, I should simply show you what an orgasm from a man who knows what he's doing feels like."

I'm hot. It must be ten thousand degrees in here because I'm sweating and flushed and I have the insane urge to rip off all of my clothes so I can cool down. Is this a pregnancy thing? Do women get hot flashes when they're pregnant?

"We can't."

He pulls back and meets my eyes. "Why not?"

"Because you're my fake husband and my brother's best friend, and we have to live together for two years. Oh, and I don't like you."

"All the more reason that I should. You don't like me, and it's not as though anything will happen again after this. What kind of husband would I be if I didn't know what my wife tastes like?"

Wow. That's a strangely valid point. No! Wait. It's not. Ah! I cover my face with my hands. "Stop talking. We said we wouldn't do this. We can't break that rule on day one."

"Skylar Fritz Davenport Hughes, I'd like to slide your dress up your thighs, drop to my knees, and eat your cunt until you come all over my face."

My hands fall and my eyes bulge. Holy motherfuck... "Did you just say that?"

"Consider it my wedding present."

I tilt my head, already soaking through my panties to the point where these fuckers are ruined. I've never been more turned on. But yet.

"I'm broken. You'll never be able to make me come. Men have tried. Trust me. They've all failed."

A glint of mischief and determination flickers in his eyes. "Challenge accepted. Hands back on the counter, thighs spread wide. I want your heels to stay on and your eyes on mine. And I want you to be a good girl and say yes. Right now."

19

Her head tilts, and her blonde hair falls over her shoulder, tickling the top of one breast. She's so sexy, and she has no clue. She's not even trying to be. It's just her. "Do I get to call you Daddy?"

I grin. She thinks I'm kidding. Or at least she's trying to play it off that I am.

"Only if you want to be my brat and get punished. Then by all means call me Daddy."

I brush her hair back and over her shoulder, dragging my hand across her neck and loving how goose bumps rise in my wake. Her breath hitches and her hands twist in her lap, but she straightens her spine, trying to be defiant.

"I know how to fake it," she threatens. "Better than anyone else. What makes you think you can tell the difference?"

"Only lazy men can't tell the difference. You fake it because you don't think you'll be able to come. They get frustrated with how long it takes you, and they don't care enough to challenge it because all they want to do is come."

She squints at me. "You're saying you don't?"

"I'm saying the whole reason we're doing this is for me to make you come, so faking is futile and doesn't help either of us. If I don't make you come, then don't come. But I *know* I can, and I will."

"How—" She clears her throat, and her pink tongue licks her equally pink lips. "How do you know?"

"Because I'm not making you come as a means to my end. I'm making you come because that's the only thing I'm after. The thing I want most."

I grip her thighs and yank her all the way to the edge of the counter while tilting them back, eliciting a surprised squeal from her. I shouldn't be doing this. Like I really fucking shouldn't. My daughter is upstairs asleep because she called me from my parents' house, sobbing and inconsolable, to pick her up before Alden and I even made it to a restaurant. Not to mention, I married Skylar under the pretense of never touching her.

But I think I have to.

I mean, I really have to taste her. And I really have to make her come. This feels like my shot at that, and I'll regret it always if I don't act. The rest of our adult problems and reasons can wait till the morning.

"It'll just be this," I tell her and myself, leaning in to drag my nose along her neck so I can smell her. My cock pulses, thick and heavy in my pants. God, I'm going to have to jerk off ten times tonight just from this.

"I'm pregnant with another man's kid."

I meet her eyes. "I don't care. You're my wife now, and I want to make you come."

I hook her legs on my hips and slide my hand up her inner thigh until I find her sweet little panties. They're cute. Pink and sexy and girly. Just like her.

"Tell me yes, Skylar." I think I might be begging now, but if she tells me no, I'll die. I have to taste her. I just have to.

"Aston..." Her voice dies, but the way she says my name makes me so fucking hard.

"That's it," I purr, running my fingers in a sweeping motion over the wet spot at her center. So warm, and when I drag lower, so wet. I force my gaze up, and when I see her face, shit... Hell. "My gorgeous wife, I'm going to make you come unless you tell me to stop right now."

She doesn't say a word. She hardly moves. But she doesn't push me away, and her eyes are drugged as they cling to mine. My hand grips the scrap covering her pussy, and I rip. It doesn't even take much effort, but they shred away from her. Now she's breathing hard. Her tits behind her dress are heaving and beautiful, and I want to see them so fucking badly.

But I won't. I just get to taste her. I just get to eat her out. I just get to make her come. That's all. And it'll have to be enough. Enough to get me through these two years.

I glance down and groan at the sight of her. Even in the dark, I can see enough, and fuck, she is *so* pretty. I bring one hand in to touch the soft skin of her pussy. Just to feel it.

She squirms against my hand, rocking ever so slightly, seeking more, so I crouch down, angle her legs onto my shoulders, feeling the scrape of her heels against my back, and bring my mouth straight onto her pussy. And *fuuuuuccckkkk*! This first taste. This first swirl of my tongue. It's not even the way she gasps or how her legs tense against my head or how her pussy drips with how fast she gets even wetter.

I'm high on her.

I don't know how we got here, and I know this isn't a good idea at all. In fact, it's likely the worst idea I've ever had, but it also feels like the best, so how wrong can it be?

My tongue plunges up into her sweet cunt and circles around, playing inside of her, feeling her like this. Her hips buck against my lips, and her hands are barely supporting her. I don't like her like this. I want her flat and naked, and I want her hands ripping at me and desperate. Or possibly tied to the bed, where she's even more at my mercy.

I want to flip her over and spank her. I want to watch her pussy gush. I want to tease and torment and own every inch of her.

But that's not how this goes.

So instead, I focus on my task. I suck her pussy into my mouth while my tongue flirts and plays with her opening.

"Ah! We shouldn't be doing this."

I pull away and peer up at her, but I press two fingers into her, pumping them slowly, working her up.

"Is that what you want? Me to stop? Are you saying no?"

Her head falls back as I fuck her with my fingers. "No," she pants. "But also, yes."

"What has you worried, Little Swan?"

"This. You touching me. You inside of me."

"It's not my cock. Trust me, sweetheart, you'd be waking me up in the middle of the night for it once I started giving you that."

She coughs a laugh and glares at me. "You're such an ass. Your arrogance doesn't do anything for me."

"Does this?" I quirk my fingers to rub her G-spot while my tongue lashes her clit.

Suddenly my face is shoved back. Hard. She grips me by the shoulder of my shirt and rips me up until I'm back on my feet. I stare down at her. Shocked and horrified, worried that I pushed her too fast for my own gain. Except her hand meets the back of my head, and she thrusts me forward until our foreheads bump.

Then she's kissing me, moaning into my mouth, and tasting her pussy on my lips.

But her kiss. God, how I love her kisses. They're magic and mystery and seduction and lust. They make me so hard. Hell, all of her makes me hard, but her kisses are something else entirely. A spell only she casts on me. It's why I wasn't going to kiss her. I knew if I did, it would fuck me sideways, and it is.

I kiss her back with everything I have, but I'm not done with her pussy yet.

"That night I first kissed you, I felt robbed when the power came back on," I whisper. "I hated it. I was so angry. I wanted to strip you naked and feel your body and fuck you so goddamn hard. Then the power came back on, and I saw who you were, and I felt like the worst sort of devil for how you made me feel."

She rips at my hair, but I press my forehead to hers, forcing my truth between her lips.

"I craved you. I was desperate. Let me show you just how much."

She gives me a shaky nod, and I return to her pussy, barely able to stay away for long. Her clit is thrumming with blood, thick and plump, and I suck it between my lips so I can work it. My fingers slide back in and out of her, but not just slide—I'm pumping, fucking, my wrist angled to drive them in and out of her. All the while my lips and tongue and teeth even eat her.

I go and go, but she's not coming despite how close she is. And she's close. I know she is. She's soaking my face and moaning and rocking and trembling.

It's mental.

Her hand slips into my hair while my fingers rub the spot that's the perfect counterpoint to where my tongue is licking. All I can taste and smell is her cunt. All I can feel are her thighs against my cheeks and her hand in my hair. I can hear her moans. They're not quiet despite Zoey being upstairs.

I pull back and smack her pussy with my wet fingers before I use them to rub her clit. She's staring down at me, watching me, but something is definitely preventing her from letting go. A wall she's constructed.

"What is it? Tell me."

She shakes her head, her blonde hair beautiful and wild. "I told you I'm broken."

"You're not broken, my sweetheart. Not even close." I rub her faster, and her eyes roll back in her head as her breathing quickens. She's holding back, or maybe this is the point that always stops her. I can't tell which, but I can tell she's too in her head, too cerebral to come the way her body needs.

I stand and kiss her, my lips against hers as I play with her, but I slow my pace.

Capturing one of her hands, I bring her palm to my chest, over my pounding heart, so she feels how excited and turned on I am.

"This is from you. You're doing this to me." I force her hand lower to my cock, where she rubs and grips. My eyes close, and my forehead presses into hers. "Skylar," I groan. "Can I jerk off?"

"I told you I can't come."

I grin. "Who said I was anywhere close to done?" My eyes open. "You're in your head, Little Swan, instead of here with me. What is it?"

She shakes her head.

"Is it more of that bullshit ugly girl syndrome?"

"What?"

I pull my fingers from her pussy and lick them before I cup her face. "You told me about it. About the things people said about you. The lies they filled your head with."

Her eyes pinch closed.

"God, Skylar. You don't see yourself the way I see you. If I could, I'd strip you down and spend hours worshiping your body to show you just how fucking gorgeous I think you are. I want you so badly. So fucking badly. You are so sexy to me. But for now, I'll prove it to you from my side."

Her eyes flash open to meet mine.

"Can I jerk off? Can I come all over your pussy while I touch you?"

She blinks about ten thousand times at me. "Why would you want to do that?"

"Because no one has ever turned me on as much as you do. Because you need to see that and feel it and know it's true. But I want us to do it together. To feel each other together."

More blinks. Even as I return my fingers to her pussy so I can continue to fuck her. "You want to come on me?"

"So badly," I tell her. "Please. I'm actually begging to."

She licks her lips and glances down.

"Can I take my cock out and rub it against your pussy until we both come together? We can watch the other come. You can see all that you do to me. There's no one else here. It's just us. More of our secrets. But you're safe with me, and I want you."

Her eyes flicker back up to mine. She still doesn't get it, so I start to undo my pants. I pull out my throbbing cock that's in so much pain I could come from one jerk.

"Do you see how hard I am? That's from you. I look at you, and I get like this."

I drag my cock up and down her soaking wet cunt, using it as her toy, getting us both to the next level. She's so perfect, and her pussy holds me just right. I smell her everywhere, and I need to come. I need to thrust inside of her and come.

But she needs this more, and I force myself to focus on that. On her.

"It's just for tonight," I remind her. "Just my wedding present. Please, Skylar. Please. Baby, I need it. I need you. Show me how you come."

The head of my cock rubs her clit, but I can't hold off anymore. I'm dying, and it's all from her.

"Fuck!" I moan loudly, despite my best efforts to stay quiet.

Except the greatest thing happens. She moves with me. She

slides her pussy up and down as I slide in tandem against her. I use my hand and work her pussy and my cock, kissing her, nipping at her, telling her all the things that fill my head. I'm soaked in her wet heat, and nothing has ever felt better.

"Shit, sweetheart. I'm so close. Can you feel that?"

She nods against me, watching the lewd display of our bodies rubbing and grinding.

My free hand grips her waist, holding on for dear life as her thighs do the same with my hips. "Give it to me, Skylar. I have to have it. I'm dying. Please, come on me. Please be my good girl and come with me."

A whimper slips past her lips, and that sound throws me over the edge. I come. Hard. Jets of white-hot cum coat her cunt, and the moment they do, her head falls back, and her eyes roll along with them. She grips the back of my head and holds me against her neck as she comes.

It's not fake. It's not a teasing joke.

My wife comes all over my cock while my cock comes all over her pussy. She grinds and rubs and rips and moans and pants. It's the greatest moment of my life other than when my child was born, and that's no exaggeration. I feel like a king. Like a triumphant warrior returning from battle.

I gave Skylar her first orgasm, and it only makes the one I'm having that much stronger.

I don't know what I'm doing, but suddenly I'm pulling her off the counter and both of us down to the floor. I just want to hold her. I just want to feel her. But with that, her pussy somehow comes straight onto my dick. It wasn't intentional. I didn't mean to put her on me like this. I didn't. But now I'm inside of her, filling her with my cum after I already came and she did too, and we're both sensitive.

She glances down at me, and I glance up at her, and oh shit. I'm inside of her when I shouldn't be. But *oh,* does she feel good. Like nothing has ever felt better than this. I just had those thoughts when I was rubbing my dick against her, but this is definitely better.

Even if this is not how I wanted it to happen for the first time. I'm not even hard, and how disappointing is that? Then again, give me two more seconds and I will be.

"What are you doing?"

I hold onto her hips, more than a little dazed but definitely still having that *oh shit* moment.

"Showing you how you'll come the next time we do this. Since I got you to come this time and all."

Yep. I'm an asshole.

She smacks my face. It's not really a smack, but a swat, and then she's climbing off me and running upstairs. My hands cover my face, and I blow out breath after breath into them. The urge to chase after her and beg for forgiveness is compelling.

But I had to do that. I would have wanted more. I would have followed her upstairs and into her bedroom and I would have fucked her in her bed followed by the shower. Then again in the morning and likely twice a day at least until she remembered she doesn't like me and doesn't want me and has a million reasons why I'm the wrong guy for her.

While I was busy falling in love with her.

Because I would have. I would have fallen in love with her in a second and then gotten my heart trampled again. Only it'd be worse this time because it's Skylar.

Just touching her like that was magic, so imagine actually having her?

She needs better than me right now. I'm barely holding my shit together.

A stupid smile hits my lips behind my hands. I made her come. I did it. She'll never be able to argue or lie it away. And

I'll have it too. Forever. Every second of what we did is burned into my memory.

Too bad I already know she'll never let me try again.

It's better this way. How it should be. She's not actually mine. If I have more of her, I'm never going to want to stop.

I 'm fuming. So tired and over the bullshit of men. I was before, and then the pregnancy happened, and I mentally slipped. I have one man who tells me he loves me while he hurts me. The other married me, said a million perfect things to me, and finally made me come, only to ruin it with his cocky boy crap like that was his agenda all along and I was just there for the ride to help his ego along.

He made me feel connected to him. Beautiful. Desired. All the things he said.

But he didn't mean any of it.

It was a ruse. A way to dupe me so he could win the challenge.

And I *hate* him for it. I hate him for making me feel this way after I swore to myself I'd never let a man do that to me again.

I hate that I married him, and if it weren't for Zoey and what's yet to come with me, I'd end that shit now. I suppose the one silver lining to last night is that I know I'm not broken. I can have an orgasm with a man, and one day when life finally decides to settle down a bit for me and I find a normal, healthy relationship, I'll have an incredible sex life.

Coming out of the shower, I wrap a towel around myself and stare at my reflection. I didn't sleep well, and it's becoming a bad pattern, especially when I'm so exhausted all the time.

A loud bang hits the door. "Skylar? I have to pee!"

A smile curls up my face, and I quickly go over to the door to unlock it. "Hey. Sorry. You're up early. I tried to finish before you woke up."

"I had to pee," she explains, like that should be obvious. She flies for the toilet, and I go to leave so she can have her privacy, but she stops me as she starts talking even while she pulls down her princess sleep pants and starts to do her business. "Daddy said he's going to take me to a movie today. Wanna come with us?"

Um, not really, but only because your dad will be there.

But I'm not sure I can say no. This was the arrangement I made.

"Is your daddy okay with that?"

The toilet flushes, and she goes to wash her hands at the sink, climbing up onto the step stool so she can reach. "Why wouldn't he be?" she asks in that blunt way kids have.

"I don't know. I'd love to go, but let me talk to him and see if the timing works out. I have plans this afternoon. Is that okay?" I check.

"Okay. But if you come with us, I'll share my popcorn with you."

I smile. "That's very nice of you. I'll share my candy with you in return."

"Reese's are my favorites."

"Mine too. Candy besties!"

"My mom liked KitKat." Her voice drops. "They're good too."

My chest pinches. "Maybe we can get a couple of different kinds then. I'm going to get dressed, and after I'll talk to your daddy more about it."

She goes for her toothbrush to brush her teeth, and I take that as my moment to flee. I scoop up my clothes from the small table in here and carry them out since I clearly won't be getting dressed in here anymore. I'm a bit old to be sharing a bathroom, but since I moved into the guest room before Aston and Zoey ever moved in, it is what it is.

I step out of the bathroom and plow straight into Aston, who was coming for the bathroom. My clothes drop to the floor as I work to secure my towel.

Our eyes meet before he registers my wet hair and the towel covering me. "Hi," he says, his voice rushed.

"Hi." I dive for my clothes on the floor at the same moment he does, and we bump heads. "Ow." I rub the top of my head as he picks up my clothes.

"You okay? That hurt. Here." He hands me my clothes one by one. My sweater, my jeans, my undershirt, my bra that he eyes, and finally my thong that he definitely eyes and runs through his fingers. Then I remember. He ripped my panties last night. Does he still have them? I don't. Or are they hanging out on the kitchen counter like a bad memory?

"I'm fine." I take my items from him and press them to my chest as I go to move around him, but he parries my dance and intercepts me. "What are you doing?"

"Last night I started thinking—"

"Could have fooled me," I cut him off.

He grunts, but there's a curl of his lips. "Yes, well, actually I was thinking you should take Micha's room and I should take the guest bedroom."

I hold my clothes tighter, using them as a shield. "Oh?"

"If anyone should be sharing a bathroom with Zoey, it's me. You'd also have more privacy that way, and I won't have to keep seeing you in nothing but a towel. How about after breakfast, after I make you breakfast," he amends, "we switch rooms."

I narrow my eyes at him. "Why are you being nice?"

"Who said I am?"

"You're smiling strangely at me. And you're talking about making me breakfast and offering me Micha's room."

"I'm not smiling strangely at you."

"You are," I counter.

That smile twists up even higher, and he rubs the back of his neck beneath his backward ball hat, making his stupid biceps bulge. "This is becoming one of my favorite looks for you, but I don't think I'm allowed to say that."

"You're not."

He gives a slow nod, then shrugs as if he doesn't care. "See. Definitely a good idea for you to take Micha's room. I'll let you get dressed. Eggs, french toast, or both?"

I snort. "Both. Obviously."

"Bacon?"

I roll my eyes. "Is that actually a question?"

Now I get a full set of pearly white teeth. It's annoying how good-looking he is. How the way he looks at me isn't real. It's just who he is and what he does. I was a pawn to him.

I move around him when he stops me again just as I reach my door. "About last night—"

"No," I sharply cut him off and face him so he sees how serious I am about this. "No. We're not doing that. We're not talking about it or giving excuses or gloating or anything. You got your wedding present, and Micha's bedroom is mine, and that's it. We're not friends or friendly, and I seriously don't like you. In fact, the less we talk to each other, the better."

His eyes search mine, and all traces of his smile are gone. He's not frowning, but he's not happy either. Tough shit. That makes two of us. He opens his mouth, closes it, and walks into the bathroom where Zoey is.

As for me, I lock the bedroom door and get myself dressed and ready. Then I pull down the two suitcases I have in here and put the things from the dresser in them. My hanging stuff, shoes, and purses I can carry down the hall. It'll take about eighty trips, but whatever. I'm glad to have Micha's bedroom and bathroom to myself.

I didn't take his bedroom when I moved in because it was still his bedroom with things in it, and it felt weird, but now I'm grateful Aston is giving it to me.

I finish getting ready and even blow out my hair, which I don't normally do, but it's cold out today and I'm killing time. I'll go down and eat with them, but I don't want to hang around the kitchen with him. One look at that counter and I'll either orgasm again or strangle him. Neither of which I want to do in front of Zoey.

"Sky, breakfast is ready!" Zoey calls up to me, and I laugh lightly. He had Zoey come and tell me. He's either respecting my wishes or is a total coward. The smell of bacon and cinnamon hits me, and my stomach churns a little. Not enough that I won't eat, but I won't be sad when this morning sickness ends. Thankfully, no throw-ups today.

I hit the bottom step, when the doorbell rings. I throw a glance over at Aston, but he looks just as confused as I am. For a moment, a flash of uneasiness hits me. What if Josh is making good on his threats to start showing up here?

"Who is it?" I ask through the door since I left my phone upstairs with the camera app on it.

"It's me. Open up. It's freezing out here," my mother replies, and I laugh. And sigh. Of course my mother is here.

When I open the door, I discover it's not just my mother, but Aston's mother too. "Surprise!" Halle sings out, racing in to give me a giant hug because that's Halle. "We were going to brunch and then thought it would be fun if everyone came."

"Grandma!" Zoey cries and races over to Halle, who scoops her up into a big hug.

"My girl." Halle drops kisses on her head. "Are you feeling better after last night?"

Zoey nods, and I wonder what happened last night that she wasn't feeling well. She seems fine now.

"Good. It smells like Daddy is already making you breakfast."

"I was," Aston confirms.

"But you can join us," my mom states, talking to me. "I'm positive there's a mimosa with your name on it."

Ohhh. Yeah, that's a toughie.

I twist my fingers. "Uh. Well."

"What is that on your hand?" Halle puts Zoey down and yanks my left hand up to her face.

"Skylar Fritz Davenport, why do you have a massive diamond on your hand along with a wedding band?" my mother practically shrieks.

Oh shit. I forgot I was wearing them. I throw a panicked look at Aston, who calmly turns off the stove, makes Zoey a plate of food, sets it on the table, and walks over to us. This was not how my mom, or even his mom, was supposed to find out. I was planning a sit-down over dinner, and after they'd already had copious amounts of wine or maybe a martini or six, then I'd tell them.

Aston comes straight to Zoey. "Your breakfast is ready for you. Go eat while I talk to Grandma and Aunt Rina."

"Can I watch on my iPad?"

"Yes. But only for a little."

"Why are Grandma and Aunt Rina so upset?"

"Because they like to over grown-up sometimes." He scrunches his nose and ruffles the top of her head. "Don't let your food get cold, kiddo."

Zoey simply shrugs in an *adult problems* way and scampers over to the table to eat.

"Why do you have a gigantic diamond on your hand?" my mother yells again.

"Shhh," I hush her and nod toward Zoey, who's now in the kitchen eating and watching on her iPad.

"Don't shush me. Tell me."

"So... weird story... I got married last night."

"Married?! As in *married*? To whom?" She looks at Aston. "Did you know about this?"

"Aston Oliver Hughes, why do you have a wedding band on your left hand?!" Now his mother is shrieking. "Was that there last night when you picked up Zoey?"

"Explain this now," my mother demands, her gaze snapping back and forth between me and Aston.

"I'm pregnant with Josh's baby, and Aston and I are married."

"What?!" she cries, and I pat the air, indicating she should calm down and lower her voice since Zoey isn't far. "How did this happen?" she asks, tempering her voice.

I sigh. Why is that everyone's first question? "How do you think it happened?"

She rolls her eyes at me. "I'm not asking *that,* and you know it. I'm asking for more details. A timeline. Anything, because I'm freaking out right now."

"Now you know how I feel?"

She points a motherly finger at me. "You're pregnant and married to Aston. I'm allowed to be a mess. Halle is a mess." She shakes her friend's shoulder. "Now tell us everything."

"I found out I was pregnant last weekend," I continue, only for Aston to cut me off.

"And I asked her to marry me."

Halle looks like she's about to pass out. "Why? How did you get involved in this?"

He bobs his head toward the study on the other side of the first floor, away from where Zoey is eating like it's her last meal.

My mother and Halle take off their coats, holding them in their arms and pinning us with impatient, demanding looks.

"Zoey has been struggling since Astrid's death. We all know this. You saw her breakdown last night. Her therapist explained she has some fear of abandonment issues and that she needs more home life stability and consistency. She needs people she cares about in her daily life, and for whatever reason, she bonded with Skylar within about two seconds of meeting her."

"I still don't understand," Halle admits. "How is that a reason to *marry* her?"

"Josh," my mother murmurs, covering her lips with her hand. "Josh isn't safe for you or the baby."

I glance down at the floor. "No. He's not."

"That motherfucker. I should have had him killed when you told us how he was with you."

Halle holds up a hand, stopping my mother before she goes on a rant. "So, you offered to marry her for protection against this Josh asshole, and in return she'll play house with Zoey."

It's not a question, but Aston answers his mother all the same. "Yes."

My mother blows out a breath, takes a step toward me, and grasps my arm. "Why didn't you come to us? Why didn't you tell us? We could have done... something to help."

"Like what? What is there to do in situations like this?"

"I don't know. Security or lawyers or, again, having him killed."

"All of that may eventually come, minus the murder, but for now, he can't use this to manipulate me or come after me. I'm married. I can't go back to him. There's nothing for him to try for there. End of story. Besides, I'm not sure..." I trail off.

"What?" my mother presses.

"You're not going to tell him it's his," Halle surmises, and I shrug. I'm still undecided. It feels wrong and yet right, and I'm conflicted with that.

"Who else knows about this?"

"Braelyn and Alden," I answer.

"Are you two..." Halle waves a finger back and forth between me and Aston.

"No," he and I both say quickly. "It's not like that between us," Aston finishes, and I sort of want to kick him in the shins for that even if it's true. But ouch. You know? After last night and all the bullshit he filled my head with. Ouch.

"Does Micha know?" my mother asks.

"I tried to tell him, but our call got cut short."

"So, he's not on a plane right now from Sudan to kill you? At least not yet."

I laugh, and so does Aston. "Not as far as I know. I told him I had something important to tell him. He had to go, so we'll see how long it is before he calls either of us back. Or shows up to kill me."

"Skylar, you're pregnant?" My mother has gone from irate and incredulous to tearful, which isn't helping me because now my hormones are kicking in and I'm choking up to the point where all I can do is nod. "How far along?"

"I haven't had an ultrasound yet. Best I can figure, about nine weeks or so."

"Jesus Harold Christmas. I'm going to be a grandmother."

"And you're married to her," Halle says, staring at Aston. "You're *married* to Skylar."

"It's not real," I press. "It's just... you know, convenient for both of us right now. It's an arrangement."

"Arrangement or not, you're married, and you're pregnant. People will assume the baby is yours." She points at Aston.

"If Skylar wants me to say it is, given the situation, I will."

I swallow thickly. I was never going to ask him for that. Not ever. But to hear him offer it so casually and calmly, it thaws some of the newly formed ice I had around my heart where he's concerned.

"Well then." Halle flips her copper-red hair back over her shoulders, resolute and getting down to business. "If we're going to make this look real, we have to announce it and throw a party for you both. It has to look as though both of your families are involved in this."

"Yes," my mom agrees. "It's how the Fritzes and the Hugheses would do it. We don't have to announce the pregnancy if that's not what you're ready to do, but we are going to throw you a wedding party."

Oh shit.

21

ASTON

Our mothers leave in a tizzy of pregnancy and wedding party planning flutter, which officially means the word is out. Our moms will tell everyone in our families, and I guess that takes the burden off us. One less awkward conversation to have.

I shut and lock the door behind them, momentarily sagging against it. I started this train, and now I'm stuck riding on it, even as the brakes seem to have blown out and it's racing down the tracks, headed straight for destruction.

A wedding party. Great. Zoey will never understand this, and I can't fathom a way this doesn't make her situation worse. Skylar's too, probably.

Skylar walks straight past me into the kitchen, where she pulls a glass out of the cabinet, fills it with water from the fridge, and downs it in three huge gulps. I have no clue what to say or how to help her with this. In fact, I'm pretty positive she's all set with my help and never wants me to speak to her again. I seem to hurt everything I touch lately. Or at the very least fuck it up somehow.

Zoey waves her fork wildly in the air. "We're going to see the movie still, right?"

I nod and push myself away from the door to head back into the kitchen. "Yup. This afternoon."

"Can I get the big popcorn? The one with the butter and stuff?" she asks, chewing with her mouth open, blissfully oblivious to all that's happening.

"Sure," I say because I don't think I can say no to her today. She saw something last night that reminded her of her mother, and she absolutely lost it. I brought her home and lay in bed with her for an hour, holding her, comforting her, until she finally cried herself to sleep. She made me promise I'd never die and leave her, which I can't obviously promise. If she asked for a Ferrari right now, I'd probably oblige.

A smile lights up her face, her lips glistening with syrup. "Sky's coming too. We're going to share popcorn and candy."

"Sweetie, Skylar might have other plans today." I go over to the stove and fix Skylar a plate. She's quiet. Hardly moving, and I have no clue what's going through her head. When the girl wants to shut down, she does it well and keeps everything roiling in her head and heart a mystery. She likes her secrets, but they're unfolding to everyone one by one.

I hand Skylar her plate. She eyes it dubiously but goes and sits down across from Zoey. She hasn't made any coffee for herself, and I don't know if she wants any, and I'd rather not ask because fuck, it's like I don't even know how to talk to her anymore, so I just make her a cup how she likes it and set it in front of her.

She eyes it for a harsh minute before mumbling, "Thank you."

"You're not coming?" Zoey asks her, crestfallen.

Skylar puts on a happy-go-lucky smile, one no one could see through.

"Of course I'm coming. Popcorn, candy, and getting to hang out with you? Sign me up."

A smile cracks my lips even as I wonder if she developed this talent from being a nurse and having to smile for kids despite knowing sometimes they won't have the best outcomes or if this comes from her childhood when kids were dicks and she had to smile and appear unfazed or if it's from covering the abuse she sustained from Josh.

All of those options piss me off, but I brush them aside. What am I doing trying to figure her out?

I shake myself out of my inane curiosity and make myself a plate minus eggs because eggs gross me out like few things in this world do, a large cup of black coffee, and sit beside Zoey. I tell myself it's to give Skylar space from me, but as I glance up at her, able to study her pretty face, I know it's so I can watch her when she doesn't realize I'm looking. Fuck. Last night has me spun.

I fell asleep with the taste and smell of her all over me. Hating myself for how I ended it while convincing myself I had no other choice. But she was the first thing on my mind this morning after being the last when I fell asleep, and that's not a new phenomenon. It's been like that since I saw her outside the bar that night on Valentine's Day. Even before that, because she made Valentine's Day her holiday for me two years ago.

I rub my forehead and take a sip of my coffee, staring at the kitchen counter, unable to stop myself from replaying last night through my head for the hundredth time since she ran upstairs on me. I've never wanted a woman like this. Never had a taste and craved more. That one kiss two years ago somehow rewired my brain into only seeing her, and what the fuck do I do about that?

Skylar isn't eating either. She's shuffling her food around on her plate, her left hand wrapped around the porcelain of the mug, and my gaze fixes on the diamonds. She's wearing them. I hadn't expected that. I thought they'd live in the jewelry box, and she'd only wear them when forced or in front of Josh.

I need to tell Zoey about this, but she's a bit fragile. Maybe tonight.

I clear my throat. "Do you have a lot of things to move?" I ask, spinning my hat around on my head so it faces forward and I can watch her from beneath the brim.

"Yes," she admits with a rueful laugh.

"You're moving?" Zoey cries in horror, completely misinterpreting.

"No way," Skylar tells her. "Your dad and I are simply switching bedrooms."

Zoey is way too relieved by that, and acid burns up my stomach lining. My lungs constrict like I'm being held underwater, but no matter how hard I try to get to the surface, I can't reach it. I just keep swimming in place and holding my breath, praying I don't drown.

"So, we're still going to the movie?"

"Absolutely. What are we seeing again?"

"*Dog Cops.*"

"Oh." Skylar's eyebrows bounce with amusement. "What's it about?"

"Talking dogs who solve crimes," I deadpan.

"No!" Zoey exclaims as if I'm an idiot. "He only talks to the girl." Then she shrugs. "And his animal friends."

"Naturally," Skylar agrees. "It sounds awesome."

Zoey wiggles in her seat and crunches on bacon when Skylar's chair suddenly screeches back from the table. All the color has drained from her face, and without a word, she gets up and races toward the powder room off the entry.

"Is she okay?" Zoey asks, dripping in concern.

"I think she has an upset tummy."

"Maybe the eggs made her sick like they do for you. Or maybe it's just these eggs."

I choke on a laugh. "Hey. What's wrong with my eggs?"

She stabs them with her fork and holds up a chunk of them for me to see. "They weren't good today. They're brown on top."

The grossness dangles from her fork, and sure enough, I burned her eggs. Clearly, I was a bit too preoccupied with thoughts of my wife.

"I'll go check on her," I offer. "You finish up and then clear your place. But be careful not to drop anything."

"Can I color with markers after that?"

"Only on your art mat."

She nods and hastily shoves food into her mouth so she can color.

"Slow down. I don't want you to choke." I kiss the top of her head and make my way down the hall to the bathroom.

"Skylar? Can I come in?"

"No. Go away."

I open the door anyway, since she once again didn't lock it, already anticipating she'd tell me that, and peek in to find her kneeling on the tile floor, her head resting on her arm that's stretched over the plastic seat. Her hair sticks to her damp forehead and falls limply behind her.

Without thinking, I kneel beside her and brush the strands back from her face.

She swats at me. "I said go away," she mumbles, but there's no force behind it. I think she's wrecked.

"And miss this glamorous moment? Never," I tease, keeping my voice light. "Can I get you anyth—"

I'm cut off as she jerks up faster than a bullet and retches into the toilet. I pull her hair back so it doesn't fall into her face as her body heaves with very little coming out. When she's done, she groans and falls back to the position she was in before.

I grab a clean cloth from the cabinet under the sink, wet it with cold water, and hand it to her. She uses one side to wipe her mouth and chin and the other across her cheeks and forehead.

"This is humiliating. And gross."

"True. How dare your body do exactly what we doctors say it will do? So inconsiderate."

"God, there's no limit to your arrogance. You're enjoying this, aren't you? Seeing me at my worst."

I crouch back down and run my fingers along her cheek. "Skylar, trust me, this isn't even close to your worst."

She rolls her eyes, but her lips twitch even as she says, "Fuck you."

"Not right now. At least not until you brush your teeth."

She sits up, scooting until she's pressed against the wall. I flush the toilet, though there's not much in there other than a few traces of water and bile.

"Thank you," she concedes grudgingly. "Even if you're still a jerk."

"Wouldn't be me with you if I wasn't."

"Fair." She sighs. "Christ, Aston. What have we gotten ourselves into? Our mothers are planning our wedding party. None of this was supposed to happen. They were going to listen as we told them what was up, and they were supposed to be quietly supportive."

I close the lid of the toilet and sit on it. "It's our mothers. We honestly should have anticipated this."

"What will Zoey think about a wedding party where people talk like we're in love and together?"

My elbows plant into my thighs, and I stare down at the floor between my feet. "I don't know. I don't even know what to say or how to phrase it, and I can't exactly ask her therapist for help on that, though I do have to tell her I'm married now."

"We had five days to figure this out between when you asked me and when we said 'I do,' and we didn't."

"It's like what Monty Python says. 'No one expects the Spanish Inquisition.'"

She snorts a laugh and sits up a little straighter. "Ain't that the truth?"

She still has the washcloth pressed to the side of her face, and just beneath it is a small freckle I've never noticed before. I have a sudden and intense urge to trace it with my finger.

"How are you feeling?" I ask instead.

"Like I got hit by a truck carrying nothing but morning sickness and regret."

"That's very poetic."

"I try." She tilts her head. "Why are you still in here?"

"I'm a father and a pediatric surgeon. Vomit doesn't scare me off."

"Good to know. How about garlic around my neck or a silver bullet?"

I smirk. "Sorry, wifey, you're stuck with me for a while. In sickness and in health, for better or worse."

"Right now, it's only the first and the latter."

"Better than till death do us part."

She pushes herself up from the floor but wobbles slightly as she gets to her feet. I shoot up and grasp her hips, steadying her.

"I'm fine." She tries to push me away, but she's not fine. Some of it might be stress, some of it might be morning sickness, but she's not fine.

"Don't fight me, okay?"

"What?" she asks as I swoop her body up into my arms bride-style, ironically enough. "Ah! What are you doing? Put me down."

"I said don't fight me. I'm carrying you up to bed."

"I can walk," she protests adamantly, going so far as to try to squirm out of my grip as I move us out of the bathroom.

"Skylar Fritz Davenport Hughes, shut up and let me carry my sick wife up the goddamn stairs," I growl at her.

"Stop with all of that already. You'll drop me."

I smirk at her. "Sweetheart, you call me a lot of things. A jerk, an asshole, cocky, and arrogant, but one thing I am is sure-handed. I will never drop you. Now stop fighting me."

Shockingly, she does. She even wraps her arms around my neck and lets me carry her up the stairs. "Josh called me a roly-poly the first and only time he picked me up and carried me."

I peer down at her. "A what?"

"They're bugs that roll into a ball and are small and well, round."

"Wow. He's seriously going to die on Monday at work. How did you stay with him so long? And I'm not judging or blaming you. I'm curious because you seem so strong and confident, and you have no issues handing me my ass when I deserve it and even sometimes when I don't."

I walk her down the hall, past her bedroom, and into mine since it'll be hers soon.

She glances around but doesn't comment. "I'm a people pleaser and was always terrified of confrontation. Plus, well, he wasn't the first to comment or tease me about that kind of stuff, so I didn't... realize what it was or how bad it was until, well, I did. I believed a lot of what he said because I didn't have the best self-image of myself."

I pause beside the bed, still holding her in my arms, and meet her eyes. "You're not a roly-poly or an ugly duckling or whatever else people said about you. You're a swan, and I'm glad you finally see that, and I'm glad you left him."

She holds my gaze for a long moment and then looks away. "I should brush my teeth."

I set her down on my bed, in my sheets. "I'll grab it for you."

"It's just morning sickness. I'll be fine."

"I know you will be," I tell her, meaning it for more than just this. "Don't move."

I scoot down the hall to the other bathroom, grab her toothbrush, toothpaste, and anything else that's blatantly hers, and bring them back into my bathroom. I'll have to clear my stuff out of here, but I'll do it later after she's rested.

"Stop being nice to me," she calls out to me, and I chuckle.

"I'm not."

"You are."

I set everything down and return to the bedroom, standing over her when what I really want to do is climb into bed beside her and hold her until everything in her world is better. I'm a doctor and by nature a caretaker, but I've never felt this level of protectiveness over someone who wasn't my child before. Not even Astrid.

"Why do you want me to stop being nice to you?"

"It's confusing."

I move some of her hair out of her face so I can see her better. Her color is already improving. "Maybe I like keeping you on your toes."

"Except I don't have the ability to trip and stumble anymore."

"What do you want me to say? That I meant everything I said to you last night except for the last thing?"

"No," she snaps. "I don't want you to say that."

"Fine. How's this then? Last night was one of the greatest nights of my life. I know it shouldn't have been. I know it's all a lie. I know it's a mess and we're a mess, and it's only going to get worse from here. I know all of that. I also say stupid shit, and I fuck up. A lot. But marrying you wasn't one of my fuck-ups. I'll be the husband you need me to be, and I'll keep my distance if that's what you tell me you need with it."

"That's the deal we made," she whispers, staring down at

her hands the way she always does when she's nervous or unsure. "It's the only way we'll get through this unscathed."

Wow. This sucks. "It is. So, I'll stand by that. It's probably for the best anyway." I head toward the door only to stop. I have to say it. I shouldn't. It falls under the category of *I say stupid shit*, but I have to say it anyway. I open my mouth, the words hanging from my tongue, but what good will setting them free do?

She doesn't want to know that I don't think there's any way I'll get through this unscathed now that I've made her my wife.

So, I shut the door and let her rest. Wondering if I'll ever get to a point in my life where not everything hurts.

I wake to the unfamiliar feel of Aston's sheets against my skin. Silky cotton that smells of cedar and something distinctly him. The room is dim, the curtains drawn, and I flop on my back, thinking of how I ended up here. The morning sickness. Him coming into the bathroom to help me. His unexpected gentleness as he carried me up here, and then his subsequent apology for last night.

My fists rub at my eyes, bleary and disoriented. I have no clue what time it is, but I feel better. Well, physically at least. My head is still a disaster, but I think that's going to be my baseline for the next... well, likely years. I snort out a choked laugh.

Christ.

I roll over in bed and bury my face in his pillow. It feels weird to be in his sheets where he slept. And unfortunately, it's kind of hot too. I'm not sure if this makes me a creeper or not, but I take a deep inhale, and immediately flashes from last night flicker through my head. His apology this morning shouldn't make it better, but like almost everything with him, somehow it does. The moment I start to hate him again, he takes a bat and bashes my animosity away.

I need to take that apology for what it was and nothing more. He doesn't regret marrying me, and he doesn't regret what we did last night. Great. All good. I'll accept his olive branch in whatever this thing is between us and ignore the something electric and dangerous that hums through my body when I think beyond that.

Eight weeks ago, I was a nurse with a crappy boyfriend. Now I'm pregnant, living and working with Aston, and married to him.

I roll over to find my phone resting on the nightstand. I didn't hear Aston bring it in for me. It's after noon. I hope they didn't go to the movies without me. I'd feel terrible since I promised Zoey.

Slowly I pull myself up and out of bed, my limbs tight as I give a stretch, my toes curling against the area rug over the hardwood floors. I stuff my phone in my pocket and open the door, immediately hearing sound downstairs.

"When are we going?" Zoey whines.

"In two hours, Zo-Zo. Be patient. And please keep your voice down, or you'll wake Skylar."

"But why is she sleeping? It's lunchtime."

"She wasn't feeling well this morning, remember?"

A smile quirks my lips, and I pad down the stairs only to practically bump into Aston, who's coming up them. His eyes widen, and he moves one step down, creating some space between us.

"You're up," he says, his voice even. He's wearing a faded Boston Rebels T-shirt, gray sweatpants, and a backward hat, leaving some of the longer pieces of his light hair sticking out the back beneath the brim. Holy shit. I think I just came again. "Feeling better?"

"Much," I answer, crossing my arms over my chest because I took off my bra before I fell asleep in his bed, and my nipples are definitely saluting him. Come to think of it, my bra is likely still on his floor. "Thanks for lending me your bed."

"It's your bed now, remember? Speaking of, did you want to do that now? Switch rooms?"

"Oh. Um. Sure," I chirp brightly, and wow, is this tense.

"Great. I'll help you move your stuff. I don't want you lifting anything heavy."

"Let's do it." I mentally smack my forehead. Did I just say that?

He follows me into my bedroom and grabs my two already packed suitcases and drags them down to his room. Or I guess it's my room now. That'll take some adjustment.

For the next hour, the two of us go back and forth, dancing awkwardly around each other as we move our stuff from one room to the other. Every time we pass each other in the hall, I'm hyperaware of the space between us and how careful we are to avoid even so much as a glancing touch.

"How many purses and pairs of shoes do you have?" he asks as he grabs a box from my bed that I filled and walks it down the hall.

"Hey," I snap. "Never comment on a woman's shoes or bags. How many hats do you own?"

"I collect them."

"Same," I throw back at him.

"Good thing the primary has the walk-in. You're going to need it."

I flip him off, and he laughs, but since he's holding my shoes and bags, I follow him into the master, where he sets them down on the bed.

"I changed the sheets for you." He juts his chin toward the king-sized bed. The guestroom has a queen, and I hadn't gotten that far yet.

"Thank you. Sorry. I wasn't as generous."

He shrugs. "It's fine. I can do it." He glances down at the box on the bed and then up to the pillows. "I should finish moving my things. I think I only have one more run, though."

"Yeah. Same."

Neither of us moves, and the air between us suddenly feels charged, thick with everything we're not saying. With all the things stuck between us that seem to get shoved into a corner or we pretend aren't there.

"I start a twenty-four-hour shift tomorrow night," he tells me, his gaze returning to mine. For a moment, it dips to my lips and holds there only for him to swallow and force it back up. "Zoey will be with my parents."

"Oh. I can watch her."

He shrugs. "She doesn't mind. They spoil her rotten. Last night was just a rough night."

"She didn't do well?"

All he does is shake his head, and I let him leave it there.

"So... what happens Monday?"

"Monday we show up wearing these and casually announce that we're married." He holds up his left hand with his thick, platinum band on it.

I stare down at the diamonds sparkling back at me. "I can't wear the rock to work. It's huge, and I'll struggle with gloves."

He takes a small step forward, his hand on my cheek as he pushes some of my hair behind my ear. "Will you wear the band?"

I swallow and nod. "That's the point of this, isn't it?"

"Good."

"Aston..." I trail off, unsure what to say. His words from this morning ring heavy in my ears.

"Can I ask... I mean, I know I shouldn't. But..." He sighs and chuckles as he adjusts his hat on his head. "Did you enjoy it?"

I quirk an eyebrow at him. "You need your massive ego padded more?"

His lips curl up, making his blue eyes sparkle. "In this case, yes. I know you... came. But was it good? The other stuff, I mean. Before I opened my mouth and fucked it all up, that is."

"Yes. It was good. Obviously since you've done what no man has done before."

He inches in ever so slightly, and my neck cranes up to his face as he stares down at me. "They were lazy, Skylar. Once you relaxed into me and got out of your head, it didn't take you all that much. And I didn't mean for you to... fall onto me the way you did. I hope you know that. I wasn't trying to take advantage or push you somewhere we hadn't discussed or you didn't want. I'd never do that."

I did know that. I didn't think he was trying to take advantage of me. He looked just as shocked by it as I was. I look down at my hands. For some reason, him saying they were lazy makes me feel both better and worse. Those guys, the ones who tried, always made me feel like it was my issue. Maybe it was their frustration or annoyance over it, and that only made it worse for me. But all they would do was rub my clit harder or whatever. They never tried talking to me the way he did. They never cared enough to know why I was having trouble.

"It doesn't matter, though."

"Right. It's better this way," he agrees sharply, his eyes intense. Resolute. "We both have enough complications right now."

He's right. I have a baby on the way, a vindictive ex to avoid, and he has a little girl still grieving her mother. Besides, I don't want to get hurt. I want to focus on myself and what's ahead for me.

"I'm not looking for anything," I promise him.

"Same. It was a moment. It doesn't have to be anything more. It *can't* be anything more."

I nod, ignoring the odd sensation that settles in my stomach at that. Probably more morning sickness. "Right. A moment." I clear my throat. "We should finish up if we're going to make that movie."

I turn away from him and go for the box of my shoes, giving him my back as I put them away. I don't even know why I brought it up again, other than I can't stop thinking about it, and then he had to go and apologize and fuck me up more.

But it's done. We've officially talked about it more than once, and it's over.

I feel his eyes on me, the weight of everything surrounding us, and despite what we just said to each other, when I glance over my shoulder at him, I see it. All the things we say on the surface and all the things we're both burying. Last night changed us, and not in a good way. We're playing a dangerous game pretending we can live together and work together, while maintaining a careful distance.

But I've made enough mistakes already, and I can't afford another. Especially not with Aston. So, I straighten my spine and continue to put away shoes and purses, and after another second, he leaves, closing the door behind him and allowing me to finally take a breath.

FOREST'S TOWNHOUSE gleams in the Sunday afternoon light, all sleek surfaces and floor-to-ceiling windows that show off the Boston skyline across the harbor we sit almost directly above. He's only been living here for a couple of months. A bribe from his parents if he moved back to Boston from LA and took over the Abbott Foundation, which my grandmother's family started generations ago. His father, Kaplan, was the CEO, but he's a surgeon at the hospital with me, so Forest's mother was essentially running it.

Forest always swore he'd never move back here. Boston

holds demons for him, but I'm happy he did even if I'm not sure he's quite sold yet.

"Do you actually live here?" I tease. We're up in his crow's nest on the third floor, and to say it's sparsely furnished is putting it mildly.

He rolls his dark eyes at me. "Yes. I haven't had time to buy a lot of furniture, and when I sold my place in LA, I sold it furnished. It's weird living here. I grew up in this townhouse. Maybe that's why I'm having trouble furnishing it."

"I get that," Crew agrees. "I haven't bought much for my place yet either."

"You would if you'd let me take you shopping for stuff," Quinn bites out at her twin.

"We should all go furniture shopping then. It'll be fun."

Hayes tilts his head at me. "What's up with you? You seem… off."

I am off. And after Aston and I told Zoey that we were wearing rings because we're special friends who care a lot about each other, she was like a different kid. Curious and not quite getting it, but happy to hear that I was going to be living with them for a while. We didn't use the term "married," but she'll hear it sooner or later, and I know Aston is worried about that and the implications of it for her.

Braelyn is keeping her face in her sub, taking a massive bite and washing it down with her soda, since this is Forest's place, and we never drink here with him since he's sober.

"You know something," Roman accuses her, staring down his best friend, trying to read her, which he's insanely good at. It's likely what makes him unstoppable as a boxer. Or an underground street fighter. Whatever you want to call what he does as a side gig.

"Ha! You're crazy," she garbles around her bite. "I know nothing, Jon Snow."

"You just misquoted *Game of Thrones*," he tells her. "That means you do."

I sigh. Might as well rip the Band-Aid off. I already did it twice this weekend, first with my mother and then with my father when he called me last night. That was a fun conversation. And yes, that's sarcasm.

"I married Aston on Friday." For some reason, that's easier to lead with than that I'm pregnant.

Everyone gapes at me, eyes wide, shock all over the damn place.

"Umm..." Quinn trails off, twirling her reddish-brown hair around her fingers. "Did you say you *married* him? Were you trashed? Is this like a Vegas thing? Like what Mason and Sorel did?"

"No. It wasn't like that. It was here in Boston."

She's flabbergasted. Everyone is. "How? Why?" She shakes her head, at a total loss.

"Wait." Hayes comes over and sits beside me. "You married Aston? As in married him, married him? You're serious?" He yanks my left hand onto his lap. I'm still wearing the diamond, but tonight it's going back in the box. "Shit, Skylar. What the actual fuck?" He holds up my left hand for everyone to see.

"That's a fucking rock he put on you." Roman blinks at me. "This is fucked up. What's going on?"

"She had to marry him," Braelyn chimes in. "She's pregnant with douchebag Josh's baby, which said douchebag doesn't know about yet, but she's scared to tell him and scared of his reaction for reasons we all know. She and Aston struck a deal since they're already temporarily living together. She'll help out with Zoey, and Dr. McBroody will help her with Josh."

I snort. "Please don't turn my life into a *Grey's Anatomy* episode. I can't handle more drama."

She holds up her hand. "Fine, but I still feel like we need a nickname for Aston. I was torn between broody and hot but couldn't think how to combine them in a way that worked."

"Fair. We'll think about it." Because asshole doesn't quite fit him anymore, even if part of me wishes it still did.

"Stop with the girl crap," Crew barks, climbing up onto his knees since his massive frame is sitting on the floor in front of the coffee table while he eats. "Reverse and explain all of this. In detail." His features soften, and he glances down at my still flat stomach. "Sky, you're pregnant? For real?"

Hayes shifts beside me so he can stare me down, holding my hand, and I take that comfort and rest my head on his shoulder. "Yes. I found out last week and have an OB appointment scheduled for this Thursday and an ultrasound in a few weeks."

"Why didn't you come to us first?" Hayes questions, hurt in his voice. "We would have helped you with this. With Josh. Hell, I would have married you if you felt that's what you needed."

"Same," Crew agrees.

"And we would have been there during it," Roman states. Forest has his head in his hands. My guys are a mess. They feel like they let me down. When I finally told them about what Josh had been like, they were similar to how they are now. It broke them that I kept so much from them, but this is different.

"I know you all would have been, and I love you for it. I didn't really plan on the whole marriage thing. Then again, I didn't exactly plan to be pregnant either. Braelyn did the test after I randomly threw up and realized I had missed my period, and Aston came home and found me crying about it on the sofa. It went from there. Zoey needs more stability at home, someone she can be close with, and I..."

"You need a buffer from Josh." Forest stands up and paces toward the window. "He doesn't know yet? About any of this?"

"No," I tell him, and he nods, keeping his back to me, his hands going to the top of his head.

"I still wish you had gotten a restraining order against him."

"I couldn't without everyone knowing what happened and having to leave my job, and I love my job. It's one of the top ICUs in the country, if not the world."

"Are you going to tell him?" Quinn asks, coming to my other side and taking my other hand.

"I haven't decided yet. Regardless, the marriage needs to look legit. Like Aston and I are actually in love."

"And the baby as his?" Hayes questions.

"Aston said he would do that if I wanted. I can't ask for that, though. The more lies we tell, the worse it'll be. For now, I'll let people assume what they want without confirming."

"Dude, you're married to Aston Hughes." Quinn hiccups out a laugh before she slaps a hand over her mouth. "I'm sorry. I'm not making light of what you're going through, but Aston Hughes!" she exclaims, fanning her face. "He's sexy as hell."

"I know, right?" Braelyn jumps in. "So hot. You should have seen him in his suit at the wedding. Damn."

"It's not like that with us." I shake my head, trying not to smile at the accuracy of this description. "Can we focus, please? Aston's looks are not why I wanted you all here."

"No, you wanted us here because you got married without telling us, and now you need our help to convince Josh and the world that it's real and not completely insane," Crew says, his usual bluntness softened by the affection in his voice.

"It's not insane," I protest weakly. "It's... an arrangement."

Six pairs of eyes stare back at me with identical expressions of disbelief.

"Fine." I sigh. "It's a little insane. But it makes sense for both of us. He needs help with Zoey, who's still struggling after losing her mom. I need Josh to back off, and hopefully, being married is more effective than a restraining order. And it's temporary. Once things settle down, we'll get a divorce and move on."

"Except you'll have a kid. Josh's kid."

I shrug at Hayes. "Not much I can do on the parentage other than possibly lie. Or go through the courts."

Roman leans forward, his fierce *no one fucks with my people* demeanor on full display. "Skylar, we're all worried about Josh. What he did to you—"

"Was abuse," Hayes finishes, his jaw tightening. "The man is a textbook narcissist and treated you like shit."

I stare down at my hands still being held by theirs, hating the way my chest constricts at the mention of my ex. "I know. That's why I left. That's why I'm not telling him about the baby. At least not yet. Maybe not ever unless I have to."

"Good," Quinn says fiercely. "He doesn't deserve to know. And if he tries anything—"

"I'll kill him," Roman states bluntly.

"I believe that, which is why I'll handle it."

"Or Aston will," Braelyn quips. "That's part of the deal."

Forest turns, his eyebrows at his hairline. "Part of the deal? So, Aston's your personal bodyguard now? I thought you hated him. Just how close are the two of you?"

I hitch a shoulder and find my knotted fingers on my lap. "I wouldn't call us close. We can barely stand each other."

"Skylar Fritz Davenport!" Quinn demands. "You little slut." She nudges my arm. "Your voice squeaked, which means you're lying. Did you fuck your new husband?"

"What? No!" Except my face flames, and yeah, I squeaked again. I clear my throat and work to even my tone. "Nothing like that. He just... he's helping me out."

"Oh yeah? I bet he is. How much is he helping out?" Crew quirks an eyebrow at me.

"You're totally fucking him." Hayes sighs. "You have your *I did something scandalous* face."

"I don't have a scandalous face. What even is that?"

He points at me. "That. That face. Ninety-nine percent of the time you're this sweet, good girl. But that one percent..." He trails off.

"You can lie all you want, but you forget I saw the kiss," Braelyn reminds me.

"Oh, the kiss!" Quinn is all over that. "Wait! Did he make you come?"

The room falls silent.

"Yes," I say in a low voice. "But before you all start getting excited or freaking out on me, he was a jerk after. He knew no one had ever... done that to me before, and he made it his mission, and he said things. He filled my head with bullshit, and I fell for it because I was stupid and vulnerable and I'm freaking pregnant! It's likely pregnancy hormones that did that to me and not him."

"Shit. I don't know whether to thank him or kick his ass." Hayes wraps his arm around me, and I sink into him. Into these people and this circle of friends and family.

"We're getting off track," I say, trying to steer us away from this. I don't want to talk about it. "It was a one-time thing and won't happen again. We've already agreed to that. So, let's move past it. I have a complicated enough life right now without adding screwing my fake husband to the list."

"Fair," Roman agrees.

"Yes, but orgasms." Braelyn simpers. "Right? I mean, you finally had one. That's pretty big, Sky."

"Woohoo. Go me." I twirl my finger around in the air. "I'm a real girl," I cry, doing a horrible impression of Pinocchio's voice.

She rolls her eyes at me and tosses the throw pillow she was resting against at me, and I throw it right back at her.

"All joking aside," Quinn says, her voice gentle, "we're here for you. Whatever you need, whenever you need it. If this arrangement with Aston is what works for you both, then we support it."

"And if Josh gives you any trouble," Crew adds, his expression hardening, "you'll tell us."

"And we'll take care of him," Roman follows up.

"The same goes for the pregnancy," Hayes throws in. "We've got you. Always. You're not alone. You've got us, and we're your family."

"Thank you. That means the world to me." Let's just hope I don't need it.

23

ASTON

I roll my head around on my neck until it makes a satisfying crack. I nearly groan at how good that feels after that surgery. My foot presses down on the pedal, and water splashes out of the faucet into the large basin. I scrub out, washing off the last three hours of grueling work. I peer up and watch as the nurses wheel the patient out toward the ICU, too critical for the PACU. He's got a long road ahead of him, but he survived this round of surgery, so I'm hopeful.

"Did you put in orders?" the scrub nurse asks from the doorway.

"Not yet. Can you put in the standard ones for now? I'll add the others after rounds." I glance up at the clock on the wall as I dry off my hands and slip my wedding band from the loop on the drawstring of my scrub pants that I tied it around. I hold it in my hand for a moment. I'm already getting used to wearing it. Liking its weight and how it feels. It's different from the last time I had one of these on me.

I should resent it more than I do. And I certainly shouldn't like it as much as I do.

I slide it onto my left hand and push away from the sink.

"I didn't know you were married," she says to me. "Rumor had it that you were divorced and your ex-wife is deceased."

"My ex-wife is," I tell her, trying to hold in my smirk.

"But you're married now?" she presses, wanting the inside scoop to feed the ever-churning gossip mill. Patients, coffee, and gossip are what keep hospitals running.

"I am." I wink at her, grab my phone from the tray we keep them on, and head toward the elevator. I pull up my text stream with Skylar. She wasn't home before I left for my shift last night, and it bothered me. I also couldn't text to see where she was.

I'm not that kind of husband to her.

When I see her, I remember I'm supposed to keep my distance. I remember that Astrid was pregnant when I fell in love and married her, but Astrid likely never loved me back. She said she did. She acted the part. But she cheated, and it seriously hurt. It messed me up for a long time. I didn't trust. I didn't want to love.

Skylar doesn't even like me. She'd be no different from Astrid. I already know this.

My issue? When I'm away from her, I can't stop thinking about her, and with that, all the reasons why I need to keep my distance get shoved to the background. It's a paradox and a mindfuck, and I have no clue how to reconcile the two.

> Me: Text me when you get to the hospital, and I'll come down and meet you.

I press the button for the elevator, wondering if I should go down to the lobby to head her off instead of the MSICU, which is where I was initially going. She replies instantly, and a stupid, *I'm an idiot* smile curls up my lips.

I have it bad for my wife.

> Skylar: Why would you do that?

I roll my eyes.

> Me: Because, my lovely wife, we should probably be seen together if we're going to sell this thing. Don't you think?

> Skylar: Fine. I'm here. I'm in the lobby.

I immediately hit the L for the lobby

> Me: Stay there and wait for me. I'll buy you a coffee.

> Skylar: Make it a lemon ginger tea, and you have a deal.

A frown instantly tugs my smile off my face.

> Me: Morning sickness?

> Skylar: Just some nausea. Hoping the tea will help it pass.

I place an order online for her tea and a large coffee for myself, as I've been going since seven last night. The elevator doors open to the chaos that is the hospital lobby. Families and healthcare workers are coming and going. A large, brightly colored sculpture takes up half of the lobby, and I work my way around it, already spotting Skylar on the other side of it.

Her blonde hair is twisted up into a tight bun, and her face is sweet with only a small touch of makeup.

"Hey." I stand close enough that I have to look down at her. She's so adorably short and looks insanely cute in her pink scrub pants and blue hospital fleece.

Her green eyes cast up to mine. "Morning. How's your shift been so far?"

"Long," I tell her, reaching up and snatching an eyelash

that's fallen to her cheek. She startles back from my touch, but I hold it out in front of her. "Make a wish."

She snorts. "I hardly know what to wish for at this point." Yet she closes her eyes and blows on my finger, making the eyelash flutter away and heat surge through my body. The way this woman affects me is like no other. I hate it as much as I love it.

"We should head up," she says. "I don't want to be late, and if possible, I want to talk to Michaela before she hears about it from someone else."

"I don't think she'll care."

Her lips curve up into an alluring smirk. "Oh, she'll care. All the nurses and doctors who wanted to be the next Mrs. Hughes will."

"It's just new guy syndrome."

"New hot billionaire guy syndrome."

I step into her, my lips dipping closer. "Is that what I am? Hot?"

"And a billionaire."

"You don't care about that. You likely have more than I do."

She shrugs. "I never said you were hot. I was simply relaying the nursing party line."

I can't stop myself from trickling my fingers along her cheek. She shudders ever so slightly, and her pupils dilate. I doubt she's even aware of it, but I know she feels this. There's no stopping it. No denying it.

I only hope we can contain it.

"Is that so?" I whisper, only to have something catch my eye off to the side. "Shit. Josh."

"What?" Alarm skitters across her face.

"Josh is heading our way." And because she's my wife and I want him to know it, I put my hand on her cheek with my band showing, dip my head, and kiss her. Her hands grip my arms—

the way she has every time I've kissed her—and she holds on tight, rippling with uncertainty and unease.

"What the fuck?" Josh barks, grabbing onto Skylar and tearing her away from me. I jar back, feigning surprise that he caught us. Even as I gather Skylar back into me, resting my hand possessively on her hip and keeping her close.

I fix my gaze on him. "Problem, Dr. Wesley?"

His expression is murderous as he ignores me and goes right after Skylar. "Why is he kissing you?"

Skylar licks her lips but straightens her spine, and I love that. I love that she's not cowering. I love that she's bold, even if I know he scares her. I love that she left him and is finally able to see her worth.

"Because I'm married to him," she states bluntly, and if I thought he was murderous a moment ago...

His eyes scan back and forth between us before narrowing down on her hand. My diamond band is there even if the rock isn't.

"I told you she was seeing someone. You weren't interested in believing me."

He looks like he's going to tear us apart. "Married?" he spits. "How the fuck can you be married to him?"

I hold up my hand. "Hey, you're in the lobby of a children's hospital. Watch your mouth and tone, Doctor."

"Fuck you," he barks at me before reaching for her, but I shift her so he can't touch her. He goes ballistic. "This is bullshit. It's not real."

"It is," she tells him.

"You're *my* fucking girlfriend, Skylar. Mine! No way this is fucking happening."

"It's already happened." And here comes our practiced lie. "Aston and I reunited after you and I broke up. You remember how I kissed him at the Valentine's Day party two years ago. Well, I never got over that."

Recognition flickers in his eyes, and I can't help the flutter in my chest. She told him about the kiss. About me. It also explains why Josh was after me about her from the first moment I set foot in this hospital. Why he's likely the one who claimed her off-limits.

"Anyway, things got serious fast between us and—"

"I moved back to Boston for her," I explain. "We fell in love, and now we're married."

I smile down at her while keeping an eye on him.

"You stupid bitch!" he snarls. "How could you do this to me? You're my girl." He shakes his head. "No way. This isn't real. I know it's not. What the hell is going on?" He goes to grab her, and I knock his hand out of the way before he can touch her.

"Skylar, can you grab our drinks from the café? They're already ordered and paid for. I'll see you upstairs. I need a moment alone with my resident."

Before she can argue or say anything, I grab Josh by the back of his neck and haul him over to the side of the lobby and into the hall that leads to the bathrooms and a storage room beyond it. I slam him into the wall, use my forearm as a band across his neck, and get right up in his face.

I want to punch him. I want to hit him so badly.

But after my ex's husband sued me for hitting him and given the fact that we're in the hospital and I'm on duty, I won't take the risk.

"Listen here," I seethe, using my extra couple of inches to my advantage. "You will never speak that way to my wife again. She broke up with you nearly two months ago. Get the fuck over it and move on. If you don't leave her alone, I will destroy you. Not just professionally, which I can do, but physically and personally. I will rip you apart with my bare hands."

His face is ruddy with anger and the fact that I'm applying some pressure to his trachea.

For a moment, he doesn't say anything. He glares defiantly up at me, weighing his response because he can tell I'm not fucking around. But he's also not the sort of guy to have his pride wounded and let it go. I press harder, wanting to kill him. I actually want to kill him for how he mistreated her. I don't understand men who feel the need to hurt women. Who get off on making them feel small or scared or weak when it's actually them who are.

Skylar's sass and confidence are undeniably some of the sexiest things about her. And he tried to steal them. To stifle them. Simply because it made his insecure, pathetic ass feel better. What a fucking loser.

He doesn't deserve her, and he sure as hell doesn't deserve her baby.

"Am I understood?"

"Yes," he rasps hoarsely, but he's smiling. It's a cocky as all fuck smile too. It's one that's telling me that despite the yes on his lips, this isn't done for him. He views Skylar as his, and a ring on her hand isn't going to change that.

I pull back, releasing him, and he sucks in a sharp breath. Before I can do something else that I shouldn't, I storm away, my fists clenched, my jaw locked, and fire seething from my pores.

I twist my band around my finger as I press the button for the elevator. People surround me, anxious to get where they need to be. Rounds start in about ten minutes, but suddenly my phone goes off. I pull it off my hip and check it.

Trauma surgery to ER stat.

Shit. It's going to be one of those kinds of days.

I have no idea if they texted Josh too, but I jog away from the lobby, around the corner, and down the hall to the emergency department. My badge swipes along the pad, and the solid double doors open, allowing me to enter the patient area.

The nurse's station is hopping with the change of shift, but one of the nurses catches my eye, and points down the hall. "Trauma two."

I throw a hand up to her and move down the hall, grabbing a trauma gown, goggles, and gloves as I go from a tray in the hall, donning them as I walk. Using my back, I enter the room to find an unconscious infant on the table. Jesus. This fucking shift.

Stone is working the case, and he gives me a quick nod, even as he works to intubate. "Eighteen-month-old unconscious and unresponsive on scene. He somehow managed to climb out of his crib this morning and went straight over the edge. He's hit his head and has a distended abdomen because he bumped the dresser. Vitals are okay but not great, with a heart rate in the one-sixties and blood pressure sixty over forty. We're trying to stabilize and get him to CT."

"Fell out of his crib?"

"Yes."

Fuck. I come over, pulling my stethoscope off and putting the earpieces in so I can listen to his abdomen. Bowel sounds are absent, and as I palpate, his belly is tense with deep purple bruising on his upper right quadrant.

"Parents found him immediately after and called nine-one-one." Stone finishes the intubation with the meter showing yellow, which means it's in the right place. "I want a C-spine X-ray and abdominal CT now. We also need a full neuro workup as well."

"Neuro is on their way to evaluate. Central line is in," one of the residents tells us.

"Fluids up and onboard," the nurse announces.

"Abdomen is rigid. He's bleeding from somewhere. Where are the parents?"

"In the waiting room," Stone states.

"Good." Because this poor little baby needs consent for surgery. What a freak thing. "Call up to the surgical floor. I want an OR prepped and ready the moment he comes out of CT. Let's also make sure he's typed and crossed."

"On it." I let the ER trauma team finish up and get him to CT while I head upstairs to get myself ready. My guess is he has a bowel and liver laceration, but I won't know for sure or how bad they are until I get in there. Once my feet hit the elevator, I type out a text to Skylar.

> Me: You okay? How's it going up there for you?

Thankfully, she replies instantly.

> Skylar: Hanging in there. Michaela was a bit snarky at first but seems fine now and says she's happy and excited for me. I didn't tell her about the pregnancy. Haven't seen Josh again. Do you want me to run your coffee up?

My lips twitch, and I throw her favorite line to me back at her.

> Me: Why are you being nice to me?

> Skylar: I'm a loving and doting wife.

> Me: Liar.

> Skylar: Fine. I'm really not. But I am thankful for what you did for me this morning. I know you've been on all night. I bet you could use it.

> Me: That would be great. I'm about to go into the OR on a poor baby who climbed and fell out of his crib.

> Skylar: Damn. I'm sorry. That's awful. I'll see
> you in a few with your coffee.

I'm looking forward to it.

I don't type that. But I am. Even when I know it's a recipe for disaster.

24

ASTON

The rest of my day didn't improve much. It was nonstop surgeries, and in one of them, an equipment failure caused a dangerous situation for the patient on the table. I ended up having to open her up instead of using the laparoscope. Then there were weird orders for one of my patients that I had to completely redo before wrong doses of medications were administered. After that, things settled a bit. Josh assisted in a surgery in the afternoon and managed to keep his mouth shut and do his job. Even if anger was pouring off his body in waves. It only fueled the whispers and gossip, but I knew that was going to happen.

I don't trust him. I know he's not finished with this, and the moment he discovers Skylar is pregnant, who knows how he'll react?

By the time I get home, every part of me is exhausted. My mom texted me two hours ago to let me know they'd dropped Zoey off with Skylar after preschool, who only had an eight-hour shift today. It was news that brought a smile to my lips. It reminded me of why I'm doing all of this. Zoey.

And when I walk inside to find the two of them in the

kitchen listening to music and singing along as Skylar makes something that smells insanely good and Zoey helps her, that reminder morphs into something else. Into a pleasure-pain so fucking sweet I can hardly breathe for how it pinches my chest and knocks the wind out of me.

My girls laugh and sing. Skylar helps Zoey use a knife to cut up a cucumber for the salad. Pride takes over Zoey's face as Skylar praises her work. For a moment, I allow my mind to drift. To wander to places it shouldn't. I picture wrapping my hand around Skylar, feeling her belly where her baby is growing while I kiss the top of Zoey's head followed by Skylar's lips.

It's corny and cliché. Like something out of a Norman Rockwell painting, and it makes me smile and inwardly laugh at myself for how ridiculous I'm being. But I also know that if this were real, if I could go into the kitchen and do that, I'd be the happiest motherfucker on the planet.

I'd feel like I finally had it all. Instead of perpetually feeling like everything is just out of my grasp or slipping through my fingers.

For now, I'll hold onto this piece for Zoey. I already know I won't get the other pieces for myself. I know it's loneliness. Simply temptation. An existential crisis or two.

I'm married, but it's not real.

I have a thing for my best friend's little sister, and it's unreciprocated.

I haven't had sex in I don't even know how long, and it doesn't seem like that's changing anytime soon.

My focus is my daughter and work, and there isn't much left after either of those things for me. That's life. It's just how it is. It won't be like this forever. I have to remember that. I can get through this if I can focus on something to hope for, but right now, I don't know what that hope is. It's a mythical notion, a vague concept, so that makes this a bit tougher.

It makes me think about and focus on things—*on people*—I shouldn't be.

Snapping myself out of my Nightmare on Hallmark Holiday moment, I take off my coat and hang it up in the closet.

"Smells good in here," I drawl as I set my bag down and head into the kitchen.

Skylar glances up and treats me to a rare smile. One that touches her green eyes and lights her face. "Zoey and I decided we wanted to try shepherd's pie. She's never had it, and I told her it was good on cold nights like this one."

"Daddy, we're supposed to get snow this weekend."

"Oh fun," I tease as I kiss her cheek and give her a hug. "I hadn't heard that yet. We'll have to play in it in the backyard."

Zoey is obsessed with snow. It's snowed a few times since we've been here, but she hasn't ever been in a storm or seen more than a few inches. Despite my playful tone, I think it will be fun to do all the snow things with her. Especially since I don't have work this weekend.

"How was the rest of your day?" I ask Skylar.

She shrugs. "It was fine. A bit crazy, as I'm positive you know. Michaela seemed fine at first and then was distant with me, if not a little weird. But other than that, quiet." She tosses the sliced cucumber into the salad bowl.

"Good. I'm glad. But why would Michaela care? I think I've spoken to her not even a handful of times, and a few of those were about you."

She peers up at me. "She thought you liked her."

I squint. "Huh? Where on earth did she get that from?"

"I told you the powers you have over the nursing staff."

I smirk. "Not over all the nurses." Unfortunately. "Can I help?"

"Sure. You can set the table."

I lean in and whisper in her ear, "You're being nice to me again."

She coughs out a laugh and jabs back to elbow me in the flank. "A momentary lapse in sanity." She turns her head over her shoulder and smirks at me. "It won't happen again."

I throw my hands out defensively. "I'm not complaining. I'm actually enjoying it. I just wanted to make sure you were aware of what you were doing."

"I'm not very good at disliking people, and you're becoming someone I don't want to dislike."

The urge to lean in and kiss her is so overwhelming I have to clench my fists. Thankfully my phone rings, pulling me away. I slip it out of my pocket and instantly blanch.

"What's wrong?"

I flip the phone around so she can see. "We should get this over with. You want to answer the phone with me?"

She chews on her lip. "No. But we have to. Pick up before we lose him."

I swipe my finger across the phone. "Hey," I answer.

"Hey!" Micha's voice comes barreling through the phone. "I'm sorry we haven't caught up. It's been one thing after another here. How's it going? How's my favorite goddaughter?"

"I'm good," Zoey singsongs. "Uncle Micha, Daddy said we could send you another care package."

"That would be amazing. You'll put crunchy peanut butter and a picture of you in there, right?"

"Obviously."

My eyes bulge. "Obviously?" I parrot. "When did you start saying that like you're fifteen?"

She shrugs. "Can I go play? Grown-up conversations are *so* boring."

"Yes, my sassy kid." I rub the top of her head. "Go ahead."

"We'll call you when dinner is ready," Skylar finishes.

"Bye, Uncle Micha."

"Bye, Zoey-Zo."

Zoey scampers off to the playroom we set up for her, and now it's down to us.

"Sky, you're there too?"

"I'm here."

"Great! How are things?"

"Well, I'm pregnant with Josh's baby, and Aston and I got married on Friday."

I throw her *a what the fuck* look, and she returns it with an *it was going to come out anyway, might as well rip off the Band-Aid* look.

"I'm sorry. What? None of that made any sense. It's probably the satellite phone acting up."

Skylar launches into an account of the last however many days it's been, while Micha sits silently on the phone.

"So… let me… fuck. Jesus fuck, are you kidding me? Aston is now my fake and temporary brother-in-law, and I'm going to be an uncle and likely have to stay in Sudan forever so I can fight extradition for murder?"

"You can't kill Aston," Skylar protests. "He's helping me."

Something warm and inappropriately comfortable rolls through me. Skylar just defended me. I'm almost tempted to look out the window to see if pigs are flying.

"I wasn't talking about him, Sky. I was talking about the asshole who shall not be named. Fuck. Aston, take me off speaker. You and I need a man-to-man, brother."

My stomach sinks, and I throw Skylar a fleeting glance as I walk into the gym Micha has off the main room.

"If you're going to yell at me—"

"Are you sleeping with my sister?"

"No," I answer easily as I sit down on the weight bench. I tuck the phone against my ear and pick up a twenty-five-pound dumbbell I have on the floor that I never put away after I used it last. I do bicep curls as I talk.

"So, you're really just helping her out in exchange for her helping you with Zoey?"

He's incredulous. I got this from my father last night, too. Because the truth is, if I had asked Skylar to help out with Zoey, Micha's goddaughter, I'm pretty positive she would have said yes. That's who she is. Everyone knows it. Skylar has a heart of gold and magic.

But I didn't do that. I didn't even offer to simply help her with Josh.

I asked her to marry me.

"He's not a safe guy," is my answer.

He sighs audibly into the phone. "I never liked him. He was the sort of guy who was combative for the sake of being combative while also trying to pretend he was your best friend and you could trust him. I can't explain it beyond that. But he was controlling while calling it love. He was critical while calling it constructive. All of those things I saw. What I didn't see and only heard about later was the behind the scenes. The things he'd say and do to her turned my blood cold. A lot of women would have stayed, but Skylar was brave and strong enough not to. If you feel that marrying her to protect her was the right call, then I trust you."

His trust is somehow a sucker punch, and I drop the barbell with a heavy clang on the rubber mat. Because I made his sister come on the kitchen counter and then was a dick to her after. I've kissed her and meant it too. I also think about her in ways that would have Micha seeing red.

It sits all wrong with me. And yet, I am protecting her. Even if it's not because Micha is my best friend and I'm playing the role of big brother in his absence.

"I'm on it," is how I reply.

"Good. Thanks. I appreciate it more than you know. Weird though, man. You've always been my brother, and now you are for real. And I'm going to be an uncle. I'll have to come home for that. I want to see her pregnant, but I also want to see the baby." He laughs with something akin to wonder and excitement in his voice. "Josh still doesn't know?"

"No. He doesn't."

"People will think the kid is yours."

I dig my elbow into my knee and rub my forehead. "I know they will." I swallow. "I'm fine with that. Especially with Josh."

"Dude, this is fucked. Like seriously fucked. I don't want him in her life anymore, and I'm glad you're there with her."

I close my eyes and nod, feeling like I'm betraying him.

"Just let me know when you plan to come home, and Zoey and I will stay at my parents'."

"Nah. It's your house now. In fact, we should discuss me selling it to you if you still want it."

I open my eyes and stare sightlessly toward the far wall. "I still want it. Are you sure?"

"Absolutely. It's where you and Zoey belong. It's why I offered it in the first place. If I ever move back to Boston, I won't need such a big place. Living here... it changes your perspective. I can't explain it. But I want Zoey to have a home again."

My chest pinches, and I'm flooded with warmth. "Thank you. I'll have my attorney draw up the paperwork. Just let him know what you want for it."

"You got it. It'll be what I paid for it and not a cent more."

I shake my head and rub my forehead. "You don't have to do that. I know it's appreciated in value, and I want you to get what it's worth."

"And I want my family to have my house, so don't argue with me."

I chuckle and shift on the bench, staring down at the black rubber between my feet. "Fine. Thank you."

"I'm glad Skylar is there with Zoey. Maybe this fake marriage will be the right thing. Just be good to her, okay? She's been through so much already, and now that she's pregnant, it's even more. Take care of her."

I cover my eyes with my hand, pressing the phone into my ear with the other hand. "I will," I promise him.

"Thanks, man. I wouldn't trust her with anyone else, but I trust her with you."

Bile rises up the back of my throat. I'm a son of a bitch. "She's safe with me."

I fly off the bench and start to pace. *Fuck!*

Tell him. Tell him the truth.

But what is the truth? That I have an ill-placed thing for a woman who doesn't want me back? Who is too young for me? Who is my best friend's little sister? Who is pregnant with a bad man's kid and has enough problems? She doesn't need me. Not in that way.

Even if I'm starting to need her more and more.

But it stops now. I vow to get myself in check and under better control. Distance. No flirting. Teasing is a thing of the past. No more fantasies either.

I owe that to Micha. But more importantly, it's what Skylar needs from me. And for that, I can sacrifice just about anything. But realistically, what choice do I have?

25

I wake to a small knee digging into my side and the screeching excitement of a five-year-old right next to my ear. "Skylar! Wake up! It's snowing!" Zoey climbs up to her feet and bounces on the bed beside me, her long, blonde hair all over the place, and her red heart pajamas a little too small.

I blink against the dull light of my room, my body heavy with the restless sleep that's become my new normal. "Zoey," I mumble, pushing myself up to my elbows before I take a quick glance down. I'm wearing a T-shirt and underwear and nothing else. Luckily the blanket covers my lower half. "What time is it?"

"Snow time!" she declares, bouncing again, this time hard enough to rock me. "Come on! Get up. Daddy is already downstairs."

I suppress a groan and reach for my phone. It's seven, and I don't have to work today, which means I could have slept for another couple of hours. Ugh.

"Can we build a snowman? And make snow angels? And have a snowball fight?" Her questions shoot at me in rapid-fire, her small hands waving above her head like she's already practicing those angels.

"Hold on, tiny tornado." I laugh, sitting up fully and pushing some of my hair out of my face before I attack the crust in my eyes. "I need to get dressed and have something to eat first." I've found that if I have something small in the morning, it helps with my morning sickness. Even if it's just giving me something to puke instead of stomach acid or dry heaving, which is the worst. "And coffee. I'll need some of that too."

"Grown-ups always need coffee," she bemoans.

"It's our fuel."

"But—"

"Zoey, you better not be where I think you are." Aston's voice carries from the hallway. "I told you to get yourself dressed and not to wake up Skylar." The door swings open, and he leans against the frame, his hair all sexy and sleep-mussed, and his white T-shirt clings a little too perfectly to his arms and chest. "Which I see you did," he finishes. "Sorry."

I hold up a hand. "It's fine. She's excited."

He brings a cup of coffee up to his lips and takes a sip to hide his amusement even as his eyes drag across me, noting my face and braless chest down to my waist, where it meets the blanket.

"She's not the only one who's excited, I see."

I follow his gaze to my chest and gasp at him. "Hey! No peeking there."

He shrugs. "Is that for me or just the chill of the morning?"

"Definitely not for you." I grab my pillow so I can chuck it at him, but I'm smiling. It's his stupid flirty way and the way my stomach flutters with it. Aston's been distant over the last few days. I thought we had hit a bit of a truce after Monday in the hospital and telling everyone we were married, but that hasn't been the case for the rest of the week. I've barely seen him, and whenever I do, he doesn't talk to me much.

He's made dinner a few nights and left it for me on the stove, but we haven't eaten together since Monday. I've caught him watching me with a furrowed brow like I'm a problem he can't quite solve. There's been a palpable shift between us, and it's created a tension that hums beneath the surface of every interaction.

It's likely for the best and will help maintain our boundaries, but still. It sits... wrongly on me. It doesn't feel good. This unfortunately does, so yeah, all around it's a mess.

The pillow lands with a thud on the floor, nowhere near my mark. "Don't quit your day job there, ace."

"We'll see who's the ace when I nail you with snowballs."

"We'll see who nails whom better."

Now my face is a fireball. I point toward the hall. "Out, flirty McFlirtster. I have to get dressed. Zoey wants a snow day." As if to prove this, she jumps up and down some more.

His smile slips. "Right. Sorry. No more flirty—whatever you called me."

"McFlirtster," I finish for him, smiling cheekily to compensate.

"It was a momentary lapse in judgment, and it won't happen again. Come on, Zoey. Breakfast time."

I try to hide my frown. I didn't mean for him to stop flirting, just to leave so I could get dressed, but whatever. Again, this is how it should be. It's me who has to remember that this isn't real. That everything we're doing is fake.

Zoey jumps off the bed and scrambles past Aston, who immediately turns and shuts the door behind him. Well then. I guess that's that. Nothing like a full snow day at home with my grumpy fake husband, who can't stand to be in the same room as me for longer than a minute.

I pull myself out of bed and head for the bathroom when my phone buzzes on my nightstand.

Michaela: Josh is in rare form today. Good thing you're

not here. He asked to see the nursing schedule and was pissed you'd changed yours around.

My skin grows tight, and the back of my neck prickles.

Me: He'll get over it. And hopefully find someone new to bother.

Though as I say that, I pity any woman who dates him. I asked my nurse manager if she could change my schedule to avoid him. She said yes without question, and we sat down and worked on it. It's impossible to avoid him completely. He's a resident, and they spend a lot of hours in the hospital. But we were able to swap some of my shifts to alternate with his.

He's been everywhere I turn, watching me without bothering to hide it. Yesterday I caught him smirking at me from across the nurses' station as if he knew something. He can't. There's no way he could know. Still, it made my skin crawl, and I had to take action. I don't think he'll show up here now that he knows I'm married and living with Aston. So, for now, it's just working to keep my distance from him at the hospital.

I do my thing in the bathroom, get dressed in warm clothes, and head downstairs. Aston is picking at a piece of turkey bacon as he leans against the counter, reading something on his phone. Zoey is at the table, contentedly eating breakfast and focused on her iPad.

He peeks up, and he gives me a once-over, though this one is short and almost perfunctory. Like he's making sure I'm wearing proper attire and my nipples are no longer showing. "Coffee?"

I nod, and he makes it for me even though I'm perfectly capable of doing it myself. I don't argue, though. Instead, I fix myself a plate of food, but when he hands me the mug, our fingers brush, and it sends a jolt through me. It must do the same for him because his breath hitches and his fingers jump. But in doing so, the mug almost slips, and I have to make a last-second adjustment so it doesn't crash to the floor. As it is, the coffee is nearly sloshing over onto my hand.

"Sorry. Static electricity or something. You okay?"

"Yeah. That was weird."

"I'm going to get dressed, and then I want to build a snowman. A huge one. The biggest ever. And I want it to have a carrot nose and sticks for arms, and he'll need a scarf so he doesn't get cold."

"Okay, Anna," he teases, using the name of the princess from *Frozen*. "Go get dressed, and we'll build a snowman." She flies out of her chair, runs her plate over to the counter by the sink, and zooms upstairs like her ass is on fire. "And put on the thermal leggings!" he calls after her, chuckling when her door slams without a reply. He gives me a shrug. "She's been talking about this storm all week."

"She sounds very ambitious about this snowman. Micha doesn't have a huge backyard."

"She also gets bored quickly, so we'll see how far we get. There are only like six inches on the ground so far."

I fork a bite of pancake and pop it into my mouth. Aston is a killer at breakfast and seems to love making it. No complaints from me. "Maybe this afternoon, we'll bake something. I wouldn't mind some chocolate."

He smirks. "I can't wait to see what you'll send me out in the middle of the night for once the cravings start."

My heart hiccups in my chest, and he must realize how that sounded because he clears his throat and looks away. Thankfully, Zoey comes back down, saving us both. Ten minutes later, after we're all bundled up, we step out onto the back deck into inches of crunchy, wet snow. Ice crystals mixed with fat flakes fall steadily from the pearl-gray sky, and everything around us is covered in layers of white as the wind whips and howls past us

Zoey charges into it with a squeal of delight and immediately falls onto her back to make a snow angel. "Sky, make one with me."

"She's been wanting to do this with you all morning."

"With me specifically?" I ask, surprised.

He brushes some of the snow sticking to my cheek and nods. "She adores you. She talks about you constantly with her friends at school and with her therapist. I know we're in an odd arrangement but thank you. It's all I wanted for her. To see her smiling and happy."

Warmth runs through me that completely eclipses the frigid temperatures.

I swallow and nod, a little choked up. Stupid pregnancy hormones. "I'm glad she's happy and okay with our... situation. I hope you know, my friendship with her won't change even when this ends."

He turns away from her to look at me, his expression unreadable. He opens his mouth to say something when Zoey nails my back with a snowball. My eyes pop open wide, and my jaw unhinges.

Aston's lips bounce. "Nice shot, kiddo!"

I sputter, bend, and pile a wad of frozen snow into my gloved hands, ball it up, but instead of retaliating against Zoey, I nail Aston right in the face.

He chokes and laughs. "Did you really just do that?"

I take a step back, my hands stretched outward toward him. "You wouldn't attack a pregnant woman."

He wipes the melting snow and ice from his face, his expression dangerous. "Wanna bet?" He charges for me, and I scream, turning to run when he swoops me up, swings me around, and takes us both down into the snow with me on his lap to shield the impact. Zoey jumps on him, pulling him back and burying him in snow.

After that, it's chaos. Snow flying and feet slipping and slid-ing. We end up building a pathetic little snowman, whom I name Baby Yoda. Zoey doesn't get the reference, but that's what he looks like to me. After far too long in the cold, we come inside, and I end up baking cookies with Zoey's help. Aston turns on the fireplace and puts on a movie that quickly calls Zoey's attention away.

"Sorry," Aston says as he comes over and pops a chocolate chip in his mouth. "I stole your baking buddy."

"It's fine. She's wiped out."

She's curled up on the sofa under the blanket, and I wouldn't be shocked if she fell asleep.

"My mom called a little while ago. They want to know what colors we want for our wedding party."

I snort out a laugh as I put dollops of dough onto the baking sheets and slide them into the oven. "Whatever will make them cringe the most."

He smiles, his eyes glittering. "Neon yellow and taupe then?"

I laugh. "My mother would collapse with those."

"You Fritz women are so difficult to please."

I lean against the counter and set the timer on my phone. "Only sometimes."

"True. I managed to please you just fine."

I arch an eyebrow up at him. "I thought we weren't doing that. Talking about it and flirting."

"I wasn't. I swear."

"Uh-huh. And that shit-eating grin on your face?"

He pushes away from the counter and cages me in, his hands on either side of me, his face inches from mine as he dips down. "I can't help it. I try. I really do. But something about you is like being on the edge of temptation to me, and no matter how long I'm good for, you always manage to turn me bad again."

"You need to work on that," I playfully reprimand, even though my heart is pounding.

"I know. And I will. I promise. I'll go back to keeping my distance. But one more taste won't kill me, right?" He murmurs that last part almost as if he's talking to himself.

Without warning, he dips and kisses me. A groan sears past his lips, and he picks me up and puts me on the counter before his hands dive into my hair, and he consumes my mouth.

He tastes like chocolate and smells like snow, and I'm instantly lost in him. In this. My hands grip his arms, and I hold on, knowing I shouldn't be doing this, but there's no way I can stop. Forget the edge of temptation, his kisses throw me straight to the edge of chaos.

His tongue swirls with mine, and he angles my head so he can deepen the exchange.

I moan, and he bites my bottom lip, almost punishingly. His tongue licks away the sting, and he pulls back, his forehead pressing to mine, his breathing labored.

"If only I didn't have such a smart, sexy wife, it might be easier to stay away."

He winks and pushes away from me to join Zoey on the sofa. And I'm smiling. I just am. The man makes me smile like the teenage girl I never was. A girl with an unfortunate crush on her fake husband.

It'd be the perfect day. You know. If any of this were real.

26

SKYLAR

"Remind me what we're doing here again?" I ask Braelyn as I glance around the industrial space coated with a layer of dust and grime. There's a crowd of people lining up, all skirting each other's eyes as if no one wants to be seen or recognized, though I do recognize several of them.

"Roman has a fight tonight. Duh."

"Yes. Clearly. How did we not talk Quinn or Crew into coming?"

"Quinn has a shift tonight, and Crew can't be seen here. He'd be kicked off the team for sure. Besides, how much longer are you going to be able to do this?"

"You mean how much longer am I going to be able to go to illegal, underground fights?"

"Yes. Soon you'll be home with a new baby. Think of all you'll be missing. All this flash and excitement. The adrenaline. The vibe. You feel it?"

"I feel it, but…" I trail off. I've been to Roman's fights before. They've all been similar to this, but there's typically a lot of pushing and shoving when things really get going.

"Don't worry." She squeezes my forearm as we walk our way along the wall of the building. "He has us in a marked-off section. You'll be safe."

"Good. Okay."

Fights aren't my thing, and this is only my second or third that I've attended. I don't like watching two guys trying to bludgeon each other. I especially hate when Roman get hit, but he rarely does. He's the one to try and beat, and I'm not sure anyone has. He's big and fast and cagey.

"Hey. You're here," Forest greets us as we reach the roped-off area. He's holding a soda and adjusts it in his hand as he gives us each a hug.

"We're here," I exclaim. "You know, it's not as though I worked a twelve-hour shift and am tired or anything."

Braelyn rolls her eyes at me as she steals Forest's Diet Coke so she can have a sip. "You agreed. I didn't drag you. And I worked a twelve too. You don't see me complaining."

"Because I didn't want you coming alone," I protest. "And you're not in your first trimester of pregnancy."

"Whatever. Wouldn't be the first time I've come alone. Roman always looks out for me."

"That's because he'd rather die than let anything happen to you," I tell her.

"That goes for all of us," she reminds me.

"How have you been feeling?" Forest asks, changing the subject, his dark eyes glancing down at my belly as if he's expecting to see a giant round beach ball. Not quite there yet, but I am starting to see a rounding and firmness of my lower belly.

"Good. Tired."

"What about the morning sickness?"

I shrug. "It's maybe starting to get better? I don't know. I haven't thrown up in a few days, so I'll take that as a win."

"Are you still waiting for your second trimester to tell people?"

I nod. My family all knows, including my grandparents. They handled it better than I thought and gave me lots of hugs. My mother and Aston's mother are going full steam with planning a party for us, and my grandmother offered to host it at the compound they live on just outside of the city.

As of right now, it's set for next weekend, and I have no clue what I'm going to wear that won't make me look, well, pregnant. Or at least severely bloated.

It's been nearly two weeks since Aston and I told people at work that we're married, and most of the rumors have died down. Probably because Aston and I are rarely together at work. Then again, we're rarely together at home either. He's been keeping a sizable and noticeable distance from me. He's pleasant and friendly enough, but there's a wall between us. No more teasing. No more flirting. Definitely no more kissing.

Other than holding my hand if we come into work together or asking if I wanted him to come for my first OB appointment —I declined—where I got to hear the heartbeat, we have a safe space between us at all times.

I've been telling myself I'm grateful for it. That it's exactly what I wanted and definitely what we needed. But still. Part of me can't help but miss all of that stuff. Miss *him*. It's dumb. I know that. He doesn't want me that way. I'm pregnant with another man's kid, for Christ's sake.

The upside is Zoey and I have a blast together. We cook and bake and hang out. She's so much fun to be with, and I know Aston is seeing that she's doing well. We made a dream catcher for her bedroom and a jar of notes she writes to her mom or even just thoughts and feelings she's having.

Aston has met with her therapist one-on-one again, and she's encouraged by Zoey's progress but is also, rightfully so, concerned about what the marriage piece will be like for Zoey. Especially when it ends.

I haven't seen much of Josh now that I've adjusted my schedule as much as possible. On the days that he's there, I stay mostly on the medical side of the floor.

That hasn't stopped him from seeking me out, but whenever he does, I flash him my ring and remind him that it's over, that I'm married to Aston, and that there's nothing he can do about it. I still haven't decided if I'm going to tell him about the baby or not. I don't like the idea of keeping a father from their child.

But I also don't like the idea of my child being around someone who is abusive and could potentially be that way with them. But he also hasn't tried anything aggressive again. If anything, he looks sad and a bit remorseful, so I don't freaking know. I just don't. I'm taking it day by day with that right now. I figure after the ultrasound I'll make my final decision.

The overhead lights dim, and chatter and excitement fill the room that already smells of sweat and blood. Fights happen typically once a month on varying nights and sometimes in different locations, but the owner of the building is not only friends with Roman, but big into boxing, so fights happen here more than other locations.

It's not exactly Vegas, but people are dressed in varying degrees of glitz and glam, and large amounts of money are exchanging hands like it's simply paper.

"Good evening, ladies and gentlemen," the host booms from the center of the clearing, bringing the cacophony of voices down to a din. "Betting closes in exactly one minute. As always, phones must stay put away. Photos, videos, or live streaming are prohibited, and you'll be escorted out, have your device confiscated, and be banned. Posting anything about this event or future events will also get you banned. If you're not familiar with our rules, there are twelve rounds total, each lasting three minutes. No weapons of any kind are allowed, as well as no hitting in the groin area or when an opponent is down. Audience interference is a bannable offense and will most likely result in worse repercussions since there is a lot of money on tonight's match, if you know what I'm saying. Now, may I present our two boxers?"

He takes a step back and waves off to the side where the two men are standing wearing nothing but gym shorts, both rippling with muscles, tattoos, and greased-up skin.

"Our challenger tonight is Diego, and our returning champion, as I'm sure you all know since he requires no introduction, is Romeo."

Romeo is Roman's fighter name to help him keep a low profile.

Both of them step into the center of the ring to cheers and hollers from the crowd. Roman meets our eyes and gives us a smirk and a wink as he walks over to us. He holds out his hand and twists pinkies with Braelyn. It's their thing. His good luck charm, I guess you'd call it, and then he's back in the ring. Braelyn grabs my hand and squeezes. I squeeze her back as nerves and adrenaline skitter through me, making me antsy.

"Gentlemen," the announcer continues, standing between them. "Fight."

He jumps out of the way, and the two men circle each other. Roman is bigger than Diego, but Diego appears lithe and mysterious. Like a cheetah against a lion.

Roman simply watches and waits, patience and brains part of his game. It works. It always freaking works because Diego gets to the point where he can no longer stand it and charges at Roman, who ducks and spins away from Diego's fist, only to swing around and nail him right in the back by one of his kidneys. Diego goes shooting forward but recovers quickly and immediately comes straight for Roman.

An arm wraps around my waist from behind, and I turn to find Hayes.

"Hey. Did I miss anything?"

"No," I tell him. "It just started."

"Great. I've got five k on Romeo taking him down before the end of the fourth round."

We never use Roman's real name here. I quirk an eyebrow. "Does he know that?"

He grins at me. "He had me put ten grand down on that."

"Jesus," I whistle through my teeth and turn back to watch. The two go back and forth, trading blows and moving around with ease, all the while the crowd shouts and jeers, vying for a better view and screaming what they want their guy to do to the other. Roman barely has a mark on him, but Diego is already bleeding from his lip, and his left eye is swelling up. The bell rings, and the two fighters pull apart, sweaty and breathing heavily.

Roman comes over to us to make sure we're okay, checking on both me and Braelyn before he heads back into the ring for more. He doesn't sip water. He doesn't get any abrasions checked. For such a beast of a man, such a brutal fighter, he's one of the most loyal and tender guys I know.

Diego charges, raging, giving Roman everything he's got. But he's no match for him. Roman knocks him down in the second and third rounds and knocks him out in the fourth. Just like he and Hayes bet. And if I know Roman, he designed it exactly that way.

After it's all over and Roman is declared the victor, we pull him off to an empty room save for a dirty table and a few folding chairs. Braelyn and I, ever the nurses that we are, get Roman patched up. We remove the bloody tape from his hands and clean up the cuts and abrasions on his fists and knuckles as well as a small laceration on his upper cheek.

"You kicked ass," I tell him, dabbing some ointment on his cut that's hardly even bleeding now.

"Thanks. It was a fun one, I guess."

"Bored already?" I tease.

He shrugs. "It's good exercise."

I snort and roll my eyes at him.

"I'm glad you came. I know these aren't your favorites."

"They're not," I agree. "But I'm glad I came too. Even if I'm not sure my blood pressure can handle another. How do you not get arrested?"

"You obviously didn't see the chief of police placing bets with the district attorney then, did you?"

I sigh, and he laughs.

"He's Romeo," Hayes states. "I don't think you can arrest him. His restaurants alone are too popular for that. No one wants the prince to fall." Roman is a Michelin-starred top chef with a very popular chain of restaurants in the city as well as in Vegas, Paris, and London. With his Fritz name—and let's face it, his good looks—networks have been trying to get him to do a TV series. He's refused. His boxing career is likely a reason for that.

He smirks and kisses my cheek. "Go home, Sky. You look beat."

I snort. "Is that meant to be ironic?"

His lips bounce. "Yes. But you do look tired. Hayes and I will make sure Braelyn gets home safely."

They each hug me, but Hayes walks me to my car. After all, we are at a warehouse at midnight. "Hey, I leave for Paris tomorrow night, but I'll be back this weekend for your wedding party."

I point at him. "You better be," I warn. "What's up in Paris? You haven't had to go there in a while." Hayes has been slowly taking over Monroe Fashions from his parents, who own the fashion empire. My cousin Serena works for them in Paris.

"Just some production and design stuff. I'll say hi to your cousin for you."

"Please do. Safe flight." I reach up onto my tiptoes and kiss his cheek.

I say goodnight to him, more than a little exhausted, and climb into my car.

The drive isn't all that long with the light traffic, but it's all I can do to stay awake, my mind more than a little fuzzy, and when I pull into the driveway, I blow out a long, silent breath followed by a hell of a yawn. I unlock the door and go upstairs, finding my way through the darkness.

I open the door to my bedroom and immediately strip out of my clothes. My shoes, jeans, and sweater hit the floor in a heap, my eyes already half-closed as I take off my bra. My phone is in my purse, and I know I need to plug it in. Hell, for that matter, I need to brush my teeth. But I'm not sure I have either effort in me.

I pull back the blanket so I can climb under the sheets. A strange noise tickles my ears, but it doesn't stop me from getting into bed and— "Ah! Oh my god!"

I hit a warm, hard wall that groans and moves against me. I pull back, taking the blanket and sheet with me so I can cover my boobs, and Aston flops onto his back, his hands on his face as he rubs his eyes.

"What are you doing in my room?" I squawk.

He emits a humorless chuckle and rolls onto his side to face me, his hair all over the place from sleep, and his body—well, I'm trying not to look at the strong lines of his shoulder muscles and chest, but yeah, sort of impossible to miss. My eyes, those traitors, keep dropping and scrolling on their own charge. He looks like hot sex and dirty promises, and my vagina remembers him all too well.

"This is my bed now, remember? We switched rooms a few weeks ago."

Shit. We did. I was so freaking tired I didn't think about it. The number of times I've walked in here over the last couple of weeks, only to remember at the last minute and go down the hall, is sad.

"Crap. I'm sorry."

"Do you always sleep like that?" he asks, eyeing how I have the blanket up against me.

"None of your business!"

"Except you're in my bed wearing nothing. So now it is my business."

"Suddenly you want to talk to me?" I throw back at him, and I don't even know where that came from.

A slow, sexy smile curls up his lips, making my stomach flutter. "Oh, my sweet little swan, have you missed me?"

Ugh. I forgot how cocky he can be. I glare at him. "Not even a little. Close your eyes."

"Why would I do that when I like everything I see?"

I puff out an annoyed breath. "So I can get out of bed without flashing you my tits and ass."

"I could do that." His arm bands around my waist, and he tugs me until I slip down the bed and I'm supine. With one smooth motion, he climbs over me, pressing his hands into the mattress on either side of my head so he can hover above me. It makes my heart race. "Or you could stay and let me play with your tits and ass."

27

———

ASTON

Skylar's eyelashes flutter against her wide eyes as she tries to work this through her head, even as a flush creeps up her face. The room is dark except for a ribbon of moonlight that peeks through the crack in the curtains, creating a silver glow along the bed. My heart is slamming against my ribs, desperate to break free.

But it's as if something inside me snapped. Broke apart. Or maybe this is what coming back together feels like.

"Why would I do that?" she whispers, throwing my words back at me, her voice barely audible despite our close proximity.

"Because it's what we both want," I tell her plainly, my cock painfully hard and my mind spinning. I know this isn't a good idea. I know I shouldn't be doing this. But she's here, and she's all but naked, and resisting her, especially like this, is impossible.

"We made a deal."

"We did. But right now, I can't think about anything other than breaking the rules of it."

Because for the last few weeks, hell, longer than that, she's all I've thought about. Kissing her, the way she smiles, how her eyes fucking sparkle, how she looked when she came for me, the way she cried—it broke me open. I've been pulling back and avoiding her. I've created space because that's what I had to do.

For her. For Micha. For myself.

But I was just fucking dreaming about her, and now she's here, naked in my bed, and for once, just this one time, I ache to throw caution to the wind and take what I want. Her. She's what I want. More than any-fucking-thing, she's what I want.

"Tell me you haven't been thinking about me, that you don't want me, and I'll lie and tell you the same. If that's what you really want, I'll climb off you and close my eyes, and you can leave, and we can go back to how things have been. Or, you can stay, pull the blanket back, and we can see where this can go."

Her breathing quickens, her chest rising and falling beneath the blanket. She doesn't speak, only stares up at me for so long with those big eyes that were just haunting my dreams. I grow impatient and frustrated. What the hell am I doing?

"Forget it. Bad idea," I growl and go to move off her when she grabs me by the back of the head and holds me in place. Not letting me go. "If I kiss you, I won't be able to stop," I warn her.

She releases a shaky breath, but a smile curls up her lips. "Who said I want you to stop?"

That's all it takes. I crash my mouth down onto hers, swallowing her small moan that sets my blood on fire. Her lips are so soft, so impossibly soft, and they part instantly for me, allowing my tongue entrance. This kiss isn't gentle. It's not exploratory. There is no more dancing between us.

It's weeks of pent-up tension exploding. It's teeth and tongues and breath. It's her hands in my hair, ripping and pulling as if she doesn't know how to control what's already building up inside her. I bite her lower lip, and she whimpers and arches up into me. But it's not enough. Not nearly enough.

I lower one forearm to the bed and turn so I can reach between us and yank the blanket and sheet away from her chest. And with that I break the kiss. I have to look. I have to see. God, the number of times I've envisioned this exact moment...

"Fuck," I hiss, taking in the sight of her. She's wearing nothing but black lace panties, her large tits peaked with rose-colored nipples. Her skin pebbles up from the cool air, and my gaze eats up those tiny bumps, my hands anxious to cover her in chills. Her stomach is smooth and soft-looking, but there's the slightest curve at her lower belly, and it chops short the breath in my lungs and makes my dick surge with blood.

The pregnancy has changed her body, and I swear to all fucking god, I've never seen a sexier woman in my life. Jesus.

"You're staring," she whispers, her voice tinted with vulnerability.

"I seem to do that with you. I can't help it," I manage, having to swallow thickly to get the words out. "Christ, Skylar, you're the most beautiful woman I've ever seen. I'm forever undone by you."

"I don't need that from you. Not again."

I peer up at her, looking straight into her eyes so she knows and she can't question or doubt me on it. "I'm serious. I was serious that night too. I've been dreaming about this for..." I laugh and rub the back of my head. "Since I first kissed you two years ago. How have you not figured it out yet? You're all I think about."

Before she can say anything else or I can reveal more than I already have, I lower my head and press a kiss to her sternum and then another on the underside of each breast. Her breath hitches, and I use that sound to guide me as my mouth climbs up to her nipple while my hand cups and squeezes her other breast.

It's heavier in my hand than I expected, her skin impossibly soft. I brush my thumb across her nipple, watching it tighten as I suck on her skin, tasting her. Rolling over so I'm partially on top of her, I take her tits in both my hands, playing with them as I capture her lips again. I was going crazy tonight. It was late, and she still wasn't home, and I knew I had no right to ask where she was.

But she's here with me, running her hands down my back and shoulders, touching me in a way that elicits sparks across my skin. I'm dying to be inside of her. To feel her around me again. Last time didn't count. Not even close. But I want to take my time. Make this incredible for her. Have her mind twisted up and craving me so she crawls and begs and needs and *knows* there is no such thing as only one time.

Not with us.

Our tongues fight, the kissing turning frantic once again. It's as if we don't know how to slow down with each other. My hand slides down her side until I grip her thigh and drag it up and over my hip while I trail kisses down her neck.

Her hips buck up as I pull on her nipple, her pussy seeking contact and friction, and it makes me smile against her thrumming pulse.

"Is my wife needy?"

She smacks my shoulder, and I chuckle.

"I want you needy. Tell me. Tell me what you want."

"Touch me," she demands, and I pull back. Her cheeks flush darker, but I hold her eyes.

"Touch you where, sweetheart? Here?" I swirl a fingertip around her nipple.

"Lower."

I grin and nibble her shoulder. "Here?" I drag my finger down the slope of her breast, my hand meeting her lower belly, feeling the firm roundness there. Something primal unexpectedly stirs in my chest. I want to press my lips to it. I want to splay my palm against it and feel more. The baby isn't mine. Skylar isn't mine for that matter. But... I still want to do that. I can't explain it, and it's not healthy for me to try, so I drag lower to the top of her lacy panties.

I glide a finger back and forth beneath the edge of the lace, watching her face as I touch her. "This?"

She makes an impatient noise and takes my hand and moves it lower until I'm cupping her bare cunt beneath the lace. "Here. Touch my pussy. Prove to me that you have more skill than a simple one-and-done orgasm."

I smile like the devil. My feisty girl. This is what I love about her.

Shit. What? No.

That trips me up, and I stare down at her, the L-word ping-ponging around through my skull like it's in a deranged pinball machine. I'm shaking, my bones rattling my muscles. Thankfully she grinds into me, urging me to put her demand into action and dragging me from my thoughts.

But I have to kiss her again. I just have to. My hand rubs up and down on her pussy as my lips consume hers. She's wet and warm and makes the best noises in the world. She's also so turned on. So incredibly responsive.

"You're so wet," I murmur against her lips before I tilt my head the other way and dive back into her mouth while using the tip of my pointer to create circles around her clit. But the last time we did this and I made her come, I didn't get to taste it. Hell, I felt it on my cock, but I didn't from the inside of her. And since I will make her come again, that's a fucking certainty, I give her lips one last kiss and work my way down her body.

"What are you doing?"

I give her an amused look as I suck one nipple into my mouth, followed by the other. Her tits. I mean, holy hell. Her fucking tits are incredible. I'm definitely going to have to fuck them. Not tonight. But another night for sure. When she's ready to really let me play with her.

"I'm going to taste you," I tell her as I swirl my tongue around her belly button and then trail the tip of it down, going lower, removing her panties along the way. I press a kiss to her inner thigh as I spread them. "I'm going to make you come with my mouth. Then I'm going to fuck you till you come on my cock."

Her eyes round. "Oh."

I smirk against her skin. "Unless you have objections."

Her head shakes quickly, her blonde hair all over the place, partially covering one breast as she holds herself up on her elbows. It's the ultimate tease. "No objections."

"Then do me a favor? Be a good little swan for me and let me fuck you the way I want to. Trust that I know you're going to love it. Turn off your mind and surrender to me. I promise, I'll take care of you."

She bites into her lip but shockingly stays quiet. After a few seconds, I get a small nod. I learned this the first time with her. Skylar needs praise. Not shocking after all she's been through, but lucky for both of us, that's exactly what I want to give her. I want her to know she's special. That I feel honored and lucky that she's doing this with me. That she's not something I take for granted.

She's my wife. In my mind, hell, in my heart, she's my wife. I wear this band, and it never leaves my finger unless I'm in the OR, and then it's never far. I tell people I'm a married man, and I mean it. Now I want to fuck my wife the way I've been imagining fucking her for two goddamn years.

"You're so perfect." I kiss her inner thighs and spread her wider for me. I start slowly, my tongue gently tickling her opening as I use my thumb to hold her open. "Look at you. So fucking pretty, Skylar." I ring her there, first with my tongue and again with my finger. Her head falls back, and she moans louder than she should. Zoey is a decent sleeper, but I'd rather her not wake up to the sound of Skylar coming.

I bite her inner thigh. "Do I need to gag you?"

Her head pops up, her lips parted. "No," she squeaks. "Wait, what? Gag me?"

"I'm not fully serious unless you want that. But you're loud."

"Sorry. It's just..."

I nod. I can feel it. "You're more responsive than last time."

"Yes." She bites her lip again. Almost like she's embarrassed by it, and that drives me mad. She's brave and confident in so many ways, and then there's still this wounded bird in her who feels the need to make concessions and apologize. It makes me want to kill all the people who hurt her.

"Don't apologize," I tell her, pumping two fingers straight into her and curling them until she arches and grinds against me. "It's amazing. It makes me so fucking hard. I love it. If I could have you screaming for me, I would. But Zoey is across the hall."

"If I get too loud, I'll use your pillow."

"Good plan. Have it ready then because I'm about to make you come so fucking hard."

I lick a path up from her dripping cunt to her clit, where I swirl around and around. All the while my fingers pump into her. Fucking her. I work her hard with them and my tongue, building her up. I want her to come fast this time. Last time I worked her slowly, and it gave her too much time to allow her mind to take over. But now she knows I can make her come. And with the way her body responds to me, I don't think there's any way she could stop it.

She's so wet and warm and feels incredible. I can't wait to have her on my cock. I can't wait to truly be inside her. To see her face as I am. She doesn't know it, and I sure as hell won't say it, but tonight I'm making her mine. Because I've already been hers.

Her pussy rocks into my hand, into my face, and it makes me smile. "Yes," I tell her. "Fuck my face, Skylar."

She moans, and suddenly her fingers thread through my hair, holding me against her as she pushes up and fucks into my mouth and chin. I could get drunk on her taste and smell. It's something so her, but right now, with her being pregnant, it's even stronger, and I can't get enough. My tongue lashes at her clit, flicking and swirling it. My fingers rub vigorously against her front wall, my hand knuckles deep. I'm fucking her hard, and she's squirming, her thighs trembling, but fuck all, she's still holding back.

What is that? That inherent lack of trust. Or is it something else? More self-consciousness.

"Come on, baby," I growl into her, sucking her clit between my lips. "I need it. Please. I need you to come for me. I need it so badly. I need to taste it. Please, Skylar."

She groans in frustration. "I... I can't. I'm close, but... I just can't."

"You can. Let go. Give yourself to me. I've got you. You're safe with me, sweetheart. I fucking swear it. I'll take such good care of you, my beautiful girl."

Her head falls back, and her grip on my hair tightens. I pull her thigh over my head and focus on her clit. Utterly starved for her. But she's there. I can feel it. The walls of her pussy are clenching against my fingers, and with one final roll of her clit with my tongue and one final thrust of my fingers, she detonates.

The pillow lands over her face to muffle her cries as she undulates her hips into my mouth and fingers, thrusting, shaking, pushing, pulling. And fuck. Just... *fuck!* The way she comes like this.

I don't let up. I work her through the waves of pleasure until she's spent and weakly pulls the pillow from her face to push me away, too sensitive for me to continue. I give her pussy one last kiss and crawl up her body, kissing and licking and touching and tasting as I go. And when I reach her eyes, I smile.

"Not a fluke."

She laughs, the sound breathless. I get an eye roll and a smack to my shoulder because that's my girl. "Not a fluke," she begrudgingly agrees.

"Now let's get you to do that again on my cock."

28

SKYLAR

My body pulses with aftershocks, my breath caught somewhere between my lungs and the ceiling. Aston hovers above me, a sinfully cocky smirk on his lips, his eyes twin dark pools ringed in blue I could drown in if I'm not careful. Dammit. That's twice now. Twice he's made me come apart in ways I never knew possible.

The realization sits heavily on my chest alongside his palm.

I have no idea what this means. What we're becoming in these stolen moments where the lines of our arrangement blur into something unrecognizable. Into something *more*. At least for me, and that's what scares me.

"Hey," he says, his voice soft while his hand comes up to my cheek and he positions himself so he's resting on his side. He tilts my face. "You okay?"

I almost wish he weren't so tender with me. And how fucked up is that after all I went through with Josh? I nod, not trusting myself to speak just yet. The truth is, I'm not sure I am okay. I'm terrified. Not of him, for a nice change of pace, but of this current that runs between us and makes my skin feel too tight and my heart too full.

I've been missing him. The thought ambushes me, the sensation unwelcome and undesired. I've been missing my fake husband, my brother's best friend, and the man who was never supposed to be more than a convenient and helpful solution to a difficult situation. I remind myself that he's done this to me before. That he's said a million perfect things to get his desired —and mine, who am I kidding—result. The praise whispered against my skin is just to make me comfortable. Just to get me off. The way he looks at me like I'm something precious is just part of the act.

His thumb traces my lower lip, his eyes following the motion. "Where'd you go just now?"

"Nowhere," I lie, turning my face into his neck. He smells like sandalwood and cedar and everything incredible that he always does. It's something specific to him that I've started craving to the point of smelling random things around the house that he leaves abandoned. Shirts or even his stupid baseball hats that I find when he takes them off. "Just... processing," I go with.

"Processing what?" He pushes me back, his smile dangerous. Seductive. Knowing. Yet he reins it in as he asks, "Do you not want to do this?"

"I do." And I really do. I don't want to think anymore. In fact, I'd seriously love to turn off this part of my brain. The overthinking part. Even if it's just for tonight. Just for a while.

My hand runs along the planes of his chest and abs. The man really is cut from fucking stone. It's wildly unfair, but right now, I'm not complaining. "Take off your briefs."

He laughs. A full-on laugh that brings a smile to my face. "So bossy." His lips find mine again, soft at first, but that only lasts a second before they grow impatient and hungry. "Help me along, Skylar. Touch me."

"Touch you?"

"I want you. I want to feel you," he murmurs against my

lips, his hands sliding down my hips where he grasps me. "All of you. Every perfect inch."

I swallow. Hard. "Then take me."

On my next heartbeat, he rolls me until I'm on top of him, straddling him completely naked. He shifts me from left to right as he pulls his briefs down and kicks them off.

"Like this to start," he says, his voice thick. "I want to see you. But I also want you in control until I decide to take it back from you."

Holy shit. He means that. And part of me craves it. His control. My mental submission. But I also like this part. The part where he wants to watch me. Because he means it. He does want that. I can see it all over him. Suddenly, I'm not nervous anymore.

"Condom?" I ask.

He gives me a lopsided grin as he tilts his head. "I don't have any. I wasn't exactly planning to have sex here. It's been a very long time since I even have, and I've been tested."

Fair. "I don't have any either, and I've been tested too. And I'm already pregnant."

His thumb finds my clit, open and exposed to him, and he rubs tight circles that instantly have me breathless. "Then put me inside you."

The way he's looking at me like I'm the most beautiful thing he's ever seen makes me shudder. I let it wash over me. I let myself believe it. I know what this is between us and what it isn't, and I'm okay with that. I honestly am. There's no room in my life right now for more complications. For more drama from men, which, let's face it, Aston comes with.

I reach between us and guide his large cock to my entrance, watching his face as I slowly sink down on him. His head falls back, and a groan sears from his throat. His eyes momentarily close but immediately reopen, smoky and half-mast, as if he doesn't want to miss a moment of this.

"Fuck," he hisses. "You feel so good. So tight and perfect around me. Better than I ever imagined."

His words wash over me, and I let myself relax and sink down deeper. His cock is thick and long, and yeah, it's a tight fit. So much so that I have to rise onto my knees and pull him almost out of me again so I can sink back down and stretch myself fully around him.

He cups my tits and gives me a firm squeeze, pressing them together as I start to move. His eyes are glued to them, watching how they bounce in his hands, overflowing them. My eyes close as his thumbs rub my nipples.

Hell. The feel of him inside of me while he's doing that...

He's still for a few minutes, letting me move, allowing me to lead. Encouraging me at every turn with things like, "That's it. Take what you need. Show me how you want it. Take me deeper. You know you want to."

And I do.

It's not even him, it's me, I realize. *I* feel beautiful. *I* feel sexy. *I* feel... unstoppable. Like the woman I always wanted to be. The one no longer hidden inside or pushed down by the words and actions of others. I'm taking charge, and I fucking love it.

My hands plant into his chest, and I use it for leverage as I angle myself forward and grind up and down his cock. It's a smooth glide. In and out. But this angle is everything. It's so good, and he's hitting this spot inside of me that has me winded and gasping for air. He takes advantage, shifting his hands to my hips and thrusting up into me. It's the first time he's done that, and holy fuck.

"Oh god!" I cry out, my eyes rolling back while my nails dig into his chest.

He captures the back of my head and brings my mouth down to his, swallowing my moans with a dizzying kiss. Our tongues tangle, and I lose myself to this. The feel of him fucking in and out of me, his hands all over me, in his breath and taste and sounds and smell.

On my next heartbeat, he flips us over until I'm on my back in the center of the bed. My legs hit his shoulders, and he bends me until his mouth is back on mine. "I want you like this now," he rasps against my lips before taking another deep, plunging kiss. "Because soon I won't be able to fuck you like this. I'll have to be careful and gentle. Tender. But not yet. I can still fuck you hard now, can't I?"

It takes me a moment to grasp what he's talking about, but when I realize he means because my belly will be too big for it, I gasp and have to bite my lip.

"Don't do that." He cups my face. "I'm going to love fucking you as your body changes and grows."

I don't know how to make sense of that. Of the way he's talking right now. With how good this feels, I don't want to. Because if I give that an inch inside of me, it'll grow and multiply, and there will be no going back. Not just physically, but he'll tear my heart to shreds and have my mind wrapped around him like he owns both.

My hands clutch the blanket above my head, and I let him pound into me. It's fast but deep and paced. Not frantic or out of control. Not for Aston. He fucks me with precision. And he does it so goddamn well.

"You have no idea how many times I've thought about this," he confesses against my lips, still holding my face so I can't escape him. "Having you in my bed, feeling you come around me."

Heat spreads through me, making my pussy clench and my fingers tingle. "Tell me," I pant as I move faster, my hips canting in time with his, chasing the building pressure, hoping it happens, hoping this is the time I come during sex.

His hand slides to my jaw, his thumb in my mouth, and I open my eyes to find his wicked smile right above me. I suck on his thumb, and his eyes smolder. "You want to hear how I jerked off thinking about you? How I've imagined these perfect tits in my hands and your sweet cunt wrapped around my cock?"

His filthy words send shockwaves through me. I've never had anyone talk to me like this. I certainly never knew how much I liked it.

"Yes." I lean up and kiss him with his thumb between our lips. "Yes. I want to know."

His hands meet the mattress on either side of my head, and his hips pound into me, rocking forward and angling up. It's dizzying. Mind-bending. His light hair is dark with sweat, and his perfect body is coated in a sheen of it.

"How about I show you?" He slides out of me and draws me off the bed until I'm standing with shaky legs. His hand presses into the back of my neck, and he pushes me flat on the bed, leaving my ass in the air. He grasps my hips, lifts them up, and slams back into me.

"Shit!" I hiss, my eyes pinching shut.

His chest meets my back, his lips by my ear, his hot breath making me quake. "That. That sound. The way your cunt feels. Being able to fuck you until all you feel is me." He moves hard, holding me down, taking over everything, so I have no choice but to feel him exactly as he said. His cock pistons in and out of me, his lower abdomen slamming against my ass and making the bed creak. "I've wanted you like this since that first night," he continues, his voice dark and dangerous. "Wanted to taste every inch of you." He licks a trail up my spine, tasting my skin and sweat. "Wanted to hear those sweet little sounds you make when you're being so fucking good for me. Like you are right now."

My eyes pinch shut as warmth spirals through me.

"Take it, my little swan. Feel it. Let me own this. Let me own you."

I shake my head because I can't let him do that, and he growls. Fisting my hair, he pulls back, arching my neck so he can kiss me. His tongue shows no mercy. Neither does his cock as he fucks me. The sting on my scalp somehow only heightens it.

"Mine," he grunts into my mouth. "Just like that. Take what I give you. You're so fucking wet for me, and your pussy is so tight, I know you love it." His grip on my hair tightens, and his other hand slides beneath me to find my clit.

I'm close, and he knows it. He feels it.

With an arrogant fucking smirk against my cheek, he says, "Your hot little cunt is about to gush all over me, and when it does, I'm going to fill you up. You'll be dripping my cum all night. You'll touch yourself, feel it there, and wake me up to beg for me to do this to you again because you can't stand not feeling my cock inside of you."

And that does it for me. The dirty as all sin words, the filthy promise, and the way he's rubbing my clit and fucking me in exactly the right place and even pulling my goddamn hair. I don't have a choice. There's no holding back or mental hang-up. I come hard and loud. My hands scrape at the blanket, and I pull away from his grasp so I can smother my face to stifle my screams. It's consuming. My whole body has been ignited.

"Fuck, fuck, fuck," he chants, his rhythm faltering. "You're squeezing me so good. So fucking good. Fuck, yes!"

Aston's arms lock around my shoulders, and he fucks me through my orgasm until he reaches the point where he can't take it anymore. He stills as he comes in me with a wounded cry. His face falls between my shoulder blades, and he jerks as he clings to me, my name spilling from his lips.

Before I know what's happening, he flips me back over and enters me again, his cock still half-hard. His forehead meets mine, and our eyes lock while our ragged breath tickles each other. He pumps lightly, a slow rolling of his hips.

"What are you doing?" I ask.

"I don't want to stop. I want to keep going. I want to do this all night." He licks my lips. "Is this okay?"

"Yes."

He kisses me, his hands on my face, holding me. He thrusts deeper now, more primal. I can feel his cum leaking out of me, but he's fucking it back into me too, and it's so dirty I can't help but moan.

"I'm getting hard again. Already." He smiles. "Do you feel it? How do you do this to me?"

The wonder in his voice has me smiling too. I've already had two orgasms, but I'm not sure that will stop my body. Not tonight. Not with him.

"You take me so well," he murmurs. "Like you were made for this. Made for me."

The words sink into me, both terrifying and thrilling. "Aston," I whimper, not even sure what I'm asking for.

"One more," he demands. "Give me one more, my swan. I want to feel you come around me again."

He fucks me like this. Fucks us both. He holds me close and kisses me and murmurs sweet and dirty things between my lips. It doesn't even take that long until we're both moaning and moving and panting.

I don't know how it's possible. How my body can take more, but somehow it does.

"I'm close," he warns. "So fucking close. Come with me, baby."

His finger finds my clit and moves in fast, mind-blowing circles while his hips slam harder, and suddenly, I am. My pussy clenches around him as another orgasm rips through me. It's deeper, more intense. I feel it in my bones. In my soul.

Aston follows me, his body rigid, his eyes wide, and his lips parted. It's a look on him I'll never forget. We collapse together, a tangle of sweaty limbs and ragged breaths. For a long moment, neither of us speaks. His heart pounds against my chest, and his arms tighten around me as if he's afraid I'll disappear.

Then reality crashes into me. I just fucked my fake husband and my brother's best friend. A man ten years older than me. This was never supposed to happen. I promised myself it wouldn't. Yet here I am, having just had the most intense and best sex of my life.

Panic rises up my throat, choking me. What have I done? What will this mean for us going forward?"

I need space. I need to think, and I need to do that without being naked, lying in his arms, and feeling things I don't want to feel.

I move away from him when his arm tightens around me. "Stay," he murmurs, his voice drowsy and sated. "Stay with me tonight."

"I can't," I tell him honestly. "I just... I need my own space."

I don't look at him as I push his arm away and gather my clothes, pulling them on with hasty, trembling hands. I know he's watching me, and suddenly the room feels too small, the air too thick.

He sits up and moves to the edge of the bed as he puts his boxer briefs back on. "Skylar—"

"It's okay. This was fun. But I need to go." Before he can respond, I'm out the door, hurrying down the hall to my own room on unsteady legs. I press the lock button on the knob and lean against the door, sliding to the floor as my knees give out.

I'm in trouble. Deep, serious trouble. And that's the last thing I can afford to be in.

29

So, here's my thinking, and it may be crazy, but I think Skylar likes me. I think she *really* likes me, and I know I sound like I'm ten or whatever, but I don't care. Why else would she have freaked out last night? If she didn't care, she would have stayed or fucked me a third time in the shower or told me she still hated me. Maybe she would have laughed at me trying to snuggle her and told me to quit being sappy.

She would have been able to look at me. But she couldn't.

She asked for space before she ran from me, and I should grant her that, but I think that's simply her fear and uncertainty talking.

I'm not uncertain.

I'm afraid, sure, but I'm not uncertain.

I've fallen in love with a pregnant woman before. I gave her my heart. I gave her my everything. And she betrayed me. She never loved me back, but worse, she lied to me and told me she did. She played the happily married wife and me for a fool. Am I setting myself up for the same type of heartache? For some-thing possibly worse?

Maybe. I honestly might be.

But how will I know what can be if I never try?

And because I know my little swan so well, I'm outside her door bright and early so she can't escape. I mean, let's face it, it's not like I was going back to sleep after last night. I was ready to charge after her the moment she left, but I stopped myself. Barely.

The thing is, I don't care that she's ten years younger than me. I don't care that she's my best friend's little sister. I don't care that I have a kid or that she's pregnant with a baby that isn't mine. I just don't care. I want her. The things that appear as obstacles or drama don't have to be. We can have it all. If she's willing to.

I have to try. I have to. I'll regret it always if I don't.

I'm not sure anything in my life has ever felt truly right except for Zoey and Skylar. When I'm with them, I'm whole. I'm complete. I'm fucking happy. Even when Skylar is driving me crazy. But it seems I'm going to have my work cut out for me getting her to accept this.

The door to her room springs open, snapping me away from my gentle pacing. She jumps back when she sees me, and a frown tugs down on her lips. She's fully dressed in a long cream sweater and leggings, and she's holding a pair of boots.

"Nope. Not happening." Before she can argue with me, I come over to her, take the boots from her hand, put them on the floor, and lift her by her hips to walk her back into her room. I kick the door shut behind me and drop her on the bed before I climb over her.

"What are you doing?!"

"What are you doing?" I throw back at her.

"I'm…"

"You're running."

"I'm not—"

"Bullshit," I charge, hovering above her. She's so pretty like this with her hair sprawled all over the place and her big green eyes wide and on me. "It's six in the fucking morning, Skylar, after you were out till midnight and then fucked me till two. You're running."

She puffs out a breath and closes her eyes, defeat all over her. "Last night—"

"I swear to God, if you tell me that last night was a mistake or it shouldn't have happened, I'm going to put you over my knee and spank your ass red. What are you doing? Why are you running from me?"

"Because I can't do this with you!" she cries, her eyes flashing, her features fierce with indignation. "I can't repeat old habits and allow myself to get swallowed up by a man who will hurt me."

"What about me? Dammit, Skylar. I sigh, shifting my weight and climbing off her. She scoots out from under me and sits against the headboard, her knees up to her chest. A protective position if ever there was one. "Wanna talk about repeating old habits? I married a pregnant woman, and once again I'm chasing after her. I know you're scared. I'm scared. There is nothing easy about us, sweetheart. But instead of pushing me away, pull me toward you. I..." I stop. I can't tell her how I feel. I can't tell her I love her. Not yet. I scrub my hands up my face in frustration before I meet her eyes with an intensity I can no longer hold back. "I don't know exactly what this is or even what it could be, but I want to find out. I don't want to run from it."

Her glassy eyes search my face, but she doesn't say anything, and I take that as my cue to keep going. I climb up onto my knees and inch toward her until I'm sitting in front of her, my hand on hers on top of her knees. "You've had it bad, and your trust in men, possibly even yourself, is shit. I get that. So hear me now, so you know." I cup her jaw with my other hand. I will never hurt you. I will never degrade you. I will always care for and respect you. I will never treat you as anything less than the beautiful, smart, funny, feisty, pain-in-the-ass, incredible woman that you are." My thumb drags along her cheek. "God, Skylar, you have so much power over me, and you don't even see it. I'm yours. Everything I've said to you has been true and not simply in the heat of sex." I hold up my hand. "Well, everything except that last stupid thing I said to you in the kitchen that night. But everything else is real."

"What are you asking of me?"

I smile softly. "Be my girlfriend and my wife?"

"What about... I mean, I'm pregnant and—"

"I'm a pediatric surgeon and a single dad. Babies don't exactly scare me." I pull her up onto my lap until she's straddling me and we're face-to-face. I wrap my arms around her and hold her tight. "Just try with me, Skylar. Try with me, and I'll try with you, and we'll take it as it comes. I don't want to play games. I don't want to have to keep fighting the way I want you. I want to kiss you, and I want that kiss to be real. I want it to mean something."

Her eyes glitter with emotion. "I want that too."

A lightness hits my chest, and I fall back onto the bed with a chuckle. "Really?"

She laughs and smacks my shoulder. "Yes, you dummy. Were you expecting me to say no?"

"No. Yes. I don't know. I'm tired. I had this whole thing built up in my head, and it involved a lot of fighting and sweet-talking."

"Maybe you should have gotten some sleep instead of planning a battle strategy."

My eyes pop open, and I stare up at her. "Maybe." I spring up and take her down onto the bed, hovering over her once more. The hem of her sweater rubs my palms as I pull it up and over her head. "Or not, since now I'm here and there's makeup sex to be had."

"What are you doing?"

I smirk down at her. "I'm fucking my girlfriend, who also happens to be my wife."

She rolls her eyes. "You and this wife thing."

My lips are layered with her. "And yet you're wearing not only my band but my engagement ring." I tap her finger where the large rock sits. It makes me stupidly happy. She doesn't wear it often.

"I don't even know why I put it on. I saw it, and I just... did."

"I'm not complaining." I can't stop staring at her lips. Her plump, pink lips. My weight goes to my forearm and elbow, and as I slide my hand up her belly, her skin quivers beneath my touch. "You're fucking gorgeous. Damn, my girlfriend is hot."

She lets out a breathy laugh as she tugs on my shirt. "That's great and all, but you're still wearing your shirt. I want to see my boyfriend's hot muscles. Not to mention, time's ticking here."

"Thanks for the reminder." I lean down to bite her nipple through her bra until she whimpers. Reaching behind my back, I pull my shirt over my head and toss it to the end of the bed. I want to spend all day with her like this, but Skylar is right. We don't exactly have that luxury, and Zoey will be up soon and anxious for her eggs. Vomit.

I capture her lips in a bruising kiss as I work on sliding her leggings down and off while she reaches behind her back to unclasp her bra. Her tits fall free, and like a man who can't help himself, I lower my head and take one nipple into my mouth so I can circle it with my tongue. She arches beneath me and grasps onto my shoulder, her nails digging in ever so slightly.

I release it with a wet pop. "Too much?"

"No," she breathes, threading her fingers through my hair to guide me back. "More. It feels so good."

Happily, I oblige, alternating between gentle suction and teasing flicks of my tongue. I can't get enough of how they feel and taste, and I squeeze her tits together so I can bury my face in them, inhaling her scent and biting gently at her soft skin. Every gasp and shudder, every time she pulls my hair when I get her in just the right way. All of it is intoxicating.

The best part is that these are mine now. All of her is. I don't have to do everything all at once because I fear I'll never have it again. I can fuck her now and make her come this afternoon and then fuck her again tonight.

And I will. I absolutely will. Every goddamn chance I get.

I slide a hand down her belly, over her small bump, until I cup her pussy. Her panties are fucking soaked, and her cunt is so warm beneath the soft satin tickling my palm. She rocks into my hand, seeking friction, seeking full contact, and I chuckle against her nipple and affectionately bite it.

"What do you need, sweetheart?" I slip her panties to the side and run my finger through her folds. "This? Is this what you want?"

"Mmm. Yes. More."

"That's your favorite word for me this morning."

"I wouldn't have to say it if you'd finally give it to me."

I glance up at her as I plunge two fingers straight into her tight heat. "Like this?"

A moan mixed with a gasp flees her lips, and her head falls back. She rips at my hair, pushing my face back into her tits, and I think it's safe to say I'm pretty much a goner for this woman.

She moves against me, her hips jerking up into my hand. "Fuck, you feel amazing. So tight and perfect around my fingers. I can't wait to feel you on my cock." I pump my fingers coated in her wetness in and out of her. She's centered on the bed, thighs wide, one hand on the blanket, the other in my hair, eyes closed, and face totally lost in pleasure. It's an image I'll have burned into my mind forever.

Twisting my wrist, I really fuck into her as I use the butt of my palm to work her clit.

"Oh! Oh, yes."

I cover her mouth with mine, swallowing her sounds that grow increasingly louder the closer she gets. One knee comes up and fans out, splaying her open wider to me. I love how she's lost any self-consciousness with me. My little swan is so sexy when she lets go and trusts me, and I intend to reward her for that.

I move my mouth to her ear and whisper, "That's my good, sweet girl. Look how beautiful you are when you come undone for me. Come for me. I want to lick your cum off my fingers so I have the taste of your cunt on my lips as I fuck you."

Curling my fingers, I hit the spot that makes her gasp as my palm presses straight onto her clit. The pressure quickens her breath and tightens her grip on me. She yanks my mouth to hers and moans and whimpers against my lips, sloppily kissing me while losing control. Her thighs tremble, and her body starts to thrash as her pussy clenches my fingers so tightly, I have no idea how my cock is going to fit in there.

"That's it," I encourage. "You're so beautiful like this, Skylar. So goddamn perfect. My girl. I can't get enough of you."

I lower my head and suck one nipple into my mouth all the while fucking her with my fingers and rubbing her clit hard. She shatters beneath me on a broken cry, her pussy pulsing around me. I work her through it, kissing and sucking and tasting her. The moment she sags into the bed, I slip my fingers from her and slide them straight into my mouth as promised.

I suck them clean, and she watches, a dirty, depraved look on her face that heats my blood and has my pulse pounding.

"That's one," I tell her, kissing along her collarbone and up her neck while shifting so I can remove my pajama pants. "I want to see how many times I can make you come today."

"Cocky," she muses, but there's no heat to it, just a lazy, satisfied smile that makes my chest clench.

"Confident," I correct, squeezing my cock and giving it a

firm jerk as I stare down at her glistening pussy. Shit. I might come on the spot. "And extremely motivated."

"I'm not complaining," she says, throwing my words back at me. She grabs the back of my head and brings me in for a kiss. I climb in between her legs and rub the head of my cock up and down, lubing myself with her cum. My hands plant into the mattress, and I rock into her, rubbing my cock up and down.

I roll down and nudge the head of my dick into her opening, and with it, I push into her slowly, wanting to savor this. "You feel so fucking good," I groan and thrust all the way in. She whimpers and props herself up onto her elbows so she can watch as I pump in and out of her.

"Jesus, Aston," she keens. "Fuck, that's deep." Her head falls back, and her mouth goes slack as she brings her knees up, her feet planted into the bed on either side of my knees. "God yes. Fuck me like that. Right like that."

"Right there?" I ask though I already know the answer since she's sitting up higher and clinging to me, clawing at my hips. I wrap her legs around me and hold up some of her weight so I can pound into her. "You take me so well, baby. I could stay inside you forever."

All she can do is nod as I use my hand on her ass to slam her body against mine and drive my cock deeper and harder into her. She feels so fucking good, I can hardly take it. Nothing has ever felt better than this. Fucking nothing. Her tits crush against my chest, bouncing lightly with the pummel of my thrusts. She pulls me in tighter and tilts her head, demanding a kiss I'm only too happy to give her.

Her orgasm hits her like an unexpected wave, expelling a shocked moan from her lungs and causing her body to clench and tighten around me. I kiss her harder and thrust faster, chasing the high I'm right on the edge of.

"Fuck. Skylar," I grunt, needing to break the kiss to catch my breath. Her teeth dig into my shoulder, and it makes my hips jerk harder into her. We cling to each other, our bodies wrapped around the other, and when we're both spent, I fall onto my back and take her with me, still inside of her.

Just as I'm about to pull out of her, a small knock comes on the door. "Skylar? I can't find Daddy. Do you know where he is?"

Our eyes meet, wide and surprised, then amused. Shit.

"Everyone's going to know the moment I don't have a glass of champagne at my own wedding party," I murmur as I adjust my lavender dress and stare up at the massive estate of my grandparents' compound.

"Yes," Aston agrees absently, his gaze on his phone, a frown tugging down his lips and his eyebrows pinched in so tight there's hardly any space between them.

"What's wrong?" I question, coming closer to him and peering down at his phone.

He blusters out a heavy breath. "There's a weird order on one of my patients. I just got a text from a floor nurse asking me about it."

"But you're off."

He glances up at me. "I didn't put the order in this way. I'm positive I didn't."

"Okaaaay," I say, elongating the word as confusion takes over. "What does that mean?"

"I don't know. This is like the second or third time some of my orders have been messed up."

"That's... weird. Are you sure you didn't click the wrong button or put it in wrong?"

He shakes his head, but uncertainty flickers across his face. "No. I mean, I don't think so. I'm always very careful with my orders, especially my medication orders. This dose is for a child more than twice the size of my patient."

I blanch. "Yeesh. That's not good. But the nurse caught it, right? The patient didn't get that dose?"

"No. She caught it. But what if she hadn't? What if she had given it to her?"

I go over to get an impatient Zoey out of the backseat while I reply to him. "I don't know. I mean, that's a scary thought, but she questioned it, and you fixed it, and no one was hurt."

"I know. It's just weird, and I'm edgy. Especially after yesterday when the needle driver failed to hold the suturing needle. I don't make mistakes, Skylar. Not at work. This was the second time a piece of equipment didn't do what it was supposed to, and I couldn't manipulate it."

I place my hand on his arm. "I know, and I get it. But everything's okay. No one was hurt in either situation."

He nods and puts his phone back into his pocket, but he's still visibly unhappy. Other than a few strange incidents at the hospital, everything else has been great. My fake husband is officially my real boyfriend. Not many people know about it. We've kind of been keeping it quiet while we see how it goes for us. A lot of that is for Zoey. We don't want to confuse her or put her in a greater position to get hurt if this doesn't work out between us.

Some is also for my own mental sanity. Aston isn't as worried about that as I am. But we've both been in positions where we thought everything was great, only to discover that it wasn't. So, I'm being cautious and taking this slow.

I have my first ultrasound on Monday, and I'm excited and nervous for it.

It's simply a lot on my plate, and right now I like having Aston like this. I like our quiet moments and pillow talk. I like him pressing me up against the walls in the house and stealing a kiss. I like him sneaking up behind me at work and smelling the back of my neck when I wear my hair up. I like all the hot, orgasm-inducing sex we're having. It feels like a dirty secret when it's actually not.

Aston wants to tell Micha, but that's not so easy to do right now, as Micha has gone to an interior part of the country that's particularly struggling, and cell service isn't happening. But telling Micha makes this serious, so I don't mind waiting a bit longer.

But that brings us back to today. To our freaking wedding party à la Fritz and Hughes.

Everyone is expected to arrive in half an hour or so, but our moms wanted us to come early to survey all they've done. So here we are.

The front door opens, and both of our parents are there, my dad already with a drink in his hand. Yeah, he's still not thrilled with all of this. His baby girl snuck off and got married. Oh, and she's pregnant with an asshole's kid.

"You all look beautiful," Halle exclaims, a bright smile lighting up her face. Zoey does a spin for about the hundredth time in her dress, loving how it fans out around her. Naturally everyone claps for her, and she preens as she runs past us toward the front of the house.

"Can I see the cake?" she asks immediately.

"Yes. Absolutely," my mother tells her. "Come with me. I'll show you where it is."

My mother takes Zoey's hand and leads her inside, and Aston and I follow after her, heading into the warmth of the house.

My dad instantly pulls me in for a hug. "You look so pretty."

I smile as I hug him back. "You can't get choked up because then I'll get choked up."

He pulls back and meets my eyes. "I just didn't expect all of this yet. You were supposed to give me another ten years at least before you decided to get married and have a baby."

I snort a laugh. "You mean before I got pregnant and fake married?"

My dad rolls his eyes at me, and Aston makes a noise behind me. I turn and catch his eye, but I can't read his expression.

"I still wish you had let me kick Josh's ass," my father quips, drawing my attention back to him.

"But then you'd likely break a hip or something, and it wouldn't change the situation with him. That's what you call a lose-lose."

My dad scoffs indignantly. "Break a hip? I'm not that old yet."

I give him a teasing *if you say so* shrug.

"Come on, Brecken," Jonah Hughes, Aston's father, says to my dad. "Let's refill your drink. Something tells me you're going to need it today."

"Yes. I mean, I'm sure it's five o'clock somewhere," I tease.

"This pregnancy is making you more of a smart-ass with your old man than usual."

I bow to my dad. "I learned from the master."

He chuckles, but after hanging up our coats, we all head through the first floor, passing sitting rooms and parlors and music rooms and libraries to the back solarium that spans a good portion of the back of the mansion, where teams of staff are setting everything up. There are cocktail tables dripping with ivory linens and topped with pale pink roses and tiny fake votives—we do have lots of small children running around—in the center of them. There are long tables for the cocktail hour with a million different kinds of food, and the bartenders are setting up at the large bar in the back of the room, abutting a set of floor-to-ceiling windows that overlook the gardens and grounds.

It has a winter wonderland feel with fairy lights, pale flowers, and elegant crystal. "I see they didn't take our suggestion for neon yellow and taupe," I murmur to Aston, who's been quiet since we entered the house.

"Shame. But this is..." He trails off, and all I can do is nod. Because yeah. It's magical. And it makes me feel guilty. I have no clue what all of my uncles, aunts, and extended cousins know or don't know about our marriage. But looking at all of this, you'd never know it was fake. And it kind of hurts my heart.

"I don't like pretending," I murmur. "We're playing at a marriage while trying to be a couple."

"I know. I don't like that either." Aston's fingers play with my rings before he gives my hand a tug, forcing me to face him. "But we are a couple. So the marriage stuff will just be a funny story we tell one day."

I scrunch my nose. "You think—"

"I know. I'm crazy about you and you're crazy about me—"

"I never said that," I quip, and he smiles.

"You didn't have to. I can tell."

I roll my eyes, but there's no heat to it. "Always so cocky, this one."

"You make me that way." He squeezes my hands. "I really am crazy about you."

I step into him and stare up at his handsome face, my chest fluttering and my body just... happy. This guy makes me happy, and I'm desperately trying to shut off the part of my brain that is waiting for the other shoe to drop.

"Good. I like you that way. And even though it'll feed your massive ego, I'm crazy about you too."

"Then we'll get through the fake part and focus on the real part."

"Sounds like a plan."

"Except..."

"Except what?" I ask, noting the sudden turbulent shift in his blue eyes.

He blows out a nervous breath, something I don't see on him often, if ever. "I have no clue what today is going to be like for either of us," he starts, looking as though he's searching for the right words even as he says them. "But, sweetheart, I don't want to keep saying it's fa—"

"Ah, there you are," my grandmother calls from across the room, cutting Aston off. "Come join me."

Octavia Abbott-Fritz is wearing a deep red dress that accentuates her regal features. Her blonde bob is as perfectly styled as it always is, and her makeup is flawless. For a woman in her nineties, she looks fabulous and spry as she sits at one of the low tables with a glass of champagne in her hand.

Aston gives me a nervous look, but we join her at the table, taking a seat with her after we each kiss her cheek.

"You're cheating," I tell her. "You get to have a drink, and I can't."

She laughs. "How is my great-grandchild doing? Growing well?"

"I hope so. I'll find out tomorrow at my ultrasound."

"And naturally you'll send your grandmother a picture of that," she demands lightly.

"Naturally," I agree.

"And you, Aston. I just had the pleasure of seeing your Zoey. She's so lovely. It warms my heart that you're officially part of the family and taking care of my granddaughter."

He grins. "Differently, but yes. Though Skylar might disagree."

"Not all the time," I tease.

"But you care for her. I can see that all over you," she says to him before a certain kind of smile lights her face.

"Yes, ma'am. I do."

The way he says that to her makes my heart thrum against my ribs. Before I can stop myself, I lean in and kiss his cheek. It shocks us both and pleases the hell out of my grandmother, but I don't care. This is not something I ever expected from Aston Hughes, but here it is. Still, I'm afraid. Afraid of fully letting go. Afraid of falling in love. It feels impossible to trust this, but I'm trying.

He's not Josh. Aston thinks I'm all the things I know I am. And when I lag on that, he pushes me and forces me to believe it again.

"Octavia, dear. I'm too old to be a ma'am." She winks at Aston. "The happiest couples take care of each other, don't they? And it seems to me you're both already doing that."

"Grandma, the marriage part isn't real."

"My darling girl, what is real versus not? The rings on your hands are as real as the documents you signed and the words you spoke. The rest may simply need time to grow. Your grandfather's and my marriage was similar in that regard. Our families brought us together, and eventually, when the time was right, we fell in love."

My cheeks warm at her inference. I go to say something, but she and Aston seem to be having some sort of private conversation with only their eyes.

Before I can question anything, people arrive, and then we're playing the part. It's a wedding party. Complete with food and dancing and pictures and cake. I hate it. It feels awful. It feels like I'm skipping a million steps with Aston, and it sits all wrong with me.

It does with him too. I can tell. Neither of us is having a particularly good time nor wants to do the posed things. I get why we're doing it. The necessity behind it. I'm a Fritz, and he's a Hughes, and if we were married in real life, we'd have a wedding. It would look exactly like this. Everyone around me is doing this for me. To protect me from the asshole I let into my life and allowed to stay for too long.

"I'm sorry," I murmur as Aston sways me on the dance floor.

"Don't be. I get to dance with you. I'm not complaining."

"But you're not having fun either," I throw back at him.

"No. I'm not."

I swallow and nod, pressing the side of my head against his chest over his steady heart.

"I don't regret it, Skylar. I already told you that."

"I know. I just feel... dumb."

He captures my chin and tilts it up, so I'm forced to look at him. "Why would you say that?"

"We're at our fake wedding party because I stayed with a bad man and got pregnant with his child. If it weren't for that, none of this would be necessary. Think of the extreme of this all because of me."

His eyes soften as he sways us around the center of the floor in my grandparents' ballroom. "I understand why you'd feel that way, but that's not how it is. There's not a person in this room who wouldn't do anything for you, and that includes attending a party for you. We all do things that make us feel dumb, but sometimes those dumb things lead to the best. I had sex with a stranger in the bathroom of a club and didn't use a condom because I was drunk and didn't care at the time. Me. A doctor. That's a pretty fucking dumb thing to do. I was smart enough to talk to her for a few minutes prior to that so she knew what my name was and was able to look me up. Imagine if I hadn't? I might have never known Zoey, and where would she be now? I was also dumb enough to believe that Astrid loved me back when she told me she did."

He runs a hand along my jaw and stares adoringly into my eyes.

"We're not perfect, Skylar. No one is. But what you did by being with Josh doesn't make you dumb. You loved someone who mistreated you, and that's on him and not you. You stayed because love isn't black and white. It's shaded in a hell of a lot of grays, and it twists and warps our minds and hearts. It's easy for people on the outside of a situation to look in on something they don't know or understand and judge it. Stop doing that to yourself."

I swallow thickly, forcing a nod. "I know. I know all of this. I do. I just... being here today like this... It's hitting differently than I thought it would. It's like it's throwing all my mistakes right in my face and not only doing it publicly but forcing others along for the ride."

"We all make mistakes. But sometimes those mistakes lead us down a path we might not have otherwise gone down. And from where I'm standing, as much as I hate that Josh was part of your story for as long as he was and that he might not ever be fully gone, all of that brought you to me."

My insides grow warm and liquid. "You're really incredible, you know that?"

He shrugs. "Sometimes I know that more than others."

I feel that. I truly do. But Aston sees me, all of me, the good and the bad, and he's still looking at me like I'm his sun. And I see him too. The good and the bad. The perfect and the imperfect. Maybe he's right. Maybe all the bad things we endure are there to learn from and help us grow and make it so that we can appreciate when the good things come along.

I drag my fingers up to his face and pull him down to kiss me. Because I have to kiss him. He feels like all the fairy tale things I imagined as a kid, only he's real. He's here. By my side and dancing with me at our fake wedding and helping me through one of the hardest situations of my life. A situation that hasn't seemed so bad this week that we've been together.

Unfortunately, we're treated to whistles and cheers and

fucking photographs. And just like that, my bubble is once again burst.

After that, we both retreat a bit. Zoey has a blast with the other kids, and I mostly try to hide out with my friends, dodging questions from curious relatives and eating my weight in canapés.

My mother doesn't push it, and neither does Aston's. By tomorrow those pictures will be out along with our wedding pictures, and that will be that. It leaves a bitter taste in my mouth. How can Aston and I grow into anything real after this level of a lie?

31

SKYLAR

Zoey releases a heavy yawn, her head heavy on Aston's shoulder as he carries her upstairs and into the bathroom.

"No. I want Skylar to do it," she whines. He sets her down in front of the sink and throws me a questioning look.

"I've got her," I tell him and enter the bathroom.

Something flickers across his features, and I close the door to give us privacy.

"Did you have fun?" I ask her as we get her into pajamas.

"So much fun. The babies were so cute."

"They were. What was your favorite cake?"

"The chocolate one," she tells me as she brushes her teeth, and I grab the brush to work on her long hair. She's loaded with tangles, and this is why I keep my hair shoulder length. I try to be as gentle as possible, feeling bad every time she winces.

"I liked that one too."

She spits into the sink and washes out her mouth. "Are you my stepmom now?"

Oh shit. That pulls me up short. I'm not sure why I didn't expect her to ask that. Aston had told her that we were special friends who wore rings for each other, but today was our wedding party. I know Aston talked to her about some of that this morning, but clearly, they didn't address this part. Or she simply didn't ask until now.

"Your dad and I..." I stop. I honestly don't know what to say. "Do you want a stepmom?"

"I want my mom."

I run my hand down her hair and meet her eyes in the mirror. "I know, sweetie." I kiss the top of her head and set the brush down. "I know you do."

"But she and my dad weren't married when she died."

"No. They weren't."

"And you're married to him now. That's what everyone was saying today."

I pick her up and put her on the counter of the sink so we can talk face-to-face. "Yes, your daddy and I are married. But it's a different kind of marriage. We care a lot about each other and are helping each other. That's what our marriage is."

"Does that make you my stepmom like it does in the stories?"

"In a way, I guess it does. But more than that, I'm your special friend. Your bestie for life."

She stares long and hard up at me. "Do you not want to be my stepmom?"

Jesus. Way to get heavy on me after an already heavy day.

"I'd like to be whatever you want me to be. I'd never want you to think I'm trying to replace your mom, though. That's not something I could ever do. But I love being with you, and if that's what you want to call me..." I stop. Shit. But looking at her... "If you want me to be your stepmom, I'm okay with that. If you don't, that's fine too."

"I'd like you to be."

A tingly warmth curls through my veins, and my eyes immediately glass over. I bring her into my arms and hug her fiercely. I don't know what's happening. I don't know where any of us are going or what's next. This could all fall apart tomorrow. But no matter what happens or doesn't happen between Aston and me, she'll always have me.

"Then that's what I'll be." I kiss her head again and pull back.

"Why are you crying?"

I laugh lightly and wipe at my cheeks. "They're happy tears. I get emotional easily these days."

She shrugs. "Okay." And just like that, all the heaviness is gone. If only adults were as easy as kids. She hops off the counter and opens the door. "Daddy! I'm ready for bed, and Skylar is my new stepmom."

He comes out of his room wearing his standard white T-shirt and sweatpants, and yeah, that's a look that will never get old. Except now his eyebrows are at his hairline.

"Oh. Okay. Um. Great. All brushed and ready?" He throws me a look, and I give him one in return that says I'll tell him later, and he takes Zoey into his arms and carries her into her room.

"Good night, Skylar."

"Night, Zoey."

I head down into my room to get myself ready for bed. A few minutes later, Aston is behind me at the sink, his eyes meeting mine in the reflection of the mirror.

"Stepmom?"

I give him a nervous look. "She asked if that's what I was, and I told her if that's what she wanted me to be, I would. I don't know. Should I not have said that? Maybe I should have brought you in there with me?"

A smile splits his lips. One that looks like he's trying and failing to contain. "I mean, I'm not complaining about it. But are you okay with it? I know she put you on the spot. When I talked to her this morning about the wedding party stuff, I didn't think about titles or designations like that. I just went over what the party was and what she might hear."

I chew on the corner of my bottom lip. "I'm okay with it."

"Yeah?"

He looks at me with the whole world in his eyes, so hot and yet so boyish, I could die. "Yeah."

In a flash, he spins me around, captures my face in his hands, and kisses me. It's a merciless, vicious storm. One I'm only too happy to get swept away in. It's lips and breath. It's sweet and smoldering. Riled with passion and filled with need. My hands loop around his neck as I lift myself up onto the balls of my feet so I can fully kiss him back. But his hands aren't happy resting in one place. They're hungry and excited as they shamelessly explore.

The zipper at the back of my dress plunges down my back, the shoulders slipping away. My fingers trickle up into the back of his hair, and I play with the soft strands before I slide down his back, feeling his strong muscles bunch and move.

I can't get enough of him. I'm starting to feel that way all the time. Every touch, every look, every teasing or even serious word. I know now it was like this even before I mistakenly crawled into his bed. He was worming himself into places I told myself I had shut off. Places I didn't want any man to enter. At least not this soon. And not him. I didn't want it to be him.

But now I know he was always going to happen. It was always going to be him. I can't imagine it being anyone else. And that scares me to the point of having me pull back. His eyes are smoky, and a thousand goose bumps cover my skin from just this one look alone.

We stare at each other for a very long moment before we both lose our patience and our minds and give in to this... tension. I jump up into him, and he catches me reflexively, our mouths devouring and our tongues swirling and thrashing. I moan into him, my nails digging into his shoulder blades.

He sets me on the counter and rips my dress off my arms where it dangled. It pools at my waist, but that's not good enough for him. He shifts me around and tears it out from under me, letting it fall to the floor before he kicks it aside. I attack his shirt with equal fervor, wanting to see him, to feel him. And he doesn't disappoint. His skin is smooth and warm and soft over hard, delicious muscles.

No one has ever made me this wild before. Has ever undone me to my core. But that's Aston Hughes. He has me forever undone. His pants hit the floor, and then he's jerking me back off the counter, flipping me around, and pressing my chest down against the cold stone.

I whimper and squirm, but he holds me still with a firm hand on the center of my back. "Stay still," he commands, and holy shit. That voice. I'll do anything he asks if he uses that voice with me.

He kisses a trail down my spine heading toward my ass. His teeth capture the thin string of my thong and pull it down over my ass and thighs, where he releases it so it can meet the floor and leave me exposed to him. Except that's not where it ends. My wrists are stretched behind my back and bound together with my thong.

Holy shit!

I arch up, searching the mirror and finding him there, watching me as he ties me up, leaving me completely vulnerable to him. I open my lips to say... something, only to close them at his expression. It's rough and animalistic, yes, but the tender, adoring note beneath the surface tells me he'll take care of me. That he'll push me, but he'll hold my hand as we explore a bit of the dark side together.

With that I relax, and a smile blooms on his lips. Once he

has me bound, he pets my hair and cheek. "My beautiful swan, you make me so proud. You're doing such a good job for me."

It makes me preen, something warm and delicious curling around my bones and muscles.

His hands trail down my back, making sure my lower belly isn't on the counter but floating in the open air, and then *smack*. It startles a gasp from my lips and widens my eyes. He watches me watch his hand come down against my skin. *Smack*. I hear it a second before I feel the sting. It's not much. It doesn't burn or make me cry out.

It's not punishing.

It's sensual. Erotic. And when he smacks my pussy from behind, my wetness leaks out. All around my ass, the junction where my thighs meet my cheeks, the seam of my pussy, my clit. He spares no spot, and I rock and grind at nothing, anxious and needy for contact. For more.

I've had fantasies about something like this. About being tied up and spanked to the point of mindless lust. He's spinning me up, and I shamelessly crave it. And trust it because I trust him.

After more spanks than I can count, his mouth is there, licking up my inner thighs and kissing the tingly sting from my skin. He parts my ass cheeks, and I squeak as his tongue swirls around my forbidden hole.

But before I can argue or even moan and beg for more, he's eating my pussy like a man starved. He groans into me, his grip on my ass tightening as he splits me open wide and devours me. All I can do is lie here and take it. My arms bound behind me, my tits squished against the stone, and he's controlling me with my legs spread and my pussy open to him. It's so much and it both scares and thrills me like nothing has before.

"Mmm. That's it. So good. Look at you dripping for me." He runs his finger around my leaking wetness, swirling around and around, and oh god, I never want him to stop. His breathing changes, growing more labored, more excited as he dives back in and thrusts his tongue straight up into me. He fucks me with it, pumping in and out, demanding and greedy as he eats me. His control is gone, and his mouth is everywhere.

I want to see him like this. His eyes lost with lust and his body tense with desperation. I want him to fuck all of that into me. A shudder shakes me as he uses a finger to rub my clit while his tongue continues between my ass and my pussy. His tongue slips and slides in and out of me. Deep swirls and plunging fucks and sensual kisses. He plays with me. Toys with pussy and ass, and I have no choice but to take it.

"Aston," I plead.

"What is it, my swan? You want to come?"

"Yes. More. I need more."

He spanks my ass. Then my pussy and I moan and writhe, but with the way he's holding me, there's only so far I can move.

"I want you begging me for it." He pushes one finger into me, but he's pumping too slowly, and he's abandoned my clit. His tongue swirls my asshole as he fucks my pussy with his finger. But he knows none of it is enough.

He wants me to beg, and he'll play with me until he gets it.

Why is that hot? It shouldn't be, right? It should infuriate me, but the truth is, I want to beg him. I want to please him because it'll please me. It's dirty and a bit depraved and I like that about us. I like that we can be that way.

"Aston, please. Please give me more. Please make me come."

"My needy wife."

My eyes pinch closed and I bite into my lip. "Yes."

He growls and eats my ass like it's the best thing he's ever tasted. All the while his fingers are in me and then rubbing my clit. But with his tongue in my ass and his fingers rubbing my clit and my now empty core clenching, there is no controlling the way my body is taking over.

"Oh god!" I cry. "Shit, Aston. I'm going to come."

He groans into me, the vibration tickling me just right, and he picks up his pace, sucking and licking and flicking and rubbing me. I explode. Detonate. Rupture. I grind against his face as he holds me tight, my hands jerking and pulling against the restraint, needing to grab something to help me through how intense this is. And the fact that I can't heightens it.

Before I fully come down from my high, his hands are on my hips, and he yanks me back as he thrusts his cock straight into me. My eyes roll into the back of my head, and a strangled noise hits my lips. Because fuck, it's tight. I don't know if it's because of my massive orgasm or what, but holy shit, I can feel him everywhere.

One hand holds tight onto my hip, and the other captures my hair and yanks me back until our eyes meet in the reflection of the mirror. His cheeks are flushed red, his lips glossy with my cum, and his eyes are volcanic. Never have I seen a sexier sight in my life. It makes my pussy flutter around him, and he moans, his chin dropping to his chest for a long moment. That is until he slides his cock almost all the way out and then pounds it back into me.

"Does that feel good?" he rasps, his grip in my hair tighter, the stretch and burn at delicious odds with the sweet warmth spiraling through me as he fucks me.

"So good," I tell him.

"I want to fuck you sweaty and fast," he tells me even though he's contradicting that by sliding slowly in and out of me. "I want you gasping my name and begging me between moans to let you come."

Jesus. "Yes," I tell him, because I want that too. All of it. "Please, Aston. Please fuck me harder."

He slaps my ass and stares down at where his cock is pushing in and out. "Look at you. Look at your cunt taking me like this. You're so fucking wet, Skylar. So perfect. You feel too good."

With his hand in my hair, he arches my back so he can kiss me. His other arm bands around my hips, and he pulls me back, using it for leverage so he can drive harder and deeper into me. I'm perched on my tiptoes, my hands bound and stuck between our bodies. I can barely kiss him. I can barely breathe. All I can do is feel all the things he's forcing me to feel all at once.

His hand releases my hair, and my head falls forward, but he's dragging down the cups of my bra, setting my tits free, and using that hand to roughly grope one. And when he has me like this, he pounds into me. Our eyes lock, and he gets lost inside of me. With my body at his mercy and him controlling me, I get lost too.

"Do you want me to come inside you? Do you want to feel that? You like dripping my cum, don't you?"

"Please," I beg. "Please, more."

At that word he unleashes himself. He fucks me. He fucks me deep and hard. The kind of fucking that makes us both sweat and moan and gasp for air that our lungs are barely able to manage. He holds me. Protects my lower belly from the brunt of the counter. But that's the only place he takes care. Everything else he's doing is pure wickedness.

He smacks my tits and my ass and bites my lip and shoulder. He pummels in and out of me, and when he gets to the point where his control is slipping, he finds my clit and forces an orgasm from me like I never knew was possible.

I scream and thrash, snapping the string of my thong. And thank god for that because now my hands can meet the glass, and I can push against it and hold on as everything in me spirals and twists and builds and crashes.

All the while he kisses my back and neck and breathes words of praise and adoration into my heart and soul. When he comes, it's like nothing else, and I stare at him, eyes glued to his gorgeous face, and it pulls more from me.

We both collapse to the floor, and he cradles me in his arms, kissing me softly, telling me how incredible that was. Then he lifts me and carries me into the shower.

"This time slow," he tells me, kissing my cheek, and my heart gives a thump. He can do whatever he wants to me right now. I'm his.

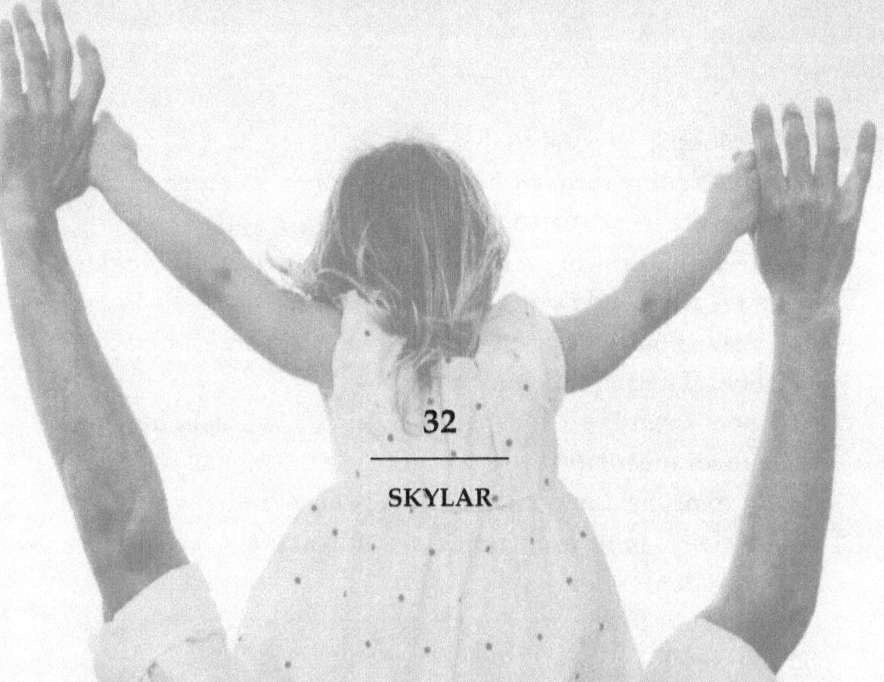

32

SKYLAR

The shower sprays down on us, filling the room with steam and relaxing my stiff shoulders and muscles. It's been a day. The wedding party took a lot out of me, and Zoey asking if I was her stepmother was another layer I wasn't expecting.

A good layer though.

One I worry about, but for now, fills the pieces of my soul that want to see her living her best life. She's not my daughter. Not really. But I love her. I do. I want her happiness and her smiles and her fun. I want her to only see rainbows and never feel the rain.

"I'm your kid's stepmother," I muse as Aston sets me down in the shower and kisses my neck from behind.

"You are. She told me when I tucked her in that she was happy you said yes."

My eyes close and a smile splits my lips, even as my heart thumps harder.

"Is this all moving too fast for you?"

Yes. No. I don't know. "We'll have to tell her about the baby. About how it's not yours," I go with instead.

He doesn't respond to that, and I can't see his face to figure out what's going through his mind. We have so much freaking drama, we're like a soap opera and a miniseries all in one.

I feel him growing hard behind me, his cock rubbing into my lower back, and I sigh and hum.

"How about it's just us for tonight. No more thinking. No questions. Life can wait until tomorrow."

I nod. I can live with that. Because life will definitely pick back up for me tomorrow and I could use the mental reprieve.

He spins me around and lifts me back up into his arms. His mouth claims mine as he walks us until I'm pressed against the shower wall.

His hands firmly grip the space between my thighs and ass. "I want this. I want you."

I can't tell how he means it. If he's talking about my body or... more.

He doesn't give me the chance to question him. His cock rubs up and down my pussy, and when he has me moaning and trying to pull him inside of me, and yes, begging, he pushes in.

There are no dirty words this time. No raunchy sex. It's slow and deep. It's kisses and breath. It's gentle and sweet. It's... loving. At least that's how it feels, and it spins my mind up and twists me into a million different directions. Our eyes hold, only closing when he hits a certain spot or I squeeze his cock with my pussy.

But it only lasts a minute before we're there again, foreheads pressing and dizzying kisses. *I could do this forever*, I think. But then he shifts, and I feel him against my bump. Reality swarms back and stings me. It bites at what this is and what we are and what's yet to come. Something we haven't talked about. Not really. Not logistically.

The baby.

It makes me choke out a gasp and cling tighter to him, not wanting to let him go. It's only been a week, but it's been the best week of my life. And the amount of time is inconsequential considering how long we've been living together and sparring. Flirting. Touching. Kissing.

He picks up his pace, his cock moving in and out of me, his hands on my ass guiding me, helping me move against him. I'm swollen inside, but somehow that only makes it better. It's a tiny bit of a sting and I like it. Sort of like when he pulls my hair.

His thumb goes back into my mouth, and I suck him down, but he pulls it out just as quickly as he pushed it in and uses it to rub my clit.

That's how I lose the battle. I wrap my arms around him and bury my face in his neck and ride his cock and finger until I come. He follows, his grip on me tightening, and I hope he leaves marks on my thighs and ass. I hope I can look in the mirror tomorrow and see his possessive fingerprints there and remember this night with him always.

The moment we're done, I climb out of his arms, but he doesn't let me get far. Shampoo is poured liberally into his palm, and he washes my hair. His fingers massage my scalp, and I moan some more. No one has ever washed me. No one has ever been this tender before. Cared this much.

He's taking care of me.

My eyes burn. Tomorrow is a big day, and I'm scared. This is throwing me over the edge. He continues to clean me, conditioning my hair and washing my body. And when we're done, we fall asleep in a heap, only sleep doesn't last long for me.

I WAKE EARLY and leave a little before dawn, needing space to think. Today is my ultrasound. I've heard the baby's heartbeat. That was an incredible moment. But I'm still walking into that ultrasound room alone. Aston has a shift this morning, and I didn't feel right asking him to come with me anyway. It's one thing to be with him when I'm pregnant. It's another to have a new baby that isn't his. I don't know what will be with us after I give birth, and we haven't talked about it. It's too soon for that anyway.

Yes, I could bring a friend or my mother or my father.

But my situation is that I have to plan this as a single mother. I can't rely on the idea that Aston will want to be part of my child's life. That we'll live happily ever after with me as Zoey's stepmother and him as the stepfather to my baby like we're the freaking Brady Bunch. Maybe that's how it'll turn out. But maybe not.

And I have to be ready for that. I have to be strong. I have to be able to handle all of this myself.

Then there's the other piece of this puzzle. The Josh piece. The one I still have yet to figure out.

After killing time in the coffee shop in the hospital lobby, I make my way over to maternal-fetal medicine. The waiting room is filled with pregnant women and their significant others, but I read on my e-reader and ignore the annoying sinking in my gut that only gets deeper as the minutes tick.

"Skylar Davenport?" the tech calls out, and I stand, my nerves all over the place, mixing with a bubbling excitement that makes my stomach roll. "I'm going to give you a gown. Please remove everything from the waist down. I'll be back in a few minutes to begin. Are we waiting for anyone else to arrive?"

"No. It's just me."

She nods and leads me to a dimly lit room with a gurney and a large ultrasound machine. I get changed and onto the bed, draping the sheet over my legs. The door opens a few minutes later, and the tech enters, walking me through the procedure for the transvaginal ultrasound. It's all very technical, and the nurse in me loves that.

"Do you want to know the baby's gender?" she asks. "We

can't always tell, and it's not a hundred percent accurate, but I'm pretty good at reading it."

I swallow, my chest fluttering and my fingers tingling. "Yes. I want to know."

"Great." She gives me a reassuring smile. "Let's get started."

I lie back and blow out a breath just as the door bursts open. My head whips over, and I squint against the harsh hallway light that filters in. Aston is in scrubs with a harried expression on his face. He spots me on the bed before he looks at the monitor and sighs in relief.

"What are you doing here?"

He comes straight over to me and takes the chair at the head of the bed, his hand on my face as he kisses my forehead and then my lips. "I ran over from the hospital. It's your first ultrasound. I wanted to be here with you. I wanted to see it. If I get a page, I'll run back over. It's just around the corner."

And that's it. That's all it freaking takes for me to fall in love with Aston Hughes.

"Are you ready for me to begin?" the tech asks, and all I can do is nod because if I speak, I'll sob or squeak or I don't even know. Dammit. I've never been so happy to have someone and so afraid to lose them at the same time.

She puts warm gel on the probe and gently inserts it inside me. It's not the most pleasant thing I've had up my vagina, but the moment the screen flickers and my blob of a uterus shows up, I no longer care about the discomfort. Measurements are taken and she clicks on a million things, but all I'm focused on is the small moving creature in the center. The one with the heartbeat pulsing like a hummingbird's wings.

Aston sucks in a deep breath and wraps his arms around me. We're both silent, mesmerized by what we're seeing. Then she narrows in on it, and we get to see arms and legs and a belly and a head. Tears pour down my face, and with every sniffle I make, Aston kisses my cheek and rubs his nose against me.

"That's my baby," I murmur.

"It is," he replies softly. "She's beautiful."

"What?" I face him, blinking a million times a minute. "She?"

He pulls back, a stricken look on his face. "Um. Well. Shit, were you not going to find out?"

I smack his shoulder. "I was, but you can't just tell me like that."

He laughs lightly. "I didn't mean to. It just came out. I saw her, you know, anatomy, and that was kind of it."

I make a displeased noise. "You can say vagina. You are a doctor."

He rolls his eyes at me. "Fine. I saw her vagina." Then he smiles the sweetest smile ever. "You're having a little girl."

I turn back to the screen as the tech measures the baby's nuchal translucency and checks out her heart, all the while pretending to ignore us. It all looks good, as best I can tell.

"I'm having a little girl."

"Don't ever run out on me again," he whispers in my ear. "You're young and you're just coming out of a bad relationship. I understand that. But I didn't like waking up to find you already gone. If you need space, you tell me. If you're spooked or scared or nervous or freaking out, you tell me. I get it. I'm having a lot of those moments, too. But I'm in this, Skylar. I'm not going anywhere. Not now. Not ever. All this means is I'll have another girl in my life to... to care for," he says, stuttering over that as if he were going to say something else. "I'm okay with that. More than okay with it. Let me be in this with you."

I nod and wrap my arms around his head and hold him. "I'm in this with you too."

I'm at a weird angle, and there is literally a woman with a probe inside of me, but in this moment, I don't care. In this moment, I feel like maybe, just maybe, it's all going to be okay. Even if the rest of me knows, this is the calm before the storm.

ASTON

I squint at the monitor, trying to make sense of what I'm seeing. Or not seeing in this case. The laparoscopic images flicker, blur, then clear for a moment before distorting again. What the absolute fuck? This is the third time in the last few weeks something like this has happened to me, and it's a different machine than the last one I had an issue with.

My jaw clenches, and I take a deep breath to rein in my ire. "The image is unstable," I announce to the OR team, keeping my voice calm despite the frustration building in my chest. "Can someone check the connections?"

The scrub tech immediately moves to inspect the equipment while I hold my position, the freaking laparoscope inside this kid's belly. It's a simple exploratory laparotomy following a fall, and I should be close to finished by now.

"Everything appears connected properly," the tech offers after a moment.

Josh shifts his weight across from me. "Maybe it's your technique. Or your eyes, perhaps." His voice drips with false concern. "Have you had your vision checked lately? It appears to me as though you're putting too much tension on the scope."

I ignore him, focusing on the screen as the image stabilizes. "There we go. Let's continue."

"I'm just saying," Josh persists, "it seems as though these incidents have happened a lot with your cases lately. Perhaps you should consider—"

"Dr. Wesley," I cut him off sharply. "I need suction here, not useless babbling and commentary from the peanut gallery."

The OR falls silent except for the steady beep of the monitors and the soft hiss of the ventilator. I proceed carefully, localizing a bleeder near the spleen, but just as I set up to apply a clip, the applicator refuses to grip.

"What the hell?" I bark, pulling back slightly. "The jaw isn't grasping."

Josh sighs dramatically. "We should have been done by now, don't you think?"

I swear, this motherfucker will die if he doesn't shut up. I glance up at the clock. It's been forty minutes, and I don't like this little guy under this long. I try again, but it's still not gripping, which means I can't apply the clip where I need it.

"I'm going to open him up. I'm not going to risk this kid's safety with malfunctioning equipment. Ten blade, please."

"Are you sure that's necessary?" Josh challenges loudly enough for everyone to hear. "Maybe if you try again with the right technique. Going open means longer recovery time, more pain—"

"I didn't ask for your thoughts, and last I checked, it's my call."

The scope is pulled from the abdomen, and everyone gets into gear to switch procedures. I'm handed a scalpel, and given where I saw the bleeder, I make the smallest incision possible that will allow me to get where I need to be to stop the bleeding.

The next twenty minutes are tense. Converting mid-procedure always is, but with Josh questioning my every move, it's worse. I feel the eyes of the entire team barreling down on me, but I'm able to locate the source of the bleeding, and with a few sutures, the leak is stopped, and the kid's vitals are pristine. Thank fuck for that.

"You can close up," I tell the intern beside me, and I stand over her as she silently works.

"Equipment fails sometimes," Josh muses with a shrug. "But three times in as many weeks, always during your procedures and no one else's? People are starting to talk."

I glare up at him, making sure the light from my headlamp flashes in his eyes. "About what?"

He squints against the light but holds steady. "About whether you're still at the top of your game. As we all know, stress can affect performance. I heard your home life is... complicated."

I laugh. "My home life has nothing to do with equipment failures," I tell him evenly. "And maybe you should leave your jealousy for my home life outside of the OR instead of spreading bullshit rumors about my performance. As it is, Dr. Wesley, you have yet to show me anything regarding a decent, let alone good, performance. Maybe if you focused more on yourself and less on me, you'd be a better surgeon."

Before he can respond, my phone goes off. The circulating nurse checks it. "There's a problem with some orders for one of your patients, Dr. Hughes."

That's been another thing. I look over at the intern. "Dr. Wesley can help you finish." Without another word, I walk out of the OR to scrub out, my jaw locked and my shoulders tense. For how amazing this week started with seeing the baby and being with Skylar, it all feels like it's going to hell now. I just want this shift to end. I just want to be with my girls and relax.

But that's not going to happen right now.

After I scrub out, I read through the text and check the orders on a computer near the nurses' station. Holy shit. This has the patient getting ten milligrams per kilogram per hour of morphine instead of ten micrograms per kilogram per hour. That's a dangerously high dose and a life-threatening mistake. How is that even possible that it was put in here like that? I didn't order it that way. I'm positive I didn't.

I always double-check my orders. Always.

Much like the equipment failure, this isn't the first time my orders have been wrong, or more like they have seemingly been changed.

I rub my hand over my head and remove my surgical cap as ice slithers through my veins. After what just happened in the OR and now seeing this, I can't help but think someone is actively trying to sabotage me. The first few times this happened, I figured it was exactly as it was. A mistake in orders. Faulty equipment. But no. This is intentional.

Josh. It has to be.

The realization hits me with such clarity that I stagger under its weight. He's trying to make me look incompetent, but more than that, he's putting patients' lives at risk. But how did he mess with my orders? The equipment wouldn't be that tough to do, but the EMR, or electronic medical record, isn't as easy to manipulate.

I spend I don't even know how long going through the rest of my patients' orders one by one, making sure everything is correct and as it should be, including for the little kid I just operated on. I'm going to need to speak to my supervisor about this, but without any proof, that can be tricky. Especially given the social situation Josh and I are in with each other.

I need to find Skylar and talk to her.

I head for the elevator and make my way to the MSICU, which is its usual busy self. I spot Michaela talking to a resident, and she turns when she notices me, giving me a wave that

I simply return with a head nod, only to have her suddenly come over to my side.

"Everything okay?"

"Huh?" I draw back, surprised she's asking me that in such a way as if we're close, which we're not. "Why wouldn't I be?"

"I heard about your patient today, and now Skylar's talking to Josh."

"What?" That pulls me up short. "She is?"

"Yes. I assumed that's why you were storming down here." She gives me a bewildered look as if she hadn't realized she was dropping a bomb on my lap. "Sorry, I thought you knew. They're in room twelve."

What the hell is happening today?

I blow past Michaela and head straight for room twelve, and sure enough, Skylar is in there with Josh.

"—not safe with him," Josh states emphatically. "I told you what happened in the OR today. It was a routine procedure, and he had to open the patient up. He's being reckless, Skylar. I'm going to have no choice but to go to my supervisor over this."

"Go away, Josh. You don't know what you're talking about," she snaps, her voice tight.

"Don't I? Ask around. Equipment failure and medication errors. Those aren't small things. All of them started after the two of you got together. He's distracted, and it's making him careless. They'll fire him, and then he'll be gone. He'll likely have to leave Boston. Then what will you do? Your job is here. Your family is here."

"Why are you saying this to me?" she asks, looking flustered, her arms folded over her chest, her hip popped out. "No one is firing Aston and he's not leaving Boston."

"You deserve better than someone who is careless and cocky with his work. I know your marriage is bullshit. I just don't know why you did it."

"It's not bullshit," she defends.

"It is. I know it is," he says with assurance. "You didn't want to break up with me. You told me so. I know you love me. You only left me because you felt I wasn't good to you."

"That's not how it was, and that's not how it is. Not anymore." She shakes her head and starts to walk away when he grabs her and holds her steady. "Let go of me."

"I can't. I love you, and I won't stand to see you throw away your life with a loser like him. You're nothing more than a glorified babysitter for his kid. Can't you see, he's using you."

She pulls her arm free of his grip before I can manually do it for her.

"What do you know of his daughter?"

Something crosses his features. "Only that he's never home with her because he's too busy fucking up here."

My heart pounds. Has he been following Skylar? Following me?

"You need to leave. I've told you I don't want to see you."

He moves in on her. "Tough shit. Because I'm not going anywhere. He is. I love you. He doesn't. I'm the real deal, and I'll do whatever it takes to prove that to you. You needed me to change, and I've changed. I've done everything you've asked of me. So cut the bullshit with him and come back to me."

"What's all this?" I step into the room, unable to listen to another second of this.

Skylar's head snaps over toward me, relief washing over her features. "Dr. Wesley and I were just—"

"Having a private conversation that doesn't involve you," Josh interrupts. "Doctor to nurse."

"Funny because it sounded like it did involve me. In fact, it seems like you sought out my wife to make up lies about me and my work."

His eyes narrow. "I'm concerned about patient safety. Something you used to care more about before you got careless."

"Patient safety?" I laugh bitterly. "That's a fucking riot coming from the guy who is actively sabotaging my procedures and changing medication orders under my name."

Skylar gasps and takes a step back, color rising on her cheeks as her eyes bounce back and forth between the two of us. "What? Is that true?"

Josh's expression doesn't change, but something flickers in his eyes. Surprise, maybe. "That's a serious accusation, Dr. Hughes. One you'd better be able to prove. As it stands, you're the one making mistakes. Not me. Everyone's seen it."

His smug look has my fists clenching, and I have to blow out a breath through my nose so I don't knock him out right here. He's fucking with my life, and that's not something I take quietly or lying down.

"Did you think I wouldn't figure it out? It won't exactly be tough to prove if you've been logging in and changing orders, and when I do, your career will be finished. Is all of this really worth it to you?"

His chin lifts defiantly. "You don't know anything about me."

I give him an arrogant as fuck grin. "I know you're after a woman who will never be yours again. A woman who wants nothing to do with your weak, pathetic ass."

Josh flies at me, and Skylar jumps in between. It pisses me off that she just did that. Josh is unpredictable, but he manages to hold himself back when she puts her hands up, outstretched toward him. Seeing that, I realize how fast my heart is racing. How tight my chest feels with this barely contained rage.

Everything right now feels like it's spiraling out of control. Again. The world I know and love is slipping through my fingers once more.

"You will not fight in my ICU. Dr. Wesley, you need to leave and cool off."

"Me?!" He points to his chest. "Tell that to your asshole husband who's spreading lies."

"Coming from the master of lies himself. Fine. We'll go." She spins around, takes my hand, and leads me out of the room. I glance over my shoulder and give him a look. One he doesn't mistake. He has no clue who he's fucking with.

34

ASTON

Skylar drags me down the hall and shoves me into an on-call room. Before the door can even click shut behind us, I'm pressing her against it. "What the hell was that?" My voice comes out rougher than I intend, adrenaline still coursing like a wildfire through my system. The on-call room is small and narrow. It fits a small desk shoved into the corner and a twin bunk bed. I've never slept in here. But when I was a resident, I used rooms like these plenty.

Her eyes flash. "He cornered me while I was clearing out the room after my patient had been sent to the step-down unit. I didn't seek him out, Aston."

"You should have paged me the second he walked in." I run my hand through my hair and take a step back, willing myself to calm down. "He's dangerous. You know this. But more than that, what I said about what he's doing isn't an exaggeration. The medication orders and the faulty equipment. It's him."

"You really think he's the one doing that?" Her voice holds a note of shock but not disbelief.

"I don't have proof. And these things don't always happen when he's in the OR with me. But it started after you and I announced we were married, and today he blatantly called me out on it in the OR in front of staff. He's trying to make me look dangerous and incompetent. And he's putting patients at risk by doing it."

She looks sightlessly into the room as she thinks. "He's jealous or whatever. I don't know why he can't let me go, but he hasn't."

"I know that," I snap, my hands going to my hips. "Is he following you? Has he shown up at the house?"

"Not that I know of, but that doesn't mean he isn't. He mentioned Zoey just now."

"I know. I heard him." I grit my teeth. "I'm going to hire security or at the very least get a PI on him."

She leans against the door, propping her foot up onto it. "First things first. If you think Josh is trying to sabotage you, you need to speak to your supervisor immediately."

"I need proof. He works for me, and I'm married to his ex that he's not shy about letting everyone know he still wants. He has access to everything I do."

"Aston, I'm not saying he's not doing it, but he'd be a moron to log in under his name and change your orders. That leaves a visible trail."

"He must be using my credentials to change orders then. I don't know how. That part isn't very clear to me, and I haven't worked it out. But obviously he has no boundaries with me and none with you. I don't want him near you again."

"That's not exactly possible, and you know it. I work with him. Though I'm thinking it's time I bite the bullet and get a restraining order. I've been avoiding it, not wanting to stir up drama or shine a spotlight on things, but at this point, I might not have a choice. Still, I'm your wife—fake or otherwise—and you still need to trust me that I can manage my own interactions with my ex."

"Fake or otherwise?" I repeat, the words stinging more than

they should. She hasn't changed her tune one bit about calling what we have fake. "Is that what this still is to you? A fake marriage?"

Her cheeks flush. "I... You know that's not what I was talking about."

"Do I?" I step closer until we're toe-to-toe, and her head tilts back to meet my gaze. "Because I'm starting to wonder what any of this means to you. What I mean to you."

We're breathing hard, the tension between us shifting into something else entirely. A palpable charge clinging to our skin and magnetizing us together.

"You mean everything to me," she whispers, her voice shaky.

Her words break me. My hands frame her face and I kiss her with all the fear, anger, and jealousy that's been building in me since I walked into that patient room and saw her with him. Hell, from when everything started going sideways in the OR. She responds immediately, her fingers digging into my arms, pulling me closer as if she too can't handle any space between us.

"I can't lose you," I murmur against her lips. "Not to him. Not to anyone."

"You won't," she promises, her hands working the top of my scrub shirt out of my pants. "It's as you said to me. I'm not going anywhere."

Our mouths attack in a frantic torrent of lips and teeth and tongues while our hands tug and pull at clothing. Her scrub top and long-sleeved shirt are wrenched up her chest above her heaving tits, while her scrub pants meet the floor in a pool around her ankles. She kicks off a clog and frees one foot, and I grab her leg and wrap it around my waist so I can grind into her.

"Someone could need this room." She gasps as my mouth trails down her neck.

"Don't care," I growl, finding the spot at the base of her throat that makes her shiver. "Need you. Now."

Her head falls back against the door with a soft thud, and I pull her panties to the side so I can touch her pussy. I circle her entrance with one finger, teasing her, rubbing her wetness all over her clit before I do it again and again. Then I shove three fingers into her, stretching her, punishing her just enough to tether her fully to me.

"Oh my god! We're seriously going to get caught. You'll have to be quick."

"Can you be?"

She blinks open her eyes. "Right now? With you? Yes."

The words are a match to gasoline. I reach between us, pull my cock free, and with my eyes on hers, I lift her up, holding her ass in my hands, and slam straight into her.

"Aston," she whimpers. "Fuck."

"You can take it," I assure her. "You can take all of me."

And I mean more than just this.

Her body is so tight around me, her thighs clinging, her arms squeezing, her pussy clenching. I have to pause, my forehead against hers as I fight for control.

"Move," she urges, digging her heels into my ass.

It makes me laugh despite how raw I'm feeling. I do as she asks. I move, setting a pace that's just on the edge of too much for both of us. Every thrust drags a small sound from her throat that she tries to muffle either against my lips or in my neck. My pounding thrusts rattle the door behind her, and I move her off it and into the wall on the opposite side. If someone comes looking for us or even for a place to crash out, they'll see us the moment they open the door. There will be no hiding it.

I can't find it in me to care. So much is falling apart right now, but I have her here in my arms. I'm inside her body. Nowhere on this planet feels better than right here with her.

"Look at me," I demand. "I want to see your eyes when you come for me."

Her gaze locks with mine, open and heated, yes, but there's more there. There's everything I'm feeling being mirrored back to me. She makes me feel like I can fly. Like I can do anything.

My cock slides in and out with fast, shallow fucks. It's not as full as I want, but if I take her to the bed, I'll never stop. I'll get her naked, and I'll keep her here. Her cunt feels so good. Her body so right in my arms.

She tries to bounce against me, but I pin her to the wall and slam into her.

"You're mine."

"Yes," she cries, her eyes closing as her face twists with pleasure. "Oh god. Oh god. Fuck, Aston."

I sure up my grip on her ass, squeezing the globes in my hands as I pound her. I don't know how to slow down. There's no controlling this. There's only the need to be in her as deep as I can be.

Changing my angle, I hit the spot inside of her that I know will push her over the edge. I pump into her, grinding against her clit with my pelvic bone. And when she tightens around me, I capture her mouth in a deep kiss, swallowing her cries as she comes apart around me.

That's all it takes for my own orgasm to hit, and I bury my face in her neck as I come, her name on my lips like a wish. Like a prayer.

"I love you," I whisper, the words slipping out before I can stop them. I freeze for a moment, and when I pull back, I find her eyes wide and her lips parted. But there's no fear with it. No worry. Just surprise, and it makes me brave. "I do. I love you."

Before she can say anything, my fucking phone goes off, and with it, the world comes crashing back down on us. I pull out of her and set her down, grabbing a wad of tissues from a box on the desk and handing them to her as I yank up my pants and go for my phone.

"Shit. It's the ER."

Skylar hastily adjusts and puts her clothes back on. "Go. We'll talk later."

I cup her face and look at her. With her tousled-by-my-hands hair and swollen pink lips, she looks like she just got fucked, and that would fill me with pride if we weren't in the middle of our shifts in the middle of a hospital.

"I meant it," I tell her.

She nods, a smile playing with the corner of her lips. "I know. Go before you get in more trouble."

I slam a kiss to her lips and fly out the door, racing down to the emergency department while I shove my scrub shirt into my pants and drag my fingers through my hair, ignoring the curiosity of the other people on the elevator with me.

When I get to the ER and race down to the trauma room, I'm shocked to find my boss, Pierce Weinberg, already here. He rarely, if ever, comes down for traumas. I throw him a curious nod but dive in on the patient along with the ER staff.

The car accident was bad, but the child was properly buckled into his seat. Thankfully, I don't think he'll be surgical, but we decide to hold him for twenty-four hours for observation in a unit bed.

That's the good news. The bad news is that my boss watches me the entire time, and when I finish with the trauma and wash my hands, he's by my side. "Got a minute?"

It's not actually a question, and unease sits heavy in my chest. "Sure," I tell him as I wipe my hands with paper towels and follow him out of the trauma room and into an empty patient room across the hall.

"You can have no illusions about why I wanted to watch you in that trauma or why I wanted to speak with you now," he starts. "I've received some concerned complaints about your work lately."

I lean against the counter, my hands on my hips. "Let me guess, they're all from Josh Wesley."

He neither confirms nor denies. "There've been reports of equipment issues only during your surgeries and at least three medication order errors."

"I never made those errors," I tell him bluntly. "And the equipment only failing for me and no one else should trigger other alarm bells for you than simply my performance."

His dark eyebrows narrow, and he adjusts the sleeve on his expensive button-down shirt. "What are you implying?"

"That someone deliberately tampered with my surgical equipment and changed medication orders under my name."

"That's a serious accusation," Weinberg says, dropping into one of the chairs and crossing his legs at the knee. "One that requires evidence."

"I'm aware of that. It's why I didn't bring it to your attention yet." I take a deep breath, keeping my voice steady. "I'd like the system logs checked for the medication changes. Never in my professional career have I put in wrong orders like that. Not ever. I'm meticulous with my work, and that goes into the OR as well."

"I checked the logs. It's your credentials that logged in."

My jaw hits the floor. "How is that possible? Someone must have my credentials. What sense would it make for me to place an order and then go in and change it? It had to be Dr. Wesley. He's been after me from the moment I arrived. As you know, I'm married to Skylar Davenport. She's Josh Wesley's ex, and he hasn't been shy about his dislike of me and his desire to win her back."

"He suggested personal issues in your life might be affecting your judgment."

At least he admitted it was Josh who came to him.

"There is nothing wrong with my home life."

"When I hired you, you were candid with me that your daughter was struggling emotionally after the loss of her mother and that, as a result, your priority was going to be her. Has that changed?"

"No," I answer honestly. "It hasn't. But she's doing better and being with Skylar has helped her with that. Regardless, Zoey is not why there were malfunctions with equipment, and she's not why someone changed my med orders. I'm being set up by a subordinate with a personal vendetta. Check the system logs. Review the staff schedule for Dr. Wesley working on the same day I had malfunctions and changed orders."

After a long moment, he releases a sigh. A sigh that says he's not at all interested in doing any of this. "We'll investigate your claims," he finally agrees. "In the meantime, I think it's best if you take a few days off to regather yourself."

The words hit like a physical blow. "You're suspending me?"

"It's PTO. Paid leave," he clarifies. "Just until we sort this out."

"And did you do this with Dr. Wesley?"

"We have no proof of your accusations, Aston, and patient safety is our priority."

"Jesus Christ. This is unbelievable."

Weinberg stands. "His allegations are strong, especially with proof of the issues." He holds up his hand as I go to argue. "The alternative is restricting you to supervised procedures and someone double-checking your orders, which would be noted in your permanent record. This way is cleaner. Take the leave, Dr. Hughes."

I cover my mouth with my hand and breathe through my fingers as I try to process what's happening. My career, the thing I've worked my entire adult life for and sacrificed almost everything for, is hanging in the balance because of a jealous ex who can't let go.

And Skylar is caught in the middle of it. He's doing whatever it takes to get rid of me and win her back. She's carrying his child, even if he doesn't know it yet.

I clench my jaw and give him one firm nod. "Fine. I'll take the rest of the week off. But I expect a full investigation, or I'll contact an attorney." With that, I leave, walking along the back of the ER to the elevator. The doors of the surgical floor open, and I'm in no better shape than I was when I stepped on.

I have to find Skylar and tell her what happened. I have to get my stuff and leave the fucking hospital. There will be rumors about this. Hell, there already are. My reputation will forever be tarnished.

As if summoning Josh from my thoughts, I find him at the far end of the hall, just outside the PACU doors. He's watching me with a barely concealed grin of satisfaction. He knows. I'm sure Weinberg told him this is what he'd do. Our gazes lock, and a strange sort of smirk curls up my lips.

I should feel afraid. I should feel defeated. And part of me does. But superseding all that is a strange calm that settles over me. He doesn't know what he just started. If he thinks this will win him Skylar back, he's in for a rude awakening. Skylar is mine.

35

SKYLAR

"Oh my god, I can't watch," my patient's mother shrieks as I start the procedure to suction the patient's ET, or endotracheal tube. My patient was working a little too hard to breathe, and when I listened with my stethoscope, I could hear the raspy, rattling of secretions, which isn't uncommon with this size of ET tube. We typically suction them every twelve hours, but this little one needed an extra go.

"Close your eyes or step out, Mom. I've got her. I promise." This is why I hate it when parents insist on staying in the room for procedures. It's not helpful for them or us.

"But she's not hooked up to the vent."

"I explained this to you before we started, and we're doing everything by the book. Michaela used the bag mask to help her body oxygenate, and her vitals are holding. Rose is doing just fine." Making sure the catheter is lined up to the correct number, I apply suction as I slowly pull the catheter back using the pill-rolling technique while keeping an eye on the patient and her vitals. Once the suction catheter is out, we put the ambu bag back on the end of the ET tube and bag her up. I give a listen with my stethoscope and nod to Michaela. "She sounds clear. Let's hook her back up to the vent."

Michaela removes the ambu bag and hooks her back up to the vent and turns it back on. I watch Rose for any signs of distress and keep an eye on her vitals.

"All looks good," I announce, and the mom races around to hug me.

"Thank you. Oh my god, this is horrible."

I hug her back. "I know. I know this is hard. But she's responding very well to treatment, and the infection appears to be clearing."

She had a spider bite on her leg that got infected, and before her parents knew what hit them or Rose, she went septic. Poor kiddo is only a year and a half old.

Michaela and I leave the room, and I blow out a breath. Sometimes pediatrics is the best, and sometimes it's the worst. "Thanks for the help," I tell her, sanitizing my hands with the station outside my room.

"No problem." Before I can go back into the room, she stops me with, "Hey, question. Is everything okay with you and Aston? Rumor has it your marriage isn't doing well and that you're unhappy with him. But you didn't say anything to me, and I know Aston is having issues in the OR and with orders?"

Before I can answer, the X-ray tech arrives.

"Hey, Skylar," Dawson greets me. "I'm here to do the portable chest on your patient."

"Great. I'll be right in," I say to him and turn back to her as Dawson heads into the patient room. "I have a lot to say about that, but the simple answer is, none of those rumors are true."

She scrunches her brow at me. "I don't know what you mean. He has had issues in the OR and has made medication order errors."

I shake my head. "No. Someone is messing with him.

They're altering the orders and screwing with the equipment. It's not Aston. In fact, I think we all know who it is."

"What do you mean?"

"Josh has been trying to ruin him because he's still trying to win me back."

She blanches, suddenly looking sick. "That's a hell of a thing to say."

I shrug unrepentantly. "Aston never put in those wrong medication orders, and equipment only malfunctioning with Aston is suspect. Whether it's Josh or someone else doing all of this, they're putting patients' lives at risk."

She shifts her weight, looking incredulous. "You're sure about that? You're sure it's not Aston messing up?"

"Positive. When I spoke to Aston earlier about it, he was a mess, and he's mentioned before that it didn't make sense what the orders were put in as. Someone had to have gone in and changed them. It has to be the same with the equipment."

She runs her fingers through her hair and shifts her weight again. "Wow. I don't know what to say. So... you and Aston..."

"Are really happy."

She blinks at me. "Then I'm happy for you."

I need to get back to my patient. "We'll talk more later, but if you hear people gossiping about that, you can tell them I said it's bullshit."

She nods and goes back to her patient.

I head back to mine to help the tech get her ready, but once he's good to image, I say, "I'll step out."

"You sure? I have an extra lead gown for you."

"No, thanks. I'll see you when you're finished."

He gives me a funny look, but I don't care, and I'm certainly not telling him I'm pregnant. I step out and walk down the hall. The X-ray won't take long.

"Hey, you're on break in ten," Suzanne tells me as she passes by.

I check my watch. Damn, this has been the slowest and longest shift ever. "Okay. Thanks for the reminder."

"All set," Dawson calls out to me, and I head back in to finish up with Rose and make sure she's settled before I go out on break. I pull my phone out as I get near the elevator to text Aston to make sure he's okay when a hand on my arm startles me.

"What do you want, Josh?" There is no hiding the aggravation in my voice.

"You stepped out."

I cock an eyebrow at him as I step onto the elevator, shaking his grip in the process. "Yeah, hence me getting onto the elevator now. I'm on lunch break."

"No. You stepped out of the room for the X-ray. I saw you. You never step out. You always stay. In all the years I've known you and worked with you, not once have you done that."

Shit. I redirect as the elevator descends. "Have you been messing with Aston's medication orders and equipment?"

The doors open at the lobby, and instead of answering, he grabs me by my elbow, his fingers digging in painfully, and he drags me out the front doors, down the street a bit, and into an alley.

"What are you doing?" I try to pull away, but his grip tightens. "Let go of me."

He pushes me against the brick wall, pins me, and gets right up in my face. "When you stepped out, it got me thinking. I looked a little harder at you. Thought more about some things I've noticed since you left me. Are you pregnant?" he asks, his voice low but fierce in a way that makes my skin crawl. Before I can answer, his other hand moves to my lower stomach, palming me. I'm not showing much, but enough that he can feel the difference in my stomach.

I swat his hand away and push myself deeper into the building. "Don't touch me."

His eyes narrow, and something dark crosses his features. "You are, aren't you? I can feel it. That's why you married him so suddenly. That's why you've been avoiding me."

"My marriage has nothing to do with you," I say firmly, though my heart is pounding against my ribs like a trapped bird desperate to break free.

"How far along are you?" he presses, leaning into me.

Shit. Fuck! This is not how I was going to do this. I knew we'd get here. I knew eventually he'd ask, and then I'd have to make a choice. Lie or tell him the truth. And I could lie. I could. But eventually, the truth would get out. It always does.

"Tell me!" he demands, bringing his hand up to my throat. It's his move. The one he's done countless times that never fails to fill my heart with dread. I used to think it was simply him being possessive, even as he spouted ugly things at me. But then there were the times he'd squeeze, and the last was the final straw. He squeezed hard enough that I was coughing and sputtering when he finally released me. The next day, we had that in-service, and then I left him.

Thankfully, he doesn't squeeze me now, but he holds my throat tightly, and when I still don't answer, he shakes me, causing the back of my head to bang against the brick and a tear to slip from my eyes.

"Get off me." I dig my nails into his hand and try to push him away, but to no avail. His weight is pressing into me, and I have no room to move or maneuver. His eyes are murderous, and they hold me in place as his nose presses in on mine, and his lips hover close enough that I can taste his breath.

"It's mine, isn't it?" He shakes me by my neck. "Answer me!"

"Fuck you!" I scrape my nails into his hand, but it's as if he doesn't even register it.

"You stupid fucking whore! You're pregnant with my kid, and you married him! Did you think I wouldn't find out?" He squeezes my throat, making me choke and my nails dig deeper, only to immediately relax his grip.

"This is why I didn't want you to know!" I bark. "Look at what you're doing. You have me by the throat, pinned to a building. You're scaring the shit out of me, and you make me feel unsafe. You treated me like shit and terrorized me for a year. A fucking year!" I slam against him, but he presses harder. "I never knew which way your moods were going to go, what to say to you because I was always afraid anything I did say would set you off. You'd throw things and call me every freaking horrible name you could think of, and you'd do this." I tap his hand. "You'd put your hand around my neck like a threat. Like you could kill me at any moment, and sometimes I even thought you might. You made me feel weak and powerless and ugly and fat and gross and stupid. You made me feel like no one could ever love me but you because I was an awful person to love. But it's you who's awful. You who's weak. I know what you did to Aston. I know," I spit. "I'm not going to let you hurt him the way you hurt me. And I sure as hell won't let you hurt my baby."

He laughs caustically in my face. "You think he gives two shits about you? Once he learns the baby is mine and not his, he'll walk. You trapped him like a poor bastard. You're nothing but a stupid slut who fucks her way from one man to the next. Only this time you fucked up. The baby is mine and not his. You think I was so mean to you? Boo-fucking-hoo, princess. I never hurt you. That was all in your head. You're a spoiled, coddled rich girl who expects the world to worship you when the truth is, you're nothing without me."

Now it's my turn to laugh, even when it's shaky and rattled by his hand on my throat and adrenaline charging through my veins and muscles. "Now who's the stupid whore? He knows whose baby it is, and he wants me anyway. He married me anyway."

His eyes flash dangerously. "Except it's my baby and not his. So that makes you mine." His teeth graze my jaw, and he pants heavily against my skin. "Why do you do this to us? I love you so much. If you think I'm going to let him have you when you're pregnant with my child, you've got another thing coming."

"That's not your call to make. It's mine. If I have to fight you tooth and nail in court over it, I will. I will use all of my resources to keep my baby safe and you out of my life."

His forehead presses into the side of my face. "You won't. You're too soft for that. You're just mad at me. But I'll change. I *have* been changing. You've seen it. I've been everything you love about me."

I thrust against him, and he finally relents, giving me an inch to breathe. "You just called me a stupid whore, squeezed my neck, and slammed my head against the wall."

He makes a dismissive noise, irritation angling his features. "I didn't *slam* your head. That's not how it happened. Jesus, Skylar, you're exaggerating again. I said those things because I was angry." He gives me a reproachful look. "You can't blame me for that. I just learned you're pregnant with my baby, and yet you're married to that fucker and not me."

He seriously doesn't see it, and that's terrifying. But more than that, I don't want to fight with him anymore. I don't want to question or doubt myself the way I did with him for so long. There is no safety in doing that, and frankly, none of it matters anymore.

"You're dangerous. Did you honestly think you could get away with altering medication orders? With fucking with equipment? You could have killed a patient."

His eyes pin mine. "Your husband's the one who fucked up, touching things that never belonged to him. There's no proof of anything other than the fact that he's incompetent. Even if there is, it won't lead to me." He grins and locks me in place once more, licking a ring around my lips and up my neck that makes bile climb up the back of my throat. "His career is finished. He's on administrative leave."

I gasp and fight to push him back. "He's what? Since when?"

He gives me a satisfied smile. "Since about twenty minutes ago. I just saw him going up to get his things from his locker before I got on the elevator with you."

"What did you do?"

Thankfully, he finally releases me, his anger ebbing just as quickly as it came on. That's how he works. A volcano erupting before he turns dormant again just as fast. It was the ultimate mindfuck. Especially when he'd become soft and remorseful and adoring after. He'd make it feel as though I imagined the entire thing.

But not anymore. And never again.

"I spoke to Weinberg about him. About my concerns."

My jaw unhinges. "Why would you do that?"

"Because he needs to go. You never would have left me if it weren't for him. And now that I know you're pregnant, I know I made the right choice with the med orders and equipment. I did what I had to do for you and for us. You never should have married him."

"You could have killed someone."

"No one got hurt, and now that he's gone, no one will."

Holy hell. I can't even with that. "Why do you want me back?" That's what I can't make sense of. The way he speaks to me, you'd think he hated me.

He steps back into me, and I press my hands into his chest to keep him at bay. "From the moment I saw you, I knew you were going to be mine. You make me crazy, Skylar. I can't think or function without you. I love you, and you walked out on me. Fine, I got angry a few times. Maybe I even said some things I shouldn't have. But you left me. I never walked away from you. And now that you're pregnant, I can't let you do that again."

My phone vibrates against my hip, and instinctively, I know

it's Aston calling to tell me what happened. I also know I have to do something about it. I can't let this stand. Josh knows about the baby now. That secret is out. So all I can do at this point is save the people I love from the man in front of me.

By staying silent, I protected Josh. Allowing my fears of others' opinions and scrutiny to rule, I hid what he did. That was wrong. If I had come forward about him sooner, maybe none of this would have happened.

"I understand," I tell him, ignoring my phone. "I need to get back."

"You didn't eat anything."

I snort because his concern over me eating is the most fucked-up and ironic thing ever. I can't pretend to understand him or his actions. Frankly, I don't. I don't get the sick obsession. I can't fathom intentionally hurting anyone in any way. But he's not well. That much is obvious. It's more than he's hurt and threatened me. He's risked innocent children with his fixation and cruelty. And he did all of that against the man I love.

"I'll be fine."

I push past him and head out of the alley.

"I'll walk with you."

"No." I turn and hold his gaze even as I walk backward toward the front entrance. "I need time alone to think about everything you said to me."

This makes him smile. He thinks I'm planning to come back to him when, actually, I'm planning to get rid of him from my life once and for all.

36

I don't call Aston back. Not yet. I only have half an hour left on my lunch break, and time is of the essence. I make it to Dr. Weinberg's office and greet his assistant. "Hi. Is he available? I just need a few minutes."

"He's in a meeting." Then she gives me a funny look. "Are you okay? Your neck is... red."

The blessing and curse of having fair skin. "That's because Dr. Josh Wesley just squeezed it."

Her eyes round and her lips part. Maybe I shouldn't have fired that one off, but oh well. Her eyes glue themselves to my neck, and she grimaces. Yikes. How bad is it? I pull out my phone and use the camera app to see it. I've got red lines across my neck that look like a handprint. I snap a quick photo of it and put my phone back in my pocket.

"I'm sorry, but his meeting will have to wait. I'm on the clock." Without waiting for her to argue with me, I burst into his office only to stumble over my feet as I come to a screeching halt. "What are you doing here?"

Michaela is sitting at the round table in the corner of the office with Weinberg directly across from her. They appear deep in conversation, and Michaela is visibly upset with tears in her eyes and staining her cheeks.

"Shut the door, Skylar," Weinberg orders, and by some miracle, I manage the task, though I can't remove my gaze from her. "Please, come have a seat. I believe you're likely here to discuss the same matter Michaela is."

My heart hammers in my chest, and my palms tingle with adrenaline as I take a seat at the table.

"What's going on?" I ask, unable to wait another second.

Weinberg holds up his hand to stop Michaela before she can speak. "It is my understanding that Dr. Hughes told you that he believes Dr. Wesley somehow altered medication orders under Dr. Hughes's name and tampered with OR equipment before his surgeries. Is that correct?"

"Yes," I utter. "Dr. Hughes and I spoke about it this morning after he had equipment issues during a surgery, followed by a changed medication order. He was very upset and adamant that he never made those errors. He was paged to the ER following our conversation, and I went back to work, only to have Dr. Wesley follow me out of the building on my lunch break. He did this"—I point to my neck where it's red—"when he squeezed my neck and pushed me harshly against a brick wall in the alley outside the hospital. He was angry with me because..." Shit. I swallow. "Because I'm pregnant with his child and didn't tell him because I didn't feel safe with him knowing yet. You see, I left him because he was emotionally and psychologically abusive with me during our relationship, and he likes to squeeze my neck, as you can see."

Michaela gasps and covers her face as she starts to cry again.

Weinberg wearily rubs his forehead.

"That's only part of why I came here right now," I continue. "The main reason, other than filing a complaint against him for his actions just now, is to inform you that Dr. Wesley admitted to me that he's the one who altered the medication orders and tampered with the equipment."

Weinberg hisses out an expletive. "You're willing to make a formal statement about all of this?"

"Absolutely. Dr. Wesley is dangerous and put patients' lives at risk to set Dr. Hughes up because he wanted to get rid of him."

"I gave Dr. Wesley Dr. Hughes's credentials," Michaela admits, and my jaw unhinges for the second time in two minutes. I shift in my chair to look at her, her expression broken and contrite. "I was jealous of you. I had liked Josh, but he went straight for you and never noticed me. Then it happened again with Aston. I told you I liked him, and three days later you were married to him, which didn't make any sense to me since you had told me you didn't even like him. Anyway, I was angry and hurt and jealous. Josh knew I used to work in the badge office before I got my RN license. He approached me about making a duplicate of Aston's badge. He told me he needed it because Aston hated him and made it impossible for him to do what he needed to do for his patients as his resident. He said if he had the badge, then he could go around Aston and wouldn't have to bother with him."

She blows out a breath and stares up at the ceiling.

We use our badges for everything. To get in and out of the floor and to log into computers and the Pyxis machine. Josh would have also needed Aston's password, but how difficult can that be to get? He could have looked over his shoulder anytime to see it.

"He... he said all these things to me and told me, well, it's stupid. I should have known better, but I've been pretty lonely, and then he said these things to me, things I had always wanted him to say, and he told me that you were unhappy and that Aston was dangerous. I thought I was helping him. I never knew he mistreated you that way." She looks at my neck. "I was bitter, and I should have known better. I should have known he wasn't trying to go around Aston by using his credentials. I should have known he was trying to hurt him. Maybe part of me did. Maybe I was getting back at you and Aston. I don't know. I didn't think Josh would ever put patients at risk. Not ever, or I never would have done it. But it's my fault, and after what you told me today about what Josh had done, I couldn't live with it anymore. It all clicked into place what he had been doing and just how dangerous he is."

I fall back in my seat, simply blinking and staring at her. I'm shocked. I never would have imagined Michaela would do something like that. I also give her a lot of credit for coming forward about it. Many would have hidden their involvement.

But more than that, part of this is my fault. I left Josh, sure, but that's all I did. I didn't tell anyone other than my friends and family what he did to me. I avoided it, hoping that by leaving him, I was solving my problem. That he'd simply fade into the background eventually and get over it. I took the easy, passive way out. I didn't file a restraining order, and other than avoiding him at work, I took no action against him.

I felt ashamed and hid from so much. But I'm not responsible for his actions. He is. And if I'm going to protect myself and my child, I can't run from what he did.

"In addition to filing a formal complaint against him," I continue, "after my shift, I'm going to be filing a restraining order with the police department."

"You do know that with your family name, that will become public," Weinberg tells me.

"I'm aware, and if that happens, then I'll face it."

Weinberg nods. "I have to speak to the chief of surgery and the resident advisor for the program, but it's safe to say that Josh Wesley won't be practicing medicine in this hospital again."

Relief floods me, but there's more to this. "What about Dr. Hughes?"

"In light of the evidence that's been brought forth to me, he'll be reinstated immediately."

Fuck yeah! I inwardly fist-pump the air but work to contain my gleeful smile. "Thank you, sir. Am I permitted to tell him?"

He grins at me, clearly seeing straight through me. "Sure. In fact, why don't you do that now? I need to finish speaking with Michaela in private."

"Right." I throw her a glance, but she's not meeting my eyes now. I still can't believe she did what she did for Josh. Then again, I know what it feels like to be on the receiving end of his excessive and effusive affection and attention. It's how he ensnared me so quickly. He knows how to create an intense emotional attachment like no one else.

I stand, and without saying anything else, I leave Weinberg's office. Then I run for the bathroom. I have like ten minutes left before I have to get to work, which right now feels impossible with all that's going on and all that's rushing through my head, but that's reality. I pull my phone out of my pocket and immediately call Aston, who picks up right away.

"Hey. Where are you? I came looking for you, and Suzanne said you were on break, but I need to tell you—"

"Dr. Aston Hughes, I'm going to need you to return to work ASAP," I interrupt. "Your administrative leave is officially over now that it's been discovered that you were in fact sabotaged by Dr. Josh Wesley."

A beat of silence. Then, "Are you serious? How would you know that?"

I launch into a fast version of what happened.

"Where are you?" he asks instead of responding to anything, his voice tight.

"Um, the bathroom outside the administrative offices on the surgical floor."

"I'll be there in two seconds."

The phone disconnects, and I put my phone back in my pocket and exit the bathroom, only to immediately get picked up by a firm set of arms. Aston's lips land straight onto mine, his arms banded tightly around me.

"Are you okay?" he murmurs around my lips.

"I'm fine. That really was like two seconds."

"I was down the hall." He rips himself back and examines my neck. I didn't look too long in the mirror, but most of the redness is already gone. Still, his jaw clenches. "I want to kill him for touching you."

I shake my head. "Not worth it."

"No. It's my job to protect you. I hate that you went through that, and I wasn't there."

"I've also learned how to protect myself. How to stand up for myself to him. He's going down already by his own hand. Literally. Between what's going to happen here in the hospital and me filing a restraining order after work, he won't be able to hurt either of us again."

He sets me down, and his fingers trickle along my neck, his lips following, kissing me softly.

My hands meet the back of his head, and I pull him back so I can see him. My heart thunders, but nothing has ever felt as right as saying, "I love you," to him. "I would have told you before, but then you got paged."

His eyes sparkle, and his expression softens. "Yeah?"

I laugh at his slightly bewildered tone. "Yep. A lot, actually."

A smile splits his face. "Does this mean I can officially call you my wife without you arguing with me about it?"

I puff a feigned annoyed breath. "If you have to."

"I have to. Because I'm so fucking in love with my wife."

"Good. Because I'm so fucking in love with my husband."

He cups my face and kisses me until we're both breathless. "Do you have to go back to work?"

I laugh. "Yes. Like right now. But incidentally, you need to go back to work too."

His fingers trickle along my jaw, and he stares into my eyes. "I don't know how to thank you. I was formulating a serious battle plan, and you just kicked its ass."

"A lot of it was Michaela, but I think it's pretty easy to say I'd do anything for you, especially tell the truth."

His forehead presses to mine, and his hand slips to my lower belly, where he holds me possessively. "I love you so much. You, Zoey, and our little girl in here are my world." His thumb glides up and down. "I couldn't handle it if anything happened to any of you."

Damn him.

I sniffle and blink, trying to will the tears back. "You mean that? Our little girl?"

He smiles. "I thought you got that yesterday at the ultrasound, but yes, my swan, ours. You're my love. My life. My family. My forever."

"I want that. I want all of that with you."

He kisses me softly. "Now I just have to tell your brother."

Oh. Right. That.

37

ASTON

I blow out a frustrated breath and set my phone back down on my nightstand. He's said next week four times now. Meanwhile, I've continued to hold off on telling him about me and Skylar because he was going to come home and I wanted to do it in person. Yet my wife's belly is growing. Our daughter is getting bigger, and we're planning things for her. And yet her brother, my best friend, still doesn't fucking know.

We've sworn Rina and Brecken to secrecy. I need to be the one to tell him. And if he reacts badly, that falls on me too.

"He canceled again. I'm going to tell him over text." I kiss a line up Skylar's neck as she curls sleepily into me.

"Go for it," she murmurs. "Serves him right for not coming home."

"He is saving lives."

"And he knows we're married and living together. How mad can he get? Or frankly, how shocked?"

"He told me to take care of you. And I told him we weren't sleeping together."

She smiles, her eyes still closed as she rolls over and hikes her thigh up and over mine. "I'm fine with you taking care of me. I am very needy."

I grin against her lips and kiss her. "You are. Does my pregnant wife need to come?"

She laughs. "What is it about you with that?"

"I'm a caveman," I admit. "You being pregnant and wanting my cock makes me fucking feral."

She reaches between us and grips my hard-on through my briefs. "So I feel. Is all of that for me?"

I laugh at her coquettish tone. She knows it's for her. Fucking her has become my favorite hobby. And thankfully for me, she wants it all the time. Her pregnancy has made her insatiable, and I have zero complaints. And when she comes—which she always does now—damn.

A million things have happened this last month. Our fake wedding pictures made the front page of national news and were buzzing everywhere, especially in the hospital. I got immediately reinstated as Skylar said, and Josh lost his position as a resident at Boston Children's Hospital. He was furious and came after Skylar in the ICU that day, only to subsequently be dragged out by security. That, along with the picture of the marks on her neck, was used when Skylar filed a restraining order against him.

She also had her attorney send him a notice informing him that if he left Skylar alone for good, she wouldn't file assault charges against him. He didn't know at the time—and neither did Skylar—but the alley he brought her into had cameras set up. The entire incident was on video, and she has a photograph of her neck following it. It wouldn't have just ruined his career. It could have sent him to jail.

Skylar is a Fritz after all.

He agreed, and we haven't seen him since. Skylar also asked him to relinquish his paternal rights to the baby and had her attorney send the paperwork for it. His other option was extensive therapy and only visitation when she allowed it and with supervision. She told him she'd use all her money and family power to keep her child safe and that the choice was his on how he wants to proceed.

So far, we haven't heard back from him on this, but Forest's guy assures us he's left Boston and moved to Atlanta. We'll take it. For now. But once the baby is born, I plan to adopt her as mine, and we'll take whatever steps we need to in order to keep both the baby and Skylar safe.

Michaela was suspended without pay for a week and put on a performance plan as well as probation. She didn't end up staying and has subsequently left the hospital. Skylar doesn't keep in touch with her, and I'm not sad about that.

Despite those things, this last month has been a dream come true. Zoey is happy and thriving. We told her about the baby and how we are going to be a family with it. It brought her to another level, and now she wants to be part of everything we do with the pregnancy and planning for the baby. Work has settled down for both of us, and Skylar's pregnancy is looking great. Bonus, she's not having any more morning sickness.

My hand slides up her thigh until I'm gripping her ass and using it to rub her over my aching cock as my mouth comes down on hers. She tastes like mint from her toothpaste and a sweetness that's all Skylar. It makes my head spin and my heart gallop in my chest. Always. No matter how many times I kiss her or touch her, it's like the first time. A kinetic pull only she has on me.

My hand glides into her hair, and I roll partially onto her, mindful of her belly, so I can deepen the kiss. I hike her thigh up higher and grind down into her, making her whimper and rub against me. It sends sparks shooting up my spine and draws my balls up with the need to come.

Her shirt, followed by mine, is pulled off, and I trail my lips down her neck, licking and sucking and tasting her skin. Her fingers rake through the strands of my hair, guiding my head where she wants it. My tongue swirls around one stiff nipple, and just as I suck it into my mouth, we hear a sound coming from downstairs, followed by the house alarm going off.

I shoot up off Skylar, immediately covering her with the blanket as I practically fall out of bed. Adrenaline takes over, charging my muscles and making my heart race.

"What the hell?" she cries, fear contorting her features. Especially as we hear more noise downstairs. "Oh my god! Someone's in the house."

"Get dressed and go into Zoey's room. Lock the door behind you. I'm going down—"

"No, you're not!" she yells, sitting up and scrambling for her shirt while I hastily shove mine on. "You're going to call the police and lock yourself in with me and Zoey."

"Skylar, for once, just listen—" My voice cuts off as the alarm does. I blink at her as she blinks at me. "How did they turn it off?"

"I'm sorry!" a voice calls from downstairs. "It's just me!"

"Micha?!" Skylar shrieks before she scrambles from bed and races for the door, not even caring—or possibly forgetting—that she's only in booty shorts and a T-shirt. The door flings open, and Skylar flies down the stairs. I head into the hall just as Zoey opens her door with a hazy and confused yawn and a rub of her eyes.

"It's okay, sweetie. It's just Uncle Micha. You can go back to bed."

"Uncle Micha is home?" Now Zoey is completely awake, and she too is heading down the stairs like her ass is on fire.

Awesome. Evidently, this is happening now, and it's also happening in front of my kid.

"Uncle Micha!"

"My favorite goddaughter! Look how beautiful you are. And big." I hear him kiss her. "But speaking of big." I turn and start down the stairs when I hear Micha exclaim, "Skylar, your belly is huge!"

Skylar laughs. "It's not that big. I'm only fifteen weeks."

"But... you have a baby growing in here. I can't believe it. I'm touching your belly, and there's a baby in there. I'm going to be an uncle."

"Yes! I'm going to have a baby sister," Zoey tells him.

That's when I hear a sharp, "What?! *You're* going to have a baby sister?"

I close my eyes, blow out a breath, and continue to the bottom of the steps, where my best friend is looking at me with fury dancing in his bright blue eyes even as his hand is still on Skylar's belly.

"Her baby sister?" he questions. "Something you haven't told me, friend?"

He's kind of a mess. His light brown hair is shaved close to his head, and he looks like he hasn't showered or shaved or slept even in days. His clothes are just as crusty-looking as the rest of him.

"The baby isn't his," Skylar says dismissively, and wow, that stings. I know how she's saying it and what she means by that, but still. She must realize this because she looks at me, and an apology instantly flickers in her eyes. She crosses the room right in front of her brother and touches my cheek. "I'm sorry. That's not how I meant it."

"I know."

"I didn't mean to imply it's not yours. I know it is. I was just explaining... ugh. You know."

I grin down at her. "I know. It's okay."

"You sure?"

I nod and bend to kiss her, and that's when Micha kind of loses it.

"Are you kidding me right now? When were you going to tell me that you're fu—er"—he glances down at Zoey—"messing around with my sister?"

Instead of addressing Micha in front of my daughter, I bend to face Zoey. "Hey, Zo-Zo, you've got school in the morning."

"But I'm not tired," she whines in protest.

"I know, but you'll get to see Uncle Micha in the morning. Give him another hug and then scoot back up to bed."

"Fine," she grumbles. "Night, Uncle Micha."

"Night, Zoey-Zo. I'll make sure I'm up in the morning to see you before school, and then after school we can hang out."

"Okay," she chirps, gives him a hug, and runs back upstairs. I'm shocked that it was so easy as it was. I was expecting a fight and tears, but right now I'll take it.

"Why don't we go into the kitchen?" I suggest. "You look like you've been flying since Jesus was an infant and could likely use a drink."

"Since Jesus was an infant?" he deadpans.

"It was my polite way of saying you look like shit."

He smirks and shakes his head but actually walks into the kitchen without an argument, and now I'm two for two. Hopefully this keeps going. Skylar squeezes my hand, and we walk into the kitchen, but I end up grabbing one of my oversized hoodies from the sofa and handing it to Skylar for her to put on, which she does with a grateful smile.

Micha heads straight for his liquor cabinet while Skylar climbs up onto one of the stools. She's smiling, not the least bit concerned with any of this. Micha pours two small glasses of whiskey and slides one across the stone counter to me.

"No poison?"

"Not yet," he tells me, and I laugh.

"Welcome home." I raise my glass to his, and we clink them before we both drink our large shots down. The whiskey is hot and harsh as it slides down my throat, and I use that to drive me forward. "Why did you tell me you weren't going to make it?"

He shrugs. "Surprise."

Skylar rolls her eyes. "Then you get what you deserve. It's after ten."

"Explain to me what's going on," he demands, leaning against the counter as he pours himself another. "Because this isn't what you told me. Neither of you."

"I love her," I tell him simply.

He stares at me for an eternity after that. "You love her?"

"And she loves me."

"I do," Skylar confirms. "It's true. He's hot and good in bed."

"Skylar, are you trying to fucking kill me right now?" Micha growls, scrubbing a hand across his face, and I can't help my laugh, especially when she throws me a wink.

She shrugs unrepentantly. "You're my brother. That's my job. But yes, we're in love and happy."

He whistles through his teeth and takes a sip. "And you're together even though she's pregnant with Josh's baby?"

"Yes," both Skylar and I say together.

"How long has this been going on?"

Skylar glances up at me. "About six or so weeks, right? Something like that."

"But it started a while back. At least for me."

Micha's lips twitch with an amusement I don't understand. "You mean following whatever happened between the two of you at the Valentine's Day party?"

"What?" both Skylar and I spew out. "How did you know?" I finish.

Micha drains his second glass and sets the empty down on the counter, where he rolls it between his hands. "I saw you. I saw both of you, actually." He points at Skylar. "I saw you leave the bedroom with Braelyn, the two of you whispering, and I heard you say the word 'kiss' to her. Then I saw you"—he points to me—"walking out of the bedroom looking insanely guilty, but there was something else to you. A sadness maybe or an anger and an awakening all at once. I can't describe it beyond that. I just know you, and you looked different, and I put it together pretty quickly. But neither of you spoke about it again. Except I know you, and you never really got together or hooked up with anyone after that. Was it because of her?"

I glance down at my hands pressing into the stone. "Partially, I guess. I wasn't looking for her, and then I kissed her, and it turned out it was Skylar. After that, it was always Skylar, no matter how sometimes I wished it weren't." I look up at him. "You knew all this time?" Guilt battles with relief inside me.

Now he's grinning like a Cheshire cat. "I knew, and I also didn't forget that Skylar was living here when I offered you and Zoey my place."

"I'm sorry, what?" Skylar barks out, her voice a dance of incredulous laughter.

"Are you serious?" I ask.

He shrugs. "Yep. I didn't want Skylar living alone after what Josh had done to her, and I also wanted you to find a life again, man. It had been years, and you were a fucking mess with everything. Plus, I knew Sky and Zoey would hit it off. I thought maybe if you kissed her once, it could lead to something else between the two of you, and lo and behold, I was right." I go to speak when he holds up his hand. "But I wish you had told me from the start, and I wish you had told me after it began."

And just like that, a fresh wave of guilt hits me. "I get that, and I'm sorry. I wanted to do it in person. I was serious about her, and that wasn't the kind of thing to mention over text."

"Wait." Skylar holds her hand up like a six-year-old in school. "Hold the phone here, Cupid. Are you telling me you orchestrated all of this?"

"Of course I did. I never liked Josh, and Aston's my best friend."

"You're unbelievable."

He grins at her. "You're welcome."

"Oh my god! I could hug you and strangle you. Who does something like that, Micha?"

"Who marries a man only to end up dating him, Skylar?" he throws back at her.

"Fair. That's fair." She shakes her head. "So, you're not mad?"

"No. I'm not mad. I'm annoyed I had to fly home in the middle of the night to find out, but I'm the opposite of mad. Aston is the best guy I know, and he'll take care of you. And your heart is the biggest one on the planet, and I know you'll take care of him and Zoey in return."

"I will," I promise him.

"Same," Skylar says.

"Good. Then we can go to bed now because I've been up for a very long time. Evidently since Jesus was an infant." His lips bounce. "In the morning you can fill me in on everything else I missed."

I walk over to him and give my best friend a hug. Because the bastard set me up, and I'm not the least bit upset about it. If anything, I owe him one. I just hope I get to one day return the favor. Until then we have a lot ahead of us. And I can't wait for any of it.

EPILOGUE
SKYLAR

Sometimes I don't know how to process the world. How to handle the meaning from moments that are meant to be meaningless. Maybe because nothing ever is. Every moment, whether we're aware of it or not, has meaning. Has an impact.

Like right now.

Leaves crunch beneath my feet, and the crisp fall air tickles my cheeks. It's a gorgeous October day. The sort that reminds me why fall is my favorite season and that I'm happy to be done with summer. Then again, being pregnant over the summer—a particularly hot summer—wasn't my favorite. Even if I'm more waddling than walking at this point.

I officially started my maternity leave three days ago when my nurse manager all but kicked me off the floor. I'm five days overdue, and no one wanted to deal with my enormous, slightly grumpy ass. But I'm not a sit-at-home-and-do-nothing person either. The nursery, which is the old guest room that alternated as a bedroom between me and then Aston, is all set up. My mother and Aston's mother did the entire thing for us, just a little excited about being grandmothers.

The laundry is done. The bags are packed. Everything is in place.

But this little girl is taking her sweet time, and to hopefully help her along, I'm out here walking. My phone rings in my purse, and I pull it out to see my attorney's number. My heart skips a beat as I answer. I haven't heard from Josh again. Not since he was literally dragged from the MSICU by security as he tried to come after me, and I subsequently had my attorney and the police serve him with the restraining order and notice that I wouldn't press charges if he stayed away.

I've had one of Forest's guys keep an eye on him just to make sure he really was done with me. But he also hasn't filed the paperwork I sent him, which means he could decide he wants visitation with the baby. It's had me on edge, and now with this call, my heart rate is through the roof.

"Hello?" I answer, picking up the pace a bit, my nerves hastening my steps.

"Skylar, good morning, it's Danny Johnson. Is this a good time to talk?"

"Yes. This works."

"Great. Well, I won't keep you in suspense. I've heard from Josh Wesley's attorney, and he sent us the signed paperwork relinquishing his parental rights."

"Oh my god" slips past my trembling lips. My legs feel like they're about to give out on me, and I press myself up against the wall of a nearby building.

"I take it this is a good reaction."

"Yes." I'm totally crying, and there is no hiding it. "I'm so relieved." I never have to deal with Josh again. And with him signing the paperwork, my child never does either.

"We're going to file the paperwork with the family courts, and then they'll review it and make an official ruling on it, but it's done. After the baby is born, Aston will be able to adopt her without any issues or holdups."

I gasp and cover my face with my hand, shaking and silently sobbing into it. "Thank you," I manage. "Thank you so much."

"It's my pleasure. Just happy we had this type of ending to this. He certainly took his time getting us this paperwork."

Because he had to exert power over me in some way or another, because that's him. But last week I had my attorney reach out and remind him that if he didn't relinquish his rights, then the moment the baby was born, we'd file paperwork with the courts demanding child support. Clearly that was Josh's tipping point, and he caved.

"But it's done now?"

"It's done. Once we have the court's paperwork, we'll be in touch."

"Thank you. I'm so grateful."

"Absolutely. Have a safe delivery, and we'll talk soon. Take care."

"You too."

He disconnects the call, and I squeal, jumping up and down on the side of the street like a crazy lady. But I don't care. I'm so freaking happy right now. It's probably why I don't realize my water broke until the front of my leggings is soaked through and it's dripping in a puddle around my boots.

Shit. Oh shit.

I'm half a mile from the house, and Aston is in surgery. He called me before I started my walk to tell me. I could call him, and the circulating nurse would put me on speaker, but I don't want to rattle him or make him nervous and rushed while he's operating. Dammit. And I can already feel that this isn't fun as I'm getting a cramp—more likely a contraction—in my side.

I think through my people for a minute. My parents don't live close and are likely both at work. Hayes is back in Paris. Quinn and Crew are in Buffalo with the team because Crew plays Thursday Night Football tonight. Braelyn is working, and

Roman—oh shit. Roundhouse is right up the block, and Roman only lives another two over.

I call his phone, and he picks up on the third ring. "Hey, what's wrong?"

I snort. "Why would you think something's wrong?"

"Because you never call me in the middle of the day. For that matter, you tend to text instead of call. What's wrong?"

"My water broke in the middle of the sidewalk and I'm a half mile from home and Aston is in surgery and—"

He curses under his breath, cutting me off. "Where are you?"

I look around and spot a street sign. "Tremont and Clarendon."

"Don't move. I'll be there in not even five minutes."

"You're the best."

"Just promise me I don't have to deliver the baby in my car."

I laugh. "You won't. I've only had one contraction so far."

"I have no clue what that means, but I'm hoping that's good. Okay. Share your location with me, and I'm on my way."

He hangs up, and I blow out a breath, but I send him my location and hang tight against the wall. Despite being as nervous as I am, I'm also bubbling with uncontainable excitement. I rub my hand over my large belly.

"No more Josh," I tell my little girl. Only Daddy Aston." I snicker at that, thinking about how I teased him by calling him Daddy. So much has happened, and yet everything now feels as it should. Like I was always going to get here with him.

A few minutes later, Roman's G-Wagon pulls up. He double-parks and gets out, not giving a fuck about anyone as he rushes over to me.

"How are you doing, kid?"

I hug him. I'm so happy to see him and so overwhelmed, and I need a hug. "I'm happy and scared."

"That goes for me too."

I laugh and smack his shoulder. "I don't want to call Aston until I'm at the hospital. He's in surgery."

"I've got you. Come on." He wraps his arm around me and helps me up into his SUV. Smart man has a thick towel on my seat, and I feel better knowing I won't ruin his leather. He hops back in and does a crazy U-turn in the middle of the road, and off we go. "Do you want me to call anyone else? Your parents or Aston's?"

"I will once I'm checked in."

"You're very calm," he tells me with a hint of teasing. "It's very un-Skylar-like."

"I know. It's freaking me out too."

He laughs and reaches over to take my hand. "You're going to be just fine. More than that, you're going to be an amazing mother."

"Thank you." I look over at my cousin. "I just have to get through the birth part first."

Ten minutes later, we're pulling up in front of the hospital, and the valet takes the car. I called my OB's office on the way over and told them I was in labor. Thankfully, they have a wheelchair and a nurse here waiting for me. I'm brought up to antepartum and admitted and then brought into a room and hooked up to monitors.

Roman has been on his phone, and I know he's texting our group chat. I've heard my phone buzzing in my purse. Aston told me he'd call when he was out of surgery, and he hasn't yet. It's making me edgy. I want him here with me.

"Your parents and Aston's are on their way."

I sigh. "That was fast."

He shrugs. "Braelyn was up in the ICU and saw your mom, and you know how she is. There was no holding her back once I texted that you're in labor."

"You should go," I tell him. "This could take hours to all night."

He gives me a dry look. "I'm not going anywhere, and you know it. Forest is on his way, Hayes is flying home tonight, and Quinn and Crew will be back tomorrow after the game that Crew already said he's going to get a touchdown in for you and the baby."

"You guys are—oh! Wow. Yeah, this hurts." My eyes pinch up tight as my belly tenses with a contraction.

"Shit. Breathe or do whatever you're supposed to do."

"I am!"

"Fuck," he hisses, but my phone rings in my purse.

"Can you get that?"

"I'm on it."

He answers and tells the person on the other end, who must be Aston, that I'm in labor and that he needs to get over here.

"He wants to talk to you," Roman tells me, and I shake my head because I'm focusing on making this hurt less, and I can't talk right now. It doesn't matter, though. Aston's on his way. And thank God for that, because when the nurse comes in and checks me, I'm already six centimeters dilated, and they end up moving me down the hall to labor and delivery.

By the time that happens, Aston is here, still in his scrubs. He shakes Roman's hand and thanks him for staying with me, and then he's by my side. Roman sees himself out, but I make him hug me first.

"I don't have my bag," I tell Aston, who's curled up next to me on the bed, his hand on my belly between the monitors.

"We'll get it. Don't worry. My parents are picking up Zoey, but she's staying with Alden tonight. They have to pack her a bag anyway, so they'll bring yours here."

"Good. Okay."

"How are you feeling?"

I give him an unimpressed look. "Like I'm in labor."

He smiles and kisses the corner of my lips. "Still feisty, though. Good thing I love you."

"I love you too." I turn to look at him. "Josh filed the papers. My attorney called me right before my water broke. We're done with him."

Something intense flickers across his face, and his hand on my belly slides so he's holding the side, and his arm is around me. "Then the moment she's born, I'll have my attorney file the adoption papers."

I get choked up. I can't help it. He's so fierce and loving and tender and just everything in my world. This man is everything. He's exactly who I want to be the father of my baby.

"I love you," I tell him, cupping his face. "So much. Forever."

He kisses me, but then a contraction takes over, and that's that. They have me walk the halls, and I labor in the tub for a bit, and hours later, when I hit eight centimeters and my contractions are eating through my body and my energy, I get an epidural with my mother watching because Aston couldn't handle being in the room when they inserted a needle into my spine.

Men. This is why women have babies. Men can't even handle a needle.

People, including Zoey, float in and out. Zoey is excited and made Alden promise to bring her back here first thing in the morning to see the baby. After that, it doesn't take long. Within the hour I feel like I have to push, and forty minutes after, the doctor says, "Call it, Dad."

"It's a girl," Aston whispers with such love and reverence I'm immediately crying. My eyes open, and I take in the squirmy, crying little thing held in the doctor's hands, and everything that I am centers in on her. Aston cuts the cord, and they place her on my chest with a blanket over her and a cream hat on her head.

I glance up at him, tears streaming down my face. "She's

here." I hold her against my chest, keeping her warm, keeping her safe. My heart has never been so full.

"She is. She's perfect." He kisses the top of her head and my lips. "My swan, you did so well. She's incredible. Our little Valentine."

She is. She's ours, and she's every bit as perfect as Aston said.

"Love you both," he murmurs, holding us, shedding his own tears. None of this was what I planned, but I can't imagine it any other way. What started with a Valentine's Day kiss has become our happily ever after. We are forever undone. Together.

BONUS EPILOGUE

ASTON

Four years ago, I kissed a pretty girl in a dark room. I touched her. It was only for a moment, but my hands memorized how she felt. My lips and breath and tongue couldn't forget. Even when the lights came back on and I saw who she was, I still knew I was a fucked man. That I was indelibly imprinted with her.

I never gave Valentine's Day much thought. I'd buy my ex-wife flowers and candy and give her an *I love you* kiss. It's a Hallmark holiday as far as I'm concerned, and I still don't care about the holiday itself. But I do care about the woman I kissed for the first time on this night.

It's been a long day. I worked, and so did Skylar. I had about six traumas, and I know Skylar had a complicated patient. I'm tired. I want to go to bed and fall into a blissful oblivion in the form of sleep and wake up tomorrow to start this all over again.

But like I said, I kissed my wife for the first time four years ago. So, I feel like I need to do something about that. Skylar doesn't seem to care. She came home before me and helped Zoey with homework and played with Valentine before she made dinner for everyone. I cleaned up the kitchen, and now the girls are watching a movie in front of the TV while Skylar looks worn out and beautiful, and I start to make dirty plans.

And in thinking about it, it's been a long two years. A happy two years, but we haven't done much together as a couple. We've been parents. Valentine is a handful at a year and a half, but a lot of fun and a total snuggler. She's also a daddy's girl. Dada was her first word—much to Skylar's chagrin—and I ate it up. Zoey is obsessed with her and loves being the big sister.

That's been our priority, but when was the last time my wife had anything special just for her? It gives me an idea. Perhaps a crazy idea, but fuck it. When have Skylar and I ever done anything the normal way? I send out a flurry of texts as I head upstairs and do what I need to do in order for all of this to work. Sometimes it's good to be a Hughes with Fritz connections.

By the next morning, everything is scheduled and set up. I'm buzzing with anticipation but holding it in as best I can. Just after breakfast is cleaned up and I'm finishing packing up the girls, the doorbell rings and I head downstairs, catching Skylar's puzzled expression.

"Are you expecting anyone?"

I smile. "I am. Be ready to leave in the next twenty minutes. I already packed your bag, but you might want to double-check my handiwork."

Her head tilts. "Come again?"

"You will. Several times. Go check. Don't question it, but kiss the girls goodbye. You won't see them again until Sunday night except over FaceTime."

Yeah, I get a look. A not-so-happy look, but she'll get over it quickly. She kisses the girls, and I open the door to her parents.

"Hi! We're here for a grandparents' weekend," Rina singsongs out. The girls fly over to her, give her hugs, and asking a million questions. Skylar is clingy with the girls, continuing to give them kisses, and hugs all the while throwing me and her mother looks.

I explain to the girls that they're going to stay with Grandma Rina and Grandpa Brecken for the weekend and have a special, magical time. Valentine is a little wobbly, but with Zoey excited, she quickly falls in line. After all, Zoey is a pro at this, and Valentne will do anything her big sister does and tries to match her same enthusiasm and emotional output.

"Bye, Mommy!" Valentine says, hugging onto her tightly. Zoey gives her a similar chime. I hug both of them, and then they're gone. No tears shed, which I'm grateful for. Otherwise, I doubt Skylar would do it.

Skylar doesn't ask questions. Probably because the girls are excited. Having this sort of social network is amazing. This is the first time she's leaving Valentine overnight. In the year and a half since we had her, she hasn't done that once. The moment the door shuts, I head upstairs for her bags. Honestly, all she needs is sexy fucking lingerie or nothing at all.

When I return downstairs, she's waiting, leaning against the wall, arms folded, and an expectant look on her pretty face.

"It's our kissaversary," I explain.

"Kissaversary? Is that even a thing?"

I cock an eyebrow. "Question me again on it and you'll find your ass getting spanked."

She shivers. "Yes, Daddy."

I smirk. "My love, you are so asking for it."

She shrugs, unconcerned. "Then give it to me."

Fuck, I love this woman. But we still have a two-hour drive north. It's not like I picked a random hotel off I-495. We're talking about a gorgeous oceanside hotel in Maine. I mean, yes, it's February and there's snow everywhere and it's too cold to go out onto our balcony, but who cares? The room has a gas fireplace, and the spa is able to accommodate our couples' massage.

By that evening, we're all set in our suite, and Skylar is finally starting to relax and welcome the idea of an adults-only getaway. The waves crash against the rocky Maine coastline, and behind me, I hear Skylar in the bathroom, getting ready for the dinner I've arranged. I adjust the sleeve of my dress shirt, my reflection in the window smiling back at me. Valentine's Day was a perfect excuse for this escape. Something I wish I had thought of ahead of time and not at the last minute. It's just us. No little hands tugging at our clothes or tiny voices calling for attention, even if we already miss them terribly.

Still, we know Zoey and Valentine are safe with Skylar's parents, probably being spoiled rotten, and for the next forty-eight hours, I have my wife all to myself.

The door clicks open, and I turn to find Skylar framed in the silhouette of light from the bathroom. My breath catches in my throat. She's wearing a midnight blue dress that hugs every curve, her hair swept up to expose the elegant line of her neck. In the soft light of the hotel room, she looks like something out of a dream. *My dream.*

Specifically, the one I never knew I was having until she walked into it.

"You're staring?" she accuses for not the first time, a small smile playing at her lips as I stare.

"Just wondering how I got so lucky," I respond, crossing the room to her. My fingers find her waist, drawing her against me. "You're beautiful, Mrs. Hughes."

Her cheeks flush with that familiar pink I can't get enough of. "You clean up pretty nice yourself," she says, adjusting my collar. "No baseball hat. Imagine that." She gives a mock gasp, a hand covering her mouth.

"Such a sweet little brat." I smack her ass only to grip it. "There's more coming for you tonight, my swan, if you continue to mouth off to me."

"But your threats aren't as scary as you like them to be." Her fingers linger at my throat, and I resist the urge to pull her straight down to the bed. We have dinner reservations. Expensive ones.

"Ready to go?" I ask, my voice already rough with wanting her.

She nods, reaching for her small clutch on the dresser. "Lead the way, Dr. Hughes."

The restaurant is on the hotel's top floor, with glass walls that showcase the dark ocean and star-scattered sky. I reserved a corner table, away from the other couples celebrating the holiday. When we're seated, Skylar looks around with wide eyes.

"How did you manage this so last minute?" she whispers, but her smile tells me she's pleased.

"I should have booked it months ago," I agree, reaching across the table to take her hand. "I should have set this all up and planned ahead. But I looked at you last night and simply wanted this time with you. But more than that, this is our night."

"You dropped the Fritz name, didn't you?"

I smile ruefully. "Hughes doesn't have as much pull."

"I'm not complaining. I didn't realize how much I needed this until you put me in the car."

"Same. We need to do things like this more often. It's easy to get lost in our jobs and all the things our girls need. But I don't simply want to steal nights and early mornings with you. I want times like these. Times when I have you all to myself with no child wake-ups or late-night interruptions."

Her expression softens at the mention of our daughters. "I love this idea. It's just tough in reality. They're growing too fast."

"Yes. But we have people to take them, and it's just a weekend."

"You're right. I love this. I love this so much, and I'm glad you made me do it because I'm not sure I would have without the push."

The waiter brings champagne, pouring two glasses before discreetly withdrawing. I lift mine in a toast. "To us. To taking the biggest fake-it-till-you-make-it risk of our lives and making it our bitch."

Skylar laughs, clinking her glass against mine. "To us," she agrees. "And to you, for somehow convincing me that marrying my brother's best friend while I was pregnant was a good idea."

"Best decision you ever made," I tease.

Her eyes meet mine over the rim of her glass. "It really was."

The dinner is everything I hoped for. Perfectly cooked seafood, rich wine, decadent dessert. But it's the way Skylar looks in the candlelight that I'm savoring. The curve of her neck as she tilts her head back in laughter. The slight dip of her dress revealing the constellation of freckles across her collarbone. The way her foot occasionally brushes against mine under the table with a promise of what's to come. The relaxed, happy smile on her lips, and knowing I put it there and plan for it to never leave her face all weekend.

By the time we finish dessert—a dark chocolate soufflé we share—with Skylar's spoon slipping between her lips in a way that makes my pants uncomfortably tight, I'm struggling to keep my hands to myself.

"Should we go back to the room?" I suggest, my voice low enough for only her to hear.

She nods, a knowing smile playing at her lips.

The elevator ride up to our floor is torture. We're alone, but it's too quick for me to do any of the things I'm thinking about. Instead, I stand close behind her, my hand at the small of her back, my lips near her ear. My other hand grazes her breasts over her dress, making sure her nipples perk up, and she starts to unconsciously pant.

"I've been thinking about getting you out of this dress all night," I murmur, pleased when I feel her shiver against me.

"What else have you been thinking about?" she asks, her voice breathy.

"All the ways I'm going to make you come tonight."

The elevator doors slide open before she can respond. I guide her down the hallway to our room, my hand never leaving her body. Inside, the room has been prepared exactly as I requested. The lights dimmed, rose petals scattered across the bed, a bottle of champagne chilling in an ice bucket, and a box of gourmet dark chocolates on the nightstand.

Skylar takes it all in, then turns to me with wide eyes. "You did all this?"

"I had help," I admit, closing the door behind us. "But the idea was mine."

"Champagne and chocolate?" She picks up a truffle, examining it with a smile. "Are you trying to seduce me, Dr. Hughes?"

I step closer, taking the chocolate from her fingers and placing it back in the box. "Is it working?"

Her answer is to rise on her toes and press her lips to mine. I respond immediately, one hand cupping the back of her head, the other at her waist, pulling her flush against me. She tastes like chocolate and wine, sweet and intoxicating. I deepen the kiss, my tongue sliding against hers, drawing a small moan from her throat that shoots straight to my dick.

"I want you," I breathe against her mouth. "So fucking badly, Skylar. I know we're here to be romantic, but I want to do dirty fucking things to you."

"Show me," she challenges, her eyes dark with desire.

I reach for the zipper at the back of her dress, slowly drawing it down to reveal inch after inch of smooth skin. The fabric pools at her feet, leaving her in nothing but a lacy black bra and matching panties. My breath catches at the sight of her.

"Fuck, you're gorgeous," I murmur, running my hands down her sides. "Look at you. Perfect tits, perfect ass, perfect everything."

She flushes under my praise but doesn't shy away. I love that she finally sees this in herself. That she doesn't just hear me say the words but knows I not only mean them but also that they're a fact.

"Your turn," she demands, her fingers working at the buttons of my shirt. I let her undress me, enjoying the way her breath quickens as she reveals my chest and stomach before pushing the shirt from my shoulders. Her hands go to my belt next and then onto my button and zipper.

When we're both stripped down to our underwear, I reach for the champagne, popping the cork and pouring two glasses. I hand one to Skylar, clinking mine against it.

"To Valentine's Day," I say. "To it being our day. The one that changed my life. And to finally getting you all to myself."

"I'll definitely drink to that." She takes a sip, her eyes never leaving mine.

I set my glass aside and select a chocolate from the box, holding it to her lips. She opens for it, taking a small bite. A drop of the cherry filling escapes, sliding down her chin. Before she can wipe it away, I lean in and lick it off, the sweet taste mixing with the salt of her skin.

"Delicious," I murmur, watching her pupils dilate.

"The chocolate or me?" she teases, her voice husky.

"Both."

I feed her the rest of the truffle, then capture her lips in another kiss, chasing the taste of chocolate on her tongue. My hands slide up her back, finding the clasp of her bra and unhooking it with a flick of my fingers. The lace falls away, and I cup her tits, feeling their weight in my palms.

"I love how sensitive these are," I tell her, brushing my

thumbs over her nipples, watching them harden at my touch. "Love how responsive your body is to me."

"Only you," she whispers, arching into my hands.

I bend to take one peak into my mouth, sucking gently at first, then harder when she moans and grasps onto me. My hand slides down her stomach, dipping beneath the waistband of her panties to find her already wet.

"So ready for me," I groan against her skin. "So fucking wet."

"Yes," she breathes, her hips pressing into my touch. "More."

I smile against her and bite her nipple hard enough for her to know that I'm the one running this tonight. My demanding little swan will get what she wants, but only when I let her.

I walk her backward until her legs hit the bed, then ease her down onto it. Kneeling between her spread thighs, I hook my fingers into her panties and draw them down her legs, tossing them aside. She's completely bare to me now, flushed and beautiful against the white hotel sheets.

"I'm going to lick this sweet cunt until you're screaming my name," I tell her, pressing kisses up her inner thigh.

Her breath catches, her legs falling wider in invitation. "Please," she whispers.

I take my time, teasing her with light kisses and gentle touches until she's writhing beneath me, her hands fisted in the sheets. Only then do I finally press my mouth to her pussy, my tongue flat against her clit.

The half gasp, half moan she makes sends heat pulsing through me. I grip her hips, holding her steady as I eat her like a man on the edge, alternating between broad strokes of my tongue and precise circles around her clit. Her taste is everything I've been craving, and I can't get enough of her.

"You taste so fucking good," I murmur against her. "I could do this for hours. All night."

"I'd—ah—I'd die," she pants, her head thrown back, neck taut.

I smile against her skin. Always so fucking sassy.

I slide one finger into her while my tongue continues its work on her clit, curling it to hit that spot inside that makes her thighs tremble. A second finger joins the first, stretching her slightly, preparing her for what's to come later.

"Aston," she gasps, her hips lifting off the bed. "I'm close. So close. Please."

I blow on her pussy, making her shiver. "Please what, baby?"

"More. Eat me harder."

Fuck, how I love her. "Good girl." I increase the pressure of my tongue in tandem with the rhythm of my fingers. I fuck into her, sucking on her clit and pounding against her front wall. "Come on my mouth, baby. Let me feel you."

Her release washes over her with a broken cry of my name, her inner walls clenching around my fingers, her body arching beautifully. I work her through it, gentling my touch as she comes down, and pressing soft kisses to her thighs.

"God," she breathes, her chest rising and falling rapidly. "That was—"

"Just the beginning," I promise, crawling up her body to claim her mouth in a deep kiss, letting her taste herself on my lips and tongue. "I'm nowhere near done with you yet."

Pulling away, I head into the bathroom and grab the small bottle of lubricant I brought with me. When I return, her eyes widen slightly, then darken with understanding and anticipation.

"Is that what you have planned?" she teases, though there's a slight tremor in her voice. It's not fear, but excitement.

"If you want it," I tell her, brushing her hair back from her flushed face. "I want to make you feel good in every way possible."

She nods, biting her lower lip in that way that drives me crazy. "I want it. You know I want it."

I kiss her again, deep and slow, before turning her gently onto her stomach. "Up on your knees, my swan," I direct, my voice hoarse.

She complies instantly, and the sight of her like this, with her perfect ass raised and her slick cunt visible, nearly undoes me. I slide my palm down the curve of her spine, feeling her shake beneath my touch.

My hand comes down in a clap, meeting directly with one ass cheek immediately followed by the other. She moans and rocks forward, her pussy visibly dripping.

"Shit," she hisses as I hit her pussy next, alternating where my hand goes so she can't expect it. So, it surprises her each time. When her ass is deliciously pink and warm, I reach for the lubricant, running it between my fingers before tracing the tight ring of muscle of her asshole.

She tenses slightly at first contact, then relaxes as I continue to gently play before gradually increasing the pressure.

"That's it," I encourage, my free hand reaching around to find her still-sensitive clit. "Relax for me, baby."

I work her open slowly, patiently, one finger at a time, never rushing. All the while, my other hand stays busy between her legs, keeping her aroused and distracted from any discomfort. When she's taking three fingers easily, her hips pushing back against my hand, I know she's ready.

"Yes," she whimpers, her face pressed into the pillow. "I need you inside me."

I shed my boxer briefs, my cock springing free, achingly hard from watching her come and being worked by my fingers. I apply more lube, stroking my cock a few times before positioning it at her entrance.

"Slow and easy," I promise, gripping her hips as I begin to push forward. "Tell me if it's too much."

The initial resistance gives way, and I slide in inch by inch, pausing whenever I feel her tense, continuing only when she relaxes again. The tight heat of her is almost unbearable, the pleasure so intense it borders on pain.

"Fuck," I groan once I'm fully seated within her. "You feel amazing. So tight around me. And the way you look right now with my cock in your ass is fucking sinful."

"Oh god," she moans. "Move." Her voice is muffled by the pillow. "Please, Aston, move."

I start with shallow thrusts, giving her time to adjust to the fullness. My hands never stop touching her. Cupping her breasts, circling her clit, stroking her thighs. I want her to feel nothing but pleasure.

"Is this good?" I ask, needing to hear her say it as I pump in and out of her, mesmerized by the sight of her ass stretched around me.

"So good," she whimpers, pushing back against me and taking me deeper.

I increase my pace, my thrusts becoming longer and deeper, still careful but less restrained. The way her body accepts me, the sounds she makes... it's overwhelming. Intoxicating.

"That's it," I praise, feeling her start to tighten around me again. "You take me so well, baby. You're so perfect for me."

I hold her hip and start to pound, my chest finding her back so I can kiss along her neck and really drive into her. Her hands push against the headboard, using it for leverage to drive back into me. Her heavy tits swing, and I slap her ass hard, loving how she moans against the sting.

My fingers find her clit again, circling with firm pressure, determined to make her come once more before I allow myself to. Her moans grow louder, less coherent, a sure sign she's close.

And with it, my own control slips. "Fuck, baby. I can't... it's too good. Fuck, Skylar, I need you to come."

All she can do is nod, but she's already there. She shatters with a cry, her entire body tenses, her inner muscles clamping down on me so tightly I see stars. It's too much. The pressure, the heat, the knowledge that I'm the one making her feel this way. With a few more thrusts, I follow her over the edge, pulling out at the last minute and shooting myself all over her ass and back, emptying myself with a groan of her name.

For a long moment, we stay frozen in place, both of us panting, trembling with aftershocks. Then I climb off the bed only to return a moment later with a warm, wet cloth. She's on her stomach, her eyes closed and her lips soft.

I smile at my girl. So fucking in love with her, just seeing her like this makes my heart beat faster.

"You okay?" I ask as I wipe her down and brush sweaty hair from her forehead.

Her cheeks are flushed, her eyes heavy-lidded with satisfaction, but her lips curve in a soft smile that makes my heart ache with how much I love her.

She nods, reaching up to trace my jawline with her fingertips. "More than okay. That was... wow."

I chuckle, pressing a kiss to her palm. "That's the best you've got?"

"Always needing your massive ego boosted." She snorts and makes a show of rolling her eyes. "It's hard to form complete sentences after you've fucked my brains out," she retorts, making me laugh again.

I pull her against me, her head tucked under my chin, our bodies fitting together like puzzle pieces designed for each other. Outside, the waves continue their endless rhythm against the shore, a soundtrack to this perfect moment. If I died right now, I'd die the happiest man. I have it all, and that's not something I ever thought I'd get.

"I love you," I murmur into her hair, even as my last thoughts sit on my chest. "So much it scares me sometimes."

She tilts her face up to mine, those eyes that first captured me now full of a love I never thought I'd be lucky enough to have. "I love you too. Even when you're being smug about your sexual prowess."

"Not smug, just honest," I correct, making her giggle. The sound is light and free, so different from the guarded woman I married for all the wrong reasons. Or maybe they were the right reasons after all, just not the ones we thought at the time.

"Happy Valentine's Day," she whispers, pressing a soft kiss to my lips.

"Happy Valentine's Day," I echo, rolling her on top of me so I can play with her hair and back, already growing hard and ready for round two.

THANK you for reading Forever Undone. Continue the series with Roman and Braelyn's story, Forever Fighting.